TWO FLAGS FOR MARCO

PATRICK PHAIR

Ten|16
PRESS

www.ten16press.com - Waukesha, WI

Two Flags for Marco
Copyrighted © 2021 Patrick Phair
ISBN 9781645383819
First Edition

Two Flags for Marco
by Patrick Phair

For information, please contact:

www.ten16press.com
Waukesha, WI

Cover design by Kaeley Dunteman

This book is dedicated to Mary, my loving partner, and my five marvelous children, Matt, Kate, Molly, Emily, Kevin, and their beautiful families.

This story is also dedicated to the men and women who have fought battles on foreign fields and battles within themselves to make this world richer and more humane. They are warriors all.

"It's not given to people to judge what's right or wrong.
People have eternally been mistaken."
(Leo Tolstoy)

"War is not paid for in wartime. The bill comes later."
(Benjamin Franklin)

"If you've met one individual with autism,
then you've met one individual with autism."
(Stephen Shore)

PROLOGUE

THE GRAY SKY HUNG LOW as a sharp northerly wind sprayed a heavy mist, covering every branch and newly formed leaf in a sheet of glistening drops. It was the first Friday in June, but the chilly air made it feel more like late March or early April. It was a little after eight in the morning, and the wrought iron gates of Riverside Cemetery were clamped wide open. One group of cars was already huddled behind the thick, maroon ninebark bushes that surrounded the open-air altar with its floating white ceramic angels. A black hearse was in the center of the throng, its back door wide open. A few people stamped their Sunday shoes under umbrellas near a freshly opened grave. A pile of sandy loam concealed by a green covering of fake grass loomed at the foot of the grave.

The couple in the Toyota sedan inched their car slowly past the hearse, trying not to distract or disturb the mourners.

"Do you remember where he's buried?" Eva whispered once they were safely by.

"Over there." John put his finger to the windshield, pointing toward a stand of embowering oak trees. "He only wanted a simple headstone, no crosses or military stuff. And shade. He insisted on shade."

The car moved quietly on the freshly black-topped lane and stopped near the trees. As they climbed out, both opened their black umbrellas. "This way," said John. He steered them to the foot of a fresh gravesite with blades of rye grass poking up from under yellow straw. The couple let their heads hang. A catbird in a nearby cedar called out. Eva leaned into the man, their umbrellas touching, drops of water silently sliding off the edges to the soft ground below.

After a few minutes, John held out his hand. "Can I have the flag?"

Eva reached inside her knee-length raincoat and handed him a small American flag rolled in plastic.

John stepped forward, unrolled the flag, and put the plastic into his pocket. He paused to look down at the headstone made of gray granite flecked with tiny pieces of crushed onyx, the same color as the sky. He carefully pushed the wooden post into the wet dirt, unfurled the flag, and stepped back.

"It'll be complete when the other flag arrives," Eva said. Then she put her hand out, and John took it softly. "I have it on order. It should come in a few days, maybe a week. We'll come back then."

They lingered for a few more minutes, then turned and slowly walked back to the car.

1

AFRIKA KORPS

October 1943

THE BATTALION AID STATION had thirty-six beds, and all were filled with injured men, forcing several newcomers to be laid on the sand between cots and a few even scattered along the main aisle. Marco had never seen so many injured people at one time. He had transported a few wounded soldiers on occasion and routinely visited the aid station to replenish first aid equipment and swallow a handful of salt pills, but this, this had the look and feel of a catastrophe, as though a plane had crashed right outside the door or a tornado had swept up a whole village and dropped the inhabitants within a few hundred yards.

Blood-stained sheets and bandages were strewn everywhere. Doctors and medics scurried between cots like worker bees. Many of the wounded couldn't find a painless position, turning like dogs round and round, searching for a comfortable spot to rest.

Marco zigzagged his way down the main path, making sure not to step on any soldiers, until he found Oskar in the penultimate cot, his eyes closed and breathing shallow. Oskar's blanket was anchored under his armpits but fell short, so his toes were visible and standing straight up like tiny mushrooms growing on two branches of a fallen tree. Though the temperature outside the tent was nearing triple digits, Oskar was shaking slightly and a small perspiration moustache appeared below his nose.

When he came up close to the cot, Marco whispered, "Can I get you a drink of water, Oskar?"

Recognizing his friend's voice, Oskar let his eyes flutter for a few seconds, opened them, and croaked, "Find me some cold beer instead."

Marco smiled broadly. "That's the bunkmate I know and love. For a while there I was worried. They tell me you've been sleeping for almost twenty-four hours."

"Is the war over?"

Marco leaned in and whispered into the right ear that had no bandage, "Not yet." Then he righted himself and said, "You took quite a knock on that thick skull. The doc thinks a fragment from a bomb caught ya right below the hairline."

"I've been trying to remember." Oskar's face took on a serious look. "Did the man I carried in make it?"

"He's still alive. But he's in pretty tough shape. The doc doesn't give him much of a chance." Marco leaned over again and stared directly into Oskar's dark, deep-set eyes. "You, on the other hand, can take a punch harder than even Max Schmeling could deliver."

"Schmeling can't punch as hard as my cows back home. They are stronger than any bomb blast."

"I'll bet."

"But I tell my cows not to kick too hard . . . or else."

"Or else what?"

"Or else it's off to the butcher they go. I warn them . . . be gentle."

"And they listen?"

"I have a secret way with animals," he answered with a forced smile.

"What secret?"

"I give them extra treats. Cows love maple syrup. Did you know that?"

"The only thing I know about cows is they give us milk."

"I pour a little maple syrup into their oats, and they love me for it. But only if they are gentle."

Marco was chuckling when a medic walked up and put a blood-stained hand on the forehead of Oskar, then stuck a thermometer in his mouth. With his other hand, he wrapped his fingers like so many tentacles around Oskar's wrist, searching for a pulse. After a moment, the medic, whose face seemed to be drawn on an egg, pulled the thermometer. "The worst is over, soldier. Your fever is down—not gone, but down—and your pulse is regular and strong. You'll be out of here in no time." Without even looking at Oskar or saying another word, the medic nodded to Marco and moved on to the next forehead.

"Did you hear that, Oskar?" Marco said delightedly. "Out in no time and back bunking with me."

Oskar's face, rosy in the glow of the hanging light bulb, held a stern pout. "If you really want to help me, Marco . . ."

"Yeah, what do you need?"

"You could talk to the head doctor and convince him I need extended recuperation."

"But the medic said you're . . ."

"In a quiet place, maybe Switzerland."

"Ah, I see. Of course!" Marco slapped his forehead. "Why didn't I think of that?"

"With lots of good food—strudel and dumplings and bacon."

Marco flashed a broad smile. "Sure, I'll make an appointment with the chief medic as soon as I leave. Anything else while I have his ear?"

"This desert is too damn hot. Everything rots in such a hurry, and the stink of death is not good for the healing. And I can't stop coughing for the dust. Have the big doc write an order to Sergeant Weishaple saying I can no longer dig graves—you either!"

"Wouldn't that be a treat."

"Wait, a single exception to that order."

"What's that?"

"I'll be happy to dig the grave for Weishaple myself!"

Two days earlier, Marco and Oskar were on perimeter guard duty when the Brits, aided by the Americans and Egyptian volunteers, launched a night attack. Caught off guard, the entire German battalion found itself rushing for defensive cover. Oskar and Marco ran from their forward foxhole once the order to retreat was given. Several explosions seemed to follow them, and when they finally took cover behind the carcass of a troop transport, Marco pulled Oskar close. "Are you hurt?"

"No. You?"

"Fine."

Within a few moments, the Germans regrouped and the lines stabilized. When a medical officer spied Oskar and Marco hiding behind the burned-out truck, he ordered them to follow, and the three hurried to the battalion aid station. "Pick up a stretcher and help move the wounded. Start with the first cot and don't stop till you have all wounded loaded in the lorries parked near the mess tent. The medics and orderlies will give you specifics. Get going!" He disappeared in the smoke and dust of pandemonium, looking for other helpers.

After several trips from the aid station to the lorries, Marco was ready to collapse. "Oskar, hold on a minute. I need to rest. Do you have any water?"

"No."

They dropped their stretcher in the sand and were sitting on it when Weishaple came up, waving his rifle over his head like a banshee. He kicked Oskar. "What the hell are you two doing? Get up and get back to the front! We're regrouping." He kicked Oskar again. "Now's the chance to drive the bastards back."

Marco looked up at Weishaple. "We were ordered to move the wounded, sir."

"I don't give a shit who ordered you to do anything. You belong to my outfit. Now get up! You too, turnip boy!"

As the three moved closer to the fighting, flashes of small arms fire could be seen in every direction. When a few bullets whizzed overhead, they slid into a foxhole with a soldier who appeared dead or badly wounded. Weishaple gave no heed to the wounded man but bolted up to the far edge of the foxhole and began firing wildly. The wounded soldier opened his crusted eyes and shouted at Weishaple, "Not that way, you fool!" He pointed in the other direction. "That way!" Weishaple shifted his rifle and started firing again, his nostrils flaring open like a sail searching for a breeze.

Oskar tended to the injured man, who had been shot in the chest. Tiny bubbles of blood were forming at the corners of his mouth. He had a scraggly brown-and-gray beard about an inch long and eyes dark and shaped like caraway seeds. His arms were at his side, but his fingers were glistening with fresh blood as if he had just cut up a pig. "Don't waste your time on me," he whispered to Oskar. "I'm going to die right here in this grave."

Oskar pulled out a bandage and stuffed it into the hole in the man's chest, then grabbed one of his hands and slapped it against the wound. "Push hard right there," Oskar shouted. "You're not done yet, not if I can help it!"

Marco was staring at Oskar and the wounded man when Weishaple turned on him, screaming. "I could use some help here!"

Since arriving in Africa, Marco had not fired his gun, at least not at an enemy. From the time the recruits joined the regular army, the campaign had spent most of the time in retreat. For all their training and the glowing reports of the Wehrmacht's victorious achievements, the new recruits couldn't staunch the flood. The Afrika Korps was in an endgame.

Weishaple screamed again, then turned back and fired at anything that moved.

Marco clambered to the edge of the foxhole, looked up, and thought he could see stars poking through the wispy clouds. Like the ancient Greeks, he believed the stars were positioned to tell him something, something profound. He could make out Scorpius with its deadly claws and poisonous tail poised to defend itself against all danger. Could it mean he was being protected? Or was Scorpius a sign of an agonizing death about to rain down upon him? He wanted to begin firing, but his fingers were cement balls and his arms like long, lifeless grass.

Before Marco could pull the trigger, another soldier staggered over the brim. Marco turned his gun toward the intruder only to watch the wounded German soldier as he rolled to the base of the foxhole. Blood was seeping from a hole in his stomach. He was gulping air, and sweat was streaming from his hatless head to the ends of his black hair, droplets falling like rice. When he finally caught his breath, he turned and shouted, "Who the hell's been shooting at our men?" He fastened his bloodshot eyes on Weishaple, who had lifted his rifle to reload.

Weishaple's eyes darted from one person to the next like a mouse caught in a round pail. He finally pointed his index finger at Marco. "That asshole over there! He's a conscript and a fucking useless soldier."

Marco screamed at the wounded man, "No, sir, I haven't even fired my rifle. Feel the barrel, it's cold."

The soldier threw aside his own carbine and scuttled like a wounded turtle to Marco. He grabbed the barrel of Marco's rifle, put the end to his nose, and took a whiff. When he realized it hadn't been fired, he turned to Weishaple. "You are a lying sack of shit! You shot me." And with that, he scrambled to his feet and lunged at Weishaple. The two men fell against the side of the foxhole, each clawing at the other, trying to rip open the vulnerable parts: the eyes, the throat, the mouth. Suddenly, a shot echoed in the foxhole like a bullet fired into an empty oil drum, and the wounded man slumped backwards and fell supine at Marco's feet. Weishaple, in a sitting position, was holding a pistol, a small but steady stream of vapors floating from the tip.

For a moment, the wind stopped blowing and the sand settled. The cacophony of fighting drifted away. Oskar and Marco stared at the blood covering the man's face. When they looked into each other's eyes, they could feel the dread pooling like rainwater. Weishaple put his fingers to the man's neck and found only a faint pulse. "If either of you speak a word of what happened here, you'll end up same as him." His malevolent face was streaked with sweat, and his lips pulled back to show his yellowed teeth. "Not a word." Neither Marco nor Oskar could think to say anything. Sounds of nearby gunfire brought the battle back into focus, and Weishaple crawled to the rim and loaded his rifle.

Suddenly, Oskar stood up and slipped his arm under the soldier with the chest wound. "I'm going to carry this man to the aid station. He may have a chance."

"Leave him be!" Weishaple's voice was high and tight like a wounded hare. "He's going to die anyway."

Oskar ignored his officer and lifted the wounded man into a fireman's carry.

Weishaple was unsure of what to do with two witnesses. "Okay, okay. Yah, get him out of here. And you," he said to Marco, "take the other guy. Maybe there's a breath of life in him. Move it before I change my mind!"

Marco followed Oskar, and together they weaved their way toward the aid station. The route was peppered with craters, empty oil drums, burning tires, collapsed tents, and a few corpses. Much of the heavy shelling had subsided, but not all. A shell exploded ten yards in front of Oskar, and he and his wounded man toppled to the ground, their faces grinding into the sand. Marco was able to stay on his feet but dropped the soldier he was carrying.

Oskar wiped the sand from his eyes, shook his head, picked up his wounded man, and continued on. Marco followed, his bleeding soldier draped over his shoulders. At the aid station, an orderly directed them to the triage section. Both bodies were lowered carefully. "This one's dead," said the orderly, pulling his finger away from the neck of the man Weishaple shot. He lingered over the other man for a long moment. "This one still has a pulse," he muttered from his knees. When the orderly stood up, he caught a glimpse of Oskar in the tent's piercing light. "You better let the doctor take a look at you, soldier."

Blood was running down the left side of Oskar's face. "Must have come from a shell fragment," Marco declared.

Oskar smiled a broad smile, sat down, and fainted.

2

OSKAR AND MARCO

A Month Earlier, 1943

SINCE BEING DRAFTED INTO THE ARMY, Oskar believed his life was no longer his own. He was a captive in the broken dreams of political leaders chasing a worldview that hung like the dirty, yellow clouds of sand invading his nose and eyes and clinging to his hair. His own memories of quiet mornings and apricot sunsets on his farm near Kiel north of Hamburg were but dust devils shimmering in the triple-digit heat. The endless plodding of thousands of worn and split boots followed the sandy tread marks left by dun-colored tanks and half-tracks.

Germany had been at war for nearly four years. The early, quick successes in Poland, France, and the Low Countries gave way to stagnation, especially in Russia, then reversed course, and now momentum was racing downhill into a dark, inescapable chasm. The loss at Leningrad seemed to be a seminal defeat. More German soldiers died or were captured in Russia than at any other place or time in German history. But calls for a bargained settlement fell not only on deaf, but retaliatory ears. To ask for peace was a coward's way out. Those who weren't willing to die for the Fatherland were not true Germans and needed to be culled from the army. Or so was the attitude of thousands of veteran soldiers.

Oskar, nineteen, broad-shouldered with eyes the color of rich Brazilian coffee, sported huge hands and short, powerful fingers. His arms and legs showed tendons and muscles from his years of farm work. However, his great size and strength did not depict a bully, because, in fact, he was gentle and soft-spoken.

Conscription forced Oskar to become a reluctant member of the feared German Wehrmacht, creators of the blitzkrieg and liberators of all German territories as set forth by the Nazi leaders. He hated it, all of it. He was living in a nightmare and hoped to awaken from it each morning. He wanted nothing more than to return to his be-loved farm life.

Oskar's great-grandfather earned a small parcel of farmland for his service in the Franco-Prussian War of 1870-71. The government, short on funds, used acreage instead of money to pay its officers. Many of the returning officers balked at receiving such a payment; they wanted cash instead. But over time, the acquisition proved fruitful.

Nearly seventy-five years later, the family still worked the thirty acres, raising oats and wheat and clover. To keep a half-dozen Holstein cows alive and profitable milk producers all year long, the clover hay was stored in the barn's loft above the stanchions and milking parlor. A pair of Belgian workhorses, a single nanny goat, three sows in farrowing pens, and rabbits, chickens, a sheep or two, and cats too numerous to name inhabited the rest of the ground floor of the barn.

The bonds Oskar made with his animals and the daily nudging against warm, moist bodies when he entered their pens was soothing. He made a point to run his large fingers through the soft fur of the rabbits, and he cupped the velvet nostrils of the horses as he offered them a carrot or sugar cube. Oskar's gentleness and love of living creatures oozed from his pores like the sap of a severed willow branch. The farm animals sensed it, his parents accepted it, the nuns at his primary school praised it, but the military machine despised it. He hated to see any of his animals in pain and mourned them silently when they died.

Oskar endured a quick basic training, with its rigorous physical maneuvers during the day and lengthy propaganda speeches echoing in his ears at night. By any military benchmark, Oskar was a poor soldier. Gunshots frightened him, the soles of his feet were constantly in pain, and he had limited mechanical skills, a rudimentary education, and almost no knowledge of the world outside his rural northern German county. Most of the officers treated him as, aside from his brute strength, a military liability.

After five short weeks, his transport ship passed through several fortified seaports and submarine-infested waters to drop him off on the tortuous sands of the Sahara, the largest desert on earth. He and his fellow conscripts were ordered to join General Erwin Rommel's highly touted and battle-weary Afrika Korps. But by the time the new arrivals got sand in their boots, victory was an illusion.

His daily assignments resulted in digging foxholes, moving a mountain of provisions from truck transports to the mess tent, hauling boxes of medical supplies to a field station, and replacing ammunition canisters to forward artillery guns.

Oskar didn't shirk from hard work. He had been taught by his strict parents to see a job to its conclusion. He could heft hay or guide the plow behind the horses or lug the bushels of milled corn from sunup to dark. During planting times, he would be careful to make sure every seed was covered with dirt and every bit of fertilizer spread evenly. Field work was difficult at times, but he relished the reward at harvesttime and the food provided to the family livestock. He loved fresh milk, fried eggs, bacon, wheat flour bread, and all the good food his mother served; in short, Oskar loved to eat and never tired of the toil it took to produce the raw ingredients.

The desert, however, not only lacked water, it had no fertility, no season, no plant life or animals he could see. The landscape was dull and the sun fierce; even the clouds lacked shape and color and richness. Most of all, there was no hope of future happiness. Why would someone want to fight or die for this dismal land? The end of fighting could not come soon enough.

Back home, Oskar had a mixed-breed dog, Fritz, no larger than a cocker spaniel, who hid under his bed long before an approaching thunderstorm could be heard by human ears. Oskar laughed when the brown-and-white furball scurried up the steps and pinched itself between the mattress and floor. Sometimes Fritz would be crammed in so awkwardly that after the storm passed, Oskar had to lift his bed to allow the dog to escape.

In the last few weeks, with his army unit retreating and the enemy gaining, he wished Fritz was with him. The dog's hearing would be an early warning of distant shelling and could be the canary in the mine shaft.

Now his days were an endless routine of marching till dark, establishing a perimeter, cleaning sand from his rifle, digging a latrine, eating dried beef and beans, and pitching a threadbare tent.

There were nights in this ocean of sand when he would ball himself up in a fetal position and hold himself so tightly he could feel his heart pulsating through every vein. Even though the enemy shelling was far off, he didn't sleep as much as lie still to keep from breaking, afraid the ground would open at any moment and swallow him whole.

At dawn, the first shafts of sunlight streamed through the holes along the tent's creases. His army blanket did little to keep the cold air at bay, and Oskar's jaw was sore from chattering. He learned if he let his teeth hit rhythmically, like a metronome, he could lose the thoughts of the war and concentrate on the sounds of the farm. The lowing of the cattle, the clucking of the hens, even the sows grunting in their farrowing pens was easier to hear and visualize. But with the light came the sounds of the camp's waking.

"Oskar! Oskar! Get up! We're going to be moving out soon." Marco stepped into the tent.

"Not today, Marco. I'm not moving again," Oskar groaned.

"Did you hear me?"

"I don't want to move."

"Fine. Then you'll be a speed bump for a British tank."

Marco was Oskar's closest and, truth be known, only friend. Having met at the conscription camp near Hamburg in the summer of 1943, they shared the same tent from day one. Marco was witty, gregarious, worldly, and well educated. He had the lithe body of a long-distance runner, narrow hips, well-defined calves, and narrow shoulders. His brown hair was thick and parted down the middle, and his eyes were gray but flashed a hint of blue when the sun crossed his face. He was a man who could walk onto a movie set or sit at a nightclub table with a lovely woman on his arm and feel completely at home.

The universe was a known entity to Marco. He grew up in a family of readers who believed learning was a lifelong endeavor. He was able to cipher the grand events playing out on several continents, including the army he detested.

Conscripted army life was to be tolerated as a means to an end, not the end of the war, but the end of the day. Marco spent most of his time following the safest paths to survival, like those large migrating animals who know instinctually which spot in the river to ford or where the nutritious spring grasses sprout. He seemed to have survival techniques built into his DNA.

When Marco marched past gravesites marked with a small pile of gray rocks or a rusted rifle pointed upside down, he swore to himself that his fate was not going to be buried in a pile of shifting sand. His daily goal was to keep Oskar, and himself, out of trouble and out of harm. So far so good. Their friendship, Marco was convinced, would keep both of them alive.

"We don't have much time, big man," Marco declared as he held out a pair of boots. "Can you believe this pair? Real leather and hardly a scuff on them." He took a long whiff, then lowered them from his nose and stuffed them into his canvas duffel. "I found them near the burial site. Can still smell the leather, no hint of death at all. The gravediggers did a poor job of scavenging, I'd say." He zipped his bag. "Hey, wait a minute! Weren't you digging graves yesterday?"

"Not yesterday. The day before," replied Oskar. Each day after the march halted, usually by late afternoon, the lorry carrying the daily dead would find a flat area within the perimeter and graves would be dug. Quick burial was mandatory in the desert. Sergeant Weishaple loved ordering Oskar to the burial ground. "If you can't shoot straight, at least you can dig straight! Get on with it!" He would toss the shovel at Oskar's feet as he stomped off.

"Well, someone must have had sand in their eyes to let these boots get away."

"Don't remind me of the sand," replied Oskar, pulling his blanket up to his nose. The wind yesterday had been strong enough to allow grit to find refuge in every human orifice. His hair felt like a colony of ants had moved in.

"Oskar, get up! Do I have to come over there and kick you in the hinder? And you know I will. No response, eh? Okay. I'm starting to count to three . . . one . . . two . . . two and a half . . ."

"I'm moving. See, I'm up." Oskar threw off the blanket in a cloud of dust and lurched to his feet. "Shit! It's so cold. How can a guy freeze in a desert, Marco? Huh? Explain it to this *rural turnip*."

"*Rural turnip*. That's a good one."

"That's Weishaple's new name for me."

"That's pretty creative for him, but don't let it get to you. He's suffering from *little man's disease*. He knows you could break him in half, and his fear shows up as having little self-respect. Remember, though, he does outrank you, and that calls for caution."

"He's evil," Oskar mumbled.

"That too. And . . . it's thermodynamics."

"What?"

"Why it's so cold. The sun's rays bounce off the sand, making it hot in the day, and at night the heat evaporates, like steam . . . phttt! Gone. No heat, so the cold sets in. Simple. Now get a move on. We have formation in fifteen minutes."

"The sea. Are we getting closer?" Oskar asked plaintively.

"I don't know. Maybe. But what I do know is if we're late for formation, asshole Weishaple will put both of us on burial and latrine duty again."

"He hates us."

"He despises anybody who's not regular army."

"Like us." Oskar turned his boots upside down and watched a stream of sand slide out like water.

Marco emptied his backpack on the ground and started to re-pack. He shoved his clothes in first, followed by socks, a razor, tins of biscuits, canned beans, a mess tin, a small first aid kit, a bayonet, twenty rounds of ammunition, paper and a pencil, a piece of stale brown bread, and just enough room left to fit in the new boots at the top and strap it all down. "Guys like Weishaple work out their hatred on the backs of others, especially us conscripts."

With a loud and angry voice, Oskar said, "He knows I hate this war! He knows I hate this place!"

"Oskar!" Marco turned to his friend with his finger over his lips. "Not so loud! How many times do I have to remind you to keep those thoughts to yourself? There are men in our own outfit who, if they hear that, could hurt you worse than an Allied bullet."

"Sorry. I'm sorry."

Marco tilted his head. "Most of the seasoned soldiers still buy into Hitler's world domination theories. They think he has some secret weapon that will kill all our enemies and save the Reich. Ignore those guys. Just roll your blanket, and let's go."

Throwing his hands in the air, Oskar said, "I'm moving as fast as I can."

Marco stepped toward the tent's door, pulling back a flap. "Hear it, Oskar? Our morning Angelus bells, right on schedule." A low rumble could be heard in the distance. The heavy artillery guns of the Brits had moved up during the night, and the first salvo was aimed at the forces of the outer perimeter. "Six in the morning, six at night. Got to hand it to those Brits, they are predictable."

During their few weeks in Africa, it became clear the army was in hasty retreat and the regular officers and soldiers were in dismal spirits. They knew disaster was about to bring them down like a couple of wolves clinging to the hindquarters of a moose. The enemy had grown stronger, aided by the influx of American soldiers and armaments, and the only hope for the Wehrmacht was to reach a Mediterranean escape route as soon as possible.

Marco looked forward to retreating. In fact, he looked forward to the end of this senseless war just as much as Oskar but was cautious enough to keep his thoughts silent. The veterans who had seen both victory and defeat and swore allegiance to the Führer were holding out for a devasting blow to the Allies that would give Germany a chance to regroup and win back everything it lost since the debacle in Russia.

"Coming down!" Marco shouted as the center beam for their makeshift tent collapsed around Oskar. "Here comes the sun!" Marco pulled the thin canvas off his bunkmate. "You'll be sweating in an hour and wishing for the cold then."

Oskar hefted his duffel over his shoulder. "Is it safe to say I hate the desert?"

"Go ahead. In fact, holler it out from the highest dune . . . you'll probably receive an ovation!"

After formation, Weishaple tracked down Oskar and ordered him to carry an extra five gallons of water. "It's either you or a mule," Weishaple yelled, "and we ain't got no mules!"

The metal water container was heavy, but no more so than a sack of cracked corn. Oskar could stack hay all day, so he accepted the extra load silently and hoped this was the only grief he'd get from Weishaple. Marco offered to help his friend, but for every forty-five minutes in an hour that Oskar carried the water, Marco managed only fifteen.

After a couple hours of marching, Marco looked over at his sweat-drenched friend. "When we stop, I'll lighten your load by drinking as much water as I can."

Oskar's face broke into a wide smile.

On they marched, talking of home and family and childhood experiences. Marco wanted to talk about girls. Since Oskar had little experience with the opposite sex, he listened attentively. When Oskar talked, it was about planting potatoes, oats, and barley and plucking brown eggs from under angry hens. They both talked about food and how much they disliked the war. Mile after dusty mile, they marched. Mutt and Jeff. Damon and Pythias.

3

DANIEL

2019

HIS MOTHER DROPPED HIM OFF in front of the doors of Oakwood High School at exactly 7:35. Pulling the JanSport backpack over his left shoulder, Daniel passed through the security doors and across the commons and veered down the main hallway toward the academic classrooms. He walked wordlessly past students drinking Mountain Dew and eating cinnamon rolls, thinking nothing could be unhealthier to start the day. He strode as close to the walls as possible to avoid any physical contact.

In his head, he clicked off the contents of his backpack: 2 pencils, a number 10 and a number 7, 3 pens 1 red ink and 2 black ink, 15 sheets of unlined paper, 1 spiral notebook with 48 lined pages, 2 apples, 1 sandwich of organic peanut butter on whole wheat bread, 2 hardboiled free-range eggs, 12 dark-chocolate-covered almonds, and 3 juggling balls, 1 orange, 1 green, and 1 yellow. His books included a calculus text, a *Governments of the World* text, a hardbound copy of *Moby Dick*, although why he was carrying it he couldn't remember since he had finished reading it days ago, and *A Brief History of Oriental Religions*.

Daniel walked to his first class, Spanish 4. He had breezed through the entire curriculum as a sophomore, so Ms. Aaronson allowed him to work independently. She assigned him the task of translating *El Cid* into English from the original Castilian dialect.

He was a senior now, and short of bringing in some of her old college textbooks, she didn't know what else would keep him stimulated. Daniel didn't mind translating since graduation was only 97 days, 9 hours, and 23 minutes away.

When he turned the corner and slipped into room 1207, he thought of Pearl Harbor, 12/07/1941, and in the year 1207, King Henry the Third of England was born, and in 1207, Genghis Khan came to power to rule all of Mongolia.

Daniel Mannheim loved numbers. To him, the world was filled with floating numbers overflowing with meaning and backstories: speed limit signs, phone numbers, address numbers, heartbeats per minute, blood pressure numbers, license plates, etc. The endless stream of numbers corresponded with history, science, mathematics, music, and a plethora of other disciplines.

Once, when Daniel and his mother had driven to Madison for a medical checkup, he regaled his mom for nearly an hour on the number 60 which he had seen on a highway speed limit sign.

"The number 60 appears 32 times in the Bible, most notably in the book of Numbers when sacrifices by the Israelites are made, consisting of 60 rams, 60 goats, and 60 lambs. The Roman Catholic rosary consists of 60 beads, and Buddha sent 60 trained and trusted disciples into the world to carry out his teachings. There are 6 games in a set of tennis, and to win 6-0 is a wipeout."

He loved facts and words and language too, though he was reticent to use many words in public conversation. He was a person with autism and understood his affliction better than most who counseled or treated him. Some experts even used the term *autistic savant* to describe Daniel Mannheim. He might even agree with their assessment. In years gone by, he may have been publicly referred to as an *idiot savant*. Rather than disparage the misinterpreted term, he adopted it because the origin of the word *idiot* comes from the Greek *idiotes*, which means private, apart from others, or to keep to oneself. He believed the Greek definition fit him like a fine suit of armor. If his classmates, especially the Neanderthals in his school, thought he was an *idiot*, well, they didn't know one word origin from the next.

Shortly after he set his backpack down on his desk in the corner of 1207, his teacher, Ms. Lisa Aaronson, walked in, toting a large book bag slung over one shoulder and a pair of black flats in her left hand. In her mid-forties, Ms. Aaronson was a twenty-year veteran teacher of Spanish. She had hair the color of caramel, and though she had not one drop of Irish blood, she wore an outfit highlighting the color green every day. Today, she had on a lime-green skirt, white blouse, and green-and-yellow scarf tied neatly at her neck. Daniel had suffered through two weeks with a substitute teacher since Ms. Aaronson recently had arthroscopy surgery on her left knee. Her return the last few days was comforting because he could now arrive before class started and escape to the corner table he used as refuge.

When Ms. Aaronson walked in, she didn't even glance in Daniel's direction. Unless he was sick, which he rarely was, he would be poring over a book or writing in his spiral notebook and rarely looked up to offer a greeting. She left her classroom door unlocked at the end of the day, knowing Daniel would arrive before her the next morning.

"Buenos días, Daniel. Frío this morning, wouldn't you say?" She plunked her book bag loudly onto her metal desk. "I put my boots on at home, thinking the snow was going to be wet, but I found everything frozen and wouldn't have really needed them." She pulled off both boots, shaking them upside down. "Such weather for March. First rain, then snow, then it all freezes up. Can't wait for spring break." She looked over to the corner and smiled. Daniel appeared to be reading, but she knew he had listened to every word she said.

She stripped off her North Face coat and draped it over the back of her desk chair. "My husband and I are going to Florida this year for the first time ever!" She sat down and put the left loafer on. "Now that the kids are old enough to stay home on their own, it'll be nice, just the two of us." She stopped suddenly. "Oh my, I have a hole in my sock! You don't darn socks, do you, Daniel?"

Daniel looked up. "You could be punished for using the word *darn* in Massachusetts in the early eighteenth century."

"You're kidding."

"It was a swear word forbidden by the Puritans."

"Humph! I'll try to remember that, though I don't think there are any Puritans within a hundred miles of here or anybody else in this building who knows the origin of that word." She held her foot up and wiggled her exposed big toe, then slipped her foot into the right shoe. "Next time, I'll stick to *mend*. Is *mend* okay?"

Daniel nodded.

"Do you mend socks?" she asked with a grin.

Daniel shook his head.

"Oh well, no one but you will know I have a hole in my sock, and I don't think you'll tell anyone." She smiled and hid her boots under the desk.

Daniel stared down at his copy of *El Cid*. He was nearly halfway through and wanted to make as much progress as possible so he could spend more time during class working on one of his own stories.

"I'm going to run down to the office to pick up today's announcements, Daniel. Be right back."

At 7:49, Ms. Aaronson walked out, and the room was quiet until 7:53 when Seth Wenton floated in. He didn't notice Daniel in the corner and started rummaging through some of the papers on Ms. Aaronson's desk. Daniel thought he was looking for a homework assignment she may have graded, but when Seth opened the desk drawers and bent over, peering into each, he knew it wasn't an assignment he wanted. He looked inside the drawers and went through the contents methodically. When Seth caught sight of Daniel, he straightened up and said, "Hey, D-squared, didn't see you back there. How they hangin'?"

Daniel didn't respond.

"Getting a little extra credit for coming in early?" Seth asked.

Daniel looked out the windows.

"Yeah, well, I was just looking for the directions to . . . ah . . . the um . . . term paper we have to have done by the end of the quarter. You don't know where the direction sheet is, do ya?" Seth took a couple steps toward the doorway. He was well over six feet tall, with broad shoulders and sandy-blond hair. "Well, I gotta go. Ciao!" He turned for the door but stopped to face Daniel. "Probably goes without saying you didn't see me here . . . if you know what's good for ya. Right?" He stared at Daniel but didn't wait for an answer and walked out.

Daniel stared at a drawing in his textbook of Babieca, the great black Andalusian stallion of the *Cid*. The horse was a magnificent animal, a warhorse that had special powers, especially in the heat of battle. Babieca could see attackers in both directions at the same time and was able to turn the *Cid* out of trouble, saving the rider's life on countless occasions. Daniel wished the horse could be his.

When Ms. Aaronson returned, she didn't suspect anyone had been through her papers or drawers. Daniel kept his gaze on his desk, staring at the same line over and over in *El Cid*. He wanted to report Seth's inappropriate actions, but he knew enough not to say anything.

4

SETH

2019

HE WAS THE LEADER OF THE NEADERTHALS, a whole tribe of male students who reversed the evolutionary food chain by using their bullying tactics and testosterone antics to put those with the smallest brains at the top. Seth had been the leader for the past two years. His slim waist, muscular chest, and bulging biceps gave him an imposing look that few were able to challenge. His face was round and smooth like a marble. He could have been a poster boy for the Aryan propaganda machine of the Third Reich.

Daniel spent the better part of his daily routine avoiding as many of the Neanderthal tribe as possible. Unfortunately, as fate would have it, his locker was right next to Seth's.

Daniel's locker was numbered 665. June 1965. The Gemini 4 space flight and the first walk in space was a thought he could roll around in his head with pleasure. Seth had locker 666. Daniel's brain almost spun out of control with so many negative thoughts on 666. Whenever Daniel visited his locker, which wasn't very often since he carried most of his necessities in his backpack, he kept his head pointed toward the floor. He didn't want to look upon 666. Seth interpreted his downward glances as supplication to his position as the alpha Neanderthal.

After Spanish 4, Daniel spent the rest of the day trying to figure out why Seth was rifling through Ms. Aaronson's desk. She rarely gave written tests, so it wasn't an answer key. Money was out of the question. Seth and his family weren't poor, at least if Daniel could believe that from the brands of clothes Seth wore and the late-model car he drove. Maybe Mrs. Aaronson had taken something from him as punishment: a cell phone, or Chromebook, or some other personal item. He definitely didn't need a term paper direction sheet; he could get that from any of his lackeys.

Daniel's last class of the day was his American Novels class. Mrs. Hunter was reading aloud the final paragraphs of the third chapter of *Moby Dick* when the final bell rang. Most students bolted from their desks, leaving Daniel alone. He had made a habit of being the final student out to avoid the jostling and congestion at the door. Once the room cleared, he headed toward the hallway.

Before he had a chance to escape, Mrs. Hunter asked, "What do you think of Melville?" She was a large woman with short, black hair flecked with silver streaks and parted on the left side. She was older than his mom, he felt certain, with big ears made even bigger with hoop earrings the size of golf balls. She wore heavy makeup and had narrow eyes with lids that drooped to make her seem sleepy all the time. She could be fifty or sixty or older.

Daniel stopped and stared at the clock above the door. He had exactly four minutes to get to his after-classes appointment. "I think Herman Melville is overrated."

"Really? How much of *Moby Dick* have you read?"

"I finished it again last week. I read it the first time when I was ten."

"Goodness, what am I going to do with you for the next two weeks?"

"I read and write on my own," he replied, still staring at the clock.

Mrs. Hunter loved the fact that Daniel would read everything required and he could write a treatise worthy of publication on her assigned essays. But she detested his unwillingness to share his genius with the other students. Daniel was convinced if she had her way, she'd strap him to a chair and use a rubber hose to force him to give his opinions about authors and their works. In her view, what good was that God-given brain if he didn't use it to everyone's benefit.

"When we finish the novel, will you at least give your opinion on the merits, or demerits, of *Moby Dick* to the whole class?" Her voice was as strident as a knife across a chalkboard.

"Does my grade depend on it?" Daniel asked.

"I can't force you . . ."

"No thank you." He stepped closer to the door.

"You could help some of the students understand Melville's themes."

"I have an appointment in 2 minutes and 43 seconds," he muttered over his shoulder and hurried out.

5

DANIEL

2019

MRS. LENORE RYAN, SCHOOL PSYCHOLOGIST, was a matronly woman with salt-and-pepper hair, smooth skin, and a blush on her cheeks. She wore smart clothes, had long pianist fingers, and wore overpowering perfume which trailed her like an invisible fog.

She looked up at the analog clock: 3:07. She had two minutes before her next appointment, and she knew Daniel Mannheim was never late. His last class ended at 3:05, and with one stop at his locker and a short trip to the water fountain, he would step in at exactly 3:09 with his mother in tow. He would sit in the left-hand chair, put his backpack on the floor to his right, check the clock and his watch, and then stare at his shoes, or out the window behind the desk, but only if the sun was not shining. If he was feeling un-usual stress, he might pull out his juggling balls and start. His mom, Denise Mannheim, would take the chair on the right, smile, and make pleasantries.

For the past two decades, Lenore had counseled the full array of high school student concerns: anxiety attacks; unwanted preg-nancies; sexual abuse; racial bullying; hearing, speech, and sight defects; and recently, gender transitioning. But in the last few years, the bulk of her time was spent with children suffering under the autistic umbrella. The symptoms of children with autism seemed to be as vast as the universe. Each month, a new study purported to claim underlying causes and offered remedies from drug therapy to diet control. Though she was a trained psychologist, her college experience hardly touched on the causes or treatments of autism. Most counselors in her age bracket needed to google the latest information, including a workable definition, which, despite all the research, still seemed to be elusive. Prescribing a workable intervention was even more challenging.

Lenore made every effort to read current journals and attend professional seminars on autism. But when push came to shove, she relied heavily on her instincts. She was motherly in a good way, not smothering or overly protective. When discipline was needed, she could be stern without anger. Most of her students and their parents respected her and believed her action plans were helpful and handed out in a spirit of positivity.

3:09. She pulled Daniel's manila folder out of her desk drawer, located a pen that worked, and, when she pulled her chair close to the desk, she looked up to find Daniel already seated and his mother, Denise, coming through the door. Denise was in her forties but had a pair of sad eyes that made her look older, though no less attractive. She had black hair pulled back as tight as wire and tied in a ponytail with a bright red scrunchy. She was dressed comfortably in jeans, a long-sleeved white shirt, and a soft, gray vest. She wore no jewelry.

Lenore opened her arms wide, palms up, and smiled broadly. "Denise and Daniel, thank you for coming in on such short notice. As you know, the district monthly evaluations need to be completed and filed by tomorrow, and I almost let March get away from me."

"Thirty days has September, April, June, and November. All the rest have 31, except February, with 28," Daniel mumbled while looking out at the gray skies.

"Thank you for reminding me, Daniel," said Lenore.

"Procrastination can add anxiety to a person's metabolism and lead to several unhealthy syndromes."

"Thanks for the warning. I'll try to be more attentive to my calendar." She pulled at her collar and sat even straighter in her chair. "So, Daniel, how are you? Grades still going strong?"

Denise proudly interjected, "Straight As, as always."

"Wonderful." Lenore nodded at Denise, then turned to Daniel. "I was a little worried about AP Calculus."

"I thought it would be harder." He shifted his gaze to his shoes. "It's boring."

"Really?"

"I ask Mr. Feldman questions he can't answer."

"As a matter of fact, I bumped into Mr. Feldman the other day, and he says you're a bit of a handful in class," Lenore replied.

Denise looked accusingly at her son. "Not disruptive, I hope?"

"No, no, Denise, nothing along those lines. Mr. Feldman just shared his frustration is all," said Lenore.

Daniel shifted in his chair and crossed both hands in his lap, though his eyes stayed focused on his low-cut black Converse. "I know calculus better than he does."

"Daniel . . ." Denise said warningly.

"When I ask a question, he uses the internet to find the answer."

Lenore crossed her arms under her breasts. "He knows you're brilliant, Daniel. He just wishes you wouldn't remind him so often."

"It's not even my favorite subject," muttered Daniel.

"It wasn't mine either when I was a senior in high school," laughed Lenore. "But that's not the point, is it? Your teachers are doing the best they can. They realize you are an exceptional student."

"The school district thinks I'm in the special education category along with cognitively disabled and behavioral students."

"The *special student* definition covers a wide array of categories," replied Lenore. "You are wonderfully gifted. That makes you special. At least I think so, and so does your mom."

"That makes two," Daniel said, his face flushed.

"He knows he's appreciated. He just won't admit it," Denise offered.

Lenore leaned forward and opened her arms as though directing an orchestra. "What *is* your favorite activity these days?"

Denise answered for him. "It appears to be writing. He spends most of his free time in his room working on short stories."

"I have a collection of 116."

"Wow! Your English teacher must be very happy with you," responded Lenore.

"Mrs. Hunter loves *Moby Dick,* but Melville is overrated. I finished the book for the second time in five days even though she gave us three weeks. Did you know Starbucks Coffee is named for the first mate?"

"I didn't," replied Lenore.

"The narrator, Ishmael, is a fascinating character, solid and strong, not weak like Starbuck. I would've named the business Ishmael Coffee," Daniel said earnestly.

"Hmmmm . . . too bad you didn't suggest that to the founder years ago."

Suddenly, Daniel jumped out of his chair and, looking out the window, hollered, "Call me Ishmael!"

Lenore snapped her head back. "Whoa! Where did that come from?"

"It's the opening line from *Moby Dick,*" Denise interjected. "Sorry if he frightened you. He's gotten into the habit of saying it when he needs to feel stronger, maybe reaffirm his identity . . . I don't know. I've heard it a lot lately."

"Not to worry, Denise. I've heard lots worse." Lenore looked down at some papers on her desk. "So, what else has been happening?"

Denise pulled on her ear and said, "Let's see, he taught himself Portuguese and Italian recently."

"Awesome," said Lenore.

Daniel, sitting once again and staring at the floor, lifted his head toward the ceiling. "Once I mastered Spanish, the others were easy."

"Now he's working on German," Denise added.

"It's based on the Celtic tradition. Not as easy." Daniel frowned.

"Being adept at foreign languages may come in handy when seeking employment after graduation," said Lenore.

In a voice attempting to mimic Mr. Tobias, the high school principal, Daniel stood with shoulders back and called out, "*Graduation! June 7th, two o'clock. Ceremony in the gym, not outdoors, because of the elements. Make sure your gown is ironed and don't forget the tassel. No tassel, no graduation.*" And with that, Daniel sat down softly and lowered his head.

Lenore smiled. "Principal Tobias would be honored to know how closely you paid attention to his message."

"He's *definitely* ready," said Denise.

Checking her papers once again, Lenore looked up squarely at the top of Daniel's lowered head. "Classes good. Graduation set. What about the senior prom? Are you planning to go?"

Daniel seemed to collapse inward. He clenched his lips and twined his fingers behind his neck. He wanted his juggling balls.

"He hasn't asked anyone yet," said Denise. "I've been encouraging him."

"It's getting late, Daniel," Lenore said in support of his mother. "There are quite a few arrangements to be made, not to mention your date may want to purchase a dress and . . ."

"I'm not going!" Daniel interrupted. He searched his backpack for his juggling balls. When he located them, he tossed them one at a time into the air and juggled while looking at Mrs. Ryan.

"Why not? It could be fun. Most of your class will be there," implored Lenore.

"My classmates think I'm weird."

Denise turned to face him and said, "Not all of them."

"It's alright, because I hate them as well."

"That's not true," said Denise. "You and Paige Bartlett worked together on several science projects. She's a lovely girl, and very polite. The two of you built that toothpick replica of the Golden Gate Bridge, remember? You won first prize as I recall."

"We were freshmen then. I'm a senior now."

"That shouldn't matter," added his mother.

Daniel stood and moved slowly about the room, juggling as he went. "She only tolerates me because you and her mother are friends. She's going to the prom with Seth Wenton, and I hate him. He's a bully and calls me Daniel Disaster, which is ironic because as the leader of the Neanderthals, he rarely uses three-syllable words."

"There are other fish in the sea," said Lenore, trying to placate.

"The average prom-goer in America spends 443 dollars for one night of revelry. I would rather spend the money on the complete set of *Starship Troopers*."

"Sit down, Daniel, and put the balls away," Denise demanded. "You have the whole *Starship* series now."

He stuffed the balls back into his backpack. "I want to watch them all in HD."

"Well, if you're *not* going to the prom, so be it," said Lenore. "But I think it's terribly important for you to work on your social skills. After high school, you'll need to earn a living, hopefully on your own, and interact with the community, wherever that may be. People with autism can find it difficult. You need to recognize the pitfalls and work at overcoming them."

"One in 68 births in America is on the autistic spectrum," Daniel said loudly and flatly like a radio emergency announcement. "It's the fastest growing developing disability in America. Thirty-five percent of post-high school autistic graduates face unemployment every year, and in the future . . ."

"Stop!" Lenore demanded. "You can recite chapter and verse, I get that, but you need to have a goal, a realistic goal."

There was a pause and a moment of quiet in the room. Finally, Daniel said, with a hint of conviction that even made Denise flinch, "I want to be a writer. A professional writer."

"Well, now, there's a start." Lenore leaned back in her chair, then shoved some papers in his folder and closed it. "What brought you to this idea?"

"I can translate my stories into five languages, six when I master German. I can create a global audience."

Putting her elbows on the desk and leaning over them, Lenore said sincerely, "Writing is a noble pursuit, Daniel, and I would be the last person to dissuade you in any way. But until your first novel, or short story collection, is published and bringing in an income, you may have to work as a waiter, or ticket taker at the movie theater, or become a barista in a coffee shop. I don't know any writers professionally, but what I do know is most aren't self-sufficient at age eighteen."

"My father sends child support," Daniel said defiantly.

"Which will end when you turn nineteen." Denise turned to Lenore. "As part of our divorce agreement."

"Have you enrolled in a school for next year?" Lenore asked.

"We're looking at the local community college," Denise responded.

"It's a good school for starters," agreed Lenore.

"The tuition is reasonable, and I can live at home," Daniel added. "That makes it attractive."

"Don't be rude, Daniel." Denise turned back to Lenore. "They offer a technical writing course and a publishing class as well."

Lenore stood and walked around her desk, extending her arm toward the door. "Daniel, I'd like to chat with your mom for a few minutes, so if you will wait out in the hall, I promise it won't be long."

Daniel stood, picked up his backpack, and sidled toward the

door. Before he exited, he turned to look out the window and then to his mom. "I hacked into the school server this morning and read the comments you made in last month's evaluation, Mom. Please try to be a bit more positive this time. I know you think the prom will be good for socialization, but forget it." And he slipped out.

Denise let out a long sigh and shook her head. "I'm sorry, Lenore. He can be terribly irritating at times. The closer we come to the end of his high school career, the more frightened he has become. I can tell. The future scares him as much as the prom."

Lenore waved her hand dismissively. "You don't need to apologize. I've grown accustomed to his quirky behaviors. He's amazing and obnoxious at the same time. I think he knows more about psychology than me or most counselors for that matter. He has a remarkable brain. But I'm preaching to the choir, I'm sure."

"He has a good heart, but sometimes he just can't hold back. He says and does things without thinking of the social backlash. The other day when we were at the library, he told a mom to check out a certain picture book for her youngster. She looked at him politely but ignored him. He continued to lecture her on the importance of brain development by reading to children under three. She finally picked up her daughter and hustled out. I couldn't blame her."

"I do worry how he'll manage socially," said Lenore as she settled into the chair Daniel vacated. "Students in high school may call him weird, but they're immature and frightened by what they don't understand."

"Adults aren't much different, I'm afraid," lamented Denise.

"Other than you, are there any other adults he interacts with?"

"Ever since the divorce, our connection with other families or even extended family members of mine has been limited. As you know, my parents are dead, and I only have one brother who lives in California. We see him once, maybe twice a year for a few days. He's accepting of Daniel, but their relationship is minimal at best."

"What about your . . . *ex*."

"Hah! Anton? If he wasn't so busy procreating a second family, he might be helpful. His second wife is pregnant again. That makes three, and they live in Ohio. I'm just grateful for the money he sends. Without that, I would probably qualify for public assistance."

"Are you dating anyone?"

Denise laughed mirthlessly. "You're joking now."

"I didn't mean to pry, Denise, I really didn't," said Lenore apologetically.

"It's a fair question, I get it. I only wish there was time, or an inclination, or a white knight who showed up at the back door. I thought a year or so after Anton took off I might be able to date again. It never happened. In fact," Denise said with a silly smirk, "if you have any suggestions, I'm all ears."

"Sorry, I lead a dull married life," Lenore giggled. "My husband is an accountant who spends six days a week at work and two weeks in November deer hunting. If there were any great single men in my life, I would've divorced Ted and grabbed them long ago." They both chuckled.

"I agree that a male role model, other than the teachers in this high school, would be great for Daniel."

Lenore stood and walked behind her desk. "You know, I might have an idea. When Daniel mentioned he was interested in learning German, I thought of a retired German teacher from Oakwood High. His name is Mark Flour, taught here for decades. I didn't know him when he was here because he retired before I moved in, but a few of the older staff remember him and claim he was very popular with students and parents."

"Are you friends with him?"

"Not exactly. As it turns out, I volunteer over at Bethlehem Retirement Community once a week, and he's a resident there. I've gotten to know him a bit, and even though he's in a wheelchair most of the time, his mind is as sharp as mine, probably better. If I were to ask him, he might be willing to meet with Daniel, as in a tutor and student situation."

"Couldn't hurt to ask. Teachers who love language are top-notch in Daniel's book."

"I'll check into it," Lenore said as she wrote herself a little note.

"We only live a few blocks from Bethlehem. Daniel could walk. He still doesn't drive."

"Doesn't drive? Really? Did he fail his road test?"

"He's not interested in taking the test, or getting his license for that matter," Denise said, her voice full of frustration.

"What high school senior doesn't want his driver's license?" Lenore asked incredulously.

"One who knows too much about safety, that's who. He insists driving a car is an accident waiting to happen and can name ten other forms of transportation that are safer, including a rickshaw."

Lenore chuckled. "So you're still carting him around?"

"Afraid so. In fact, when he rides in a car, he always sits in the back seat right behind the driver. He's determined it's the safest spot in the vehicle. I believe he would sit in a child's car seat if they made one big enough!"

Lenore let out a loud snort. "Oh my, that's Daniel for you. A lovable eccentric."

"It is, but I'm used to it," Denise added lightheartedly. "He's gotten into the habit of calling me Hoke ever since he watched the movie *Driving Miss Daisy*."

"Hoke?"

"Morgan Freeman's character, the chauffeur. From his seat in the back, Daniel likes to mimic Miss Daisy. *Careful, the traffic light is changing color, Hoke!* Or *Slow down, Hoke, we're in a school zone!*"

Laughing loudly, Lenore hurried around her desk to stand in front of Denise. "You deserve a hug and then a medal, in that order."

Denise rose to accept Lenore's hug. "Aren't autistic children just the best? Damn, you've done a marvelous job, Denise."

"One day at a time is all I can handle," Denise pointed out.

Lenore slipped her arm through Denise's elbow and guided her to the door. "I'll contact you next week about the 'German Project.' Something good may come of it."

"Thanks, Lenore. You've been a great help these last four years. Daniel will never say so, but I'm sure he'll miss your guidance."

"It's been a pleasure . . . most of the time." She giggled. "Until next month, drive safely, Hoke!"

6

OSKAR AND MARCO

November 1943

THE THOUSANDS OF PRISONERS FROM ROMMEL'S AFRIKA KORPS who crossed the Mediterranean from North Africa into southern Italy now awaited further assignment. Since neither France nor England were equipped to handle the burgeoning number of POWs, much of the responsibility fell on America and Canada. Several *Liberty* class ships docked at Naples just days after the fighting moved north, and the large natural harbor was secured.

American personnel set up processing stations on the outskirts of Naples while the POWs languished in the hot autumn sun. After months of surviving the grueling Sahara, the heat was a mere inconvenience. Two lines of shirtless soldiers queued up in front of wooden desks staffed with clerks who checked each prisoner for name, rank, and where they were captured. A medical doctor and a few corpsmen gave each prisoner a cursory inspection. Most men were suffering from sunburn on their exposed skin and blisters on the soles of their feet. Some having suffered from dysentery for months were as thin as scarecrows. A few had an arm in a sling or a bandage around their head, but most with serious wounds or sicknesses had already been culled. Those awaiting embarkment were in fairly good health.

As each soldier passed through the medical line, he was ordered

to raise both arms and pirouette for the local MP. The Waffen SS had
dedicated themselves to the Nazi cause by tattooing their blood type,
such as O or AB, under their left arm as a sign of fidelity and broth-
erhood. When an SS was identified, he was pulled out and placed
in a separate enclosure. Most faced a future prison term beyond the
scope of the war or, if more serious charges were leveled, a war crimes
tribunal.

Oskar and Marco neared the front of the sunburned bodies with
their arms above their heads. "I am so thirsty I could drink a bottle of
seawater," Marco whispered to Oskar.

"Don't remind me," replied Oskar. "I can still taste sand in my
throat, and my stomach is groaning." They moved slowly toward
the American MP. "The only good thing about this medical exam
is we'll be rid of Weishaple. He has that tattoo under his arm. You
ever see it?"

"Let's hope the Amis MPs don't miss it," Marco answered.

"I thought only the SS were allowed to have a blood tattoo?"

"Weishaple joined the SS at the beginning of the war but was
kicked out."

"Kicked out?"

"He made off with one of the officers' mistresses or something.
That's what I heard."

"We had to put up with his shit for making eyes at some officer's
whore?" Oskar groaned.

"Afraid so. Aren't we the lucky ones."

Weishaple was only four or five men ahead of them as the line
serpentined forward. When it came time for Weishaple to spin
around for the MP—who was a short man, no taller than five foot
two, with droopy eyes and a bored expression—Weishaple flicked
his bony hips, and his trousers dropped. The MP guffawed at first,
then snarled at Weishaple, who had lowered his left hand to pull up
his pants and hopped forward amidst the mounting laughter. It all

happened in a few seconds, but for Weishaple, his antics allowed him to escape the discovery of the SS marking, and he proceeded with the rest of the prisoners.

"Did you see that?" Marco whispered anxiously.

Oskar nodded slightly and lowered his bushy eyebrows as far as possible.

"Don't say anything," Marco pleaded.

"I won't. I won't," Oskar replied with a bit of fear rising in his voice.

For now, Weishaple was to remain in their company. Repugnant as it was, no recruit would call out an SS member. Weishaple had a cadre of friends, and they would certainly take their revenge on a snitch.

America was poorly equipped to transport large numbers of either men or equipment overseas at the beginning of the war, as most available navy ships for transport were leftovers from World War I and were either obsolete or in poor running condition. In 1936, President Roosevelt signed the Merchant Marine Act, and in short order, new ships were hurriedly being built to transport aid to England, which in 1940 seemed to be on the edge of defeat by Hitler and his incessant bombing campaign. Once the U.S. entered the war in 1941, shipbuilding became a frenzied activity.

Eighteen American shipbuilders between 1941 and 1945 produced 2700 *Liberty* ships to carry men and munitions around the globe. In 1941, the average length of time to build a seaworthy *Liberty* ship took 230 days. By the end of the war, the average was forty-two days. One ship was built in California in under five days. Each ship was constructed in assembly-line fashion, not unlike Henry Ford's car plants. All 2700 *Liberty* ships were built according to the same construction plan so parts could be manufactured throughout the country and sent by rail or truck to the dry docks for assembly. Over two hundred *Liberty* ships were fitted with extra latrines and larger mess halls to double as troop carriers, supplies going out and wounded or relieved soldiers coming home. Designed to carry up to five hundred men, by the end of the war several *Liberty* ships were known to carry as many as a thousand.

By September of 1943, the American *Liberty* ship SS *Ambrose Bierce* had already crossed the Atlantic three times, carrying tanks, jeeps, ammunition, food stuffs, and other military items as well as a crew of forty-four. As part of several convoys protected by U.S. destroyers, it had survived U-boat attacks and near-hurricane-force storms. The latest crossing experienced the only damage, a minor collision with a French cargo ship in the harbor of Dakar, Senegal. Repairs were completed within a week, and the ship steamed on to Italy.

When the food and medical provisions for the American army were safely unloaded in Sicily, the SS *Ambrose Bierce* was ordered to Naples to pick up wounded American soldiers and fill up the remaining space with prisoners of war. On November 7th, 1943, the SS *Ambrose Bierce* lowered anchor in the calm waters of Naples harbor.

The shadow of Naples' Castel dell'Ovo, overlooking the harbor, covered a large portion of the barbed-wire enclosure hastily erected by the American Military Police to hold German POWs before final inspection and boarding. Built in the twelfth century by the Normans who captured Naples, the site of the castle had many owners prior to the Norman takeover. The Middle Ages castle, built as a harbor fortification similar to what might be found in England or Scotland, received its unusual name, the Egg Castle, from a legend attributed to the great Roman author Virgil. According to Virgil, if the defenders of the castle placed an egg inside, and if the egg remained unbroken, the city of Naples would remain safe. Many believed the legend to be true as the castle survived unscathed during the Nazi occupation and the retaking of Naples by the Allies. After the battle, several dozen unbroken eggs were found throughout the castle.

In the Naples harbor, the SS *Ambrose Bierce* refueled and took on enough provisions to keep several hundred POWs alive for an Atlantic crossing. The crew, having returned from a week layover, were sated with the tastes of Italian wine and cuisine and the company of local women who welcomed the American "heroes" with open arms.

Once the processing of the prisoners was finished, the human cargo was separated into several large groups awaiting the order to embark. Three centuries earlier, Spanish and Portuguese ships crammed hundreds of Africans into their dark holds from similar harbors. The POWs wore the same palpable fear on their faces in 1943. They were to be carried to an unknown destination by a hostile captor and kept for an indeterminate amount of time, and the Atlantic crossing was still dangerous. The open sea was a vast hunting ground for submarines, and even in a protected convoy, safe passage was never certain.

The fateful city of Pompeii, located a short distance from Naples at the base of Vesuvius and buried in ash for centuries, was a constant reminder of the fragility of life. What seemed so secure and familiar for thousands living in Pompeii disappeared in an instant eruption of fire and ash. The stories of the Vesuvius eruption were heard everywhere in Naples, and though they couldn't visit the volcano's artifacts, the German POWs seemed to know that life on their home continent had come to a calamitous end, and some feared they may never set foot on European soil again.

There was little noise as the ravaged captives plodded in single file up the gangplank, like circus animals returning to their train cars, or ants on the move. Heads slumped and arms at their sides, they disappeared into the dark cavities of the ship.

On November 14th, the SS *Ambrose Bierce* raised anchor and steamed out of Naples' harbor. The peak of Mount Vesuvius was visible for an hour or more before it hid among the cirrus clouds long and thin like orange peelings in the gloam of the day.

After a few days at sea, the dank and metallic holds of the *Bierce* were muggy and smelled of urine, vomit, and sweat. Mold quickly formed on the inside of socks and on the edges of worn leather boots. Soldiers were strewn wherever they could find a space large enough to sit or lie down. Some had their backs to the bulkheads and could feel the vibrations of the two 2500 horsepower steam engines as they turned the sixteen-foot propellers. *Liberty* ships were welded for quicker construction, unlike most ships of their class which were individually riveted. Though not as strong as the rivets, the welding did create smoother walls, and those walls were soon coveted by the men for their comfort as a place to lean against.

Each *Liberty* ship was equipped with a sound system that allowed the crew to communicate from bow to stern, and, for several hours at a time, the captain turned on the American Forces Radio to hear the latest in news reports of the war and listen to contemporary music. Bing Crosby and the Andrews Sisters were singing a rousing version of "Don't Fence Me In" when Marco elbowed Oskar. "I love American music."

"What do they call this music?" Oskar asked.

"I think it's called *swing*," he answered. The two were sitting back-to-back and swaying slightly to the rhythm.

"*Swing*? What the hell does *swing* mean?"

Marco turned his head slightly and said into Oskar's ear, "I think it's because you can dance to it and *swing* your partner." He stood up and looked down at his buddy with his hand outstretched. "Want me to show you how to *swing*?"

"On this tub? Are you crazy?" Looking cautiously at the men sprinkled nearby, Oskar whispered, "They already think I'm a sissy."

"Forget them," Marco said dismissively. "Dancing is a noble hobby. Besides, it's good exercise." With that, Marco bent his knees and moved his arms up and down in some sort of homemade calisthenic while singing softly, *"Don't fence me in* . . . come on, Oskar, time to work the stiffness out."

Oskar stood up but remained motionless, watching Marco flash his self-assured smile. After a moment, he admitted, "I've never danced."

Marco stopped bending. "Not even to a polka at Oktoberfest?"

"Nope."

"Proves you are a country turnip!" Marco said with a laugh.

Oskar could feel the stares of men on his back like a thousand pinpricks. He caught sight of several faces fixed with malicious sneers. "Can we sit down again?" he asked, his voice catching.

"Sure, okay." And with that, they resumed their back-to-back positioning. Oskar folded his arms over his chest but could feel Marco still swaying slightly to the music.

"Damn, I wish I knew how to speak English like you, Marco."

"You'll be fine. I'll help you. Be thankful we won't have to learn Russian. We wouldn't be listening to swing music if we were headed to Siberia."

"You can understand and talk to the Amis. I saw you talking to one of the guards up on the deck."

"Nice guy, too. His name is Kervin. I asked him why this ship was named the *Ambrose Bierce*. Know what he said?"

Oskar answered bitterly, "Of course I don't know what he said. I don't know English. Did you forget already? And why not ask him something important like, can we get more food? I'm always hungry."

"Easy, partner, I get it. But speaking English doesn't mean I have any special privileges or anything. I eat the same food and sleep against the same cold steel as you."

Oskar rested his chin on his chest. "I didn't mean it that way. I

just meant you're so much smarter." He sulked for only a few minutes. "So, why is the ship named the *Ambrose Bierce*?"

Marco turned, his mouth forming a large grin. "That's the funny
thing. Kervin had no idea. None. As far as he's concerned, the name
Ambrose Bierce could belong to a gangster or a movie star or a truck
driver."

"Or a farmer," Oskar chipped in.

"Exactly. But guess what, Oskar? I know who Ambrose Bierce
is," Marco said, his eyes shining brightly and his smile expanding to
the entire width of his face.

"How do you know?"

"You just said I was smart, didn't you? I thought everyone would
know Ambrose Bierce."

Oskar punched him on the upper arm. "Liar. You're making this
up."

"Ow! I'm not. Remember I told you my dad's brother lived in
England, and every summer for years before the war, we visited?"

"Yeah, where you learned English. So?"

"Well, my uncle loved to read, and he especially loved to read
stories about American cowboys and Indians with titles like *Riders
of the Purple Sage*, *The Last Rider*, *Sunset Pass*, *Valley of the Wild
Horses* . . . the books were always displayed on tables or shelves. So,
one day I picked up a story called *A Horseman in the Sky* and read it.
It was good, too. And it turns out the author was . . ."

"Ambrose Bierce!" Oskar declared.

"See how smart you are?"

"Did you tell Kervin the guard that this bucket of steel is named
for a writer?"

"Nah," said Marco with a dismissive tone. "Better to keep certain
things to one's self and stay out of trouble. Maybe it'll come in handy
later. Who knows?"

Soon they returned to leaning back-to-back like a couple of high school boys in a Norman Rockwell painting. After a few minutes, a solemn look appeared on Oskar's face. "You think the Americans will torture us?"

Marco shook his head. "Why would they do that? We don't know anything important. We aren't officers. We're just a couple of foot soldiers, conscripts. For the first time since we found ourselves in this lousy war, being lowly draftees might keep us safe. It shows we didn't want to be here. At least we didn't *volunteer* to be here."

"That's true, I guess. But I'm still scared."

"Truth be told, so am I. So is everyone on this boat."

Oskar seemed to think about that for a long moment before blurting, "I don't want to die in a strange country."

"Oskar, you just turned twenty years old, you're not injured, you're not sick, and you're not going to die!" Marco turned his head and spoke directly into Oskar's left ear, the one that showed recent pink scars from the shell blast. "We're prisoners of war, not murderers being sent to the gallows. There's a thing called the Geneva Convention, and the Amis have to treat us with some kind of, I don't know . . . rules. And torture is not one of them."

Oskar closed his eyes tightly and turned ever so slightly. "What about Weishaple? He's a murderer. We both know that."

"And we need to keep that information between us," Marco whispered.

"But he and his buddies are on this ship."

"Just ignore them."

Cupping his hand over his mouth, Oskar spoke in a voice almost inaudible. "Some of the older soldiers here frighten me more than the Amis. I see the way they look at me. The way they laugh when I walk past. They think I'm a coward just because I never fired my rifle in battle. Not once. They know I ran when the firing got close."

"Everybody ran at the end," reminded Marco. "Weishaple and his gang like to spread lies to cover their own consciences. Weishaple is a bully looking for a scapegoat. He gave up like the rest of us. Guys who didn't run are in some sandy grave in the desert. There are no cowards or heroes in here, Oskar. We're all prisoners, that's it."

After another long pause, Oskar continued, "You have more courage than I do, Marco. You're smart and know who Ambrose Bierce is, things I'll never know. You have a girlfriend . . ."

Marco stopped him. "*Had*. I *had* a girlfriend."

"Right, *had*. What was her name again?"

"Martina, and she was very pretty."

"She broke your heart?"

"Not really. Maybe . . . I don't know, it seemed it was over before we had a chance to know what love is all about."

Oskar asked sympathetically, "She ended it?"

"She moved. Her father was a member of the National Socialists and got called away to Berlin. Last I heard, he had a fancy job in an armament factory. I tried to write, but she didn't respond, then the war got in the way . . . you know."

"Yeah, I guess." After a minute thinking about girls, Oskar admitted, "Girls are still a bit of a . . . mystery to me."

Marco shook his head in agreement. "Me too, Oskar. Me too."

Oskar changed subjects. "Do you ever think how much we would be missing in our lives if a torpedo hit us right now and we ended up as fish food?"

Marco called up as much bravado as he could muster. "I don't plan on missing a thing once this war is over. We've made it this far, haven't we? We lasted through basic training, then the desert, and Italy—you and me, Oskar, we'll survive in America, too. I have faith."

"If we aren't blown up first."

"We can't control U-boats, not that I think a torpedo will hit us, but try to worry about things you can control . . ."

"Like my stomach?"

"Exactly!"

The loudspeaker crackled, and the music stopped. A few seconds later, the following news announcement blared:

This is the Armed Forces Radio with an up-to-the-minute report: American and British forces have landed at Anzio, Italy, and caught the German army by surprise. The Huns are on the run! American tanks are racing toward Rome. Soon all of Italy will be liberated . . . stay tuned!

Since the radio news came regularly, most of the POWs paid no attention. What they listened for were calls for chow or a trip to the upper deck. Every eight hours or so, POWs were escorted to the open decks to exercise and breathe in a bit of ocean air. On sunny days, they were blinded like miners when they emerged out of the darkling depths. Many held their hands over their eyes for several minutes of adjustment. Some even pulled their cotton shirts with the large PW stenciled on the back over their heads to be used as a cap. On cold days, the wind lashed at them like shoestrings and they scurried about the deck looking for a leeward spot to keep warm.

Whatever the conditions, the endless ocean and the salty air were a balm, a chance to exhale the stink of the ship's basement quarters and walk without stepping over each other. It was a short viewing of the horizon at dusk, with its purple and pink cloud formations more brilliant than a nighttime firefight. Sometimes seabirds crossed the decks, searching for scraps of bread or potato peelings. A pod of dolphins often zipped through the ship's wake, hunting the small fish pushed to the surface by the propeller's commotion. When the thirty-minute recess was over, a chorus of groans could be heard like those from elementary students forced to return from recess.

But for one soldier, the ocean was an irresistible Siren more attractive than what Odysseus faced on his voyage home from Troy. The green waves broke like a pair of welcoming arms, and the bubbly, foam-like fingers were too irresistible.

The lonely soldier, tormented by dreams of desert scorpions and mangled bodies and endless shelling, heard the Siren's seductive voice and stepped between the lifeboats, away from the eyes of the guards, and climbed to the top rail. Witnesses claimed his face was content, with a hint of a smile, as he spread his arms open like a priest about to give a blessing. Without a word, he leaped as far into the air as possible, then disappeared like a torpedo to the fate of the underworld, leaving behind but one tiny splash.

"Did you know that guy who went overboard?" Oskar asked Marco.

"I didn't know his name. He was from Cologne, I think. I heard him talk about it once."

"Cologne, your hometown?"

"Yeah. He was part of a tank crew and saw lots of action, at least that's what I heard."

"Was he the guy who was always talking to himself at night?"

"That's the guy. He was troubled, Oskar." Marco shook his head and frowned. "Don't take any lessons from him."

Oskar nodded. "He'll sleep better now."

The next squawk from the loudspeaker ordered chow lines to be formed. Men who seemed listless and lost in idle thoughts, or playing solitaire, suddenly moved like a school of minnows when a hungry predator comes into view. They scurried toward the stairs, even knocking each other aside in the process. Shouts and occasional shoving took place under the guards' lazy eyes.

As long as nothing escalated to the point of spilling blood, budging in line was tolerated. Oskar tried to get a spot toward the front of the line. Not only was he perpetually hungry, but he remembered the days when the Wehrmacht dished food by rank and the conscripts were always last. Some days in Africa, the bread was mostly crust and moldy, the soup a thin broth at best. Marco kept reminding him this wasn't the Wehrmacht, but Oskar still wanted to be up front.

Weishaple and a few friends budged in front of Oskar; they chuckled among themselves and ignored the angry stares from others. One of the bullies pushed Oskar backwards, and when he tried to get out of the way, he stumbled and fell. As Oskar was going down, he flailed his arms and hit the bully square on the cheek. Weishaple rushed over, and before Oskar had a chance to gain his footing, Weishaple jerked him upwards by the neckline of his t-shirt and jabbed him in the nose. He bent low, and with his face a few inches from Oskar, said, "I don't like you . . . coward! From now on, I want to see you at the end of the line." Oskar could smell the stench of his unbrushed mouth and watched as his nostrils opened and closed like tiny pink clams. "We have ways of makin' troublemakers and disloyal soldiers disappear." The gang of bullies snickered and slapped each other on the back. "You think about that man who jumped overboard and ask yourself if you might be next."

Oskar trembled with rage and fear.

"Got it?" Weishaple pushed Oskar and watched as he flopped back against the stairs.

By the time one of the guards closed in, Weishaple had already slithered away and Oskar was on his feet, his hand flat against his face. The guard, a young soldier with so many freckles he looked like human camouflage, asked Oskar what happened, but by then, Marco intervened and told the guard in English that Oskar was fine. Marco put his arm around Oskar's broad shoulders and turned and walked toward the end of the line. Oskar's pupils were large ink spots, but he said nothing. When they were out of earshot of the others, Marco said, "You're okay, Oskar. They can't really hurt you." Marco didn't believe his own words but couldn't think of anything else. "Even if we're last in line, the Americans always give everyone the same amount of food. They seem to always have enough. Rank doesn't mean a thing in here."

When Oskar's hand fell away from his face, a few drops of blood showed above his upper lip like tiny pimples. Oskar pulled the sleeve of his shirt up and wiped them away. He turned and watched the last of the line move to the stairs. "I've been hit harder by a horse, Marco, enough to knock me out. His punch was nothing. I hate him."

Marco whispered, "He thinks because he's SS he has the right. But he doesn't, not anymore!" As they walked slowly toward the stairs, Marco gave Oskar some good news. "The guard, Kervin, told me we're gonna dock tomorrow. You won't have to deal with Weishaple and his thugs once we're in America."

"We've heard that docking rumor for over a week," said Oskar sullenly.

"Not from a guard."

"Did he say where?"

"New York," answered Marco.

"Is it warm there?"

"I don't know, but it doesn't matter. We'll be shipped to the interior."

As Oskar took the first stair, he looked back and found Marco grinning. "What's so funny?"

"Not funny, really, but Kervin said we're headed for a place called Wisconsin. When I asked him what the weather was like, he said it's supposed to be very much the same as Germany, and they're supposed to have lots of dairy cows."

With that, Oskar's face brightened in the light shaft streaming down the staircase. There was only a hint of blood in one nostril. "I like cows," he said and hurried up toward the chow line.

7

STANLEY

November 1943

"I TAKE IT, SERGEANT STANLEY, you've never been to Milwaukee."

"No, sir, first time. Does it show that much?"

"Your head is moving like a bobber in a school of hungry perch."

"Sorry, sir, but this city is *big*! I've been to Green Bay and Oshkosh, but they don't compare."

"See that clock tower over to your right?" asked driver Albert Davel, Commandant of Central Wisconsin POW camps.

Stanley bent over and stared out the windshield. "Yes, sir, I do. I think it reads 2:35."

"Well, that's where we're headed. Union Station, home of the Milwaukee Road. When that tower was built way back in 1880 or so, the face of the clock was the largest in America," he said with obvious pride.

"You don't say."

"Uh huh. Probably not the biggest anymore," Albert mused. "I had an uncle who was a bricklayer and worked on that tower."

"Really?" said Stanley.

"He lived straight south of here, on Oklahoma Avenue. Started out as a hod carrier and worked his way up to become a master bricklayer and president of the local masonry union."

"Impressive." Stanley had no idea what a hod carrier was, or what a president of a union's duties entailed for that matter, having grown up on a farm in Outagamie County. But he did know how to keep Albert and those in authority, especially officers of higher rank, happy by listening to their stories and laughing at their jokes.

Sergeant Stanley, age twenty-four, was christened Ogle Washington Stanley after his grandfather. He hated the name Ogle and preferred everyone just call him Stanley. His black hair and a pencil moustache made him look like a silent movie actor. His body was wiry like a lightweight boxer, and his face was thin with eyes the color of weak green tea set wide apart. His crisp uniform was perfectly creased.

Stanley joined the Army Reserve when his admission to the regular army was denied. Born with a heart murmur, every doctor who listened to his chest since he was a youngster warned him against too much physical exertion. As it turned out, not once had he ever felt any pain or believed his heart weaker than any of the other children at school or on the farm, but when he thought it was to his advantage, he would play his "trump" card: no lifting heavy bales of hay in summer's heat, no plowing through snowdrifts with a shovel, no pulling a dead cow from the manure-layered stall. He slid into the avoidance of difficult work as easy as an alcoholic can find his next glass of beer.

Stanley's health, in general, was excellent, and when it served his purposes, he was quick to show his stamina and athleticism. But at the Army recruiting station, he argued with the doctor, claiming he was fit as a fiddle to serve, his heart never faltering. The old country GP who donated his time to give physicals to inductees in central Wisconsin listened to Stanley's heart murmur and endured his boisterous pleas, but in the end, conferred a medical deferment for active duty. Army Reserve was his only option.

"I'll park the car across from the entrance over there on Juneau Street," Albert said. "You go on in and head right to the stationmaster's office. It's not hard to find. You're looking for the arrival of the special Hiawatha troop train from New York. Find out what track it's on and if it's late or on time."

"Yes, sir."

"I'll find the driver of the bus, let him know we're here. Then I'll join you. Any questions?"

"No, sir. Looking forward to it."

Albert glanced over and caught the crooked smile on Stanley's face. "You seem eager enough. This your first assignment?"

"First of any consequence. I've been stuck at a desk doing background checks for the last month or so. Meeting the enemy face-to-face on our own turf will allow a little payback."

"I don't think these men will pose any threats."

"How many of them, sir? I mean, in the group?" Stanley asked.

"You'll be in charge of thirty-two. And when this war is over, you need to return the same thirty-two. Got it?"

"You can count on me, sir."

"I hope so, Sergeant."

8

COMMANDANT ALBERT DAVEL

November 1943

DAVEL DODGED A FEW PEDESTRIANS carrying suitcases and pulled the ten-year-old Pontiac to the curb. "Okay, out you go, Sergeant." And with that, Stanley loped off and disappeared into the bustling station.

Albert was a small man, not over a hundred thirty pounds, bald with large chocolate-colored liver spots sprinkled about his head. He had gentle eyes and a quick smile, like he was always ready to accept a clever remark or good joke. He was born in Germany in 1887, but at the age of six weeks emigrated with his parents to America, ending up in Thorton, a small farming town in central Wisconsin.

In his early twenties, he married an Irishwoman, opened a dry goods store on Main Street, and became the father of eleven children. A devout believer in the power of education, he insisted that every one of his tribe receive some schooling beyond high school. There was nothing a man or woman couldn't achieve in the few decades of the twentieth century, and he pushed his family to be a part of the American success.

Albert Davel was arguably the most civic-minded and patriotic man in town, and in 1912 was elected mayor of Thorton. But when the First World War erupted, despite being freely elected, he was forced to resign. Nationalistic prejudice was like a fog that seeped in overnight. Being German-born was enough to fuel the fears of small minds.

Twenty-five years later, the sentiment behind the slogan "We All Need to Pitch In to Defeat the Fascists" was strong enough to overshadow Albert's birthplace, and the Army Reserve welcomed him with open arms. Because of his leadership roles in city government and organizational skills as a small business owner, he advanced quickly and was named Central Wisconsin Commandant by the War Office, overseeing the placement and well-being of over two thousand prisoners of war, mostly Germans.

His years behind a grocer's counter allowed him to easily offer a toothy smile, and he served his staff and the prisoners as he might his customers, fairly and courteously. He held no grudges against the POWs, nor did he believe they should receive any special treatment given that he, too, was of German parents. He carried out his orders willingly and efficiently, finding suitable locations in rural areas, converting them into habitable POW camps, and supplying decent food and fruitful jobs for those prisoners who were in good health and willing to work.

Union Station was alive with hundreds of men and a few women in uniform scrambling from one platform to the next or scurrying out the exits to waiting taxis. Most of the soldiers struggled with overloaded canvas bags pulled tight at the top and lettered with their name, rank, and outfit. Some dragged wooden footlockers with black handles and black clasps. Representatives of all branches of the service seemed to be in perpetual motion, as though the war might be won or lost before they reached their destinations.

Women and children, grandparents and friends waved handkerchiefs and small American flags to soldiers already boarded on long, yellow train cars, their faces pressed against the windows. One train began to move as a line of khaki-sleeved arms protruding from open windows jiggled fingers in a last sign of departure. Mothers cried and dabbed at their eyes. Wives threw kisses and called out remembrances. Everyone hoped they would see each other in one piece again.

Albert spied Stanley striding through the maze of tracks and joined him on the platform. The stationmaster informed Stanley that the Hiawatha prisoner train had already pulled in and was sitting on Track 7.

Several reservists in butternut uniforms and felt caps were waiting to escort the prisoners. Steam rolled out from under several of the mustard-colored passenger cars and a cluster of blue-and-gold uniformed porters waited for instructions.

Albert gathered the reservists to attention and gave them the procedure for disembarking. They listened with bored expressions before disappearing onto the waiting train. As commandant, Albert waited on the platform, looking up at the faces of unshaven men peering through the foggy windows. When they rubbed the moisture away, he could see the signs of sleeplessness upon hollow cheeks. They looked upon their new destination with big eyes and staid expressions, not knowing whether they should be happy or fearful.

Many of these men had been enthusiastic in war, then had broken slowly through boredom and unfamiliarity to the point where they kept all emotions in check. They had traveled thousands of miles for resettlement and were now close to the finish line. Albert turned to Sergeant Stanley and said, "Well, Sergeant, now you'll get a chance to see the enemy up close and personal."

A few minutes later, a column of men in olive-green shirts and gray cotton trousers slowly stepped down from the steel cars. On the back of each shirt, the large letters PW were visible as though lit by neon. Some were limping, a few brandished bandages across a forehead or around an elbow or ankle. But most appeared healthy enough that in another setting they could've been mistaken for a defeated football team after suffering a loss on a cold and soggy field. They moved slowly and deliberately, forming several uneven lines. In 1865, they could've been Union soldiers returning from years of marching and physical degradation, survivors of war's worst encounters.

Hungry, tired, disillusioned, and void of any hope, some carried a book or small shaving kit, photos, or a small canvas bag cinched at the top. They were silent except for an occasional cough, and their dour expressions were plastered to their faces as though part of the PW uniform. For two days, they had seen only the inside of a train car and fleeting glimpses of rural Midwest America. The name Milwaukee meant no more to them than Singapore, or Toronto, or Buenos Aires. They were the defeated, the vanquished, the strangers in a strange land.

Albert checked his clipboard, then ordered the guards to take the thirty-two out the side door of the terminal to the waiting bus. "Don't let any of the civilians talk to them. Make sure they all have water now if they need it and escort any that might need to use the restroom. There'll be no stopping once the bus is rolling." After twenty minutes, the column moved like a giant caterpillar toward the rear parking area, Sergeant Stanley in the lead.

As they queued up in front of the bus, their names were read loudly by an Army reservist: "Gross . . . Gunther . . . Hauptman . . . Helms . . . Holman . . . Heger . . . Eisnentraut . . . Finklemun . . . Schwiber . . . Weishaple . . . Weber . . . where is Weber?" he shouted.

Stanley hustled over to the reservist holding the clipboard. "Weber!" Stanley barked as he walked down the column. "Where is Weber?" A thin man with sunken gray eyes and a long, bulbous nose raised his hand and moved cautiously toward Stanley. "Are ya deaf? Get on the bus, you lousy Kraut!" He cuffed Weber behind the ear. "You ain't the mighty Wehrmacht here. *Schnell! Schnell!*" Weber stumbled, regained his footing, and hurried onto the bus. "And that goes for the rest of you! Move when your name is called!"

A few minutes later, Stanley returned to Albert's side. Albert cautioned him, "Let's not hurt anyone before they get to the camp, Sergeant. You'll be supervising these men till the war is over, and I want all thirty-two returned in one piece."

"You don't need to lose any sleep over that, sir. None of these cabbageheads will get away."

"I wasn't worried about escape, not unless they can swim like dolphins. I was referring to their physical health. Anyone dies, and the Army brass will be on us like ticks on a mangy dog. Got it?"

"Yes, sir."

A moment later, the bus driver came off the vehicle waving his thick arms over his bullet-shaped head. "That's it! I can't put any more on!"

Stanley snapped his clipboard to his chest. "Sure you can. I only see two more slackers, there. Stuff them in."

"Nope. It's already overloaded," the driver insisted.

"Can't be that bad."

"My bus was built to haul twenty-four passengers, and there must be close to thirty crammed in there now, and that ain't counting the guards. Any more and I could lose a couple to suffocation."

"What's one more dead Nazi, eh?" replied Stanley with a smirk. "Just two more."

"Not on my conscience. I don't care who they are."

Stanley added in a soft voice, "Look, they had a nice cushy ride from New York on a passenger train, not a cattle car. A few hours stuffed in like cordwood won't kill 'em."

"No, sir. I'm contracted to drive 'em, not bury 'em."

Albert strolled up and said, "Throw the last two in with you, Sergeant Stanley. The Army's loaned you a truck. They won't bite!"

Stanley's face turned pale. "Okay. Okay." He turned to the bus driver. "I'll take the last two in the military pickup and follow you. No stops! I want to be home by dinnertime, got it?"

The bus driver turned to go. "If we don't break down," he said over his shoulder.

"Just a minute, Mr. Bus Driver!" shouted a woman who came crisscrossing through the crowd carrying a large, white duffel bag over one shoulder. "If you don't mind, I have something for your passengers." She skidded to a stop, her bag rolling off her back like a huge mushroom. She was wearing a gray wool skirt with red piping and a matching waistcoat over a light-blue blouse. A large red cross was stitched boldly above her right coat pocket, and above her curly, dark hair sat a red and white felt hat held on by several bobby pins. "I have care packages from the Red Cross for the POWs. Can I give them out before you leave?" she asked plaintively.

The bus driver hesitated for a moment before pointing toward Stanley and Albert. "You'll have to ask them, miss. The bus is about to shove off in a few minutes." And he sauntered off.

Rose Callahan turned and walked up to the officers standing together in their matching tan uniforms. "Excuse me, sirs . . . oh, Stanley! I didn't recognize you in that fancy outfit. How . . . ah . . . how are you?" she stammered. But before he could answer, she blurted, "Are you coming or going? I mean, are you waiting for a train or just off?"

Stanley brought both feet together as though he should stand at attention when answering. "I'm here to pick up some . . . um . . . baggage. Nice to see you, Rose." He didn't offer his hand.

Albert cleared his throat. "Stanley? Who might this young lady be?"

"Sorry, sir, this is Rose Callahan. I believe . . ." He scanned her uniform. ". . . she's here with the Red Cross. Rose, this is Commandant Albert Davel."

Albert held out his hand as Rose pushed her bundle to the side with her foot and accepted his hand with a wide smile. "Pleasure to meet you, sir. I was wondering if I could deliver the Red Cross POW care packages before the bus leaves. I promise to be quick."

"I don't see why not," replied Albert. "Sergeant Stanley assures me the POWs aren't going anywhere without him. And as he's still standing here, there should be a few minutes before they head out. You know Sergeant Stanley, I take it?"

Stanley interjected, "We do . . . know each other." Before Albert could respond, Stanley turned to Rose and asked with the same sincerity he might ask youngsters selling lemonade on the corner, "How long have you been working with the Red Cross, Rose?"

"A little over a year now. It isn't much, but everybody's got to pitch in . . . right?"

Albert nodded. "That's the spirit, young lady. What's in the duffel?"

Rose bent over and fished out a small paper bag tied off with twine at the top. "Each of these has a few chocolate chip cookies, a little candy, soap, and reading material, just to tide the POWs over." She straightened up and asked, "As Commandant, are you in charge of the POWs?"

"For those assigned to central Wisconsin, I am. A couple thousand at last count, but the way the fighting's going, I wouldn't be surprised if that number goes up."

Rose bent to retrieve her duffel. Albert stepped up, asking, "Can I give you a hand?"

"Oh, no thanks, sir. I've got it. My volunteers will definitely have to make up more packages. I only have about fifty left."

"That'll cover the Krauts on the bus," Stanley said. "Total of thirty-two." His voice was stern, and his fists clenched.

"Thank you, Sergeant," she said coldly, then looked to Albert with a returning smile. "Nice meeting you, Commandant." She turned and headed toward the waiting bus.

After a few steps, Albert stopped her. "Miss! There are only thirty POWs on the bus, and a couple will be riding with Sergeant Stanley. If you want to catch the last two, you'll have to come back."

"Thank you, sir. I'll be as quick as I can and then head back."

Stanley turned his back on her as she hurried off, his tongue making his upper lip wriggle like a red worm.

9

ROSE AND STANLEY

1930s

STANLEY WAS A COUPLE YEARS OLDER THAN ROSE
but had a crush on her the moment she stepped into high school as a
freshman. For two years, he admired her from a distance, until finally
as a senior and Rose a sophomore, he screwed up his courage and
asked her out to see a movie matinee. She didn't show much interest
at first, but after he persisted, she said she would.

Stanley borrowed his father's rusted out Dodge pickup truck,
and together they drove over to Oshkosh to see a picture starring
Clark Gable and Myrna Loy titled *Test Pilot*. The plot was simple.
Gable, the test pilot, has a drinking problem and is forced to land a
plane in rural Kansas, where he meets a farm girl, Myrna Loy, who
tries to straighten him out and get him sober for good. During their
time together, the sparks of love are set aglow.

Rose found the film entertaining and loved watching Clark
Gable. Ever since *Gone With The Wind*, he had emerged as America's
male heartthrob, and Rose was not about to argue the point. Stanley
believed the movie was a road map to his future. As a senior about
to graduate, he was planning to enter the military and confront
America's enemies looming on the horizon. He was hoping, before
heading off for basic training, to find a girl to keep his home fires
burning. Little did Stanley realize that Rose had no intention of living the life of a farm wife. She was smart, adventurous, and curious

about the world. She wanted to see and taste the fruits of what the earth had to offer.

On the way home from *Test Pilot*, Stanley turned the car into a small county park that was on the shores of Lake Emily. The skies were clear, and the sun was still warm. He hoped maybe they could take off their shoes and wade in the shallows of the sandy-bottomed lake. It was May. The willows were leafed out, and the poplar trees along the shores were dropping their cottony seeds. A pair of mallard drakes scooted across the surface and out to the deep water when they walked to the lake's edge.

They shed their shoes and socks, and though the water was cold, walking in the lake was a treat after a long winter. As they slowly ambled along, the shallow waters swirled like feathery clouds behind them.

"War may be coming soon," Stanley said. "That's what all the papers are saying."

Rose broke from her reverie and looked up at him. His face was stoic, and his eyes focused out over the lake. "I hope it doesn't happen," Rose responded. "My mother's younger brother was in the last war, Uncle Michael. He's never been the same since. He doesn't work. He's not married. My grandma and grandpa have to take care of him."

She raised one thin ankle and splashed at a black water bug skittering across the emerald water. "They claim Uncle Mike was a wonderful person before he left for France. I'm afraid to go near him now." They moved past a fallen birch log as two small painted turtles slipped silently off. Rose's guilt was palpable. "I know I shouldn't, but I just can't help it. He's always talking to himself and claims to see horrible things."

"Not all veterans are like that."

"Of course not," Rose said, her voice rising, "but what good comes from war? Seems like it's all about the egos of a few leaders, male leaders. What did we, here in rural Wisconsin, gain from World War I?"

"Sometimes it's inevitable." When she didn't respond, he continued, "If we do get dragged into a war, I hope to play my part."

She looked at him and said quizzically, "You want a war?"

He answered with a bit too much bravado. "Not really. But I'll be ready. I've been practicing shooting with my father's rifle. I can hit a full can of peaches from forty yards, sometimes fifty. You should see how the peaches in the can explode when the bullet strikes ... it's ... it's ... like a firecracker going off in a toad's mouth. Guts flying everywhere!"

Rose stopped suddenly and put her hand to her mouth. "That's awful!" she said through her fingers.

"What is?" He gave her a perplexed look.

"I hope you never did such a thing to a toad. I like toads. I like frogs too. They eat lots of bugs and are fun to watch. Several tree frogs with those little suction cups for fingers visit my window every night." She turned and walked quickly ahead.

He hurried to catch up. "I've only done it a few times," he said contritely.

"Once is too many."

He backpedaled as best he could. "Don't be sore. I was just making a point about my shooting."

"I think you made a point about a lot more." She turned suddenly and headed back toward the Dodge. "I need to get home before supper." And the conversation was over. Stanley tried unsuccessfully to make amends on the drive home, but he stumbled and stammered, and the idea of future dates dissipated like the ripples on the lake.

10

DANIEL

2019

"I KNOW YOU DON'T WANT TO, DANIEL, but could you please pick up the phone?" Denise called out as she stirred a pot of linguini noodles with one hand and with the other jabbed at strips of chicken frying in a cast-iron spider. It was nearly six o'clock. "I'm sort of busy at the moment!" After a pause, she continued, "Daniel, I'm begging!"

Denise and Daniel lived in a modest ranch-style two-bedroom home built in a Millcraft factory. Every house on the block was the same design, but over the years, neighbors added a second garage or a family room out the back or raised the roof for additional bedrooms. The Mannheim house looked the same as the day the carpenters put in the final nail. The living area was small, but Daniel didn't complain since he had his own bedroom, and that was all the space needed for a single bed, small desk, and his own television to play his video games without being disturbed. His closet was no bigger than a phone booth found on an old movie set, but since he wore the same half-dozen outfits, it was adequate.

"Daniel!" A moment later, the ringing stopped, and Denise could hear Daniel's muffled voice as he spoke a few terse words. He rarely used the landline, and even rarer was there a call for him. It was an inconvenient noise when it rang, and he often put his hands over his ears until it stopped. When forced to answer, Daniel listened and

66

usually responded with single-word comments, then at the conclusion replaced the receiver without a goodbye.

Denise stood over the avocado-green gas stove holding stir forks. "Who is it?" Her voice echoed down the hallway but met no response. She went back to browning the chicken. She would ask him later.

At exactly six o'clock, Daniel walked into the kitchen and asked, "Did you use organic noodles?"

"Of course, though I could've bought twice as many of the non-organic ones for the same price."

"And the chicken's free-range?"

"I ran it down in the backyard myself."

"I know that was a joke."

"You ask me about the chicken every time, and the answer is always the same. So, who was on the phone?"

"It's time to eat. It's already 6:01."

"First tell me about the phone call."

He hesitated. Supper always started at 6:00. For every minute past the hour, he believed his digestive system had to work harder and his vitamin intake would be suppressed. He never ate after 7:00 p.m. even if there was an emergency. If supper wasn't served on time, he would fast until morning. "I'm ready to eat now."

"So am I. But I also want to know who was on the phone. Quid pro quo," Denise said, her voice rising slightly.

"Did you cook the chicken all the way through? I don't want to come down with salmonella."

"I think you're safe." She asked again, louder this time, "The phone? Who was on the phone?"

"Dad."

"Thank you. That wasn't so hard. And what did Mr. Mannheim have to say?" She set the chicken on a cutting board and started slicing. "Did he want to talk to me?"

"No."

"Of course not," she said with resignation. "Did he want to invite us to a baby shower?"

"He said his wife is due on June 15ᵗʰ, 93 days from now. Neil Patrick Harris, aka Doogie Howser, was born on June 15ᵗʰ, so was baseball great Billy Williams, and . . ."

"Stop right there. I don't need a litany of famous people born on the date of your father's second-family offspring, okay?"

Pointing at the cutting board, he shouted, "Cubes, Mom, not strips! I don't want to perform the Heimlich maneuver."

"Really? Are you sure you wouldn't want a good excuse to punch your dear ol' mom in the stomach?" Daniel flinched. When he took his seat at the table, she could tell he had been hurt by her remark and apologized. "Sorry, that was uncalled for. A bad joke on my part." She dished up the noodles and chicken on two plates, set one in front of Daniel, and sat down with the other. "What else did your dad say?"

"He wondered if I was still on track to graduate in June."

"Hah!" Denise chortled. "Did you tell him you're the valedictorian?"

"I don't think he believes me."

"Did he say he was going to be here for the graduation?"

"He said he would try, but . . ."

"But he's *so* busy with his new wife and new family it would be *so* difficult." She raised her hands in front of her and shook them back and forth. "His way of saying he's not coming."

Daniel stared at her with resignation. "He said he'd try."

She pulled off her apron and tossed it toward the sink. "He *tried* to get here for Christmas, and he *tried* to get away at Thanksgiving, and he *tried* to work us in during his vacation last summer. Look where that got us! He's not coming, and that's that."

"He knows you will accompany me up to the stage at graduation. Not everyone will have two parents."

"Of course I will walk up with you, Daniel. I wouldn't miss it for the world. I'm so proud of you. And you're right, other students only have one parent. Some are deceased, others divorced like us. It'll be simply fine."

"I've tried my graduation gown on. It fits."

Denise didn't seem to hear. She was still angry with her ex. "I don't care if he doesn't come for me, but I feel sorry for him. He hasn't seen you in over a year, or kept up with your schooling. He can't grasp how wonderful a student you truly are. His loss. I'd be surprised if he could pick you out of a lineup." She pushed her chair back, scraping the linoleum floor like nails being pulled from a tin roof.

"I'm not a felon, Mom. I shouldn't be in a lineup."

"Of course not, I'm sorry. You are a wonderful, intelligent, and nearly perfect son. And that's what he'll miss."

"Not *perfect* because I'm autistic?" he asked flatly.

"Don't be silly. I love you just the way you are . . . but . . ."

"What?"

Raising her eyebrows in a Groucho Marx manner, she asked, "You want to know what would make you perfect in my eyes?"

"I would."

"Well, you'd be perfect in my eyes . . . if you had a date for prom," she said and grinned a Cheshire cat grin.

Daniel stabbed at his noodles and twirled a few strands on his fork. "Dad asked me about prom too. You must have talked to him. Prom is why he called, isn't it?"

"Your father may not live with us, and for that matter may not know much about what's going on in our daily lives, but he does think you need more social interaction. He and I can agree on that." She picked up the pepper shaker and shook it roughly over the noodles. When she reached for the salt, Daniel snatched it and held it close to his chest, keeping his eyes focused on his plate.

"A woman of your years should limit salt intake," he said with defiance. "It can lead to hypertension."

"Give it to me!" Denise demanded. "It's nice to know you are concerned about my health, but if I have problems with high blood pressure, it's because a certain teenage boy, who shall remain nameless, is too smart for his own britches and can drive me bonkers! Now, hand it over."

After a long pause, he set the salt back in the middle of the table. "If your kidneys fail, don't blame me."

With a triumphant smile, she picked up the saltshaker and shook a heavy dose onto her noodles, then stuffed a large forkful into her mouth. "These are so good with just the right amount of seasoning."

When the conversation about her ex was over, Denise watched as Daniel picked daintily at his cubed chicken. He masked most of his feelings from strangers, but she knew the concern for her health came from a great fear he had of living without her. As brilliant as he was, he had trouble coping with the mundane; he would one day have to fix his own meals, always organic, wash his own clothes in baking soda, transport himself somehow, even make his own bed, leaving the sheets exactly ten inches from the headboard.

She fought with herself to avoid being overprotective, but for nearly two decades, she provided his creature comforts, and the end of his living at home was coming into focus. Though he seemed unconcerned about the future, she knew better, and occasionally the separation anxiety she anticipated shook her awake in the middle of the night and filled her with dread.

11

DANIEL

2019

FRIDAY AFTER SCHOOL, Denise and Daniel walked through the sliding glass doors of the Bethlehem Retirement Community, a skilled nursing home built in 1963 according to the numbers etched into the smooth concrete cornerstone. The one-story cream-colored brick building was licensed for seventy-eight residents and had a long waiting list. A majority of residents were rural people previously residing within a twenty-mile radius. BRC had become an essential business as well as an integral health care facility to the small town of Oakwood, which couldn't thrive without a school system, one grocery store, a handful of taverns, the nursing home, and a plethora of churches.

In the lobby of the BRC was a large aviary with a polished wooden frame backlit with fluorescent tube lighting. The rear panel was a painted scene of vanishing green fields topped with purple and orange and pink clouds floating above distant dark mountains, and if you looked closely, you could spot a tiny waterfall tumbling through a green river valley.

Several colorful birds flitted from one nesting box to the next. Others jumped or flew through artificial tree branches strategically placed throughout. Flat, wooden feeding trays near the floor held seeds that looked like thistle or sesame but were artificial and filled with a high-protein recipe. A small plastic container hanging from the outer wire dispensed wax worms, and strewn on the floor were a few crusts of organic baked cornmeal that looked like they were left over from the morning breakfast.

Daniel walked to the center of the cage. His eyes sparkled like two fireflies on a hot July evening. His fascination with birds and animals of all kinds started when he was very young. He could spend an hour trailing after an ant as it moved a tiny piece of dirt from one hole to the next, or wonder for hours how a grasshopper, with its gargantuan steely legs that seemed so out of proportion with its soft body, could leap with more ease than a well-engineered rocket machine.

There were mysteries in the smallest of creatures, and he tried to cipher them. He wondered how a slug, without feet, could move up and down a smooth concrete basement wall. Or how a mouse could fit between an air vent grate in his bedroom, but he couldn't push a pencil through the same opening. Once while walking through Riverside Park, Daniel came upon a large, black snapping turtle laying pink, glistening eggs in a shallow sandy hole. It was September, and the days had begun to turn cold. He wondered how long it would take before the eggs would hatch. He begged his mother to take him to the park whenever possible, and for weeks he hoped to catch the new turtles as they hatched. Nothing happened.

By chance, the next April, he was in the park and spied the little black creatures clawing their way out of the sand and scrambling down the grassy riverbank. He refused to go home until every one of the newly hatched turtles made it safely to the water. Winter's frost in his part of the world reached anywhere from 18 to 36 inches underground, turning the soft sand to concrete. How could the little turtles survive subzero temperatures for months on end with seemingly no protection? Next time, he promised himself, he would steal one egg and put it in his mom's freezer. Would it develop? Could he bring it to life in the warm April sun?

Lenore Ryan sailed into the lobby of the nursing home and greeted Denise warmly. "First time in the BRC?"

"It is," she answered.

"I think you'll find it quite welcoming. Most of the residents are alert and friendly. They like having company. Lots of school groups come here to put in community service hours: Girl Scouts, Boy Scouts, church groups, the National Honor Society from the high school. Seems there's someone showing up every week." Lenore caught a glimpse of Daniel pressed up against the aviary. "I see Daniel has latched on to our feathered friends."

"He's always enjoyed watching animals. If it moves, or wiggles, or flies, he can spend hours observing."

"Does he have any pets?"

"No. I tried a gecko once when he was in about fourth grade, but he became so entranced he didn't want to go to school. One day when he was at school, please don't tell him this, I let the lizard go in the backyard and convinced him it escaped on its own. Plus, I hated feeding the thing live insects. Yuck!"

"Can't blame you. I read somewhere that children with autism have an easy time bonding with the natural world. Horse whisperers, veterinarians, Native American shamans, a lot of them have autistic characteristics."

"The Temple Grandin syndrome. Unfortunately, most people with autism don't have a movie made about their lives."

"So true." Lenore took a step toward the aviary. "Daniel, time to go." Daniel stepped back from the caged birds but kept his eyes fixed on their movements. "Do you recognize any of the bird species?"

He answered methodically as though reciting a simple haiku. "6 Java finch, 9 zebra finch, 5 yellow canaries, 2 blue-and-white parakeets, both males, and 2 rare Gouldian finches."

"Which are the rare ones?" asked his mother, peering over his shoulder.

"The two on the branch in the upper left corner. John Gould, a British ornithologist, named them in 1841 for his wife. Their official name is Lady Gouldian Finch. They're native to Australia, and fewer than 2500 are thought to be living in the wild."

"The residents love them," Lenore said, "all of them." She paused for a moment, then continued, "Can we walk this way? Our host is waiting in the day room."

The three of them entered a brightly lit communal room complete with a few stuffed chairs, a round Formica-topped table with an unfinished jigsaw puzzle, a sink and refrigerator, and floor-to-ceiling bookshelves stuffed with board games, used magazines, and cribbage boards. A long, rectangular table with eight brightly colored plastic chairs was on the far side of the room.

A man, hunched in a wheelchair, was positioned near sliding glass doors that looked out onto a cement patio surrounded by rhododendron and forsythia bushes. Several bird feeders filled with black sunflower seeds and suet were being attacked by a couple of cardinals, several slate-colored juncos, and a pair of gray-crowned tufted titmouse.

Daniel walked over to the patio doors without acknowledging the man in the wheelchair. He fixed his eyes on the birds as Lenore came up behind the wheelchair. Mark Flour was paging through a *Travel + Leisure* magazine. His full head of thick hair was the color of cream cheese frosting sprinkled with cinnamon. His Roman nose protruded through two round, rosy cheeks, and he had a cleft chin covered with beard stubble that must have felt like an emery board. His eyes sparkled like sun-flecked ice when he looked up at Lenore.

"Mark, I want you to meet Mrs. Denise Mannheim, and over there is her son, Daniel."

Mark broke into a wide, toothy smile. "My pleasure, Mrs. Mannheim." He offered his hand.

"Thank you for giving us your time," Denise said and turned to Daniel. "Daniel, would you come over here, please?"

Mark offered his hand with the same smile, but when Daniel hesitated, he added, "I promise not to bite, and I used germ-free soap less than an hour ago." At first, Daniel stared up at the ceiling, but then raised his hand and allowed Mark to take it and give it a soft squeeze. "*Guten tag*. Or should I say *Guten abend*?"

"Guten tag," Daniel answered flatly. "It's not late enough for *Guten abend*."

"I believe you're right. It's still afternoon. Well, I'm looking forward to working with you, Daniel."

After a short conversation covering meeting times and days, Denise and Lenore made a hasty retreat, leaving the student and mentor to get to know each other. "Do you want to sit down?" Mark pointed to one of the stuffed chairs.

Daniel took a long look at the chair, then back to the birds pecking away at the black sunflower seeds. "No." After a pause, he added, "Cardinals are not born with any red feathers. They get their color from the pigment of red fruit."

Mark smiled. "Is that so? I wonder what they would look like if they ate nothing but green grapes." Daniel turned his head slightly and nodded, as if trying to imagine such a thing. Mark waited a moment, then spoke. "There may be a cold soda in the fridge if you're interested. I don't know who it belongs to, but we all tend to share."

"I only drink water and unfiltered fruit juice."

"Sounds healthy."

Daniel moved slowly around the room, taking inventory with his eyes and sense of touch. Mark watched without comment as this willowy teenager allowed his index finger and eyes to drift across backs of chairs, tabletops, rims of lamp shades, and finally coming to a stop near the counter close to the sink. "Artesian water is best. There's no chloride or human handling."

"Closest we have is bottled water from Evian. It's there in the fridge."

"I'm fine."

"If you don't mind, could you dig out an Evian for me? There should be several."

Daniel looked at Mark fully for the first time and stared at his face as though it were a Renaissance painting or Native American wood carving. He noticed each wrinkle, some as deep as a volcanic fissure, and liver spots that looked like wet sand had been flung at him. The left eyebrow was lighter than the right, and his ears had tiny gray hairs sagging from a dark hole. His neck skin hung like a Galapagos turtle, and his head bobbed forward when he talked like a turkey bending to peck at a cricket. "If it's not too much trouble," Mark repeated.

Just as Daniel opened the refrigerator door and disappeared behind it, searching for the Evian, a health aid walked into the room. "Hey, Mr. Flour! How they hangin'?"

Mark swung his head toward the visitor. "Still attached, thank you, Seth."

"Glad to hear it." Seth Wenton, dressed in orderly whites, was carrying a metal water pitcher in each hand. He had taken the job a year ago as a health aid at BRC because, according to him, the money was good, the work easy, and on occasion he could extract a healthy tip from some of the *old codgers* whose vision couldn't detect the difference between a dollar and a C-note. "Gotta get some ice for *Salt and Pepper.*"

"Who?" Mark asked.

"You know, Salzman and Peprosky. *Salt and Pepper.* 306 and 308? They get real cranky if their water isn't cold." He turned toward the fridge only to find someone standing behind the door. "Whoa! Mannheim . . . that you?" Daniel took several quick steps away from the fridge and stared at his shoes. "Whataya doin' here?"

Daniel pulled three juggling balls out of his pockets and started to juggle. Seth gave Mark a sideways glance. "What's up, Mark? You know this guy?"

"He's here to see me." Mark's voice was strong.

"Really? Mannheim? He a relative?"

"No, just a friend."

Daniel moved quietly toward the sliding doors.

Seth raised his eyebrows and screwed up his face. "If you say so, Mr. Flour." After he poured ice from a bag in the freezer into his pitchers, he sidled to the sink and turned on the tap. "I'll shove off as soon as these are filled. Leave you two to settle world affairs."

When he straightened up, he gave Daniel a long perusal before heading toward the exit. At the door, he stopped and stared back at Mark with a contorted look. "I guess everyone needs a friend. Maybe even a juggling friend." He walked out, shaking his head.

"See you later," Mark said to the empty doorway.

Daniel juggled for several minutes after Seth left before stuffing the leather juggling balls back into his jeans. He returned to the fridge, took out a bottle of Evian, then walked over and offered it to Mark.

"I take it you know Seth?"

"We're both seniors." A tiny spider moved along the baseboard near the patio door. It was probably a weaver spider, common in buildings like this, and he watched as it moved slowly along the baseboard edge before disappearing behind a curtain.

"Do you want to tell me about the juggling?" asked Mark.

Daniel brought his head up, then pulled the balls from his pocket. He held them out as though in need of inspection. Mark looked at them but didn't say anything. "They help me stay calm in stressful situations," Daniel said softly.

"And Seth makes you uncomfortable?"

"Most of the time."

A former classroom teacher of high school seniors, Mark recognized the signs of anxiety, perhaps anxiety tinged with fear. He
might have the chance to talk to this young man about it someday,
but for now, he said, "I think you're safe in here. You can put the
balls away." After Daniel returned them to his trouser pockets, Mark
said, "Mrs. Ryan says you want to improve your German. Is that
your intent?"

"I already learned the basics." Daniel stopped wandering and
pulled up a plastic kitchen chair but didn't sit.

"You learned on your own?"

"Yes."

"Impressive," replied Mark, his eyes open wide enough so Daniel
could see the gray irises with a hint of green, like grass growing around
a smooth river stone. "Tell me, Daniel, don't they teach German at
Oakwood High anymore?"

"Only Spanish," he answered dismissively.

"Hmmm . . . that's a shame." The thought rolled around in his
brain before he continued, "This part of Wisconsin is rich with German ethnic residents. Its history is steeped in German culture. How
do you think we became the beer and brat capital of America?"

"I don't drink beer, and brats are filled with too much sodium
and empty calories."

"I wasn't implying that you . . . did drink . . . oh, never mind. Did
you take Spanish?"

"I passed out of Spanish 4 in my freshman year."

Mark put both hands on the wheels of his chair and moved closer to Daniel. "I see. Please, sit."

Daniel shoved his backpack to the left of the chair and sat down
as though the chair were a bed of nails.

Mark unscrewed the Evian and took a drink. A few drops dribbled onto the front of his sweater, which was buttoned up to his
neck. "Do you credit your ease of languages to your autism?" He be-

lieved the direct approach was the best. "Mrs. Ryan told me. I hope you don't mind."

Daniel seemed nonplussed. "I don't know why my brain works differently than others. I remember written facts from any source I lay my eyes on. I love numbers. I can recall every daily event I have experienced since I was two years old."

"And language?"

"It seems to flow like a long sentence or paragraph in my head. After I learn a few vocabulary words and understand the structure, I can read it like a book. Words I don't already know I figure out through context and retain for future use."

"Does Mrs. Ryan think you're a savant?"

"She sometimes calls me an autistic savant."

"People in my generation weren't quite so courteous with their labels . . . you might have heard . . ." Mark stopped, hesitant to finish his thought.

Daniel finished it for him. "I would have been called an *idiot* savant. That's what you were going to say."

Mark nodded slowly. "I'm afraid so."

"I don't really mind that term because the word idiot comes from the Greek *idiotes* which means *to be alone*, or *apart from others*. I fit both concepts."

"That's a very mature perspective you have," Mark said and breathed deeply. "You cherish your privacy?"

"Yes."

Mark looked into Daniel's youthful eyes and tried to imagine the routines in his life, especially the gymnastics he must perform in his head. He appeared to be brilliant, yet all the good wishes of others did little to bolster his confidence. When Seth had entered the room, his reaction was visceral. Daniel, like a bat that suddenly finds itself trapped inside a house, became desperate . . . and the juggling balls appeared.

Mark envisioned Daniel as the lonely albatross in Coleridge's *The Rime of the Ancient Mariner* hoping to rest on a ship's mast after weeks alone at sea. But if Seth's attitude toward Daniel was any indication of his high school peers, his quirky behavior brought on by his autism was hanging around his neck like the fallen albatross.

Mark decided to take a new tack. "I'll bet you're a wiz at chess."

"I play against the computer most of the time."

"And ... ?"

"I generally win."

"Mrs. Ryan organizes a trivia game for the residents here at the BRC about once a month. She makes up the teams, and we try to outscore each other to win silly little prizes. Last week, our team won a subscription to *People* magazine. There were four on our team, so I guess I get to look at one week out of a month. You'd make a great *phone a friend*," Mark said with a wide smile.

"I don't answer the phone unless I have to."

"Not even for friends?"

"I don't have any friends, just my mom."

Mark replaced the cap on the bottled water without comment. After rolling his chair back a few feet, he said, "Well, I suppose we should think about how we're going to approach our study of the German language. Do you want to study German from a literary and grammatical point of view or just conversational? It doesn't matter to me. I'll wait upon your wishes."

Daniel looked up at the ceiling before answering. "Do you live here?"

"In this room? No. This is an all-purpose room. I live down the hall in room 409."

"409." His eyes focused on a crack that ran from the fluorescent light fixture in the center of the ceiling to the nearest wall and reminded him of the Nile running from Khartoum to the delta near Cairo.

He lowered his eyes to look at Mark. "409. Theodosius the Second ruled the Roman Empire in 409 . . . April 9th . . . F. Scott Fitzgerald published *The Great Gatsby* on April 9th, 1925."

"A memorization from school?"

"I like numbers. They play like musical notes in my head." He bent his head back to look again at the Nile. "How long have you lived here?"

"It'll be nine years next month. I moved in after my health took a turn for the worse. I'll be ninety-five years old pretty soon."

"The number nine keeps coming up."

"I hadn't noticed."

"It must be a special number for you."

"Other than my age, yeah, I guess you could call it special."

"It is special."

The way Daniel stared at the ceiling, Mark wondered if this young man saw him as a fixture on the landscape, like a small blemish on the side of a rocky mountain, a reminder of how old the earth really is.

Looking away from Khartoum, Daniel asked, "Do you believe like Native Americans that everything in life is circular?"

Mark's eyes drew tight and narrowed. "I don't know. Never thought much about Native American culture. I was brought up a Lutheran. I'm not a big believer in mysticism, if that's what you're asking."

Daniel looked back at Mark's hands folded on his lap. The fingers were gnarled and splotchy like buttermilk, the nails long and curving inward, hiding the edges.

Staring up again at the long, meandering Nile, Daniel spoke in a slow monotone. "Nine can be magical . . . is magical. Nine and a circle are one in the same. 360 degrees, 3 plus 6 plus 0 equals 9. Cut a circle in half, 180 degrees, 1 plus 8 plus 0 equals 9, slice it in half again equals 45-degree angles, 4 plus 5 equals 9, and again equals

22.5-degree angles or 2 plus 2 plus 5 equals 9. Every time you cut it in half, the numbers of the angle always come up 9 . . . I could go on."

"I must say, I never thought of circles as being that interesting, or the number 9. You've got me thinking though because my birthday is September 9th."

"9th day of the 9th month."

Mark believed Daniel wasn't trying to impress, but was simply reciting like the human computer he appeared to be. He seemed oblivious to his own breadth of knowledge and how it might astound those around him. Mark was both excited and a bit fearful to work with this teenage savant, for what else could he call him?

Daniel continued his treatise on the number 9. "Any number multiplied by 9 equals 9. 9 times 9 equals 81. 8 plus 1 equals 9. 9 times 4 equals 36. 3 plus 6 equals 9. Any number works. You try."

Flummoxed, Mark thought, then said, "23."

"9 times 23 equals 207. 2 plus 0 plus 7 equals 9."

Mark shouted hoarsely, "47!"

"423."

Mark laughed as he spit out, "4 plus 2 plus 3 equals 9. I got it now."

When Mark looked at Daniel, a silly smile was nibbling at the corners of his mouth. "You're good. I give up." He raised his arms slightly. "When it comes to numbers, you're the cat's meow. I hope you're around when I have to balance my checkbook, though there aren't any big numbers to worry about. But what about German? You didn't answer my question on how you want to approach German."

Daniel didn't appear to hear the question. "You must be acclimated to the smell of this building."

"How's that? The smell? Is it that bad?"

Daniel surveyed the room and took a deep breath through his nose. "Pine-Sol, linoleum wax, hairspray, and . . . urine."

"Ouch!" Mark exclaimed. "With a nose like that, you must be able to track pheasants."

"I don't have a hunting license," Daniel replied with a straight face.

There it was. For all his facts and memories, his ease of history and numbers and language and animals, he couldn't see the humor in a social joke, a mundane reference outside his experience. Like a horse wearing blinders to protect it from sidelong distractions, Daniel Mannheim had put on social blinders. He avoided as many person-to-person interactions as possible. When he couldn't tolerate physical situations, he wrapped himself securely in his cerebellum, complete with mystical numbers and brilliant colors and Arabian perfumes and soothing facts—a bolt hole to calm himself whenever he needed it. His juggling balls were nothing more than a flare sent up announcing a potentially difficult or embarrassing situation on the horizon—time to take cover.

Mark laughed quietly. "That was said in jest, young man. A joke. Something you and I will work on, perhaps even in German. *Hast du verstanden?*"

"*Jawohl, Mannlicher Lehrer,*" Daniel answered with a millisecond flash of excitement crossing his boyish face.

12

STANLEY AND ROSE

November 1943

"PRIVATE!" STANLEY SHOUTED AT ONE OF THE RE-SERVISTS. "Bring the last two German POWs over here." The young reservist, who looked like he was in the tenth grade, turned to carry out the order. Before he was out of earshot, Stanley added, "If they give you any trouble, even look cross-eyed at you, give 'em a kick in the balls, young man. They ain't the master race in this country." The private saluted with one finger and rushed off with a large smile ballooning on his face.

"Well, I guess I can give you the roster sheet," said Albert. "Things seem pretty well under control here." He handed a clipboard to Stanley. "I'll meet you this evening at the camp. I've had the beds all set up and alerted the cook to be ready with some grub. I'm sure these men will be hungry."

"Yes, sir," said Stanley. "I'll have them there."

"When you finish getting them settled, stop by my office and we'll go over the job assignments. I have a few new requests from local farmers, and I hope this whole group of thirty-two will be jobbed out within a couple days. Speaking of thirty-two, here come the two you're taking in the pickup."

The scarecrow-thin reservist, with his carbine at his hip, was marshalling the last two POWs. Civilians couldn't help but gawk at the sight of German soldiers, now prisoners, in their midst. A few pointed and whispered behind hands placed over their mouths.

"Hold them right here while I use the head," Stanley said to the private and handed him the clipboard. "Don't let them get too close to any civilians. We don't want to frighten the women and children." The teenaged private nodded as he slung his gun over his shoulder. Stanley turned to Albert. "Have a safe trip, sir." They saluted each other and walked in opposite directions.

A moment later, Rose reappeared and asked the guard if she could give the POWs their care packages. "I don't know. The Sarge will be back soon," he said passively. "He told me to keep them away from civilians."

"And you're doing a good job of it. But I'm with the Red Cross, and we have access to most prisoners."

The guard pulled on his chin. "Okay then. But you better hurry because the sergeant said women shouldn't get too close to the prisoners."

"Thanks." She reached into her nearly empty duffel, pulled out a couple of small bags, and gave one to each POW. Her voice was filled with a lilt of kindness. "There's not much in these bags, just a few cookies and chocolate bars and crackers and, oh yeah, a little prayer book written in English. Seems a bit out of sorts, written in English, I mean, but it has pictures. Might help to pass the time."

"Thank you," said the shorter of the two prisoners.

"Oh, you speak English," said Rose.

"Yes, ma'am, a little," he replied.

Rose smiled, recalling the little German she learned from her upbringing. "I only know a few words of German. My grandpa on my mom's side was born in Germany. Am I talking too fast?"

"No, ma'am. I understand."

"Wonderful. My grandpa came to America when he was a baby, just a couple years old. That's a long time ago. He's passed on now, but when he would stay at our house, he always greeted us at the breakfast table with *guten morgen*."

"Of course, good morning."

"Unfortunately, that and a few other expressions are the only German I know."

"We appreciate the gifts. Thank you."

Rose smiled. "The Red Cross supplies them, we just hand them out. So, what's your name?"

"I'm Marco, and this man is Oskar, but he doesn't speak much English." She looked at Oskar, who smiled and nodded his head like it was on a spring. He held up his bag. "Thank . . . yoou."

Rose set the duffel down and put her finger to her chin in a moment of thought. "I think I've seen those names somewhere before. Let me think . . . Marco and Oskar, Marco and Oskar." She turned to the guard. "Private, do you have the manifest?"

"Yes, ma'am. Right here." He held the clipboard out with his left hand.

"Can you find the names Oskar and Marco on there? Probably don't need their last names right now."

Studying the clipboard as if it were written in hieroglyphics, he squinted and ran his finger down the list. "Oskar and Marco . . . Oskar and Marco . . . here they are! I actually found them," he said, his voice triumphant.

"Does it say anything else?"

He pointed with his index finger to a spot on the page. "Seems these two are assigned"—his finger crossed the page to a new column—"to the Red Callahan farm."

"Of course, my uncle!" Rose pushed her hair behind her ears with both hands. "You are the two farmhands Uncle Red requested. That's where I saw your names. I hope you boys like cows?"

Marco smiled and turned to Oskar to translate. When he finished, Oskar's face lit up, thinking of his days at home in Germany. Marco said to Rose, "We love farm work. Oskar grew up on a farm, and I love milk and cheese. Oskar, well, he eats anything," he chuckled.

"Be prepared for hard work," said Rose. "To get that milk, you'll have to haul tons of oats and clover and corn. And don't forget the manure. You'll be mucking out the stanchions every day."

"We don't mind hard work, do we, Oskar?" Oskar shook his head with every syllable.

"I believe I'll see the two of you real often. My name is Rose, by the way, and I live on Butternut Road, just a stone's throw from my uncle's place on Rocky River Road," she added.

Marco seemed a bit confused. "A stone's throw?"

"Oh, sorry, it means to be really close, distance-wise. Here, I'll show you." She walked up to Oskar and took him by the elbow.

"Excuse me, ma'am," interjected the private. "I don't think you should get too close."

"I'm fine," Rose replied, and the private stepped back. Turning to Oskar, she moved him a few steps away from Marco. "This is where I live on Butternut Road, and here . . ." She took Marco by the arm and moved him a half-dozen steps in the other direction. ". . . this is my Uncle Red's farm . . . a *stone's throw* away. It means close by, see?"

Stanley saw Rose with her hand on the shorter POW and raced through the crowded lobby. "Get away from her!" He shoved Marco with enough force to see him tumble over Rose's duffel and land on his back. Stanley pulled out his pistol, and before he could contain the situation, a woman screamed and several men dressed in business attire and carrying leather briefcases scampered away, setting off a mild stampede. A tall man with two small children at his side lifted them to his chest. The little girl screeched, and soon the entire lobby was focusing its eyes on Stanley and the two frightened men dressed in government-issued PW shirts.

"Stanley! Stop!" Rose hissed. "We were just communicating a bit. Put your gun away."

After a moment, Stanley, realizing there was no threat, felt like he had stepped through a stage door in the middle of a production and the audience was staring and wondering what he was doing. He turned to the guard. "I thought I told you to keep the civilians away."

Rose tried to explain. "It's not his fault. I wanted to give the Red Cross care packages to these two men. He was just kind enough to let me."

Stanley's face was as red as a Cherry Belle radish. He turned, grabbed the clipboard, and barked into the guard's face, "Take these two POWs and put them in the back of my pickup truck. It's parked next to the bus. Think you can handle that? Or do I have to do it myself?"

"No, sir, I can do it." The scarecrow held his rifle with both hands in front of him and pushed Marco and Oskar toward the parking lot. "Move! Get moving!"

After they disappeared and the crowd dispersed, Stanley holstered his pistol and turned his anger on Rose. "Are you crazy?" he said venomously. "Those men are enemy combatants, not hotel guests. They're rotten Nazis for chrissake. Murderers!"

Rose picked up her belongings. She hefted the duffel over her shoulder. "You're overreacting, Stanley. Those two men remind me of the same kind of boys we grew up with and went to school with."

"They're Nazis," he insisted.

"My friend Camille Putzer works at the courthouse and told me all the card-carrying Nazis have been separated out and sent to maximum-security camps." She straightened her hat and dusted her skirt as she spoke. "Maybe you should do a little research of your own. These are only regular soldiers who have been captured, and I hope our own GIs are treated as kindly if they find themselves in a prison in some enemy country." Her anger was palpable.

Stanley straightened his own shirt and fitted his own hat. "As long as they're wearing PW on their backs, I'm treating them as dangerous. As should you. If one of them breaks outta camp and visits your bedroom in the middle of the night, you might sing a different tune."

"You sound more jealous than protective, Stanley. Don't let that uniform go to your head." And with that, she turned on her heel and joined the throng of civilians hurrying to a platform or a waiting auto.

13

DANIEL

2019

AFTER A COUPLE WEEKS, Herr Flour took stock of the time spent teaching and learning with Daniel. He had never met anyone with such brainpower as Daniel's; his data-collecting abilities and memory skills were phenomenal. He recalled watching an old Alfred Hitchcock movie, *The 39 Steps,* about a group of German spies trying to spirit defense secrets out of London in 1935 and into the hands of Hitler's scientists. When the plot is unraveled, it's a young savant who has been recruited by the spy ring to memorize an entire secret jet propulsion plan and all the mathematical equations that go with it. The savant's brain became the suitcase that would pass from country to country. Of course, the plot was foiled, but Mark believed Daniel Mannheim could have played the part of the actor savant. Once he looked over those plans, he could have regurgitated them flawlessly.

What Daniel couldn't do was win over the beautiful young woman who played opposite the hero. Daniel's social skills were still receiving a D grade—*needs work.* Mark tried to get him to engage in conversation with other BRC residents and staff, but so far had met with little success. Daniel's love of language was the common denominator in the German-learning adventure. Over the past several weeks, their relationship had deepened and moved beyond a typical student/teacher scenario. Mark believed he could ask a few personal questions in hopes to carry on normal conversation.

The German/English thesaurus set down on the coffee table, Mark asked, "Tell me about your family. What's your mother like?"

Daniel slipped the No. 2 pencil behind his right ear and looked at his shoes. At first, Mark thought he may have overstepped, but then Daniel answered matter-of-factly, "I'm the only child of a divorced couple." There was a lengthy pause. "The only *living* child of a divorced couple."

"I see. Do you want to talk about it?"

"Do you know what the divorce rate is for this state?"

"No. I haven't a clue."

"Just under forty percent."

"That seems high. But . . . I come from a prehistoric generation that didn't tolerate divorce as easily."

"My mom works at the public library, the 8-to-3 shift, mostly shelving books. She picks me up every day at school at 3:09." An automatic answer.

"What if she's late?"

"She's never late."

Mark looked up from his glasses and asked pensively, "What if you're late?"

"I'm never late."

"Not even if you stop to chat with another student or teacher?" Before Daniel could answer, or even bend his eyes up from the tops of his shoes, Mark continued, "That's right, you don't have any friends." A quiet settled between them like lightly falling snow, the ticking of the analog clock over the sink the only noise. Finally, Mark spoke up. "Even Seth Wenton, your Neanderthal nemesis, recognizes the need to have friends."

Before Mark could stop him, Daniel was up and juggling. "He doesn't have friends, he has followers," Daniel said. The colored balls began flying in a bright circle as if they were riding an invisible Ferris wheel. Daniel dodged the coffee table and headed toward the sink, balls still in rhythm.

"Seems to me you might try to round up a few *followers* of your own. Couldn't hurt."

Daniel let the balls fall to the ground. They didn't bounce but sounded like hard-boiled eggs without the shells. Daniel looked down at them and then up at Mark with a face like a baby bird. "Is it necessary?"

"Is what necessary?" Mark asked.

"Having friends." He stooped onto one knee and picked up the balls. "The adults in my world harp on the need for friends. I have my mom. I have my German teacher. I have my short stories. What more is needed?"

"It's a question of quality. No man is an island."

"John Donne said that."

"Did he?"

"He died in 1631, but his poems weren't published till 1633, two years after he died."

"Hope his wife had an income."

"She died after giving birth to their twelfth child."

"Oh my. That's sad." Mark took off his reading glasses, pulled out a clean handkerchief from his sleeve, and began cleaning them. After a minute, he held the lenses to the fluorescent light to check for cleanliness. He fixed them back on the end of his nose and looked over to Daniel. "Speaking of children, do you want to talk about your sibling?"

Daniel put the balls in flight again and walked over to the window and back, then stopped a few feet in front of Mark's wheelchair, caught the balls, and stuffed them in his pants. He looked at his shoes, bent over, and flicked off a small piece of mud. When he stood up, Mark took in his beautiful, smooth face, white as a seashell and flecked with pink. *He's a kind boy*, Mark thought, *shy and awkward and yearning for acceptance.*

Mark waited a full minute.

Finally, Daniel turned to him and said, "My favorite heroes died on January 17th ... T.H. White, who wrote the King Arthur stories, I can recite three from memory ... the story of Arthur pulling the sword from the stone, the story of Arthur meeting Merlin for the first time, and Arthur walking into Camelot and placing the crown on his head and announcing . . ." Daniel shouted with a maniacal grin, "I AM THE KING!" He stopped juggling and sat down.

It seemed out of character to hear him so boisterous, but so appropriate at the same time. His eyes were dark as ink spots and fluttering like two crows taking wing in the morning sky. Mark sensed the teenager could be himself in this nursing home with a man who, if he were captured in a black-and-white photo, was fading to gray. Mark was no threat. He was not a peer. He was not a relative. He was a soul mate, a lover of language, a confidant if Daniel wanted one.

Mark waited patiently, then whispered, "And your other heroes?"

"Bobby Fischer. He died on January 17th too. He was the greatest chess player America ever produced. The greatest in the world for a while. I read his biography and studied his game strategies." Daniel's voice grew strong and clear now, as though the question broke through the ice. "You can play against Bobby Fischer in a computer-simulated game. His moves are beautiful. I haven't beaten him . . . not yet."

"No doubt you will someday," Mark said.

Daniel shifted in his chair and searched the ceiling for the ever-flowing Nile. Then he blurted, like air escaping a balloon, "And my sister, Maggie, she died on January 17th, all because of me."

For the first time, Mark noticed water collecting in Daniel's eyes. Daniel pulled the sleeve of his shirt over his right hand and wiped both eyes roughly, as though cleaning them of dust or some foreign object that had no business being there. He leaned back in the chair and focused on Khartoum. "I haven't told anybody, except my mom, what happened that day." He found the river current rushing through the Sudanese desert and followed it north all the way to Cairo.

"I'm a good listener," Mark said softly. "And I have nowhere to go for hours."

"Did you know in the time of the Egyptian pharaohs, luxurious barges were built to carry them and were rowed by twenty singing virgins?"

Mark shook his head. "I don't know much about ancient Egypt."

"My mom homeschooled me for the first few years of schooling. She fixed up a space in our basement as a classroom. I read about the gods of ancient Greece and the pharaohs who built the pyramids and Oden and Valhalla. I called our learning area the 'Bomb Shelter' because I became fascinated with the private shelters people built in their basements in the '50s and '60s to survive an atomic blast. I even made one of those yellow-and-black radioactive signs and hung it up at the top of the stairs.

"Mom made sure the Bomb Shelter had plenty of books and blankets and water and snacks, and we would start my lessons every morning at 8:30. I insisted. We worked till noon, then ate, then napped, then finished exactly at three o'clock. Maggie was too young to do too much learning, so she mostly bugged me and played with mom. She was a *normal* kid. Not like me."

When Daniel paused, Mark said, "Normalcy's not all it's cracked up to be."

"My mom was with us every minute we were in the Bomb Shelter . . . except Friday afternoons from one till three when she would go to the hairdresser. I don't think her hair ever changed shape or color, but she would not miss an appointment. She needed to talk to adults, I suppose. Our neighbor, Mrs. Olsen, relieved Mom and stayed with us those two hours. When Mom was gone, Maggie mostly napped and I read or did some other quiet work.

"On January 17th, Mrs. Olsen came as usual. She was wearing jeans and a yellow sweater with a gray collar. After my mom drove off, Mrs. Olsen received a phone call. She spoke into the receiver very loudly and seemed frantic. I was reading *Treasure Island* by Robert Louis Stevenson. I was just starting chapter 9, page 99. I should have paid more attention to the number significance. After the phone call, Mrs. Olsen came to me with a frightened look on her face. 'I have to go home right now! There's smoke coming out my kitchen window.' She placed her hand on the top of my head, which she never did. 'You have to watch your sister for a few minutes. I'll be back as soon as I can.' She ran up the stairs, and 7 seconds later, I heard the back door slam.

"With all the shouting, Maggie woke up crying and with a wet diaper. I led her up the stairs to the bathroom but didn't know what to do, exactly. I was only nine. She was almost three and wanted to do everything herself, so she pulled off her wet diaper, and instead of wanting a dry one, she dashed out of the bathroom, down the hall, and out the back door which Mrs. Olsen had left unlatched.

"It was a warm day for January. Maggie should have had a coat and hat on. From the kitchen window, I saw her pulling handfuls of snow from a snowbank for a full minute. My feet were made of cement. Then I saw Mrs. Olsen coming back . . . she usually walked since she only lived five houses away. But it was winter, and sidewalks were slippery . . . after putting out a grease fire on her stove, she turned her shiny Buick into our driveway. She seemed distracted because she left without calling my mom and was driving too fast and not expecting a nearly three-year-old to be anywhere nearby . . . I watched as my sister disappeared at 2:07 p.m. under her black-and-silver station wagon." Daniel lowered his eyes. "2 plus 0 plus 7 equals 9."

After a long pause, Daniel added, "It was as if the gods opened up the gates of the underworld. I watched as Acheron ferried her across the River Styx."

The ticking of the clock seemed to be loud enough to rattle the windowpanes.

"My mom and dad divorced shortly after that. My mom has for-given me, but I know she wanted another child . . . a normal . . . a normal . . . a normal . . ." His voice trailed off like an echo over a calm lake.

Mark waited patiently. Finally, Daniel continued, "My father, on the other hand, blamed me and could not see himself as the father of a *weird kid*, his words, for the next couple of decades. He ran."

For several minutes, both Daniel and Mark stared at the ceiling. One was drifting precariously into the deep waters along the sands of a distant desert, the other wondering how far he could throw a life buoy.

Daniel quickly packed his things into his backpack and head-ed toward the door without another word. When he stopped and looked back over his shoulder, his eyes were dry but still full of life. "Tomorrow." It was a statement, not a question.

Mark saluted with one finger to his temple, and Daniel was gone.

14

DANIEL AND MARK

2019

IDIOMS CAN BE DIFFICULT TO DECIPHER. Imagine trying to explain to a student learning English what "walk the plank" means, or "ride the gravy train," or, one of my favorites, Mark thought, *"give someone the third degree." German idioms can be just as tricky.*

Mark was sitting in his blue-and-green La-Z-Boy in room 409. A red-white-and-blue afghan was tossed over his thin legs, and his feet were covered with orange-and-yellow socks. He could have been mistaken for a crumpled rainbow. After meeting for a month, Daniel was comfortable enough to park on the side of Mark's bed, feet barely touching the floor, notebook and *Grumman's Conversational German* opened on his lap, waiting for Mark to start. With two fingers, Mark pulled out a sheet of paper stuck between pages in his book of poetry by Robert Bly. "I've made a list. See if you can figure this one out: *Morgenstend hat Gold Mund?*"

Daniel curled his nose. "Finding gold in the morning light?"

"Not bad. It's said as a statement comparable to 'The early bird catches the worm.'" Daniel scribbled in his notebook. "Try this one: *Hunde die beller beichen nicht.*"

"Something to do with a dog and his bark."

"Close again. We would say, 'His bark is worse than his bite.' I should try that one on John Mancuso some time. I mean in German, he wouldn't understand, and therefore wouldn't hurt his ego."

"Who is John Mancuso?"

"Another resident down the hall. You'll meet him sometime. How about: *Tomaten auf den Augen haben*?"

Daniel chortled. "Tomatoes in your eyes. Is it because someone has been up all night and has red eyes?"

Mark smiled. "Tomatoes in the eyes is the literal, but it means the tomatoes have blinded you from seeing the obvious." As Daniel was transcribing in his notebook, Mark added, "Sort of like you and the social world."

Daniel's head shot up. He closed his textbook and placed it on the floor. "Has my mother been talking to you?"

"We've talked. She was asking how you're progressing." He smiled and continued, "After all, my services don't come free of charge."

"Is she paying you?"

"That was a joke, my boy. Although she promised to make me a fine dinner someday. She says she's a good cook."

"Most of the time she uses too much salt. I've warned her."

"She just wants you to be more engaged with others. More open to the world around you. Wouldn't hurt to try. She's thinking of your welfare, not her own."

Daniel shoved the No. 7 pencil behind his left ear. His voice flat, carrying a hint of long-term sadness, he said, "I know."

"Outside of school and academics, do you have any hobbies, other interests? What about girls?"

Surprisingly, Daniel's hands did not plunge for the juggling balls. "Only chess. I don't have any hobbies, and autism falls short of being a chick magnet."

"Is attracting girls a goal of yours?"

Daniel pulled at a small spot of mud from the cuff of his loose-fitting khaki pants. "My mom thinks it should be a goal. She's threatening to lock up my video games if I don't ask someone to prom."

"Ah yes, 'tis the season for prom." Mark pulled the chair's recliner bar and sat back, his feet shooting up. "How soon is the big event?"

"37 days and 4 hours."

"Hmmm. A little over a month."

"My mom wants a photo on the hallway wall to go along with my middle school photo, my senior photo, and my baptismal photo. I told her I would rent a tuxedo and she could take my picture and then I would photoshop in a nice-looking girl in a prom dress."

Mark laughed. "I'll bet your mom thought that was a really bad idea."

This time, it was Daniel who smiled an authentic smile. "Uh huh."

Mark offered a bit of advice. "Most women are romantics, and you shouldn't spoil your mother's dreams. Going to the prom, even with a girl you don't know all that well, isn't punishment. You might find it to be fun."

"I doubt it," he said sullenly.

"Well, even if it's not the most exciting event, treat it as a socialization project."

"That's what my school counselor, Mrs. Ryan, says." Daniel flicked more mud from his cuff.

"Your mother wants the best for you. I'm sure Mrs. Ryan wants the best as well, your teachers too. Those of us who are nearing the end of our lives realize a few important things, and making friends is one. Regardless of your physical skills and mental abilities, there are feelings that need to be talked over once in a while, talked over with someone who is a peer, not a relative. You're bright enough to understand that." Mark adjusted his glasses on his nose and folded his hands in his lap. "I don't mean to lecture."

"Do you have friends?" Daniel asked.

"I do. In fact, a few of them belong to a writing club I helped form here at the BRC. We meet on Wednesdays in the day room at that table at the far end of the room. We call ourselves the Alzheimer's Round Table, or ART for short."

"I've seen that table. It's not round," Daniel said.

"It's not, but the name is a takeoff on . . ."

Daniel interrupted. "The writers who met in New York City in the '20s."

"That's right. At the Algonquin Hotel. This is a far cry from a fancy hotel, but the name seemed to fit."

"I read some short stories by Dorothy Parker."

"And . . . ?"

"They were okay. Witty. If you like that sort of clever stuff."

"Not your cup of tea, eh?"

"I hate green tea. Earl Grey and Ceylon Black are my favorites."

Mark laughed. "Now I know you're trying to take advantage of an old man." He pointed his finger at Daniel's nose.

Daniel smiled, stood, and crossed the room, looked out at the bird feeders, came back, sat down in a chair, and pushed his legs underneath. "I've written 116 stories. I hope to be a professional writer."

"That's quite an ambitious goal. 116? You amaze me." He twisted his lips. "And here I thought I was helping you learn German so you could be the next Oakwood High School German teacher."

"High school teachers have to deal with too many dumb students," Daniel replied mirthlessly.

"Neanderthals, you mean?"

"Among other tribes," he answered.

Mark took the opportunity to probe a bit. "What about brilliant students? They can be a bit of a handful, from my experience. What do you think?"

The question seemed to hit a nerve in Daniel. He thought about his exceptional status in a class setting and how difficult it would be for an average teacher to stimulate him intellectually. He breathed in deeply and for a moment seemed at a loss for an answer.

His brilliance, a liability? Was it possible teachers didn't appreciate him, but rather thought of him as a sideshow, a freak, a distraction who needed to be avoided by crossing the street when he drew near? His words came out like spitting stones. "Um . . . maybe . . . I guess."

Mark sensed his internal battle and quickly added, "For what it's worth, I always admired my brightest students."

Daniel stood, pulled the balls from his pockets, and started to juggle, turning his back to Mark, who watched and wondered if he had pushed a bit beyond the pale. He had only known this young man for a few weeks and wasn't a counselor. Minutes later, Daniel returned to his chair and held the balls, peering at Mark with laser eyes. "I want to be a writer." He stuffed the balls in his pockets.

"Since you are an aficionado of writing, perhaps you would like to join the ART group?"

"Join?" Daniel looked at Mark with a curious expression.

"We're open to new members. You might even enjoy the company."

Daniel had received few invitations to join any kind of social gathering in his life, and he appeared puzzled. He picked up the German textbook and opened it to a random page, scanning it with his index finger as though looking for a hidden answer. Finally, he raised his eyes just above the top of the book. "You wouldn't throw me to the lions?"

Mark's voice caught in his throat. "Nice idiom, and no, you needn't worry about that."

"Can I bring my juggling balls?"

"Of course."

15

THE ALZHEIMER'S ROUND TABLE

2019

JOHN MANCUSO PULLED HIS CHAIR OUT and slammed the papers he was carrying onto the table. "Greetings, fellow writers! How are the *ARTists* doing on this fine spring day?" He sat down heavily as the four women seated around him nodded or muttered perfunctory responses. John and Mark were the only men in the Alzheimer's Round Table. All were residents of BRC except for Eva, who was the daughter of Marie. "Nice to see you again, Eva," John declared happily.

"Thank you, John," she replied.

Eva was a plain-looking woman with shoulder-length brown hair cut straight across—including her bangs, as though a carpenter's T-square was used, giving her face a boxed-in look. She had dark-green eyes, wide shoulders, and was thick in the hips and waist. Her wardrobe was twenty years outdated and she wore no jewelry or makeup of any kind. She was sixty years old and very attentive to her mother, arriving each Wednesday afternoon to assist Marie at the ART meeting, as her mom was showing more signs of the A.

Eva loved to bake and rarely appeared without a container filled with cookies or lemon bars or fudge brownies. Her specialty was rum cake. All the ART members slept better after a meeting when rum cake was served. Today, she brought a plate of chocolate chip muffins slathered with vanilla frosting.

"Look at those blueberry muffins," John said, his eyes round and wide like a miner who just spotted a golden nugget. "My mouth is watering already."

Eva smiled. "They're chocolate chip muffins, John. And, of course, there're no nuts in them because I know how easily they can get caught in your dentures." She picked up the plate and passed it in John's direction.

Helen, the tallest woman in the group and chairperson of the meeting, clapped her hands. "Can we get started? Mark will be here in a few minutes, and he told me he is bringing a guest with him."

"Whoever it is, they can't hold a candle to these cupcakes," John said as crumbs bounced on the table like raindrops.

"As most of you are aware," continued Helen, ignoring John, "Mark's been tutoring a high school student for the last month or so, and as it turns out, the young man wants to be a writer."

John guffawed. "Did you recommend he seek out a group of *real* writers, preferably young people and not old hacks like us . . . oh, sorry, Eva."

Helen frowned and scanned the faces of the other women. "To the contrary, I told Mark it would be perfectly acceptable to have him sit in on our meetings. I expect them to be here any minute . . ."

Over Helen's shoulder, John spied Mark's wheelchair. "Speak of the devils."

All eyes turned and looked toward the newcomer. Daniel pushed Mark's wheelchair to the end of the table, then stood to the side of an empty chair as though at a bus stop waiting for the driver to open the door. A gold-and-green Green Bay Packers cotton throw, stained and frayed, lay across Mark's bony legs. However, the covering fell short of Mark's feet, and Daniel stared at his toes, which pushed out of his leather sandals like skinny albino slugs. His toenails were as yellow as fading dandelions.

"Go ahead and sit, kid. We don't bite," laughed John. "We growl a little, but we don't bite."

Mark waved Daniel down, and he pulled the chair up to the table's edge and settled in. "Thank you for letting my student crash our little group."

As the ART members fixed their eyes on Daniel, he pulled his shoulders in and let his hands fall near his pockets, but so far the juggling balls were out of sight. "This is Daniel Mannheim, and I would appreciate it if each of you could introduce yourself and say a bit about who you are in twenty-five words or less."

Helen took the cue and turned to Daniel. "I'd love to start." She was articulate and handsome with her Katherine Hepburn face and the lithe body to go with it. As a younger woman, she could have been a dancer or professional golfer or swimmer. She sported close-set eyes which rested on top of high Grecian cheekbones. "My name is Helen, and I grew up in Milwaukee. I had six children, only four are still living. My husband worked for the railroad and died twenty years ago. I got my college degree when I was in my fifties and worked in real estate until I retired. I've always liked to write. Thank you for joining us today." She folded her hands on the table and looked to John sitting on her left.

But before John could say anything, Daniel muttered to no one in particular, "That was 60 words."

Helen turned and gave him a quizzical look. "Really?"

"He got ya there, Helen. I'll try to keep my remarks in the ballpark for ya, kid," said John, whose large, rough hands and short fingers complemented his thick arms and neck. His voice was always loud; even when he whispered, it came out amplified. His ears were too big for his small head, and he was bald as an egg. John seemed to wear a permanent three-day-old beard and reminded one of Yasir Arafat or Chicago Cubs manager Joe Maddon.

"My name is John Mancuso, Italian if you're interested. Built homes most of my working life. Married Maureen but divorced. Five grandkids. I don't especially like to write, but someday my grandkids might want to know more about my life experiences, which is mostly about work, which they can't understand cause not a one of 'em can change a tire or drive a nail straight. I'm afraid you won't find any Nobel winners in this group, but the treats are terrific." He gave Eva a dramatic wink and then waved his left hand dismissively. "That's it."

Daniel muttered again, "83."

"Beat ya, Helen."

Mark turned to Daniel with kind and forgiving eyes. "*Twenty-five words or less* is just an expression."

Next was Emma. A tiny person all her life, Emma was now south of a hundred pounds. She wore a red cardigan sweater with silver patches on the elbows. Her head was mostly covered with a blue-and-white paisley scarf, revealing only a few curls of hair the color of cigarette ash. She had a pixie face to go with her diminutive body, but her voice was strong and clear, and she flashed bright, ice-blue eyes. "Hi, Daniel. My name is Emma, and I'm so happy you decided to join us . . ."

"Oh, I almost forgot!" bellowed John. "I served in the Marines and am a proud veteran of the Korean War, which the history books now call a *Police Action*, which is a shitty way of saying it's easy to forget. Should've allowed MacArthur to call the shots and use a few more A-bombs on the Chinese. Anyway, I earned a few ribbons but wasn't near the soldier as that guy you wheeled in here . . . there's a hero for you."

Everyone at the table remained silent for a long moment until Emma started in again, tongue in cheek, "Thank you, John."

"Don't mention it."

She turned and confided to Daniel, "He interrupts all the time, claiming his hearing is bad, but we know differently. Anyway, as I started to say, my name is Emma, and I'm ninety-two. I was born near here but spent most of my life living in Hollywood, California."

"The movie star!" John yelled.

"I worked behind the cameras mostly . . . costumes, sets, makeup, and that sort of thing. I was in a few movies, but only when the director needed extras, usually as a townsperson. I never married. I always liked to write. When I was in grade school, we had to write an essay a week. I still remember some of those. So now I'm trying to do the same thing; one a week, that's my goal."

"And you have been very successful, Emma," Mark said, nodding with a genuine smile.

The last participant was Eva's mom. "I'm Marie, and I'm also ninety-two. This is my daughter, Eva. She comes to help. I can't remember much anymore, so she fills in the gaps when she can." Eva smiled and looked at her mom with a hint of sadness.

Marie wore heavy blood-red lipstick, and her silver hair was perfectly coiffed. She wore a blue cotton dress with a wide embroidered collar and a string of faux pearls. Her love of clothing and makeup was a stark contrast to her organic daughter. Until the last couple of years, Marie had worn high heels each time she appeared outside her room. "I was born in Hungary and came to America after the Second World War."

John let out another bombast. "That was the big war, kid. She's too polite to tell you she's a genuine survivor of the Holocaust! Got the tattoo and everything. Lousy Nazis murdered her whole damn family."

Marie pulled the long sleeve of her dress tightly over her right arm and continued. "I married a Canadian serviceman in 1948, or maybe '49?" She looked up at Eva.

"Spring of '49," Eva said.

"That's right. Later, we came to Wisconsin because my husband had family living near Manitowoc . . ."

Eva interjected, "Oconomowoc, Mother. Near Milwaukee."

"Ah . . . I can't remember a thing. Anyway, I lived there most of my life. After my husband died, I came up here to be closer to Eva. She's been a godsend." Marie laid her hand, which trembled slightly, over her daughter's as a tear cut a tiny white path down her rouge-coated cheek. "A godsend."

Helen waited for a moment and sensed no one else had anything to say. "Should we begin with today's story?" She picked up a stapled sheaf of papers and added, "I think all of you will find a copy in front of you. Daniel, you'll have to share with Mark."

John set the story down and leaned his elbows on the table and shouted, "Speaking of backgrounds, what about you, kid? What's your story?"

Mark held up his palms and said defensively, "I'm not sure Daniel wants to share . . ."

But before he could finish his response, Daniel said, "I'm a person with autism."

John raised one eyebrow. "Well, I'm arthritic, glad to meet ya." Everyone sat perfectly still. "What's atavism mean?"

Helen looked hard at John. "He said *autism*, John, and you are not his counselor."

"Sorry. Do you have to have a Ph.D. to ask a question?"

"It's personal, John," Helen answered stridently.

"Well, so are my bunions, but anyone can ask about them, even look at them if they want."

Daniel responded quietly in the way he had a thousand times, "Autism is a congenital brain abnormality."

John gave a look of understanding. "Got it. Your brain is screwed up, kind of like mongolism."

"I believe it's referred to as Down syndrome these days, John," said Eva forcefully but without anger.

John was confused. "Same difference." He sat back in his chair, wearing a heavy frown.

Daniel continued, "Autism has no cure, but certain behaviors can be altered." He turned and caught John's eyes scanning the ceiling. "Your bunions are caused by stress on the joints of the big toe.

No cure is available for bunions either, but certain holistic remedies can relieve the pain."

"Really?" John sat forward, showing renewed interest.

"Soaking your feet in Epsom salts and boiled ginseng root proves best. Try orthotic socks and open-toe shoes," Daniel concluded.

"I'll be damned! You give Doogie Howser a run for his money," John said with a huge grin.

Helen clapped her hands once again and said, "I don't want to interrupt the medical reports, but we have a story by Emma to read and talk about."

The ART members glanced at the papers in front of them and began to read silently. Mark passed his copy to Daniel, who read as well. After a few minutes, a lively discussion started on the merits of the story and the possible changes for improvement. Now and then, Mark offered some poignant remarks.

Daniel found a window near the bookshelves and stared out at an inner courtyard. A woman in a spring jacket was pushing a wheelchair with a resident so bundled up that they could be taken as a chair full of blankets being wheeled to the laundry. Though he didn't look at the ART members through most of their discussion, he listened to every word and was surprised by their sincerity, wit, and camaraderie. When his high school English teachers tried to foster a discussion of literature of any kind, his fellow students usually clammed up, afraid their thoughts might be grounds for laughter or jeering. He listened with a tight smile and let his fingers tap at the table as though sending Morse code.

When the discussion seemed to die a natural death, Emma looked over at Daniel. She spoke in a calm and sincere voice. "Can I ask our newest member a question?"

Daniel turned and looked back at Emma. "Yes."

"I understand you like to write, at least that's what Mark told us. What do you like to write about?"

Daniel shifted in his chair and stopped tapping with his fingers. "Dystopia, mostly."

John scowled before shouting. "Did he say *dysentery*?" He pushed his chair back from the table. "I haven't had that in months, and I for one don't want anyone bringing it in here."

"He said *dystopia*, John, not dysentery," Helen explained.

"Oh, yeah . . . okay . . . so . . . what is dystopia exactly?" John pulled himself back to the table.

Eva answered while looking into John's gray eyes. "It means he sets his storyline in a futuristic world, a world that generally turns out to be rather unpleasant."

"Unpleasant, huh? Sort of like *Planet of the Apes* when Charlton Heston finds out he's really on Earth?"

"Yes, sort of," Eva answered.

"I've written 116 dystopian stories." For a moment, Daniel's voice quieted the room. Only the analog clock hanging above the refrigerator could be heard.

Emma smiled sweetly, but also skeptically. "Oh my. 116? That's an awful lot of stories, young man."

Maybe he intended to impress, or maybe it was the atmosphere of the ART group, but whatever it was, Daniel felt comfortable talking. He hadn't had a real conversation, with the exception of his mother, for quite some time. His teachers rarely called on him, or he refused to get involved because the subject matter was too dull or at the very least something he had learned eons ago. But these residents were caring and kind. Even John, with his wild outbursts, seemed content to allow him to be himself in their midst. Different intellectually, six decades younger, and having no previous interaction, Daniel felt like a small bird waltzing across the hide of a wild animal looking for tiny insects. He was doing a service by sharing. "Most of my stories are set on a dying planet called Lightstar 8 which is experiencing a drastic change in the atmosphere caused by warring groups of Morlocks and

Franthems. The wars have caused catastrophic changes in the atmosphere, and most of the oxygen has been destroyed. All the civilians on Lightstar 8 must ration the use of oxygen. If they use too much, they could be arrested, and the punishment is the removal of one lung."

John couldn't let that go without comment. "That would suck! Get it? Suck!" And he took in great gulps of air before falling into a coughing fit.

The ART members found John insufferable but smiled anyway. Daniel allowed a rare smile as well. "We get it, John," said Helen.

"That sounds like an awful place, Daniel," chipped in Marie.

"There's a great demand for science fiction stories and novels. Twenty-eight percent of popular paperbacks sold are in the sci-fi genre."

Before Daniel could elaborate, Mark explained how the group exchanged stories from the ART members on a rotating basis. And then suggested Daniel could bring a story for the next meeting, and he would make copies for each.

"I could give you a story right now," Daniel offered.

Eva snapped her head back in amazement. "You brought a story with you?"

"No," Daniel answered. "But I could recite it."

"You memorized the whole story?" Helen asked.

Daniel looked at Mark's fingers. They were braided as though constructed of white palm fronds. When he looked up and focused on the window again, he said flatly, "I memorized all 116 of them. Each one has 2,790 words, give or take 10."

John's face registered amazement, his lower lip dropping as though a lead sinker were attached. "Damn! I have only a couple stories and I can hardly remember the names of my own characters . . . and they're mostly family members."

Marie turned to her daughter. "Did I hear that right? He memorized them all?"

"You heard it right, Mother," Eva said incredulously.

Daniel added, "I have an eidetic memory."

Helen held up her hand, facing John before he could utter a word. "That means he has a photographic memory." She watched as John's eyes widened and he nodded, his wisecracks at a loss.

Helen wanted nothing more than to probe this young man's brain for a sampling, but she said, "I'm sorry, Daniel, we don't have time to listen to your story today. But if you could get one of them to Mark sometime later this week, he'll make copies for us in time to read it and we can discuss it next week."

"I will do that," Daniel replied.

"That will be wonderful. For now, it's already past five o'clock."

There was a loud scratching of a chair as John rose. "My bladder needs some quick relief. Nice meeting ya, kid." He gave Daniel a finger-to-the-forehead salute. "Glad you're going to join us. Don't think I'll have to bring my pocket dictionary anymore."

The others said their goodbyes, and the meeting was over. Eva stood and put a hand under her mother, helping her to her feet, then opened her walker with the yellow tennis balls covering the walker's feet, and they headed toward the dining area. Emma was close behind, a black cane with a worn rubber tip in her right hand. Helen was last to gather her papers. When the others were out of earshot, she turned to Daniel and said, "Daniel, perhaps you could help Mark with the writing of his memoir, when you're not working on your German, that is. He seems to have trouble getting over his writer's block. We've tried, but nothing so far." She didn't wait for a response but smiled and walked lightly away.

When they were alone, Mark looked at the clock. "Your mom will be here soon."

"14 minutes."

"Will you pick up that plate of extra muffins and then push me over to the fridge? I'll put them in a plastic container."

Daniel opened the door of the fridge. "Why have you had trouble writing your memoir?"

"As long as you're in there, grab an Evian for me. Thanks."

"Your memoir?" Daniel repeated. "Helen says you need help,"

Mark held the bottle out. "Could you?" Daniel twisted off the cap and gave it back to Mark, who took a long swallow. "I can't type anymore; my fingers are a haven for arthritis. Truth is, I was never a very fast typer back in the day. And it hurts these days to simply hold a pen for very long. The thought of writing anything of length sends a shiver all the way to my toes."

"There are computer programs that type as you dictate. They used to cost thousands of dollars, but now cost hundreds."

"Talking to a machine seems a bit cold to me. It would probably be a waste of time."

"I can type sixty words a minute," Daniel stated factually.

"Thanks . . . if that was an offer. But no. How did you like the ART group?"

"I like them." His mind seemed to carry to a peaceful place as he continued. "They're old, but kind. They remind me of woolly creatures who spend most of the afternoon sitting in the warm sun soaking up Vitamin D to stay healthy."

"Interesting observation. Do you have any grandparents?"

"No."

"Too bad. If I learned anything with age, I believe the older one gets, the more tolerant we become, and if you had four, or even two, grandparents fawning over you, it would be extremely rewarding."

"Can I juggle?"

Shifting his reading glasses to the top of his head, Mark asked, "Stressed?"

"No, just tired of sitting." Mark nodded his approval, and Daniel juggled while moving about the room. First two balls, then three. Every so often, he flipped one from behind his back without missing a beat. "Juggling is one of the oldest sports," Daniel said as he wandered. Mark thought, *This young man could be wearing red, green, and gold pantaloons and a long purple stocking cap and fit right into Picasso's Juggling Clowns painting.*

"Storytellers in the Middles Ages would travel around the European countryside using juggling as a way of attracting a crowd," Daniel continued. "Pretty soon, there were juggling contests, and children learned how to juggle from a young age, like teaching soccer or baseball to five- and six-year-olds today. Buskers have used juggling since classical times. The word *busker* comes from the Italian and means *to seek*. I think the seeking was all about drawing a crowd and passing the hat."

Mark guffawed. "But you aren't wearing a hat!"

Daniel grabbed all three balls out of the air and turned to Mark. "Humorous, very humorous." Daniel's face was soft, and his lips parted. He started juggling again. "So, John thinks you're a war hero. Are you?"

"John tends to embellish the facts."

"Were you a soldier?"

Mark frowned. "Yes, I was. "

"In the Second World War?"

"Uh huh."

Daniel stopped juggling and pushed the balls into his pockets. "Did you kill anyone?"

Mark cleared his throat and thought about his answer. He hadn't been asked a question about his wartime actions in so long he had to rake his memory and then wonder why this autistic teen would ask. For the past seventy years, he had kept the war year memories off-limits, caged up in a tight pen with watchtowers and an electric fence running around the perimeter. Each time he was reminded by a newspaper article or movie scene of some aspect of World War II, the electric current would surge and he would back off any thoughts of war.

But this boy was an anomaly. He wanted to know someone, perhaps anyone, to the core. Someone who he could trust and then share his own fears and desires. He wanted desperately to have a true friend. Mark could see the symptoms, but he couldn't provide the cure, at least for any length of time, not at his age. "Would it make a difference if I said I did kill someone?"

Daniel cocked his head to the side and glanced out the patio doors. A rusty pickup truck was racing down the street with a large American flag flying from a pole stuck in the box. He didn't know what to make of people who flaunted patriotism. They reminded him of bowlers who wore shirts with their names embroidered in two-inch letters above their front pockets. He guessed it was so when they looked into a mirror, they could be reminded how important they were.

"Soldiers in the Storm Brigade in my stories kill other people all the time. They're trained to be warriors. When the young people on Lightstar 8 turn eighteen, they are drafted into the military under punishment of death."

"Conscription is a hideous device used since the beginning of time," Mark said sadly. "And what is the purpose of the Storm Brigade?"

"They are the defenders of justice."

Mark squinted. "I thought your stories portrayed a dystopia. Defending justice seems positive to me."

"The defenders of justice fight the enemy but never succeed," Daniel answered passively.

"And why is that?"

Daniel sat in the chair opposite Mark and focused on Mark's unkempt, gray hair, which seemed thinner than the first day they met. "Their brains are wired to trick them into thinking they can win, but when they face the enemy . . ."

Mark finished his thought. "They lose."

"There's no way out for the defenders of justice."

"Like there's no way out from being autistic?" Mark asked solemnly.

"I guess." Daniel looked to the bird feeders. A large fox squirrel was suspended upside down on the metal stabilizing pole, his front paws pulling black sunflower seeds from the feeder to his mouth. He was an acrobat, thought Daniel, but a bully at the same time. With each seed he captured, there were a half dozen spilled onto the ground.

Mark added, "And some of us have a past we can't escape."

16

ROSE

Spring 1944

THE CALLAHAN FARM CONSISTED OF EIGHTY ACRES of sandy loam yielding bountiful crops when the growing season was rainy and poor outcomes during hot, dry summers. Oats, corn, and red clover were planted to feed the twenty Holsteins and Jersey milk cows. There were fifteen acres of rocky pasture and a small woodlot to keep the stoves burning in winter. Until the mid-1930s, Red Callahan used horses, as did his father, to plant, cultivate, and bring in the hay. The harvesting of corn and oats was too strenuous for the workhorses and was jobbed out to traveling steam-driven combines.

After his father passed on, Red purchased a ten-year-old Allis-Chalmers tractor. Though his father loved his Belgian workhorses, Red sold them one week after his dad died and a week later proudly drove into the yard with the Super A tractor. Within a week, he constructed a makeshift roof between two twelve-foot-high wooden corncribs as a prominent parking stall for the newly acquired machine with the shiny, Persian-orange paint. On Sunday afternoons, when the weather permitted, he rolled the AC into the yard and with a bucket of soapy water washed it as best as he could.

Now that he was older, and since he and Emily had no children, Red Callahan needed help to do the daily chores. The war had taken most of the local young men to faraway places, and aside from his niece, Red continued to do most of the heavy work as best he could, but the farm and fields in general were beginning to show their age as well. The fences needed mending, along with the wooden corncribs, firewood always needed cutting and splitting, the weeds in the corn were higher than they should be, the barn roof was leaking . . . the need for rehabilitation to the buildings and fields was evident in a score of ways.

The opportunity to hire a couple of German POWs came at just the right time as far as Rose was concerned. She found an advertisement in the *Wisconsin Farm Journal* and insisted her uncle go through the background checks and paperwork to hire on a couple workers.

Now, a few minutes after eight each morning, Monday through Saturday, the tired, old, refitted POW school bus stopped at the end of the driveway to let out Marco and Oskar. The two young men would saunter up the drive, or run quickly in winter, and enter into the kitchen door, remove their hats, and take in a hearty breakfast of fresh bread with strawberry preserves, real hot coffee, and scrambled eggs with cheese and thick bacon. Emily Callahan loved to cook, and the field hands loved to eat, a symbiotic relationship from the start.

Red Callahan was an affable man with drooping eyes and thin hair that was once as orange as a carrot but was now the color of weathered rose hips. He was quick with a smile and had a gap between his front teeth wide enough for spittle to come shooting through when he laughed. And he loved to laugh. His hands were as rough as sandpaper, and the fingernails on his pinkie and ring finger of his left hand were permanently missing.

Red herded the milk cows into their stanchions and gave each a scoop of ground oats and corn before Marco and Oskar arrived. Then he joined them for breakfast. When the dishes had been carried to the sink, Red followed the boys out to begin the daily chores. Before milking, Oskar would pitch yesterday's cow manure into a wheelbarrow and wheel it out and dump it onto a pile near the cement silo. Marco cleaned the cow's teats and rinsed the milk pails and set the stools. Red filled the first pail with warm milk and poured some into a saucer for the barn cats that miraculously appeared from every direction. While they milked, Red would tell stories to Marco, mostly about his years growing up on the farm and how his father worked exclusively with horses. Marco translated as best he could for Oskar. As the days and months wore on, the two POWS became more than field hands, they became close as family.

In late April, the temperature turned unusually warm. Marco and Oskar arrived with light jackets but soon shed them as the sun rose over the metal barn roof. When the milking and barn cleaning were complete, Red believed it was time to start the spring fieldwork, the snow having all but disappeared.

The three men pulled rocks from the cornfield and mended a stretch of fence where a winter blizzard had left a fallen maple limb. After lunch, Red backed the planter, cultivator, rake, and other equipment out of the machine shed to grease the chains, wheels, and other moving parts. It was then his niece pulled into the yard driving her red International pickup truck.

"*Guten tag*, Marco. *Guten tag*, Oskar," Rose said with a smile as wide as the horizon.

"*Guten tag*," Oskar and Marco answered in unison.

"Don't forget me," Red said.

"Afternoon, Uncle. Of course I won't forget you." She sauntered over and gave him a kiss on the cheek. She was carrying a large thermos and asked if anyone would like some fresh-squeezed lemonade.

"Thank you for the lemonade," Marco said.

"You're welcome."

"Thank . . . you . . . kindly," Oskar said with a smile, his chest puffed out like a male robin.

"Well done, Oskar." She patted him on the shoulder.

"I'm teaching him English at night," said Marco. "It makes the time go faster."

Rose turned to Oskar. "You are a good . . . student . . . Oskar. Uncle Red says you are . . . both . . . good workers."

"Here, here," Red chipped in, raising his lemonade.

"I am . . . best." Oskar beamed.

Marco chuckled. "I won't argue with you, Oskar. I'm happy being the second-place worker."

Rose smiled coyly at Marco. "You're not being overlooked, Marco."

"I know," he said.

"I like . . . cows," Oskar added.

"So do I," Rose said with glee. "As do most of the residents of rural Wisconsin." Clapping her hands, she added, "But enough of cows. I stopped by to extend an invitation to a party. Aunt Emily's birthday is on Saturday, and I wondered if you would join a few of the neighbors and us for supper and cake afterwards."

"Will the party be here?" asked Marco.

"Right here, and I'll be bringing a chocolate layered cake, and Emily will make her famous dumplings . . . well . . . she will if I ask her. So, what do ya think?"

Red overheard most of the conversation and hollered from behind the grain drill, "Don't wait too long to answer. There are lots of others who would love to eat my Emily's dumplings."

Marco translated for Oskar, who nodded emphatically. "But the bus comes for us at four thirty," said Marco.

Rose gave him a wistful smile. "Uncle Red knows the commandant at the camp." She turned to Red. "Don't you, Uncle?"

"I'll call and ask for permission. Shouldn't be a problem." Red picked up the oil cans and trotted over to the machine shed to put them away.

"What about the guards?" Marco whispered.

"No guards. I haven't talked to Uncle about that yet, but don't worry, he and the commandant trust each other. It can be done. So . . . will you come?"

Marco grinned with a shine in his eyes. "Yes, of course we'll come. Eh, Oskar? Saturday? Supper here? Food?"

"Chicken and dumplings!" Rose interjected.

Oskar nodded frantically. "Food! You . . . bet! Thank you kindly."

Marco laughed heartily and turned to Rose. "Thank your aunt and uncle for their kind invitation."

Rose gathered up the lemonade glasses and thermos and hopped into her truck. Before starting the engine, she rolled down the window and said with a stern look, "I warn you now, bring a big appetite."

"We will," Marco called back. "Oskar eats enough for two." Oskar stepped close to Marco and whispered into his ear. Marco grinned, then turned to look up at Rose. "Oskar wants to know if we can listen to some swing music?"

"Good idea, Oskar. I'll bring over some records." With that, she waved and headed down the driveway, her back tires kicking up the gravel.

"She is a . . . very . . . nice . . . *Gehrl*," Oskar said softly.

"She is a very beautiful *fraulein*, Oskar."

17

STANLEY

Spring 1944

ALBERT DAVEL PLACED A COLD BOTTLE OF PABST in front of Stanley, took out a church key, opened the bottle, and walked back behind his desk and opened one for himself. He glanced out the window to see the evening sun drifting behind a bank of dark thunderclouds. A bolt of bright lightning like a large vein of white quartz split the black clouds into a dozen sections. The humidity was palpable. Water rings formed at the base of both beer bottles.

Stanley took a long draught from his beer. "As officers, we are responsible for the well-being of the POWs. Albert, I understand Army orders. But that doesn't mean I have to like 'em." He shook his head and took another gulp of beer. "Especially here in Wisconsin."

"Ah, they aren't such bad blokes. They've proven to be good workers. Lots of the local farms would be in deep financial trouble if they didn't have the extra manpower. With gas as hard as it is to get and without the migrant workers coming up from Texas and Mexico, why, we're fortunate. My buddy, Lee Simmons up in Door County, told me he wouldn't have any apples this season if it weren't for the POWs picking them."

"Needing workers is one thing, but treating them like long-lost relatives is another. They're prisoners for chrissake! Most of the locals look at the POWs like they're some kind of exotic species. Some even feel sorry for 'em."

Albert wiped the water ring from his desk. "Better to have a problem with our civilians being too friendly than the two groups being at each other's throats."

Stanley picked up his Pabst and drained the rest in one long swallow, belched, then stood and began shadowboxing his way around the room. "If any prisoner gives me back talk, or shows disrespect, you can bet I'll leave a black-and-blue mark as a reminder of who's boss." The sun suddenly poked out of the thunderclouds, and a shaft of light created a shadow of Albert's profile on the wall. "See, here I go." He gave a couple quick jabs with his left hand to the shadow, followed by an uppercut with his right that caught Albert's shadow right under the chin. "Just like that!"

"We don't need to kill anyone," Albert said emphatically. "The Army muckety-mucks will be all over us if one of these POWs should die. Not to mention the newspaper people. The press is already itching for a story." He fished under the desk and pulled out two more bottles of beer from a pail of ice water. "Another?" Stanley nodded, and Albert opened both and passed one over.

Albert picked a newspaper off his desk and held it up for Stanley. "You ever read the *County Chronicle*?"

"Once in a blue moon."

"There's a woman reporter over there, name of Arlene Howard, ever heard of her?" Stanley shook his head. "She called out here the other day and wondered if she could interview me about the POWs for a feature story she wants to run in a Sunday edition. I told her there would be no interview and I didn't want to see any article on the POWs in her paper."

Stanley took a drink of beer and asked, "What did she have to say to that?"

"She got a little huffy and reminded me about the freedom of the press and rights under the Constitution and on and on. Now, I can't disagree, in fact I believe in the freedom of the press, but I reminded her that we are at war and the world has changed a lot since Pearl Harbor."

"Ain't that the truth." Stanley sat back down and pulled on his beer.

"I called a guy I know from the local Army headquarters in Milwaukee, and he said he'd give this Howard character a call. Told me if any newspaper printed an article about our prisoners without the Army's permission, they'd shut the newspaper down immediately. They'd just as soon ensure that most of the townsfolk don't know anything about who's living under their noses." Albert narrowed his eyes and pointed a finger at Stanley. "And we want to keep it that way."

"I get the message." Stanley lifted his boots onto the desk sole to sole with Albert's. "But everybody in town will find out if people like Rose Callahan and other do-gooders keep treating the Krauts like school chums. She invited two of them Nazis to dinner tonight at her aunt and uncle's place." His voice rose in anger. "Did you know that, Albert?"

"Relax, Stanley. Red Callahan called me and told me all about it. It's his wife's birthday is all. A few neighbors, Rose, the POWs who he claims are good, trustworthy workers . . . it's not a big deal." On reflection, he added, "Besides, it'll save on our meal budget."

Stanley finished his second beer and set the empty on the desk. "Got any more beer?"

"No, sorry, that's it."

"A bit too cozy, if you ask me," Stanley growled. "One of those POWs is probably hoping to shack up with Rose when her uncle ain't looking."

"Most of the POWs are just boys who were pulled off their own farms or outta schools back in Germany. If it weren't for my dad's father emigrating from Bremen, Germany, at the end of the last century, I'd probably be in the same predicament . . . and you too!" He laughed.

"Don't put me in the same bed as those scumbags!" Stanley grimaced as if he had to swallow castor oil.

Albert pulled his feet off the desk and placed his empty in the pail. Then he leaned back and crossed his arms over his chest. "Didn't you tell me your grandparents still speak German at home? Mueller, isn't that your grandpa's name?"

"I'm an American, Albert," Stanley answered defiantly. "And so are all my relatives."

"My point is, half the people in Wisconsin come from German stock. That's the main reason I was placed in charge of this operation. I know the culture, the language, the people. Army's way of trying to head off any problems before they happen."

Frowning, Stanley shook his head and was about to respond when the phone on the desk rang. Albert reached over, picked it up, and listened for a minute, then talked into the receiver. "That's right, I gave Callahan permission. Two, that's right, let 'em in. Okay . . ." Albert caught Stanley waving his arms to stop. "Hang on a moment, Private." He placed his hand over the receiver. "What?"

"Albert, let's have a little fun with these two late dinner guests. Tell the private to send them over here and we can do a little questioning. Find out the details."

Albert hesitated for a moment, then replied imperiously, "Alright, but mind you, I have to be in bed by 2200 hours. I'm back here tomorrow morning at 0600." Stanley smiled and nodded like a teenager who was just given the keys to the family car.

Ten minutes later, Marco and Oskar were escorted into the office. Stanley walked behind the desk and stood at Albert's shoulder. When the guard was dismissed, Stanley plucked the newspaper off the desk and rolled it into a tight baton. He strutted around to the front of the desk and barked, "Stand at attention! Eyes forward!" Marco and Oskar stood straight as pencils, eyes focused on the far wall. Stanley stopped behind Marco and slapped him behind his left

ear with the newspaper. "Tell the commandant how grateful you are
to have been allowed to have dinner outside the camp."

Marco cleared his throat. "Thank you, sir, for allowing us to miss
curfew."

Stanley turned to Oskar and cuffed him behind the ear. "You
too!"

Oskar looked over at Marco, who nodded. Then he stammered,
"Thank you . . . kindly."

Turning quickly, Stanley hit Oskar across the cheek, the newspaper unrolling slightly. "Thank you kindly . . . *what*?"

Oskar's eyes darted back and forth between Marco and Stanley
as though he were watching a tennis match. Then he turned to the
commandant. "Thank you . . . kindly . . . what."

Stanley laughed manically and shook his head. "No wonder
their army is losing on all fronts, Albert. And these guys thought
they could rule the world? Just a bunch of sausage heads." He turned
and swatted Oskar again, this time on the back of the neck. "Again.
You're addressing an officer, call him *sir*!"

Marco interjected, "He doesn't understand, sir."

Stanley's eyes shot up, and he slithered in front of Marco, coming
nose to nose, and growled, "You speak when I say." He slapped him
with the newspaper hard across the face, turning Marco's right cheek
a bright scarlet. Marco flinched but kept his eyes cast forward, the
sour smell of beer and sweat piercing his nostrils. He bit his tongue
so hard he could taste the blood.

Oskar clenched and unclenched his fists, trying to look at Marco
without moving his head. The sergeant was like so many officers he
had put up with in the German army, their rank giving them rights
to use physical punishment whenever they wanted. He caught the
look on Stanley's face, the same look Weishaple and his thugs wore
when they cornered him on the SS *Ambrose Bierce*.

Albert brought his hands together on the desk and leaned

forward, his chair creaking loudly. "Careful Stanley. I don't want to write up an incident report or send anyone to the infirmary with injuries of a questionable nature."

Stanley grinned and held the newspaper baton up high like a lit torch in a tunnel. "Never laid a finger on him, sir. This newspaper got rolled up by a dust devil." He threw the paper onto the desk. "Look it over, no blood," he gloated.

Albert looked down at the paper and frowned. "Humph. Let's find out about the dinner, Stanley. Mrs. Callahan is said to be one of the best cooks in the area." He tapped his finger to his watch.

"Yes, sir. I'm getting to that." Stanley pushed the two chairs in front of the desk against the wainscoted wall and looked over at Oskar. "You! Come right here." He pointed to a spot directly in front of the desk and opposite Albert. "Now get on all fours. Here! Now!" Oskar turned to Marco quizzically. "You." Stanley nodded at Marco. "You're the English professor, tell him." Marco quickly translated for Oskar, who hurried down onto his hands and knees.

"Now you, Professor, come over here and sit on his back facing the commandant. And don't let your feet touch the floor." Marco did as he was told. "Comfy?" Stanley asked, tongue in cheek. Marco nodded. "Perfect."

Stanley stood behind Marco, gloating. "Sir, I didn't want either of these two to leave a stain or mark on one of your fine office chairs or, for that matter, an after-smell that could work its way into the wood."

Albert flashed a tight smile and leaned back in his chair. He feared he had unleashed an attack dog as he watched Stanley move about with the eyes of a predator who had cornered his prey. "Ten minutes, Stanley, then we have to bring the curtain down."

"Will do, sir." He turned to Marco and asked pleasantly, "So, how was dinner?"

"Good, sir."

"That's all you have to say . . . it was *goot*?"

"We ate chicken and dumplings," Marco added with a straight face.

"Now we're getting somewhere. How about dessert?"

Marco hesitated for a moment. "Birthday cake. Chocolate with chocolate frosting."

Stanley walked back behind Albert. "Sounds delicious, doesn't it, Albert? And speaking of dumplings . . . what about Rose Callahan?"

A band of tiny beads of sweat broke out above Marco's upper lip. "Sir?"

"Was Rose at the dinner?"

"Yes, sir."

"Did she sit next to you at the table?"

Marco hesitated and blinked several times.

"I can call Mr. Callahan and ask."

"She sat across from me," Marco said.

"Let's get back to the dumplings for a minute. Did you like Mrs. Callahan's dumplings?"

"They were . . . er . . . delicious, sir."

"And the dumpling sitting across from you. The dumpling with the dark hair and beautiful eyes. Did you find her delicious as well?"

Marco stammered, "No . . . I mean . . ." He searched for the right answer. "She is very beautiful, sir."

Stanley walked behind Marco and fingered the collar of his work shirt. He leaned over and put his nose an inch from the fabric and gave a loud sniff. "Hmmm . . . despite the normal stink you POWs give off, I'm picking up a whiff of perfume." Sniffing loudly again and winking at Albert, he added, "Could be honeysuckle or maybe lilac. How did that lovely perfume smell get on your shirt, Kraut?

"I think it's sweat, sir."

Stanley jerked his head and smiled lasciviously. "Are you calling me a liar?"

Marco shook his head slightly. "No, sir."

"Were you giving free German lessons to Rose? Perhaps up in the bedroom after dinner?"

"No, sir."

"How about the easy chair, the fool here." Stanley tapped Oskar on the back of his head. "Was he trying out his American expressions on the farm girl?"

"We work very hard, Oskar and me, for Mr. Callahan's dairy farm."

"He thinks so, I'll give you that. He even let you join his little party. But I'm not so sure your thoughts are always on the cows. The perfume on your shirt says something else to me." Turning, he asked, "Albert, what is the punishment for one of our POWs if they're found *fraternizing* with one of the locals?"

"If it's corroborated, it could result in solitary confinement or a transfer to a maximum-security camp."

Stanley's face lit up like a child opening a present. "No more chicken and dumplings. No more spying on the beautiful Rose Callahan and wondering what if . . . eh, Professor?"

Albert pushed his chair back and stood up with a loud sigh. "But I don't think a transfer's warranted in this case, Sergeant Stanley. No, I don't think so. You've had your fun, now it's time to get these men back to their barracks. They have to be on the bus at 0700 tomorrow, and I need my beauty sleep too." He turned to Oskar. "On your feet, young man."

Stanley walked to the door and put his hand on the knob. "If I see either of you getting too close to Rose or any other American girl, I will have you put in solitary confinement before you can say 'Heil Hitler.'" Marco nodded for the both of them. Stanley pulled the door wide. "Now get out of here, both of ya! Dumb bastards!" He gave each a kick in the rump as they scrambled out.

Albert straightened a few things on his desk and pushed in his chair. "I take it you don't get along with the English speaker?"

"He gives me indigestion. I see how he looks at Rose, and it just ain't right. American boys fighting over there while these POWs get to flirt with the girls here ..." Stanley shook his head. "It just rubs me the wrong way."

Albert leaned over to turn off a lamp on his desk. "Well, I hope tonight you got it out of your system." As he flipped the switch, the room fell into shadows.

In the darkness, Stanley said, "I'm afraid he and I might have just started."

18

DANIEL

2019

ON A COOL WEDNESDAY AFTERNOON, Daniel sloshed his way to the BRC through the remnants of a late winter snowstorm which left 6 inches of snow carried by 32-mile-per-hour winds and a barometric pressure drop to 28 millibars. The start of classes at Oakwood High were delayed 1 and 1/2 hours. Daniel spent the extra morning time in his bedroom finishing his 117th story. When it was time to go, his mother's cautious driving through the slippery roads took 7 minutes longer than normal. Several students came in tardy to Mrs. Aaronson's Spanish 4 class, disrupting the lesson.

A hectic day for some, a disaster for Daniel. He loved his regimen; deviations caused him to feel anxious, even nauseous at times. He couldn't wait for the final afternoon bell. It was Wednesday, and he looked forward to joining the ART group. He pleaded with his mom to drive him to the BRC, but she refused, claiming the exercise would do him good.

His black, low-cut Converse were not well-suited to keeping his white socks dry. In fact, his feet were soaked. Several stretches of sidewalk were not shoveled, and the cuffs on his chinos quickly filled with heavy snow. He had warned his mother not to put away his winter jacket, but on the first of April, she insisted, claiming she had enough of winter, and the coats were packed away in a plastic tub in the basement until next October. "You won't melt," she had said at breakfast. "No one freezes to death in April!"

It *was* spring and had been for 23 days and 7 hours, but the TV weather people kept talking about the effects of a late *winter* storm. Who would hire a weather reporter who didn't know the end of one season and the beginning of another? Did TV meteorologists even understand the significance of the March equinox . . . 12 hours of daylight and 12 of darkness, the harbinger of a new season? Why was that a difficult concept?

After reading Dante's *Divine Comedy* three years ago, Daniel was in the habit of rereading the whole thing during the day before, the day of, and the day after the equinox. Even though he wasn't a churchgoer, he understood the fundamentals of major world religions and the symbolic meaning of moving from darkness to light during the Christian Easter season. It was Dante Alighieri's masterpiece of balance and numerology.

The weather conditions today were hardly Easter-like. The dirty melting snow on the sidewalk reminded him of level three in the *Inferno,* the level of the gluttons who were bloated souls wallowing in a putrid mess of freezing rain and dirty snow. Because they overindulged in food and drink during their lives on earth, gluttons were forever stuck in the offal of the underworld. The day's weather conditions prompted Daniel to imagine he could see the obese souls like Ciacco the Hog half-buried beneath the snowbanks at the end of each driveway.

Inside the sliding doors of the BRC, Daniel stomped his Converse several times. Pieces of road salt had been dragged in and were strewn about on the plastic rugs. After giving the aviary a quick inspection and finding the Gouldian finches in good shape, he headed to the day room. He was exactly twelve minutes early, but he knew Mark would be waiting. Daniel was anxious to discuss the writing competition his mother had convinced him to enter.

Two CNAs said hello as he walked, but he ignored their remarks. He kept his head down as he moved, focusing instead on the water spots left by dirty slush atop the linoleum.

When he stepped into the day room, he pulled up suddenly. Seth Wenton had his hands on the back of Mark's wheelchair. He was leaning over Mark's shoulder, apparently listening to Mark. "This is far enough, Seth."

"You sure? I could wheel you over and put you at the head of the table, the godfather's chair. You're the man."

"I'm early. This is fine."

"Okay," said Seth, slightly disappointed. "Whatever, man."

He was about to take his leave when Mark said, "By the way, there's a cold beer waiting in my room. Actually, in the bathroom behind the door. Help yourself."

Seth grinned from oversized ear to oversized ear. He looked a bit like a child's jack-o'-lantern carving. If a front tooth were missing, the image would be complete. "Wow, thanks, dude. I gotta say, you know how to keep a guy on your good side."

Mark didn't look up. "It's only beer, not the hard stuff. Still, let's not spread it around to the other staff, okay?"

"Right," he said conspiratorially. "Just between us men of the world." He laughed at his own lame witticism. Then he pivoted on his Sketchers and took a step to the door when he spied Daniel, who already had the juggling balls in the air. "Whoa! Your juggling buddy is here, Mark."

Mark was facing the opposite direction but said blindly, "Welcome, Daniel. Come on in."

"Time for me to vamoose." Seth walked to the door as Daniel gave ground. "How they hangin', D-squared?" Seth waited for a response, but there was none. "'Bout normal, I guess. Later, dudes." Seth gave Daniel a silly wink, then disappeared.

"You can put the juggling balls away. He won't be back anytime soon." Mark turned his wheelchair and looked squarely at Daniel. "Why do you let him, the leader of the Neanderthals as you call him, get under your skin? You have a universe of talent compared to him. You are a Rembrandt compared to his kindergarten finger painting."

Daniel plucked the balls out of the air and pulled a chair close to Mark. He set the balls on the table and fell into the seat. "I like coming here. I like the ART group. But I don't like him."

"If it makes any difference, I don't care for him either. But at my age, I can't be choosy about who is willing to help me get on and off the toilet." Mark took a deep breath and let it out slowly. "What's the 'D-squared' all about?"

"Daniel Disaster . . . DD . . . D-squared. In the Neanderthal world, anyone Seth doesn't like earns a nickname. His way of making a person into an object."

Mark glowered. "There are others?"

"In my AP Biology class, there's a girl with pronounced acne. He calls her 'Crater Face.' In my Physics class, there's a sophomore girl who is smart, not as smart as me, but a good student. She's shy and doesn't have many friends. He calls her 'Debbie Don't.' I'm not positive, but I think it's because he believes she's a virgin."

"That's awful."

"In my homeroom, there's a freshman boy who has a congenital foot problem. He wears a special orthotic shoe and walks with a distinct gait. Seth refers to him as 'Lawrence the Limp.'"

"I had no idea he could be so vulgar," Mark said in disgust.

Daniel suddenly sat up straight and pointed his finger at Mark. "Did you just offer Seth a beer?"

"Sort of," Mark answered. "But it's not what you think."

"Unless you're his parent or appointed guardian, providing alcohol to minors is illegal and punishable with jail time up to six months or a fine of a thousand dollars. You can also lose your . . ."

"Stop! Stop right there, Mr. Attorney General." Mark was smiling broadly. "I occasionally give Seth a bottle of his favorite brand of *root beer*. I don't think that's illegal."

"You can buy root beer today as potent as a Budweiser," Daniel warned. "I would read the label very carefully."

Mark's giggle sounded more like a wheeze. He held both palms together as if to pray. "It's A&W."

"Most dark sodas are filled with too much sugar and caffeine. I know students who are addicted. Even my mom drinks more Pepsi than she should. Did you know A&W stands for Awful and Wasteful?"

Mark flinched and turned to look straight into Daniel's eyes. "That's not true!" He was almost shouting.

Daniel produced a real smile, even showing his front teeth. "That was a joke."

Mark stared at Daniel for a moment then broke out laughing so hard his cough turned into a spasm. He pulled out a tan hanky from his shirtsleeve and held it over his mouth. For a full minute, he fought to gain control. He shook a finger at Daniel and spoke as his cough slowed. "You got me. You got me so good it almost killed me." His breathing became more regular, but he couldn't help but go on laughing like a tickled child. When he looked up, his watery eyes focused on the face of the young jokester sporting a subtle grin like he just swallowed the canary. "Now, I suppose you're going to tell me about the real A&W, aren't you?"

"Their names were Allen and Wright. They received the patent in 1919. Made a fortune right after the First World War. It had such a low alcohol content it was classified as a *small* beer."

"So, I won't get arrested for serving it to Seth?"

Daniel shook his head. "Does he chug his A&W?"

Mark wrinkled his nose. "Sometimes, yes. Why?"

Rising from his chair, Daniel walked over to the patio doors looking for birds but saw none. "Seth likes to show off in the commons at school by chugging a sixteen-ounce Gatorade during the lunch period. His band of boors cheer him on. It's become quite a noon-hour spectacle egged on by dozens of students who would've been great fans in the Roman Coliseum when the lions were turned loose on the Christians." Daniel held both hands out wide and slowly turned his thumbs down.

"Enough about Seth and his tribe. What about you? Have you changed your mind about prom? Do you have a date?"

"May 24th, nine till midnight, Riverview Country Club."

"Not that kind of date, and yes, I caught the humor, but I meant have you asked a girl?" Mark put his hand up before Daniel could answer. "You don't have to start juggling, I'm just asking."

Daniel eyed Mark warily then returned to his chair. "My mom thinks it may be too late. Besides, I have to concentrate on my writing."

"Your writing can be worked on most any time. A senior prom comes around but once in a lifetime. And I know how fleeting a lifetime is."

"I don't want to spend the money. I'm saving up to go to Las Vegas next year for a Star Trek convention. It might be my only chance."

"Planning to have a selfie with Doctor Spock?"

"Leonard Nimoy died in 2015. I want to see George Takei. He played Hikaru Sulu and has written several dystopian stories. I might get some tips."

"Wouldn't you rather have a night of dancing with a beautiful partner?"

"I don't care to dance, especially if I have to touch anybody." Daniel found the Nile moving slowly away from Lake Victoria, winding its way through the green forests of Botswana before reaching the desert. He followed it to the flooded delta and eventually out into the Mediterranean. He swayed back and forth on his chair, keeping in rhythm to the gentle movement of the river.

Mark interrupted his reverie. "Our ART members will be here anytime now."

Daniel glanced at his watch, a Timex Expedition that glowed in the dark. "Three minutes if they're on time. I have a new writing project," he said as an afterthought.

Mark opened his eyes wide and asked, "A new Lightstar 8 story?"

"No. My mom talked me into entering the Wisconsin Young Writers Contest. The first-place winner will receive a tuition-free semester to any public college in the state." He held his hands in his lap and brought his head down, staring at the floor. "We don't have a lot of money. Mom thinks I can help her out by winning."

"That's a wonderful idea," said Mark.

"Mom thinks my dystopian stories are too dark. Plus, they have no local connection, and since this is a Wisconsin contest, she thinks I should find a different topic. Something that would convince the provincial judges."

"Makes sense," agreed Mark. "What other topics are you interested in?"

It took a moment for Daniel to answer. He moved his nose back and forth and pursed his lips. "Maybe something to do with cadavers. I like the idea of dissection."

"On a darkness scale, that seems like jumping from the frying pan into the fire!"

A moment later, John's voice could be heard coming from the hallway. "I hear the others," Mark said. "How about we ask the ART group for suggestions. They're the epitome of local. Push me over to the table and we'll see what happens."

After the group took their places, Helen called the meeting to order, her hands clapping loudly as usual. She asked if everyone had a chance to read Emma's story. When she was satisfied they had, she asked each member to comment. John started with a mouth full of Eva's homemade toffee bars. "The title doesn't make much sense to me . . . *Dreams Without Action*. You wrote about watching John Wayne from behind the set. He was the greatest actor of his time. He was the real Mr. Action. Where do the dreams without action come in?" He slurped water from a Styrofoam cup. "These bars are terrific, Eva. Glad I don't have diabetes."

Marie jumped in. "I think she was talking symbolically, John."

"I know action when I see it," he responded, "and when JW hit somebody and he goes flying across the room or off a barstool, well, that ain't no stunt. He was . . ."

"Those scenes were all choreographed," Emma interrupted. "No one ever got hurt, at least not on purpose."

"Sorry to burst your bubble," Helen added with a smile.

Emma said, "It's Hollywood, John. It wasn't real life."

"You're killing me, Emma. If a guy can't believe in JW . . . well . . ." John waved both hands in disgust and shook his head in disappointment. His face turned the color of a ripe Delicious apple, and he remained silent for longer than anyone could remember.

The rest of the ART members carried on the discussion of Emma's work for the next thirty minutes. When the table grew silent, Mark asked to change the subject. He looked over the faces at the table and spoke slowly. "Our newest member, Daniel, needs some help, and I thought we might be able to give it to him." Mark looked over to Daniel. "Do you want to explain?"

"No, you can."

Mark nodded and continued. "Daniel's mother has encouraged him to enter a writing contest for young Wisconsin writers. There's some money in it for the winner, and if he is fortunate to be the winner, it will go a long way toward helping him with college costs. He's decided to forego the Lightstar 8 stories and try something else."

John stopped pouting and roared. "And I was about to donate a lung for some poor sucker in one of your stories! Get it? Sucker!" And he made loud inhaling sounds again.

When Daniel flashed a smile, the entire table chuckled. "I understand the humor, Mr. Mancuso," Daniel said.

"Good boy!" John hollered.

"If I could continue," Mark said. "Since this is a regional competition, as all the contestants need to be a resident of the state, his mother thinks a local experience or local subject might be appropriate. Daniel's dystopian stories aren't quite what's needed here, so I thought the ART group might help him flesh out an appropriate topic."

"I think it's wonderful of you to enter the contest, Daniel," said Helen. The other women nodded as well.

John shook his finger at the teenager. "What you need is a good page-turner. Something everybody can relate to, like sex and violence. Works every time."

"No, no, John. He's too young for that," Marie scolded. She turned to Daniel. "What about a *famous first* topic. You know . . . first day at school, first birthday, first time you found out Santa Claus was real . . ."

Eva interjected, "*Wasn't* real, she means."

"I think that first experience stuff has been overdone," Emma said. "How about a childhood experience that stands out, Daniel? A family vacation or camping trip? You could set the story in one of Wisconsin's state parks." She looked at him with anticipation.

"My dad left when I was eight. And I hate sleeping outdoors, especially . . ."

"The darkness scare ya?" John interrupted.

"I'm allergic to mosquitoes. Their saliva produces an anticoagulant which reacts to the low level of carbon dioxide in my skin, which gives me hives." He scratched his arm with the thought.

"Okay, I guess camping is out," John said with resignation.

After a short pause, Helen spoke up. "I'm just thinking out loud, but since all of us are writing memoirs, which is a form of history, there might be something of interest here."

"Anything we've written would be boring unless you're a relative. And even then it's not gonna win any prize," said John. "Marie probably has the most interesting background with her Holocaust prison stuff but . . ." He stopped and let the thought drift away.

Eva pulled on the collar of her plain gray cotton blouse and faced Daniel. "Mother's ability to remember things during that time is not very good," she said as delicately as she could. Marie agreed by shaking her head. "It fades in and out." Eva smiled at her mom, then turned back to Daniel. "When do you need to be done with your story?"

"It needs to be postmarked by five o'clock May 15th. 33 days and 42 minutes from now."

Helen came back to the topic search. "Writing about an influential person in your life can be interesting. A grandparent? Or a pastor? Or a teacher maybe?"

"If his mom ain't a saint," interjected John, "I don't know who is."

Daniel shook his head. "No."

John's face quivered with excitement. "I know! How about writing about a war hero. That guy in the wheelchair next to you is the real deal. If you can get him to talk to you, that is. People love old vet stories. That'd be a winner for sure."

Mark cleared his throat and said, "I'm not that interesting, John."

John continued as if he hadn't heard the last remark. "Did he tell you he was a POW? I'll bet he left that part out, didn't you, Mark?"

Eva's eyes shot up, and she asked, "Is that true? Were you a POW?"

Mark held up both hands as if trying to ward off any more questions. "I was. But I don't think . . ."

"There you go, Daniel," John said. "You got the hero and the violence of a war and the sex . . . well, that part can be watered down . . . but it's a winning combination for sure."

Emma spoke with a strong voice. "Mark, you are the only World

War II veteran and certainly the only former POW living under this roof, perhaps in all of central Wisconsin. The experiences you incurred would be a writer's dream. Why not work with this young man?"

Mark continued to shake his head. "You are all very kind, and I appreciate your compliments, I do, but you know I can't hold a pen anymore due to my arthritis. I joined the ART group to read your stories and once in a while offer a critique or suggestion that might be helpful. That's my reason for being here. And I've enjoyed every minute. But . . ."

"I can type faster than you can talk," Daniel uttered, his head down but his tone hopeful.

"I'm flattered," Mark said. "But . . ."

"No more buts!" It was Marie this time, and she was adamant. "If my memory wasn't like Swiss cheese, I would insist on having my story told. I don't want anyone to forget the war days and the tough times some of us went through. I can't remember. You can. Just do it, Mark. Just do it." Her watery eyes gave away her emotion.

Mark was hesitant to respond. He let his hands fall into his lap and his fingers twine like coiled yarn. He looked hard at Marie, her face a statue of resolve. "Many things happened back then that people today . . . might . . . well . . . not find acceptable or maybe even offensive."

John couldn't hold back. "You were a POW, for God's sake! Whoever finds that offensive is un-American!"

"Tell your story to Daniel," Helen implored. "Let him judge whether to use it or not. He's young and talented. He can make it work, I'm sure."

"Not to mention it would help his mom," Emma added.

"And God knows she can use the help," John said. "Daniel's smart, sure, but a real handful I'll bet. No offense, kid."

Emma said, "I have a Smith Corona in my closet. It's a manual, but I think it still works. You can have it, Daniel, and I have lots of extra typing paper." She fidgeted with a blue pocket folder on the table in front of her. "Here, take this." She shoved the paper across to Daniel, who stuffed it into his backpack.

Mark's face was flush with apprehension. "I don't know . . ."

"We could start now," Daniel said, glancing at the analog clock. "My mother won't be here for 12 minutes."

Helen clapped her hands and smiled. "No excuse now, Mark. Off you go, boys. The Alzheimer's Round Table looks forward to the next great American short story."

Mark seemed resigned. He was still shaking his head. "We'll try, that's all I can promise."

Daniel stood and guided Mark's chair toward the door. "Happy trails!" shouted John and waved his pen back and forth. After they were in the hallway, John turned to the others. "I don't think Mark looked so good."

"I hope we didn't push too hard. He's avoided talking about his own story for a long time," Helen added.

Marie reminded them that Mark sits across from her at the dinner table. "The last week or so his appetite hasn't been very strong. Right now, I eat more than he does." She looked at Eva, who was straightening her mother's sweater to cover both shoulders. "He was always a good eater," Marie added.

John shouted out, "Storm clouds are gathering, fellow writers . . . my doc says a bad appetite is a bad sign!"

19

SETH

DANIEL STOOD AND WALKED TO THE PATIO DOORS, pushing his nose so close to the glass a small cloud of condensation formed like fog. He was trying to understand Mark's reason for escaping his past. What was in his past? Could a man be in his nineties and still be haunted by something that had happened more than a half century ago? The thought bounced around in his head like an uncut gemstone when he heard someone come into the room.

"Hey, D-squared! That you standin' and starin'?" Seth strolled toward the center of the room. "I think yer ol' lady is waitin' in the lobby. Sure looked like her." He collapsed into one of the overstuffed chairs and hefted his feet onto a coffee table. "Don't wanna keep her waiting."

Daniel was quivering and at a loss for words. Mark knew the juggling was about to start up. "Daniel's joined our writing group."

Seth grinned and looked Daniel up and down. "Really?"

Bowing his head, Daniel walked quickly toward the exit. "My mother is 7 minutes early." His eyes followed the seams in the linoleum floor. He tilted his head, glanced at Mark, and scurried out like a janitor caught mopping the floor of the board room when the CEO strolls in.

Mark shrugged and raised his eyes. "See you at the next ART meeting, I hope." But his words fell on an empty doorway.

"See ya, Mannheim!" Seth shouted, then raised his hand over his head and waved at nobody, his eyes landing on Mark. "I gotta tell ya, Mark, that Daniel Mannheim is one weird guy. I can't believe he's gonna be in your writing group. He hardly says two words to anybody at school."

"Writing is another way of communication. It comes easily to Daniel."

"Yeah, I get that. But what's he got to say of interest? He comes to school every day at 7:35 and leaves at 3:09. You can set your watch to his comin' and goin'. I sometimes think *time* is his god . . . Wow, that's kinda heavy, huh? I mean, I'm an atheist and all, but I can see where someone could create their own god." Proud of his own clever thought, Seth let his feet plunk loudly to the linoleum and crossed his arms over his chest, his smile as wide as a watermelon rind.

Mark's face turned dark as though a cloud just blotted out the sun. "He's a person with autism, Seth."

Waving his hand in front of his nose, Seth said, "He's somethin' alright."

"Being autistic is not a choice."

"Sure, sure, I get that. Just ain't natural, that's all I'm saying. Like being born with six fingers. My uncle was born with an extra finger, but had it removed. He was a little, how should I say it . . . *slow*, know what I mean? Don't think he could ever count to a hundred without gettin' confused. Mannheim is just like a lotta people born with defects, kinda like a car that comes off the assembly line and won't run right. Nobody's fault, just a defect."

"You can't remove autism like a sixth finger. He's trying to fit in, but students like you just make it harder," Mark said sternly. "In fact, his mother wants him to go to prom."

Seth let out a loud snort. "I'd pay money to see that." Mark didn't respond, so he added, "You're kidding, right?"

"I think the prom, with the dance and the dinner and renting of clothes and corsages, would be a wonderful social experience for Daniel. Most of his classmates will be there, not to mention parent chaperones; everyone is a little awkward. He could blend in. He doesn't have to perform or appear in front of the group. It could be a real turning point."

"He'd have to have a date. A *live* one," Seth grunted.

"Let's not be rude." Mark's anger was lying just beneath the surface. "What about you? Are you going to the prom?"

"Am I going to the prom? You kiddin'? I wouldn't miss it." With a spoonful of machismo, he bragged, "Takin' a hot little number too. And between us men, I'm hoping to make prom the beginning of a week-long party."

"Week-long?"

Pulling his chair closer, Seth looked over his shoulder and whispered, "Me and a few of my buds are renting a cottage on Lake Eleanor. It's like a Hollywood palace—five bedrooms, five bathrooms, fireplace, wine cellar . . . the works! My buddy Justin has an older brother who takes care of the place during the off-season, and he talked to the owners, and we rented it from the day of the prom for a whole week. We're gonna invite lots of friends, drink a little beer, maybe even have some live music. I got my eye on the hot tub. It's a big one, who knows . . . skinny-dipping, anyone? And only a thousand bucks."

"Only?"

Seth sat back and answered loudly, "Man, that's cheap! During the summer, it goes for five Benjamins a night. I mean, this place is like bitchin.'"

Mark screwed up his face. "Benjamins?"

"Hundred-dollar bills."

"A thousand dollars is still a lot of money."

"Not a big deal, dude. We gotta fundraiser goin'. We'll have the cash in no time." Seth flashed a confident smile and stared at the ceiling as though basking in the morning sun.

"Don't tell me you're having a bake sale."

Lowering his head, Seth replied, "Maybe that would work in your day, Mr. Flour, but we gotta be a bit more creative in the modern world. Like you say, a grand is real money, so we gotta push a good product with lots of profit . . . and do it quickly. We can't wait for summer jobs. Besides, the *love palace* won't be available in summer anyway . . . nah, we gotta act now while the ladies are romantically inclined."

"And what is your product?"

"That I can't reveal. If I did, I'd have to kill ya." The smile blew off his lips like a shadow, and for one eerie moment, Mark believed he wasn't kidding.

"What about Daniel?"

Seth's head jerked back, and his eyebrows shot up. "What about . . . *his highness*?"

"You've been on dates before, I'm sure. You know the ropes. Maybe you could give him a few tips?"

Seth tried to talk and laugh at the same time and ended in a coughing fit. "Get real, man. I'd sooner double with you and one of the old gals from here. At least we'd talk to each other."

"That sounds a little harsh," Mark scolded.

"Look, man." Sitting up and resting his hands on his thighs, he looked squarely into Mark's troubled eyes. "I know you get along with him, but Daniel Mannheim is a guy who's just not put together right, ya know? Besides, he's got no future. I mean, he's staring at a life sentence in a group home with other guys like him or some mental health clinic or a welfare ranch out west. I read about one of those places where they use horses and other animals to try and get the guys back on reality street. Tell you straight—he gives me the creeps most of the time."

"Has he ever acted up at school?"

"*Acted up*. That's an old-timey term I guess, huh? Here's the scoop. Daniel Mannheim is what I call a wall-walker. Whenever I spy him in the hallway, he's moving with one shoulder scraping the wall like he's trying to rub the paint off or something. I swear if he loses contact with that wall, he's gonna keel over. You gotta watch out for guys like that. He doesn't want anybody to touch him, and he never says, 'Hey.'"

Mark said defensively, "Did you ever think he might just be shy in a crowd? Some people suffer from anxiety when there's a lot of commotion."

"Nah. He's too smart to be shy. He's a conniver. He gets straight As because teachers feel sorry for him."

"Really?"

"I swear he's got ESP or something. He knows the answers before the teacher even asks the question. Me? I gotta work for my grades, which I might add are . . . okay. I can't sit around and talk to myself and write in a little green notebook and stare at ridiculous low-cut Converse and expect to pass. No way! Daniel Mannheim, though, can get away with it. He's the teacher's pet."

Mark shook his head as he spoke. "But certainly you can accept that people are different. And not just in physical appearance."

Seth held his palms forward as though shielding himself from a bad odor. "We hear that song and dance all the time at school. Di . . . ver . . . si . . . ty. That's the buzzword these days. Well, between us guys, Mr. Flour, it's a bunch of crap. I got friends, you got friends . . . as long as everybody hangs out with their own kind, everything is kosher. Hey, there you see I used a Jewish term, *kosher*, a good example of di . . . ver . . . si . . . ty."

With resignation and a somber face, Mark queried, "Could a *normal* guy like you get up off your white Anglo-Saxon butt and roll me back to my room? Chalk it up to your use of diversity by helping one elderly member of the community who happens to be of German descent."

"You got it, ol' dude." Seth leaped up and swung the wheelchair toward the door. "Your wish is my command." And they rolled out the door, Mark seething and Seth giggling.

20

MARCO AND OSKAR

Spring 1945

ON APRIL 30^{TH,} 1945, ADOLPH HITLER WAS REPORTED DEAD. Headlines around the world heralded his death with exuberance and joy. Thousands of civilians and soldiers took to the streets in New York and London and Toronto and Paris to toast the Führer's demise. But the news of Hitler's death brought a sense of anxiety for some of the POWs in Wisconsin. Men who had been working the fields and orchards and canning factories for nearly two years in relatively peaceful conditions were going to be shipped out. But where? To France? Or Belgium? Or maybe all the way to Germany? And when? Would they be accepted back home (if there was still a home), or would they be imprisoned once again by the British, French, or, God forbid, the Russians?

The first two weeks of May in 1945 were hot by Wisconsin standards. Daytime temps rose above seventy, and the air was thick with moisture carried on southerly winds all the way from the Gulf of Mexico. Red Callahan was preparing for the planting season. He had driven over to the Tomorrow River Co-op to pick up seed corn and oats and a fertilizer mix made mostly from potash and nitrogen. He also ordered a couple ton of crushed lime, which would be delivered by truck in the next week or so.

Red directed Oskar and Marco to load the piles of winter manure onto his spreader, and when it was overflowing, he climbed up on his Allis-Chalmers, fixed his wide-brimmed straw hat, and drove out to fling it onto the cornfields.

While Red was in the fields, Oskar and Marco washed down stanchions and cleaned the stainless-steel milking pails. They swept out the barn and even wiped down the windows. It was *spring cleaning* according to Red. "Emily takes care of the house, and we take care of the barn and the equipment. Been a long winter, and now it's time to give back to Mother Nature all the shit she threw at us during the frozen months." He laughed with his whole belly shaking, his face as red as his hair.

After lunch, Marco climbed the ladder to the second story of the barn and used a pitchfork and broom to clean the remnants of last season's hay. Flecks of dust danced in the shafts of sunlight pouring through the cracks in the cedar shake roof. After Oskar greased the haybine, he walked into the barn and shouted up to see if Marco needed help. "I'm almost done," Marco answered. "Not much of last year's hay left. Good thing the pasture's turning green."

Oskar wiped his oily hands on an oily rag and folded his thick arms across his sweat-stained t-shirt, waiting for Marco to climb down. Later, they repaired stalls in the loafing shed, drops of sweat streaming down both their backs. When the wooden slats of the pen seemed solid enough to withstand a good scratching from a half-ton cow, Oskar laid his ball-peen hammer aside. "So, have you given any more thought to what we talked about?"

Marco pulled a kerchief from his back pocket and wiped his brow. "Let's go outside and find a breeze." Under the giant basswood tree near the machine shed, they dropped to the soft grass, their backs resting against the red barn boards. Before Marco responded to Oskar's question, Rose spied them through the kitchen window. She hurried down the porch steps, carrying a pitcher of water in one hand and three glasses in the other.

"Ah! What a sight for thirsty men. Thank you, Rose," said Marco with a smile wide enough to show his teeth. Rose poured the glasses full for each.

Oskar wriggled in the grass and addressed Rose. "You are the . . . cat's talking." He looked at Marco and asked, "That okay?"

Rose laughed and touched her hand to Oskar's head as the two men followed her to the porch and sat on the steps. "Close, Oskar. But we say the cat's *meow*. It's the word that means the sound the cat makes."

Oskar nodded and looked up. "Meow. Meow. You are . . . cat's . . . meow!"

All three laughed and drank their water. Rose settled into a wicker rocker. "Your English is getting better, Oskar. You'll be talking like a true Wisconsin farmer in no time."

"I like . . . cows . . . I like cheese," he said, and they laughed again.

After a short conversation on the hot weather and the need for rain and the planting of corn and oats, Marco turned to Rose and said, "Rose, we've heard rumors."

"Rumors?" she asked.

"About the war. Some of the guards at the camp say Hitler is dead. Is this true, or are they just trying to confuse or hurt us?"

Rose set her glass on a small wooden table and leaned forward in her rocker. She straightened her light-blue denim trousers with both hands and breathed in deeply. "If the news reports are true, Hitler died about ten days ago. The radio said he committed suicide before the Russians could catch him. His body was burned, but they were able to determine it was really Adolph Hitler."

Oskar spat on the ground. "Gut! Hitler, dead!" Marco and Rose both stared at the contemptuous act. "Happy . . . he's dead," Oskar continued. Then he looked up at Rose with dubious eyes. "But . . . what . . . now?"

Marco explained, "What Oskar means is, well, is the war over?"

"From what I can gather listening to the radio, it's not official yet, but an announcement could come anytime." Rose rocked back, her cheeks pink and her long hair hanging over both shoulders. "We're all hoping."

Marco turned to Oskar. "Do you understand?" Oskar nodded, and Marco swung back to Rose. "We've been talking, Oskar and me, and we've decided we don't want to go home. We want to stay here, on Red's farm, or somewhere else in Wisconsin. At the very least we want to stay in America. There's nothing left for us in Germany."

Rose wasn't sure what to say. "But your homes are in Germany. What about your parents, your families?"

"I'm an only child," answered Marco, "and my parents have relatives in London, my dad's brother, and he's got lots of money. Last I heard, my parents were hoping to get visas for Sweden and from there to England. They speak good English and have visited England many times." He nodded his head thoughtfully. "It shouldn't be difficult for them to start a new life once they reach England."

Rose folded her hands in her lap. "And Oskar? What about Oskar?"

Oskar's face held an anxious look as Marco answered for him. "Oskar's father was in the army and killed in the first invasion of Poland in 1939."

"I'm sorry for you, Oskar." Rose's voice was filled with sincerity.

Oskar looked at his dusty shoes that were wearing thin. He didn't know how to respond in English except to say, "Thank . . . you."

Marco continued, "His mother sold the family farm after Oskar was drafted, and she and his sisters moved to Berlin. When the Allies started bombing Berlin, they moved again, this time to Holland where his mother has cousins. He thinks she's remarried to a Dutchman and moved in with her new husband . . . but he's not sure. He hasn't heard from her in over a year. They should be safe, wherever they are."

"Thank God," Rose uttered.

Oskar tapped his fat fingers on the pine boards of the porch step. He finished his water and set the glass on the top step, then scraped at the dirt under his nails. He didn't understand what Marco was saying word for word, but he knew enough to allow tears to seep into his large, brown eyes. "We like . . . farm. We like Red . . . and Emily. People . . . good to us."

"I'm pleased you're happy here, Oskar. And everyone likes you as well."

After a moment, he added angrily, "We . . . no like . . . Stanley."

"You're not alone," said Rose, nodding in agreement.

Marco went on, "There is nothing in Germany for us anymore. There's only rubble and misery. We have no future there. But here . . . " Marco swept his arm, indicating the whole farm. "There's hope."

"We work . . . for Red, and . . . Aunt Emily cook . . . I love . . . food," Oskar said cheerfully.

"I'll tell her you said so, Oskar. And I'll tell her you complimented her in English too."

Oskar couldn't stop. "We love . . . cows . . . and milk . . . and Uncle Red."

"Thank you, that's very kind of you to say." She turned to Marco with a wrinkled brow and a serious tone. "But the Army says every POW who came to America has to leave and return to Europe."

Marco stood up, his voice animated. "Isn't there some sort of paper we can sign to say we give up our German citizenship and will become American citizens? I know many of the people we've met here have family that came from Germany. The guard who has the night shift at our barracks told me his grandpa came from a town not ten miles from where I grew up. Can't we just stay?"

Rose stood up and paced across the porch. "I don't know. I can ask my uncle. I know he wants you to stay and help with the farm, so he'll do what he can . . . but I just don't know."

"Oskar will learn English. He can't be much different from the people who immigrated to Wisconsin before the war. Plus, he comes from a farm and has worked here for a year and a half learning American farming," Marco pleaded. "What farmer wouldn't want him?"

Before Rose could say another word, she heard her uncle's voice coming from down the driveway. He was walking briskly with Sergeant Stanley at his side. When Red spied his niece, he wildly waved his round hat that could have been taken off the set of *The Wizard of Oz*. "Rosie! Rosie!" He galloped into the circle drive. "It's over! The war is over! Woo-hoo!"

By the time he stepped onto the porch, he was gulping air. "It's official! According to Sergeant Stanley here, Edward R. Murrow announced it on the radio."

Red took Rose in his arms and gave her a bear hug that lifted her a foot off the ground, twirling her several times. "Four long years, and now it's behind us. Oh, I can't wait to tell your aunt." He pulled his blue polka-dotted hanky from the back pocket of his overalls and mopped his brow. Then he looked at the prisoners. "Boys, I'm gonna run over to the Simpson's to tell my Emily. When I get back, we'll do some real celebrating . . . okay? I have some beer in the root cellar, and I do believe we need to uncork it!" He whispered in a loud aside, "Don't tell Sergeant Stanley!" Red laughed and punched Oskar on the arm as he went down the steps and headed over to his truck. "Hoopdy-do! It's over! By God, we did it!" They all watched as he climbed into the pickup, stuck his elbow out the open window, and shouted, "Maybe we'll have two beers! You too, Rosie!" The truck kicked up a cloud of dust as it roared off.

After Red left, Rose smiled at Marco, whose face was a cross between joy and uncertainty. She then turned to Sergeant Stanley. "Were you just driving by, Stanley, or did you plan this visit?" Before he could answer, she offered him water. "It's not beer, but it's cold."

Marco and Oskar moved aside, and Stanley walked up and sat in the rocker. "Thanks, Rose." His uniform shirt had half-moon stains under the arms, and a dark stripe was forming down his back. He took off his hat and threw it down on the table. His oily, black hair clung to his forehead in tight curls. "So, now it's official." He stared at the POWs as he took a long gulp of water. "I've been telling these cabbage-eaters all along, they joined up with a bunch of losers, every last one of 'em. And their great fascist leader . . . he's nothing more than a pile of ashes." He lifted his glass to eye level. "Let's drink to that, Rose."

Rose put her hands on her hips and leaned against the porch railing. "What happens to the POWs, Marco and Oskar here? What happens to them?"

Stanley wiped his lips on the back of his hand. "Nothing changes for them. They were criminals when they came here, and they're still criminals. Only thing that's different is it's hotter now than when they arrived," he said with a smirk.

"But the war is over . . . and . . . they have been good, trustworthy workers for my uncle. Can't they fill out some papers if they want to stay?"

"Hah! Stay? Don't make me laugh! Here's the skinny, Rose." He leaned forward, placing his elbows on his knees. "They're not wanted, never were. America only took these rascals in 'cause no one else would. I mean, think about it. We feed 'em and house 'em and give 'em cozy work to make the time go faster . . . and what do we get out of it? A little farm help and a few hundred bushels of picked apples. If it were up to me, I'd put them all on road crews or quarry work or hauling fieldstones and give them just enough water and food to keep them alive, that's all."

"Thankfully that's not the opinion of everyone," Rose replied petulantly.

"You're right. There're a few do-gooders like the Callahans who've lost sight of who their enemies are." Stanley stood up and headed toward the steps. "These two members," he said, tilting his head at Oskar and Marco, "of the *former* master race are heading back to Europe. And guess what? Europe's in no mood to treat them as nicely as you and your uncle and aunt." He turned his back on her, walked down the steps into the yard, and stopped. "When these two hit the coast of France or England or cross into other countries occupied by Germany, every woman who lost a husband or brother or father will be happy to spit in their faces. Now that the war's over, there's no Geneva Convention to protect 'em. They'll be seen as common criminals, not war prisoners. The camps they'll end up in . . . well . . . they'll be treated as slave laborers, and many of the guards will look the other way when it comes to punishment."

Rose put two hands on the railing and leaned over, her hair falling across her face. "You're just trying to scare two hardworking men," she said sternly.

Stanley laughed with a coldness he reserved just for this moment. "You think I'm making this all up? Read the papers, Rose. When the transport ship carrying POWs sails into international waters, the U.S. government will have no authority and quite honestly won't care what happens next. Maybe they'll go to some camps that require a shower first, like the kind they gave those Jews and Gypsies and homosexuals in the death camps we're reading about. After all, these two are in the same class."

"That's a horrible thing to say!" Rose shouted.

"Really? This bunch of fascist sympathizers are about to get their just rewards."

Rose was on the verge of crying but held back. Her throat was so constricted her words came out in a sound even she was surprised to hear. "When? When are they going home?"

Stanley bent over and wiped the dust off his shoes with his hanky. "Don't know yet. A couple weeks, a couple months. I heard some scuttlebutt about cleaning the lot of 'em out by the middle of summer."

"What about the farms that need workers? We've just starting planting."

"Can't be helped. They gotta go, simple as that."

"I don't think my uncle can keep the farm going without help."

Stanley fixed his hat on his head and shoved his hanky back into his pocket. "Borrowing the last line from that movie *Gone With the Wind* starring your heartthrob Clark Gable, *Frankly, my dear, I don't give a damn …*"

Snapping together the heels of his black, shiny shoes, Stanley saluted, turned on his heel, and trotted down the driveway.

21

DANIEL

2019

LUNCH WAS A TREK TO ROOM 1104, Mr. Jensen's Current World Affairs and World Governments classroom. 1104, November 4th, birthdate of Will Rogers, who never met a man he didn't like, and Walter Cronkite, whose voice Daniel enjoyed listening to in the old World War II newsreels. November 4th, 2008, America elected its first African American president. Room 1104 was his favorite room number of the day.

Oakwood High had two lunch breaks. Daniel was scheduled in 5A, the first lunch, and it was followed by his 5B class with Mr. Jensen, who wore cardigan sweaters and had a reddish beard flecked with gray. His room was always unlocked, but Daniel was the only student who ventured in alone. Daniel carried his lunch in an airtight container, which included fresh fruit, a sandwich made with unleavened bread, a can of V8, and a sugarless cookie if he could cajole his mom into baking some. Otherwise he had raisins and pecans. He ate his food soon after entering 1104 so he would have the maximum time for digestion. Good digestion was a strong component of good health.

Mr. Jensen usually walked to the cafeteria and returned with a plastic tray full of pizza, fish sticks, or hot dogs topped off with canned baked beans or peas and Jell-O or boxed chocolate pudding for dessert. Daniel couldn't understand how he survived into his mid-fifties on his diet of processed, salty, sugary food, and Daniel was not about to let him forget.

"Mr. Jensen, the AMA warns people about the dangers of eating the type of processed foods found on your tray. I hope you have Mercy Hospital's emergency room on speed dial."

"Ah, Daniel, I'm into my sixth decade and I feel great, never better. The AMA needs to do a reassessment of what good food looks like. Care for a bite of meatless pork cutlet?"

Daniel preferred to look at a picture of Karl Marx above the chalkboard. "Did you know the Nazis had a plan to kill all the prisoners at Auschwitz by serving food injected with poison?"

Mr. Jensen frowned. "I didn't know that . . . did they invent the hot dogs?" He broke into a vigorous laugh.

Though Paul Jensen had two master's degrees and nearly twenty-five years of teaching experience in both high school and community college, Daniel was the most challenging student he had encountered. Rather than be intimidated by the breadth of Daniel's knowledge and recall abilities, Paul was exhilarated by his precociousness. As a teacher, Paul was not afraid to tackle controversial discussion topics, which often led to lively debates. His curriculum covered world religions, totalitarian governments, segregation, supreme court decisions, ethnic cleansing, and more. Daniel rarely opened up when there were other students present, but when they were lunching alone, there was no topic out-of-bounds.

Daniel kept a straight face when he said, "You should always know what you put into a well-designed machine like your body. You wouldn't put wood alcohol into your Lexus. Why put empty calories into your stomach?"

"I can't argue with you, except to say I can't afford a Lexus and life is short and sometimes it just feels good to eat a hot dog or French fries or deep fried onion rings. Don't you eat certain foods for pleasure?"

Daniel thought for a moment. "I splurge on kiwi when I can convince my mom to pay for one. Sometimes we have an organically grown Angus porterhouse steak," he said without modulation.

Mr. Jensen raised his palms out in front of his chest. "I concede. That's why you are so healthy and smart and will probably live to be a hundred. The rest of us plebeians will be lucky to make it through the month."

"Roman Emperor Augustus ordered up circuses and bread for the plebeians so they wouldn't riot. He recognized the power of the masses when they weren't fed properly."

Mr. Jensen smiled broadly. "Yes, Augustus did. And it was probably organically grown, unleavened bread . . . don't you think?"

Daniel let a slight smirk form and nodded. "I would hope so."

Mr. Jensen set his empty tray to the side of his heavy wooden desk, took out a handkerchief, and wiped his mouth. "So, what did you think of yesterday's discussion on Muhammad and the Koran?" Daniel had become a regular sounding board for Mr. Jensen. He was astute, honest to a fault, and not afraid to say so when the topic was not going over very well. "Do you think your peers got anything out of it?"

Daniel turned again to study the photos of Karl Marx and Albert Einstein above the whiteboard. They were similar to the pictures of Walt Whitman in his literature classroom, and he began to wonder if genius required unruly hair. All three seemed to have avoided a barber for much of their adult life. His own hair was short and straight and wouldn't stand on end even if given an extra dose of gel.

"The information you provided was fine. The students could understand the readings about Muhammad but didn't show much interest in knowing about him. They don't see any connection to the Muslim culture and their lives here in central Wisconsin. They are Christian plebeians for the most part."

"You and I come from the same Midwestern background, and we recognize the importance of learning about world religions. Why can't the other students and, more importantly, their parents?"

"You and I believe all knowledge is good," Daniel said dismissively.

"Ah, yes, your pat answer to a difficult question." Mr. Jensen leaned forward in his desk chair, opened the top right drawer, and pulled out a copy of an email. "You might be interested in knowing that at least one student was engaged enough in yesterday's discussion that this morning I received this email." He slid on a pair of reading glasses and read:

"*Mr. Jensen, We live in a Christian country and yet you continue to spread anti-Christian ideas to your students. Do you think the 9/11 bombing was an isolated incident? The Arabs want to dominate the world and we should do everything possible to keep Islam out of the public schools. If your students want to learn about the Koran and Muhammad, tell them to join a mosque. Signed, An Angry Mom.*"

Daniel forced out a thin smile but didn't say anything.

"If I had a nickel for every 'Angry Mom' email I've received over the years, I could retire a rich man." With that, he crumpled the paper and threw it toward the blue recycling wastebasket in the back of the room—missing by six feet. "Enough of my complaints. What's up with you, my *literati* friend?" He leaned back in his wooden desk chair, which gave out a piercing squeak as though in terrible pain. "Still reading up on mollusks, or black holes? I've forgotten."

"I finished *The Mollusks of North America*. I've turned my attention to the paintings of the early cave dwellers of Southern France."

"Wonderful! One of my favorite topics. The Lascaux Cave drawings?"

"Among others."

"Excellent. You know, many years ago I was in France and visited several of the caves and loved it. The Hall of the Bulls was so impressive. I think I still have photos if you want to look at them."

They spent the next twenty minutes talking about cave paintings, Mr. Jensen in an animated state as he recalled the highlights of his trip and Daniel doing most of the listening. A few minutes before the bell, Mr. Jensen searched Daniel's face and asked, "So why the interest in the drawings?"

Daniel took his time in answering. "There's debate about who the cave artists were. One theory is they were early Neanderthals, and I've been thinking a lot about Neanderthals lately."

"You have?"

"In fact, I've been practicing the drawings myself. Crude, but I think I caught the essence. I'm sure you'll get a chance to see them."

"I'd love to. Do you have them with you?"

"No. I drew them on a permanent surface."

The bell interrupted any more conversation as Daniel hurried out the door before Mr. Jensen could ask another question.

22

DANIEL

2019

AT 1:44, DANIEL WAS IN SIXTH HOUR PHY ED playing pickleball, or at least he was holding a paddle and swatting at the ball on occasion. He was teamed up with a sophomore girl who was arguably less coordinated than Daniel, if that was possible. The instructor, Ms. Weber, had arranged a class tournament, and Daniel and his partner, Cathy, were in the losers bracket. The only points they managed to score were unforced errors by their opponents. When the game ended 15-3, Ms. Weber walked over and took the paddle from Daniel's hand. "I'll fill in for you while you head to the guidance office. I received a call, and you're to report there right away. Better get a move on." Cathy was smiling from ear to ear. She wanted to win and assumed that with the teacher as her partner it might just happen.

The clock in the hallway read 1:44. 1 plus 4 plus 4 equals 9. A hollow feeling came over Daniel as he trotted toward Guidance.

When Daniel walked into Mrs. Ryan's office, his mother was standing near Lenore's desk still wearing her jacket, her arms tightly crossed over her chest. She turned to him with an expression that was unsettling, somewhere between anger and fear. She had no time for a greeting. "Why have we been summoned here? I received a call at the library and had to ask for an early leave, and my boss was none too happy. I thought you might be sick or injured."

"I'm fine," he said quietly. He sat in his usual chair and placed his backpack on the floor to the side of the chair's left leg.

"So, tell me why we're here."

Daniel lifted his backpack onto his lap, pulled out his juggling balls, and started up.

"Oh no!" Denise said plaintively. "What have you done?" When he didn't answer, she stepped in front of him and tried to catch one of the flying balls, but missed. He turned away from her, and she shouted angrily, "Stop! Right this instant!" He plucked the balls out of the air and held them. He was afraid to look into her eyes. "Were you disrespectful to a teacher?"

"No."

"Did you get in a fight with another student?"

"You know I hate physical contact."

Denise backed away and pulled up the other chair. "Well, something's up. Lenore wouldn't call me in the middle of my work-day for no good reason." She sat silently for a moment, her fists clenched as tightly as her jaw. She focused on something behind Lenore's desk, and when Daniel glanced over, he could see the blue veins in her neck pulsing.

Daniel could handle the stares from peers and the snide remarks from passing Neanderthals, but when his mother was angry with him, it made him weak. He wanted her always to be his ally, his an-chor, his true north. His stomach churned when she was unhappy, and he couldn't control the constriction in his throat. He wanted to take back anything he had ever done to disappoint her. He tried to diffuse the situation. "Maybe . . ." he whispered. "Maybe I'm going to receive the student of the month award."

"Hah!" she chortled with a faux smile and watery eyes.

Daniel continued, "It's usually given to a student who is warm and friendly and popular."

This time, she howled and put her hand over her mouth. "Good try, son. To make fun of oneself is a sure sign of maturing, I'll give you that." Her eyebrows darted up. "But I think Attila the Hun would have a better chance of being chosen student of the month."

"Do you want to know how Attila died?"

Her face softened, and her cheeks faded from radish red to rose pink. "Not really, but I suspect you're going to tell me anyway. So, how?"

He brought his head up and looked at her. "After the wedding to his second wife, Attila threw a big party and got so drunk he tripped, which caused a nosebleed, and he drowned in his own blood."

"Lovely," she said and chuckled. "A fitting end to a not-so-nice guy."

Daniel looked up at the analog clock and back at his watch. "She is 4 minutes late."

"If you're referring to Lenore, keep in mind that adults in authority can come and go on their own schedule. The sooner you learn that, the easier college life will be, and, for that matter, your working life as well." Her voice carried no humor.

"He wasn't all that bad."

"Who?"

"Attila. He was responsible for the creation of Venice."

Resigned to hear him out, Denise asked, "Okay, how did he help create Venice?"

"Attila's armies had destroyed many cities in northern Italy, so when Attila came close to the Venetians, they hid out in the swamps and eventually remained and built the modern-day Venice."

"And for enduring their days in the swamps, they should thank the *Scourge of Rome*? Is that what you're saying?"

"It's a fact of history."

"Have you given any thought to being a travel agent?" Now she flashed a real smile as she knew the job would require meeting and talking to strangers and he would be the last person on earth to be so inclined.

He smiled back at her. He loved this sort of repartee. "I could be a writer of travelogues. You could book the flights, hotels, side tours, restaurants, and I could write the backgrounds to cities, churches, Roman ruins, and more."

"Kill two birds with one stone, or rather one stroke of the pen. Good plan, but I think my working career is destined to be in the public library till I retire."

She leaned back and ran her hands through her hair, and despite her being away from work, despite her son's transgression, and most of all despite the rest of society turning their back on him, she chuckled softly. When she looked over, he was laughing too, out loud. She laughed harder. What was she ever going to do with this young man, or worse, what was she going to do without him? The sobering thought brought her to tears, but she wiped them away quickly just as Lenore swept in, followed by Principal Dale Tobias and Seth Wenton.

Daniel stood and moved close to the window.

Lenore made a quick apology. "I'm so sorry to you both. I know how important punctuality is to you, Daniel." She sat in her chair and set a cup of coffee and a manila folder in front of her. She plucked a pen from a Roy Rogers cup on her blotter. "Denise, I promise we won't be long. I know this is a workday for you. I was meeting with Mr. Tobias, and we waited for Seth to come down from his algebra class. You know Seth Wenton, Denise?"

"I'm sure we met somewhere along the line. Hello, Seth."

He gave a nod. "Mrs. Mannheim."

"And, of course, we all know the principal, so I'll turn the floor over to him."

Dale Tobias was a tall man, well over six feet, wearing a blue sport jacket, khaki slacks, a white shirt, and a pale-yellow Jerry

Garcia tie. His thick chest pulled the buttons on his shirt to the point of popping. He had big hands and gray eyes, waves of thick tawny-colored hair, and he wore pointed leather cowboy boots. If there was a prototype appearance for a high school principal, he had it. Few students, or anyone else for that matter, could intimidate him physically. Despite his size, his voice was soft and pleasing. "Mrs. Mannheim, thank you for coming in on such short notice."

"Please, call me Denise."

"Of course, Denise." He smiled and continued, "A rather serious allegation has come to my attention, and I thought it important we deal with it before it festers or causes any other problems. It seems someone, and we believe it to be Daniel, broke into Seth's locker and painted graffiti on the door and shelves."

Before Denise could react, Seth interjected, "It's not that big a deal. A little graffiti ain't so bad, really."

Denise turned to Daniel, who was staring out the window watching a cardinal flit along a branch on an ornamental crabapple tree ten feet from the building. The sky was gray, and a few clouds the color of day-old bruises moved slowly to the east. The cardinal pulled one of the shriveled fruits and swallowed it whole. Now there were only 74 crabapples left rocking on the branch. He brought his gaze in and settled on his shoes. "It's not graffiti."

"You wrote graffiti on his locker?" Denise asked.

Daniel repeated with more force, "It's not graffiti."

"It may not be graffiti in the true sense of the word," Mr. Tobias said, "but it's defaced whatever you call it."

Denise's lower lip quivered. "Nothing profane, I hope?"

"Nah, nothing like that, Mrs. M., more like a bunch of stick men riding horses carrying spears and bows and arrows chasing after an elephant," said Seth.

Daniel was still staring at his shoes. "It's not an elephant. It's a mastodon."

"Whatever," Seth replied with a dismissive wave of his hand.

"The subject doesn't matter to me," added Mr. Tobias. He pushed the reading glasses on his nose as far up as they could go. "I want Daniel to apologize to Seth."

Denise concurred. "Absolutely. Daniel?"

After a moment of silence, Daniel muttered flatly, "I'm sorry for drawing on your locker, Seth."

Seth pulled on the collar of his turtleneck, and his lips brandished a cross between a smile and a sneer. "No hard feelings, man. Everything's cool. You were just being you. I know you can't help it."

"Well, if that's settled, then I think Seth can return to class," said Mr. Tobias.

Seth jumped up, headed for the door, and then turned back. "Is it alright if I stop and pee first? Had a lotta Gatorade for lunch."

"Yes, yes, of course. Then straight to class," Mr. Tobias commanded.

After he was out of the room, a pall seemed to backfill like a morning fog. Denise took a deep breath and broke the silence by letting it out slowly. "Ohhhh . . . Daniel."

Daniel pulled his juggling balls out and got them spinning before his mom could stop him. He focused on the balls while talking. "I didn't deface the locker. I enhanced it. I've been practicing the drawings of the early cave art of the Neanderthals of Southern France. I drew my finished products on his locker since it was my intention to make Seth's locker more pleasing to his eye. A feng shui experience."

Lenore stopped taking notes for a moment and said, "Nice of you to be so concerned for Seth's well-being, but I, for one, don't believe it."

Daniel took one ball out of circulation. "He's in my Art Appreciation class and doesn't even try to understand the beauty or power of great pieces of art. I thought his brain might relax a bit if his locker reflected his learning capacity." He plucked the last two balls and sat down with enough force to move the chair noisily about two inches across the tiled floor.

Principal Tobias looked straight into Denise's eyes. "Seth can be a bit of a handful, I'll concede the point. I can see the humor in Daniel's actions and might even be able to overlook it as a silly prank. But my concern here, Denise, is one student going into another student's locked space without consent. It can't be tolerated for any reason."

Denise turned quickly and asked Daniel, "Did you take anything from Seth's locker?"

"No."

"I believe Daniel's telling the truth," said Mr. Tobias. "I had Seth do an inventory, and he claims there's nothing missing."

Daniel looked out to find the cardinal, but it was gone. However, the number of crabapples dropped to 73. "As often as Seth looks at a textbook, it could be weeks before he realized one was missing."

Mr. Tobias ignored Daniel's remark and spoke directly to Denise. "We try to ensure all our students' materials are safe when properly locked in their lockers."

Denise nodded. "Of course. I couldn't agree more."

"Good. I knew you would understand." He stood, turned, and with both hands on his hips, asked, "I'm curious, Daniel. Our lockers were installed only a few years ago, and our supplier assured me they were state of the art and the safest on the market. Seth claims it was locked all day. So, how did you get in?"

The cardinal returned, or maybe it was another one. It's red plumage would receive a fresh coating of color from the pigment in the wrinkled apples, only 72 left. 7 plus 2 equals 9. "Daniel!" His mother was staring at him, but he didn't want to take his eyes from the bird. "Daniel! Answer Mr. Tobias." She stamped her foot at the same time.

When he spoke, it seemed he was reading from a technical manual on how to crack open a lock. "There are 2,660,448 combinations based on two turns to the right and one to the left. A simple algorithm eliminates most possibilities, and since students often give away the third number by not spinning the dial when they leave, I only need to figure out two numbers. I can open any locker within ten minutes, twenty if they remember to spin the dial."

"And Seth's locker?" asked the principal.

"Neanderthals never spin the knob."

Dale stepped back and rested one hip on the corner of Lenore's desk. "I see. I'm going to ask your mother, or both of you, to pay for the time it takes the custodial staff to remove the graffiti. The whole locker will need to be repainted."

"Of course we'll pay," said Denise without hesitation. She scowled at Daniel. "Right, Daniel?" He shrugged and checked for birds in the branches, then nodded.

"Good. I'll let the business manager know to send you the bill. And finally, I want you, Daniel," Mr. Tobias said, peering down at him with principal sternness, "while you are still a student here, to promise not to invade the private space of any locker other than your own."

Daniel shrugged. "I promise."

Principal Tobias continued, "As you know, graduation is only..."

"28 days, 5 hours, and ... 12 minutes from now," Daniel said emphatically. "And yes, I have my cap and gown complete with tassel."

Stepping toward the door, Dale responded, "Then I believe we're finished here. Thank you, Denise, for taking the time to come in. Lenore ... Daniel." He nodded at each and strode out.

After a minute, Lenore spoke, only to break the silence of the room. "I must say, never a dull moment with Daniel Mannheim. Next year will seem mediocre without him."

Denise put her head in her hands. "I'm so disappointed in you, Daniel. Whether Seth had it coming or not, you can't break into a person's private locker."

"I'm sorry, Mom."

She stood and touched him on the shoulder. "Though the cave paintings of Southern France were a nice touch." She managed a smile as she spoke.

Lenore closed her folder and walked out from behind her desk. "As long as you're both here, we'll count this little get-together as our monthly autism conference. That way, Denise, you won't have to make arrangements for a future date."

"Thanks, Lenore."

"I do have one tiny issue before you go. Mr. Raplinger, Daniel's physics teacher, talked to me the other day because Daniel seems to be distracted in class lately. I'm not sure if it's senioritis or he's bored, but I thought I'd pass it along."

Daniel insisted, "I had the highest test scores on the pre-AP test. I only had two incorrect answers, and I showed Mr. Raplinger the errors in the data the questions gave. In one, they used Celsius instead of Fahrenheit, and in the other, the algorithm was based on incorrect numbers. I suggested he call the national testing company and have them correct the questions or throw them out and form two new ones."

Lenore turned to Denise and said with confidence, "I think his grade is still intact."

Denise asked, "What did Mr. Raplinger say was the reason for being distracted?"

"Apparently, he's spending most of his class time writing in his notebook."

Daniel stood and walked closer to the window. He put his nose up to the pane and looked in both directions, frowned, and turned to face Mrs. Ryan. "In 19 days and 8 hours, my story for the competition has to be typed in its final form and postmarked."

"Of course," Denise said apologetically. "I should have told you, Lenore, I encouraged Daniel to enter a young writers contest sponsored by the Wisconsin Humanities Board. He's been working with Mark Flour at BRC, and apparently they are making progress."

"What happened to the German lessons?"

"We spend a few minutes conversing in German," Daniel said. "But I'm on a deadline. Mark laughs when I use the word *deadline*. He thinks it's a harbinger of things to come."

"Really? Why's that?" Lenore asked.

"His health is not so great these days."

Lenore folded her arms across her chest. "Sorry to hear that. I hope it's temporary."

Daniel smiled and said, "Mark says at his age everything is temporary." His smile slowly evaporated.

Daniel looked forward to his trips to BRC with more enthusiasm than almost any activity he could think of. The writing of his competitive story was important, but his time spent with Mark was more important. Learning German had become a good excuse to sit and converse with Mark. There was something in his gentleness, the way he made Daniel feel welcome, no, not just welcome, but accepted, a feeling he had not received from anyone other than his mom. His teachers either wanted to put him under a microscope and pick at him with sharp objects or were envious and intimidated because he understood academic concepts better than they did. Even his own father treated him like a stranger, an outlier, an oddity that he was legally responsible for but had no more of a bond with than the caterpillar did the butterfly.

While Daniel drifted into reverie, Lenore asked Denise, "Any headway on the prom?"

"Nothing yet. I'm still working on him."

"Good. And with that, I'll see you next month, our last regularly scheduled meeting."

23

MARCO AND OSKAR

Spring 1945

"HERE COMES ... BUS ... MARCO." Oskar stood up from the steps of Emily and Red's front porch and walked toward the driveway. "Come on ... not want ... miss ... to eat." The late afternoon was dark with thunderclouds in the west and a stiff breeze rippling the tops of the silver maples. Oskar carried his felt hat in his hand and slapped it across his thigh, creating a small puff of dust. Suddenly, he pulled up and shouted again in English, "Oh no ... it's not bus ... is neighbor ... is Mr. Gunderson ... pulling hay wagon!"

In a moment, Oskar was back on his porch step. He looked up at a sulking Marco, who hadn't moved, and patted him on the knee. With no one else around, he fell into his native language. "Can you smell the rain? It's coming, and when it does, the corn will be popping. What's the expression Red says all the time ... we want the corn to be knee-high by the Fourth of July." Oskar laughed and slapped Marco's knee harder. "I think it might just happen. The corn, I mean. Oh! ... Did you see that?" He pointed with his left hand. "A lightning strike. That's a good sign. My father always said if you see lightning during the day, the growing gods will smile on your crops."

Marco nodded and let his head slip back into his palm, his arm resting on his knee. "I saw it."

"Why the sourpuss? It's Friday. Red said he only needs us for a

172

half day tomorrow. Once we finish with milking and cleaning up, we'll have a day and a half of free time."

"*Free time*. That's funny coming from you, a POW. Or have you forgotten?"

"Of course I haven't. I'm just happy it's Friday. What's your problem?"

"No problem. Everything's fine." He turned his head away and leaned back on his elbows.

Oskar peered at Marco, then picked up a small stone and threw it at a couple pigeons pecking at some fallen oat seeds in the yard. They jumped and looked toward Oskar but didn't fly away. The second time a stone whizzed by, they bolted straight up and flew to the peak of the barn, landing next to a metal weathervane. "I don't like those birds. We don't have them back home, and I'm glad. All they do is make a mess in the hayloft and eat all the grain we drop."

"Some people shoot them and eat them," said Marco nonchalantly.

"Those ugly birds?"

"They call them *squab* if you order one in a restaurant."

"Those birds are called *squab*?"

"Out here on the farm, they're pigeons. When they're cooked, they change names, but they're the same bird."

"Why do they do that? Change the names?" Oskar's face screwed into wrinkles.

"I guess so you don't think you're eating a pigeon."

Oskar seemed stumped by that. "Huh. That's weird."

"Like snails when cooked are called escargot. Same thing."

Oskar sat up straight quickly. "People eat...snails?"

Marco bobbed his head. "People eat a lot of strange things. Someday you'll be in a restaurant and see something on the menu you don't understand..."

Oskar interrupted. "I've never been ... in a restaurant."

"Oh . . . I didn't know that."

"Before the war, we always ate at home or the home of one of my relatives. My grandma was a great cook. Her potato dumplings were second to none. And my grandpa made the best rye bread with caraway seeds. We'd fight to see who could cut the first end piece, the *shatzel*. Fresh bread and fresh butter, nothing in the world better."

Marco was listening with only one ear. "Someday you will eat at a restaurant. If it's an ethnic restaurant, you know, foods from a different country, well, there's likely to be lots of dishes they serve that you won't know what it is unless you ask. Like squab, or escargot, or lasagna, or mutton." Marco stood up and took a few steps toward the driveway. He looked out at the thunderclouds rolling closer. The thoughts of food made him think of home and the wonderful meals his mother made. He walked back toward the porch, "Do you miss your mother, Oskar?"

Oskar stood and sidled up to Marco, and the two began a slow walk down the driveway. "Sometimes. She adored life on the farm. She taught me to care for the land and love the animals. My dad . . . he just saw the farm as a workplace, something he had to do every morning. He didn't hate it, but it was never a place he was fond of.

"But my mom, that's another story. She loves the outdoors. She had a big garden, half flowers and half vegetables. Whenever she could, she would make an excuse to walk out into the fields to see how the hay was being cut or bring us cold water or fresh-baked cookies. If she's in Holland, I hope she can go on hikes and walk along the ocean. She'd like that. And grow a garden, even if it's only in a small space." After a long moment, he added wistfully, "I hope she's happy wherever she is."

"A real outdoor woman, eh?"

"Yeah, loves all creatures . . . except birds!"

"No birds?"

"She likes them," Oskar corrected, "but at a distance, not up close."

"Seems odd to me," Marco said.

Oskar stopped and held both palms up, feeling for the first raindrops. The wind had died, and the air was heavy and clung like wet moss. "One morning when Mom went to the kitchen to start breakfast, she found a sparrow sitting on the kitchen table. She scared it, and it started flying around the room. My mom ran out screaming and made my sister and me corner it, and then I threw a dish towel over it and carried it outside. When I went back in the house, I found my mom in the parlor with the door locked. She wouldn't come out until I assured her the bird was gone."

Marco chuckled. "Imagine if it had been one of those pigeons, or a crow. She'd probably have had heart failure."

"But when it came to milking a cow or helping a sow farrow or holding the horse's leg while the farrier did his work, my mom was fearless." Oskar was smiling with pride. "She did something even the veterinarian couldn't believe."

Marco turned to him. "What was that?"

"We had a big Hampshire sow named Princess, longest pig I've ever seen. One time when she was giving birth, she suddenly stopped after she had already popped out six or seven little piglets. My mom knew there were more little ones inside her but couldn't figure out why they didn't come out. She thought maybe Princess was just taking a little rest. After a couple hours, we called Doc Kardin, the local vet. He examined Princess and then told us that one of the little pigs must be caught somehow on the way out, and if it wasn't removed, Princess could die. So . . . my mom . . ." Oskar held his arm high and pantomimed rolling up his sleeve. ". . . rolled up her sleeve, washed her hand and arm, and reached inside that sow all the way up to her armpit and pulled out a dead piglet."

"You're lying," said Marco incredulously.

"I'm not. After that, another four or five live piglets came squirting out, and everybody was fine. My mom couldn't stop smiling, and old Doc Kardin whistled and slapped her on the back. He told her anytime she wanted a job off the farm, he'd be happy to have her as an assistant."

Marco shook his head in amazement. He felt the first drops of rain as distant thunder cracked and the ground jiggled slightly. "Maybe we should head back to the porch." They turned and dashed, ducking under the roof just as the rain came in sheets. A few minutes later, the downpour leveled off and became a steady soaking rain. The yard filled with puddles, and the scarlet peonies growing along the house fell flat to the ground. A fecal smell from the barn wafted across the yard, strong in the humid air but not irritating. The cows were in their stanchions, and most were lying on clean straw.

Suddenly, Marco turned to his friend and said with conviction, "I don't want to go home, Oskar, you know that. I want to stay here. My family is safe in England or Sweden. Your mom and sisters are in Holland, your farm is probably gone, and my life in Cologne is over."

Oskar knew where his thoughts were headed. And he knew Marco was trying to reassure the both of them in the process. "Our families will be alright. They're strong and know how to survive. I love my mom and my sisters, but I don't want to go back either."

"So what do we do?"

"We know the Army will send us back home soon. You have to come up with a plan, Marco." Oskar was pleading now. "You're smart. You can think of something." The rain tapered off to a light shower.

"Staying here is all I've been thinking about . . . but . . . I don't know." Marco was agonizing over every word. "We are not Americans. Where would we go? How would we live? We'd have to find food, and if we were hungry all the time . . . you wouldn't like that."

Oskar stiffened his shoulders. "I'm stronger than you think."

"You are, I'm sorry. But we would need help. We can't just walk away."

"Have you asked Rose?"

"No." A few shards of golden sunlight fell on the roof of the barn like a spotlight on a darkened stage. "I haven't had the courage to approach her."

"She likes you. I see the way she smiles when she looks your way."

Marco placed his hands on the top of his head and looked at Oskar. "I like her too, but I can't put her life in jeopardy."

"You can ask, that won't hurt. Please." Oskar's face seemed as though it might shatter if he got the wrong response. "She might say yes. She might even be waiting for you to ask for help."

Marco looked directly into Oskar's eyes. "Just talking like this is dangerous. If Stanley or some of the other men heard us, like Weishaple, we'd be in big trouble."

Oskar put his large hands on Marco's shoulders. "It's worth the risk. You'll come up with a great plan. And if it doesn't work . . . what more can they do but send us back to Europe, which is what they're planning anyway."

"I wasn't thinking about how *we* might be hurt. But Rose and her family would be humiliated, shunned, maybe even put in prison if the authorities find out they helped us. We couldn't do that to them after all the kindness they've shown us." He pulled away and looked out onto the black clouds sinking into the east. Lightning, like far-away camera flashes, moved back and forth across the horizon.

"There's nobody else. She likes you. Make a plan." Oskar's voice was filled with a sense of hope and urgency.

"Make a plan. Make a plan . . . okay . . . okay...I'll think about it, but no promises."

Both men were quiet as the rain stopped and the dripping from the roof onto the puddles below became the only sound. Even the cows in the barn were silent. The sun was sinking behind a line of birch trees that ran along the edge of the road. The late-afternoon shadows crept upon them.

Oskar put his palm out and caught a handful of rainwater, then rubbed his hands together to clean off some dirt. "I'm more frightened to go home now that the war's over than I was when we were captured in North Africa. I like Wisconsin. I like working in the barn and the fields and Emily's cooking and Red's jokes. Red promised he would let me drive his Allis-Chalmers." There was a long pause. "I won't be able to do any of those things in Germany."

"There are lots of dairy farms in Germany." But Marco's words rang hollow.

"I know. But how long will we be prisoners in Europe? And what if we end up in a place where the people hate us? There won't be a Red Callahan farm waiting for us over there, you can be sure of that."

A few minutes later, the bus arrived, and they jogged through the wet gravel, avoiding as many puddles as possible while stepping up onto the crowded converted school bus. The windows were steamed, and the air inside was fetid from the wet clothing, sweat, bovine smell, and manure-laden boots worn by a score of tired men.

Marco and Oskar shuffled to the rear seat and squeezed together. The bus jerked as its gears shifted to a cruising speed.

They gazed out at the poplar and birch and chestnut trees that lined the roadside, glistening in the afternoon light, and crossed the Tomorrow River twice on narrow bridges with wooden planking. They rode in silence as the bus bumped and tossed all the way back to camp.

24

SETH

2019

THREE DAYS AFTER THE CONFERENCE in Mrs. Ryan's office, Seth was leaning up against his newly painted locker. The hallway was empty. It was a few minutes before three o'clock, and all the classroom doors were closed and locked until the final bell. He was twirling a fidget spinner. His hair was pulled back into a noticeably short ponytail barely touching the collar of his football jersey, number 89, with the tiger mascot on the chest and WENTON sprawled across his back shoulders.

His football days ended inauspiciously when he got into a fistfight. An hour after the final game of the season, both teams were milling around the parking lot, loading onto their respective buses. An opposing player, a running back, came over to Seth and swore at him for giving a cheap shot during the game. Seth merely grinned and asked what he wanted to do about it. The other player didn't back down but did try to avoid a fight by explaining that he should've been given an unsportsmanlike conduct penalty and thrown out of the game. Seth hit him with a left jab to the nose before his rival had stopped talking, and the two grappled to the pavement and rolled under one of the buses. It took coaches from both teams to break it up. Seth bragged to his friends that he broke the rival's nose with one punch and the loser would probably have a crooked nose for life. Because of the altercation, Seth didn't receive any postseason honors or athletic scholarships but was satisfied to be labeled a *badass player*.

Seth liked wearing his football jersey when he had group business to attend to. And in a few minutes, he and D-squared needed to settle a few differences. He knew the nerd would be along any minute because he had one of his buddies deliver a note to Mrs. Hunter, his eighth hour teacher, with a forged signature of the principal saying DD should report to his locker. Teachers were used to Daniel being called out of class. Sometimes he had to take a special brain test or meet with Mrs. Ryan. Daniel was so weird he could almost come and go as he pleased; teachers seemingly didn't care, and most students were happy when he disappeared.

Daniel arrived at his locker, notepaper in hand, 9 minutes before the final bell. His senses were on high alert. When he turned the corner to his locker and spied Seth, he walked with his head down, following a small crack in the floor tiles. Since there was no adult around, he feared Seth had set him up. In front of his locker, he came to a stop but said nothing. Seth eyed him up and down for a long moment. "You got my message, I see. Mrs. Hunter give you any trouble?"

"Why did you send the note?" Daniel's voice was barely above a whisper.

"'Cause I needed to discuss a couple things with you. Especially after that little get-together in Ryan's office. Thought this was as good a time as any, seein' as you are on your way home to Mommy before most kids can even get to their lockers."

Daniel didn't blink and remained as still as a coffin.

"Are you listening to me, D-squared?" Seth pulled a small plastic coffee container with a bright-red top from his locker and held it out under Daniel's nose. "You opened my locker without permission and drew a bunch of shit on the door. I could forgive you for that. But you looked inside this container, didn't you?"

Daniel said nothing.

"Look at me, D-squared." He towered above a bent-over Daniel and pushed the canister up against his chin, forcing his head up. "Know what's in here?"

Daniel turned his head quickly, and the canister banged against his ear.

"Did you take anything from this can?"

"No," Daniel hissed.

"Can't hear ya!" He pushed it harder against his ear.

"No!" Daniel shouted.

"But you know what's in here?" Seth pulled on his shirt collar to make Daniel look at him.

"Yes."

Seth shoved the can back on the locker's top shelf. "Yeah, you know. Of course you know. In fact, you could probably tell me all the medical names and uses for those pills, couldn't you?" Daniel turned away, but Seth continued. "The problem is . . . DD . . . you stumbled on a little fundraiser we got going to finance our prom week. It's expensive to go to prom. But I don't think you give a shit about that. You probably haven't even given prom a second of your time, girls either, have you?" He chuckled. "Me and the boys collected these pills, voluntarily for the most part, from students with ADD and a few other weird *non-normal* stuff like you got. You know, kids with weird problems are loaded with drugs, valuable ones too."

Seth glanced both ways down the hall and said in a conspiratorial voice, "I also *found* a few pain pills the old buzzards at the BRC *misplaced*. Between you and me, DD, when one of them ol' dudes kicks the bucket, I get to clean their room, and sometimes there's a treasure trove of goodies to be found. So, what's in that coffee container is pretty valuable on the street. And I don't want anybody telling Tobias or any other authority about my money stream, which is gonna pay for the beer and a love shack on the lake. Got it?"

Seth paused and stared into Daniel's dark, watery eyes. "You are the only one who can fuck up our plans. But I don't think you will because you want to graduate, don't you? And make all the teachers and counselors in this school proud of their trained dog, the student with all the answers who barks when ordered and fetches answers like a tennis ball." Seth mimicked the animal's yelps. "Yip! Yip! Yip! You'll shuffle across the stage, and all the adults will clap and cheer because they believe they had a hand in your training."

A small tear was forming in Daniel's right eye, but he wiped it away quickly. At this moment, he wanted to be a falcon, the fastest bird on earth, and dive with talons open into the face of Seth. He wanted to be a scorpion and sting him or a great grizzly bear and stand ten feet tall and swat him with razor claws. But instead he let his shoulders slouch even more.

Seth took both hands and pushed on Daniel's shoulders, making him sit, his back to the locker. "Take off that backpack," he commanded. Daniel refused. "Really? You're gonna make me?" Daniel clutched the straps as hard as he could but was unable to stop Seth from yanking it over his head and tearing it away. "Let's see what kind of crap you keep in here."

"Nothing of yours," Daniel whimpered.

"I'll see about that."

Seth unzipped the main zipper, turned the bag upside down, and shook violently, scattering the contents across the width of the hallway. Daniel's juggling balls went rolling in three directions, his lunch container shattered, sending tiny pieces of glass flying. The book from the library on Southern France cave paintings toppled out and opened to a page showing a color photo of drawings similar to those drawn on locker 666. Seth pulled roughly at the page, tearing it in the process. "So this is where you got the big idea to draw that crazy elephant on my locker." He pulled the book closer to his face as though proximity would help him understand and appreciate.

Instead, he shook his head. "Bunch of shitty stick men and horses. Big deal. This is why I don't read books." And he tossed it ten feet down the hall.

Seth scoured the backpack for hidden treasures. "How about these little pockets? Got any valuables?" He unzipped the first and found a handkerchief neatly folded, then flipped it aside. In the second, he pulled out a billfold and with two fingers held up a twenty-dollar bill and flashed a salacious smile. "Nice. This is something I will take as payment for the pain and suffering you caused by writing graffiti all over my locker." He pushed the bill into the back pocket of his jeans.

When Seth could find nothing else of value, he was about to throw the backpack aside but caught sight of something taped to the inside of the main pocket. "Woah! What's this?" He plucked out a photo and grinned. "Double D, is this your ol' lady? Huh? Now I ask you, what senior carries around a picture of his mommy?" Daniel let his chin touch his chest. "No answer? Well, I'll tell you who. A weird, fucked-up pussy, that's who. One who's dumb enough to keep a picture of his mom handy and clever enough to keep his mouth shut about the little *chat* we had here today. Right, DD?" He flipped the photo at Daniel, hitting him in the back of the head.

Just then, the final bell of the day rang. "Better get busy cleaning up your stuff, Mannheim, before the animals trample all your valuables."

Doors up and down the hall opened, and students rushed out. Seth strode away quickly as Daniel scurried after his red ball, then the yellow, but a student kicked the green, and then another student joined in, and before he could corral it, it had been kicked all the way down the hall and out of sight. Daniel crawled on all fours and put his arms out wide around his books and papers and pencils and broken glass lunch container like a mother bird shielding her young. After a few minutes, the majority of students had passed, and he was able to scrape everything together and shovel it into his backpack. No student stopped to help; in fact, most laughed or walked past as though he wasn't even there.

If he hurried, he could still meet his ride by 3:09. He would pick up the green ball on the way.

25

STANLEY

Spring 1945

**STANLEY HAD ALL THIRTY-TWO MEN STAND AT AT-
TENTION** in front of the barracks at the Kocher Valley County
Fairgrounds. It was six o'clock on Sunday morning, the day of rest.
Rousted from their cots, the POWs were dressed in an array of boxer
shorts and wrinkled olive-green undershirts. Most were barefoot,
but a few had time to slip on boots, their untied laces dangling like
worms that had come up during the rainy night.

A heavy mist was leaving tiny drops on everything it touched.
Gunmetal clouds moved slowly, if at all. Rain during the night had
left large pools of standing water, which reflected the legs and feet of
the POWs. The men shifted their weight from side to side as those
without shoes watched the mud ooze through their toes.

Stanley stood in front of the two shivering lines of sixteen, taking attendance. When he finished, he tapped a black wooden baton
against his thigh for several seconds. The pleats on his dress uniform
trousers were straight as a stretched string, and his black hair was
tucked behind his ears and under his cap. He cleared his throat and
looked slowly from one end of the columns to the other. His eyes
were black and menacing like a cockroach. "I will only say this once,"
he warned, his voice loud but squeaky, and the POWs leaned in to
hear him. "This morning, Mrs. Reeves, the woman in charge of the
canteen, informed me that two cartons of Lucky Strikes were stolen

yesterday during your free time. I want to know who's the asshole who stole them."

Even though the POWs had been in Wisconsin for over a year, Stanley refused to remember names; he just needed thirty-two bodies each morning. He encouraged the chasm between vanquished and victor to be wide and impersonal. Sometimes he made up his own appellations: Fathead, Lazy, Butch, Stupid, Cabbagehead, whatever suited his mood at the time. This morning, he raised his baton and pointed it at one of the men. "You! Dumbo, third from the end in the second row, come up here!" The POW didn't move. Stanley turned, pointed at Marco, and hollered, "Professor! Translate what I just said to Dumbo over there. I know *you* understand English."

Marco took a step forward and looked at the other men with a straight face. He spoke in German to the POW as best as he remembered, and the man moved up to the front. Stanley continued, "Dumbo, did you steal the Lucky Strikes?" The POW looked around, fear radiating from every pore, and then shook his head wildly without saying a word. "Do you know who did steal the cigarettes?" The man kept shaking even as Marco translated. Stanley spoke loud enough for all to hear. "If I have to turn every mattress upside down and keep every single man standing here till tomorrow morning, I will. Tell them!" He nodded at Marco, who translated. "Alright, Dumbo, get back in the line." He slapped his baton on the POW's ass as the man turned to go.

"I'll be lenient if the thief gives himself up—now. But if I find out later, if I have to spend my time looking through your barracks, going through your personal letters and shitty clothing and girly pictures to find the culprit . . . it'll be solitary confinement for five days for the thief." His baton was slapping like a metronome against his left palm. Marco scowled but continued to translate as the whole group focused on him. When Marco finished, he turned to Stanley and asked, "What do you mean by *lenient*?"

"None of your goddamn business what I mean," Stanley bellowed. "Let everyone know they have one minute to come up with the guilty party. Tell them!" He raised his left wrist and stared at his wristwatch.

Marco talked quickly, then stepped back into formation. There was a moment of silence as the men turned anxiously from one to the other. A few whispers could be heard, but Stanley kept his eyes fixed on the sweep of his second hand. "Ten seconds. Nine, eight, seven, six . . ."

Finally, an arm from one of the men in the back row slowly rose above his shoulder. Stanley stopped his count and raced to stand face-to-face with the POW. "You have something to say, Kraut?"

The POW spoke quietly, so quiet that Stanley couldn't hear. "Speak up!" Spittle flew onto the POW's face. "Did you take the cigarettes?"

"Oskar Wurtz," said the POW.

"Are you Oskar Wurtz? Huh?"

The POW's eyes darted to the left, then he raised his finger and pointed to another soldier. It was the POW standing next to Marco. Stanley rushed over and said sardonically, "My friend the cow lover from the Callahan farm. We meet again. Is your last name Wurtz?"

Oskar's hands trembled, and his face flushed like a boy who accidentally walked into a ladies' restroom. "I Wurtz, but I no . . ."

Stanley used his baton and jabbed Oskar in the stomach. Then he turned to the informer, "Is this the man who stole the cigarettes?"

"Oskar Wurtz," the informer repeated and rocked his grizzled chin up and down, a slight smirk unfolding.

Before Oskar could utter another sound, Stanley yanked him by the collar and snarled, "You're coming with me, plow boy." Oskar looked plaintively at Marco, but there was little his friend could do.

Marco blurted to Stanley, "Excuse me, Sergeant, but Oskar doesn't smoke."

Stanley stopped, turned, and glared. "Shut the fuck up! I'll deal with you later. For now, stand at attention till I get back . . . all of you, at attention!" He frog-marched Oskar up the steps and into the building. A few minutes later, he stormed out, pushing Oskar in the back with the butt of his baton. In his left hand, Stanley held up the cigarette cartons like a trophy he had just earned, or a game bird he had just shot. At the base of the steps, he whipped his baton against the back of Oskar's legs hard enough to make Oskar fall, his face plowing into the soft dirt.

Stanley walked in front of the thirty-one and pointed at Oskar. "This piece of shit will be cleaning the other shit from the latrine till next Sunday, and if his work doesn't meet my inspection, he'll be doing it again the following week. This is what you can expect if you break any of my rules. Translate, Professor!"

Oskar pulled himself up and scuttled off to his place in line next to Marco as Stanley harangued the prisoners. "You are nothing more than a band of snitches, thieves, and cowards, not a *master race* of wonder soldiers that little paperhanger from Austria promised. Don't translate, Professor. Not worth your breath." Instead, he walked slowly toward the administrative building and put his foot on the first step, then turned as though he had forgotten something insignificant. "Oh, yes . . ." he hollered maniacally, ". . . everyone, except the Professor . . . DISMISSED!"

The POWs scurried away, leaving Marco standing like a solitary oak tree in a field of corn. The morning was warming quickly as the sun peeked over the white pines, which ran two abreast along the edges of the fairgrounds. A few cumulus clouds folded in from the west, a touch of pink in the reflected sunlight. Two purple finches flitted from the roof of the barracks to a large puddle, dipping their beaks for a morning drink and then wading into the brown water for a quick bath. Marco heard the men in the barracks as they dressed and chatted, then watched as they slowly formed the chow line to his left. Oskar took a glimpse at Marco but mostly kept his head down and followed the queue.

After breakfast, Stanley sauntered out of his office and walked past Marco without uttering a sound. The cuffs on his khaki pants were stiff with starch and showed no dirt at all. As he walked, his black boots left deep impressions in the mud all the way to a waiting jeep. He climbed in and roared off without so much as a glance in Marco's direction.

A few minutes later, Oskar appeared at Marco's side. "How long will he keep you at attention?"

"I don't know. But you shouldn't be seen talking to me. He has spies."

"Okay. I'll go. But it was Weishaple. He set me up. One of the other men saw him put the cigarettes under my bed."

Marco frowned, his forehead wrinkles deep and dark. "We'll get even, Oskar. We'll get even."

Stanley returned midafternoon. He strode close to Marco, heading toward his office, then pirouetted and put his lips within a few inches of Marco's ear. "If you try to help your friend scrub the latrines, I will have you at attention for twenty-four hours." Then Stanley slowly backed up six feet and shouted at the top of his lungs, "DISSS . . . MISSED!"

26

OSKAR

April 1943

WEISHAPLE WAITED UNTIL THE LATRINE WAS QUIET, then slipped in the side door with a full bladder and a lopsided grin. An hour ago, he drank a full quart of water on top of the apple juice he had pilfered from the mess hall. His plan was simple—to make scrubbing the wooden trough even harder for that fucking Wurtz, the lily-livered conscript who was a discredit to every true German soldier. It didn't matter they were all POWs, the coward seemed to enjoy the work his captors on the farm made him do and even boasted about how nice the owner and his wife treated him. He was a stooge blinded by three squares a day and a barn full of milk cows. What a pathetic excuse for a soldier. It was sickening, and Wurtz needed to be taught a lesson of remembrance; he was, after all, an Aryan, a member of the proud Wehrmacht, not a slave to the mongrel Americans. Forced labor was expected, but willingness and enjoyment of prison life were unpatriotic.

Oskar leaned back on his ankles and dipped his brush into the pail of soapy water. His t-shirt was dark with sweat and water stains, his fingers red and wrinkled. When he heard footsteps, he turned to see who was coming.

"Here's the cigarette snatcher, on his knees. How appropriate." Weishaple walked behind Oskar and kicked him in the butt. Oskar rolled on his side, his pail of water spilling on the floor. "Cleaning the shit and piss to keep your captors happy. Seems it's about all you're good for. Ever since your desert days . . . you are a disgrace to the Fatherland."

Oskar winced from the kick but kept his mouth shut. He was stronger than Weishaple but knew his punishment would be far worse if caught fighting. Instead, he righted his pail and started to wipe up the spill with a towel. In a whisper, he said, "You put those cigarettes under my bed."

"Oh, you think so, do ya? Well, that's not what the Sergeant thinks. In fact, he and I have something in common. Neither one of us can stand the sight of you, and that's all that counts."

Oskar's voice rose in anger. "Why would you set me up? I've never bothered you."

Weishaple had a deep purple scar that ran from his right earlobe to the bottom of his chin. It seemed to pulsate in the dim light. "You bother me by being alive. You bother me because you are a coward and should never have been able to wear the uniform. You bother me because you don't know how to hate your enemy. To you, this is like some kind of school outing, isn't it? Learning all about another country, another language, trying out new foods and listening to new music. Well, let me tell you, you are not one of them and never will be. You are a German and shouldn't apologize!"

Oskar lashed out, "I know who I am. I know I'm German. But I didn't start this stupid war, and I don't hate these people."

"No? You can fool yourself all you want, but given a chance, these farmers would drop a bomb on your house or my house and do it with a smile. Hell, their planes are bombing our women and children every day while you're here pulling their cows' teats."

Oskar pulled the brush from the bottom of the pail and continued scrubbing. He crawled closer to the wall beneath the leaky trough and worked his brush feverishly as though trying to take the grain right out of the pine boards.

"Don't let me interrupt your important task. In fact . . ." Weishaple drew closer to Oskar. "I'm here to give you more opportunity to shine in front of your friends the Amis." And with that, he unzipped his fly and sprayed piss everywhere but in the trough. "Ahhhh . . . that feels soooo good."

Weishaple laughed triumphantly and headed for the exit but stopped suddenly. "You know, I think I'll ask a few of my friends to come over all week and work on their pissing marksmanship. Remember what the drill instructor told us so many months ago . . . practice makes perfect when it comes to aiming and finding the right target." He flicked his fingers in a lurid manner and said, "*Auf Wiedersehen*!"

27

DANIEL

2019

DANIEL BURST INTO MARK'S ROOM and flung his back-pack on the floor at the foot of the bed. Mark opened his eyes with a start, trying to comprehend where he was, but his mind was cloudy and he pictured himself in the bowels of the *Ambrose Bierce*. Was it a mine or a torpedo? For a split second, he mouthed the name Oskar. Where was Oskar? Could Oskar swim?

When his eyes refocused, Oskar was nowhere to be seen, but instead Mark found Daniel sitting cross-legged on the end of his bed, wearing a red, collared shirt with a gray, sleeveless sweater. No torpedo had exploded, and the fluorescent light on the ceiling reminded him he wasn't in the dark cavern of an ocean liner.

"You gave me a scare, young man. I must have been dozing, a common occurrence for old men in the late afternoons." Sliding his legs over the side of the bed, Mark tumbled into the La-Z-Boy. His afghan slipped to the floor, and he groped for it as Daniel watched with a sullen look, then decided to help.

"I'll get it."

"Thank you."

After he returned to the bed, Daniel announced, "You don't have to say anything . . . I'm not going to start juggling."

"Alright, I won't." Mark pulled the afghan up close to his neck, then folded his arms comfortably across his chest. "I know you want to juggle. What's keeping you from doing it?"

"Seth."

"Your nemesis, yes, I know. What about the Neanderthal leader?"

"He's a thief."

"A thief? And how did you come upon this conclusion?"

"I did a little decorating of his locker at school and found something I shouldn't have."

"You decorated his locker? I'm trying to picture that, but my mind is still fuzzy."

Daniel sighed heavily and then started in on how he had used cave paintings to enhance Seth's artistic understanding, his call to the office, his apology, and the Saturday morning cleanup he and his mother conducted under the watchful eyes of the school janitor.

"I'll bet your mother was fit to be tied."

"She was. But we made up."

"How did Seth take your little show of rebellion?"

"Seth forged a note that called me out of class to meet at his locker." Daniel went on to explain what happened and how Seth threatened him. While he was talking, tiny tears glistened in the corners of his eyes. He wanted desperately to pull out the balls and juggle but used every ounce of restraint to keep them in check.

"Are you going to do anything with this information about the stolen pills?"

"I don't know."

"Did you tell the principal? Or Mrs. Ryan?"

'No.'

"Does your mom know about the locker incident?"

"No."

"Are you going to tell her?"

Daniel didn't answer right away but shrugged and stared out the window. The view from room 409 was not very interesting. It took in the parking lot of a strip mall next door, and only one scrawny tree, a box elder, could be seen. Fortunately, someone installed a bird feeder a few feet from the building, but Mark took no responsibility in filling it with any feed, so Daniel had his mother pick up a bag of thistle seed and he routinely checked it before coming into the building. He even carried a small container of replacement seed in his backpack. Today, two goldfinches were sitting on the tiny perches helping themselves to a meal.

"My mom doesn't understand how easily Seth can needle me and make me angry."

"I'll bet she understands alright but is in no position to do much about it. After all, she can't follow you around in school. So, tell me more about the thief."

Daniel sat on the edge of the bed and dropped his legs over the side. "He and his followers have been extorting prescription pills from students with ADD and other health issues and selling the drugs to other students who want to get high. I think he's been stealing some pain pills from here as well."

"The BRC? And you know this because . . ."

"Like I said, while I was decorating his locker, I came across a container full of pills. I looked at the markings and recognized most of the chemical compounds. Some weren't the type of drugs prescribed for teenagers. He admitted he likes cleaning BRC resident rooms after they . . . well . . . you know . . ."

"You can say *die*. It happens to people in my age bracket all the time."

"I also caught Seth rummaging through one of the teacher's desks. At first I thought he was looking for answers, but then I realized it was the desk of a teacher who had recently returned from knee surgery and he was after opioid pills she might have brought to school."

Mark uncrossed his arms and leaned forward. "Do you think he's doing this for himself? I mean, is he using drugs?"

"I think he and his tribe might use drugs occasionally, but he told me he's doing it for the money. He and his clan have big plans for prom."

Mark's eyes shot up, and his eyes sparkled. "That makes sense, now that you say it. Earlier this week, Seth told me about a cottage he's renting the weekend of the prom. Some palatial estate with lots of bedrooms and a fancy in-house theatre room. He mentioned how much it was going to cost, and I must say, I was amazed. When I asked how he could afford it, he wouldn't tell me. *I'd have to kill you first,* those were his words."

"Now you know where the money for his big party is coming from."

Mark scratched his chin and breathed deeply. He rolled the words around in his mouth before speaking aloud, "What's to be done with this information?"

Daniel was silent for a long time. He stared at his shoes, then out the window, then back to his shoes. "I don't have a plan. Seth threatened me if I go to the authorities. He and his minions could be difficult to live with if I tell the principal."

"He'd like nothing better than to make your life a living hell, I understand that now." Mark wrung his hands for a moment, then said, "Why don't you let me think on it a bit, and maybe I can help in some way that won't put you in jeopardy. I still have a few contacts in this community, ex-students mostly. Maybe one of them can help."

Daniel nodded and reached for his backpack. The expectation of Mark doing anything to help win his war against the Neanderthals wasn't very reassuring. He was in his nineties and wheelchair-bound most of the time.

Mark took a book from his side table and held it up. "Shall we?"

Pulling out his conversational German from his backpack, Daniel opened it to a bookmark. "*Ich mein Deutsch uben.*"

"Wirklich?"

"Ich mache is Ernst."

"Oh! Das is gut."

28

MARK AND JOHN

2019

MARK ROLLED UP TO JOHN MANCUSO'S OPEN DOOR
to find him lying on his side in his bed, watching *The Simpsons* on
TV. The sitcom was playing, but the sound was off. Mark asked,
"Hey there, homo erectus, want to take a walk to the sunroom?"

John coughed and sat up. "Sure. I've seen this episode a half-
dozen times."

"Either you need to turn it up or I need new hearing aids."

"Don't need the sound. I know most of the lines. Let me slip on
my moccasins." He swung his legs around and slipped his bare feet
into a pair of worn black-and-red moccasins fringed with dirty white
faux fur. Then he pushed himself off the bed with a loud groan and
limped over to the dresser to splash on a little Irish Spring aftershave.
He glanced in the mirror, touched a couple fingers to his mouth,
then flattened a ridge of unruly eyebrow hairs and said, "Never can
tell who we might run into."

"Sophia Loren is still alive, I think. She'd be just about your age."

"Too old. I need a jolt of youth."

Mark turned his wheelchair back toward the hall. "Next week, a
class of kindergartners are scheduled. They'll give you a jolt."

John let that comment pass. "Wasn't thinking about them, though
they're cute." Instead, his eyebrows arched up and his lips formed a silly grin. "Was hoping maybe to run into Eva and a package of goodies."

"Oh . . . oh, that kind of a jolt." Mark collected his thoughts, then said with a deeper voice, "I get it, your testosterone is still active. Okay, that's great."

"And it wants to be more active."

Mark thought for a moment, then offered a little advice. "She's unmarried and a good cook, two great selling points."

"And I believe she still has a twinkle in her eye, if you get my drift."

"I do. I do. If I catch sight of her, I'll holler out like a sailor looking for land."

The hallway was awash with wheelchairs parked in random ways like cars after a pileup on the freeway. Most of the drivers sat or slumped listlessly, some covered with brightly colored lap blankets, others clutching stuffed animals. A few walking residents moved so slowly it was like watching a film at one-quarter speed.

John was a good driver. His big hands, despite the swollen knuckles, were clutched tightly to the wheelchair handles as he avoided obstacles. "I like pushing a wheelchair better than using a walker," he said. "Gives me better stability and makes me feel good back here, still upright, not on my butt all day . . . no offense."

"No offense taken. It's a pride thing."

"Yeah."

Mark turned and looked over his left shoulder. "Our bodies tend to give out one nail at a time until the whole frame seems to be coming apart. Don't apologize. I wish I could still walk. I wish I could still do a lot of things."

The sunroom was nearly empty when John parked Mark in front of a large picture window that overlooked a small pond in the courtyard. John flipped the brake levers on the wheels and walked up close to the window. "Nice day. We could slip outside if you want," he offered.

"This is fine, John." Mark shielded his eyes from the bright sunlight. "Haven't seen your heartthrob yet."

"She'll be here with treats. As long as Eva's mother's alive, she'll be around."

"Does she know you have the hots for her?" It was Mark's turn to give a bawdy grin.

John plunked down into one of the overstuffed wing chairs. "I'm taking it slow, my friend."

"Of course. Don't want your heart to get pumping too fast. A man of your age has to pace himself, not overload the old ticker. Keep giving her compliments on her treats. You can't go wrong in that department."

John chuckled and brought his feet up onto a gray-and-white checkered ottoman. "Speaking of food, I've been meaning to ask you . . . Eva's mother says you aren't eatin' very well. What's that all about?"

"Nothing tastes good."

"Nothing's tasted good since we moved into this place, but that never stopped you before."

"I don't know. Appetite's gone to hell."

John turned to look him in the eye. "So, you're saying it's just the appetite, you're not doing anything . . . stupid?"

"Stupid?"

"Like starving yourself to death?"

"No, I'm not doing that."

"Good." John closed his eyes and crossed his arms over his chest. "I don't want to be the last man standing."

"You don't need to worry. I'll call the kitchen and order smaller portions from now on. Marie will think I'm eating better." Both men grinned, and then Mark gazed out the window silently.

"Did you ever think you would go first?" John asked.

"First?"

"I didn't think my wife Maureen would die before me." John opened his eyes and looked down at his moccasins. "I mean, we were divorced and all, but we were still friends and continued to see each other quite a bit. She was still a good friend. She was so healthy and strong all the time till one day she didn't feel good, and the next thing I know, the doctors tell her she only has a month left. She would have been able to cope with living alone much better than me. Our kids and grandkids adored her.

"Maureen left me to try and hold everyone together, and I was horrible at that. Not being a dedicated father when I was younger came back to haunt me." John stood and paced in front of the window, his face filled with a sadness that grows like lichen on the loneliness of old men. "I always thought I'd go first. Figured whenever the kids or grandkids needed her she'd be there. Goddammit, Mark, I never thought I would live longer than her. I mean, the statistics say men should die first, right?"

"Right. And most men get their wish."

"Me and you are just unlucky, I guess. I can handle the long days, but the nights are the worst. I don't like sleeping alone. Never did. Neither did Maureen, bless her heart, so we got together occasionally, even slept together, after the divorce, I mean. The kids didn't know we were seeing each other, but what the hell. We needed each other from time to time, just not every day."

He turned away from the window. "When I was a kid, I grew up with three brothers, all close to me in age. When we were little tykes, the four of us slept in a small bedroom with two double beds. George and Alfred in one, and me and Mike in the other. Later, we had two sets of bunks, but for years we were very close . . ." His voice suddenly fell flat, and he wiped his eyes with the palms of his hands. "Sorry, just blubbering here."

"Blubber away, my friendly wheelchair driver. I understand." Mark thought of his own wife and felt his throat constrict. Both men fell silent for a few minutes.

Mark was thinking of Rose as he stared out the window when he shouted, "Land ho! I see Eva sailing in carrying a cake pan."

John rushed to the window, his nose almost touching the glass. "I hope it's that rum cake with the real rum on the bottom."

"Everyone feels a little giddy after a couple pieces."

"I had three pieces last time and felt great," said John.

Both men watched as Eva disappeared through the front door. "Do you mind if we change the subject before we head back?" asked Mark.

John moved to an overstuffed rocker and plunked down. "Shoot."

"What do you think of our teenage guest at the ART meetings?"

"Daniel? I like that kid. He's a real pistol. Smart as a whip, but a pistol." He pointed his finger at Mark and wagged it emphatically. "Now, I know he's got some social issues, but he's so damn smart. He doesn't even seem to know how smart. I would give my right arm for half his brainpower."

"And he'd probably give his left arm for your ease in talking and socializing with others, especially the ladies."

"Ain't that something? I mean, I never thought talking to strangers or going to a party or applying for a job or a million other day-to-day things would be a problem for a smart kid like him."

"Many of his peers think he's weird. They can't, or won't, take the time to understand him."

"He's not that bad a kid! I knew a lotta jerks in my day, and that young man is definitely not a jerk."

"His mother wants him to go to the prom, being his senior year and all, but he wants none of it. I'm convinced that underneath Daniel wants to fit in with his peers, most of them anyway. Not the bullies, but most of them. He just can't seem to break through."

"I give him a lot of credit for writing all those futuristic stories or whatever he calls 'em. He's got a lotta gumption and stick-to-it-ness." John snickered and smiled. "I know I get under his skin sometimes, but I do like him. Sometimes he reminds me a little of myself when I was young . . ."

"I'll bet it wasn't the times you showed your report card to your parents."

"Hah, hardly." Both men laughed. "No, I can remember being antisocial at times, you know . . . skipping school once in a while, hating church services, hiding things from my parents, that sort of thing. But I sorta feel sorry for him."

"He doesn't want pity," Mark said forcefully.

"No. No. You're right. I don't want it either, even though I see it sometimes in the eyes of my grandkids."

"Pity follows most old people like a cloud. Like that *Peanuts* character, Pig-Pen. Wherever we go, there's someone muttering under their breath, 'Oh, I remember when he was so much stronger,' or 'He can't remember birthdays anymore,' or . . .'"

John finished the thought, "Or 'He was so handsome once. Now look at him.'" And both men withdrew into fading memories.

The sun slipped under a gray cumulus cloud, and the courtyard fell into a daytime darkness. A tall nursing assistant with short blond curls and small hands was pushing a resident up to the lilac bushes, which were in full bloom. The woman in the wheelchair leaned over, put her nose in a lavender-colored clump, and inhaled deeply.

Mark said, "Speaking of the prom . . ."

"Were we?"

"Daniel tells me that Seth, our health aid, has been stealing prescription drugs and selling them to other students."

John's lower lip dropped open as he snapped up and made a fist in his right hand, then slammed it into his left palm. "Damn! I'll bet that's what happened to the painkillers I had in a bottle in my room. That ass! You remember last month when I stubbed my toe so badly on the corner of my bed and could hardly walk? Well, I got a prescription to help with the pain but only used a few of them since that stuff gives me constipation in a hurry. I thought I just lost the bottle or threw it away by mistake."

"Seth, the Eddie Haskell of the assistants, no doubt lifted it with the intent to sell the contents. He and his cronies are shaking down students to get prescription drugs and then selling them to raise enough money to rent some fancy cottage for the prom weekend. They plan to extend the party for several days."

"We should turn the sneaky bastard over to the authorities." John was receiving that jolt he wanted.

"Careful, John. If Seth finds out Daniel told us about the pills, and then we rat out Seth, he'll take it out on Daniel and it might get out of control."

"Yeah, yeah, you're right. Last thing that kid needs is a guy like Seth wanting to beat his ass."

Mark lifted the brake levers and turned his chair to face John. "Let's think on it. Maybe there's a way we can expose Seth without pointing the finger at Daniel."

John nodded. "Count me in."

Mark swiveled his chair toward the hall. "But for now . . ."

"It's cake and rum time!"

29

STANLEY

Summer 1945

"MRS. WELCH, WHERE'S MY TRANSLATOR? I asked for him a half hour ago." Stanley was standing in front of a trestle table in the outer office of the POW camp headquarters. In truth, the main office space was a converted hog barn and show area at the Kocher Valley Fairgrounds. The commandant's office was the former supply room, and Mrs. Welch's reception area the attached ticket booth with the small exchange window covered over with cardboard.

Stanley put both hands on the table, leaned forward, and said quietly but firmly, "Mrs. Welch? Did you hear me?"

"I was waiting for a civil tone." Mrs. Welch was in her mid-sixties and a former schoolteacher. Her hair was gray and held high on her head by a series of silver bobby pins. She wore a light beige, cream, or maroon sweater every day regardless of the temperature. She loved costume jewelry and wore an orange-and-brown necklace that clattered when she moved. Her desk was covered with piles of papers, vanilla folders, and a Campbell's soup can filled with pencils. She was pecking away on a black Smith Corona typewriter as Stanley stared down at her.

When she finally peered up over her wire-rimmed glasses, her bushy eyebrows rising like a matching pair of hand-tied trout flies, she said, "He should be here any minute. The bus driver had to go all the way out to Fountain Lake Road to drop off two workers at the

Fish Hatchery and said he'd pick up the man you asked for on the way back."

"Send *that man* into my office as soon as he shows," Stanley commanded.

"You mean Commandant Davel's office, don't you?" she corrected him.

"Yes, that office."

She lowered her fingers back to the keyboard. "Will do."

Stanley stepped back into the commandant's office, closed the door, and frowned at the POW sitting in the chair directly in front of the desk. "The translator will be here in a few minutes. You'll just have to sit there and try not to leave a stain on the chair, ya dumb son of a bitch." Stanley walked behind the POW. "Talking to you is like talking to a fence post. You can't understand a word, can you?" He came around to stand in front of the POW. "You are a dumb Kraut." A long silence followed. "See? You don't even change your expression."

Stanley slowly strolled around the desk, sat down, and lifted his boots onto the desktop. A moment later, the door opened, and a young American reservist stepped in and stood at attention. He had the black hair of a matador cut in the same bowl fashion. He couldn't have been out of his teens. His uniform was at least two sizes too large, and his laced boots were covered with mud. *This kid could be an extra in a Keystone Cops movie,* Stanley thought.

"Are you Hazen?" Stanley asked.

"Yes, sir, Private Robert Hazen."

"Can you speak German?"

"Yes, sir. Not as good as my parents, but I understand most everything. My parents were born in Bavaria and emigrated . . ."

Stanley dropped his feet and cut him off. "Yeah, yeah, forget that. Pull up that chair in the corner and sit next to that POW. But don't get too close. He might have rabies."

Hazen stopped suddenly and was about to say something when Stanley said, "I'm kidding, okay?"

"Yes, sir. I understand, sir," he answered, though not entirely convinced. He set the chair an extra foot away from the POW.

"I wanna question this POW, Hazen, and I need you to translate everything I say. Got it?"

"I'll try, sir."

"Don't *try*, just do it. It's not too damn difficult. Alright . . . start by getting his name, rank, and where he comes from."

For the first few minutes, Hazen and the POW carried on a steady conversation. Hazen turned to Stanley. "His name is Felix Weishaple, and he was born in Munich. He's a private and was captured in Africa. He's been a POW for over a year, and he says he loves Wisconsin."

"Yeah, I'll bet," Stanley quipped, tongue in cheek. He wrote the POW's name on a piece of paper, then said to Hazen, "Are you having any trouble understanding him?"

"No, sir. I think I got it all."

"Good. One of the night guards seems to think this Kraut wants to talk to me. Ask him why he requested to see me."

Hazen raised his eyebrows. "Is he an informant?"

"Beats me, Hazen, just get on with it."

After an animated conversation with Weishaple, Hazen reported, "He says a couple of men in his bunkhouse are planning to escape, sir, and he thought you would want to know."

"Well, of course I want to know, but let's cut to the chase. Why's he ratting out two of his comrades?"

Hazen conversed quietly with Weishaple for several minutes. "Okay, Sergeant, here's what I got. In exchange for giving you the names of the guys who are planning to escape, he's hoping to get some sort of reward for his information."

Stanley put his pencil down and placed both elbows on the table. "Of course he is. Ask him what sort of reward."

A moment later, Hazen replied, "He hopes you can reassign him to a new work duty. He doesn't want to go back to the cannery. Seems the conditions are hot and dirty, and he hates it there. He would prefer to work on a private farm. He claims he has worked with animals before."

Stanley leaned back in his chair and locked his hands behind his head. "Tell him, Private, in no uncertain terms that he will get nothing if he doesn't first give me the names and the details of this escape plan. Then we'll see about changing his job. Go ahead."

A few minutes later, Hazen smiled and said, "Here are the names . . ."

"Wait, I have to write this down."

Hazen continued, "The planners are Marco Mehlman and Oskar Wurtz. They are planning to escape from the Callahan farm on Friday."

"The day after tomorrow?"

"Correct." Hazen added, "The milk truck makes its weekly pickup every Friday, and the two POWs are planning to overtake the driver and steal the truck. Then they hope to drive to Milwaukee and from there head east, I guess."

Stanley listened and digested the information while sucking on the end of his pencil. He wasn't surprised someone wanted to escape; that's what he would do if he were captured. But Mehlman and Wurtz? They didn't seem the type. In fact, he believed Mehlman and Rose Callahan may be sweet on each other.

Stanley came around his desk and stopped in front of Weishaple. Private Hazen stood up too. Stanley leaned over, pulled Weishaple up by the collar, and said through closed lips, "You wouldn't be lying to me now, would you, cabbagehead?" Weishaple's eyes opened wide but showed no fear. "Have you got a trick up your sleeve?"

"Do you want me to translate, sir?" Hazen asked.

"No. I'm sure he gets my meaning even if he doesn't understand a word of it." Stanley pushed Weishaple back into the chair, then ordered Hazen to escort Weishaple back to his barracks. Before they passed through the door, Stanley said to Hazen, "Not a word of this to anyone, Private."

"No, sir." And the two of them marched out.

After they were gone, Stanley picked up the phone and called Commandant Davel. "I think I need to be at the Callahan farm on Friday morning."

30

STANLEY

Summer 1945

THE SUN PEEKED through a bank of slate-colored clouds, and the wind whipped through the maples, sending hundreds of seed pods whirling in every direction. An overnight rain had given way to cool Canadian air, and the mercury was still clinging to the high fifties. It was June, the height of pollen season, giving the edges of the roadway puddles a tawny streak. Hank Felmington rolled down the window of his Kocher Valley Co-op milk truck, held a finger to one nostril, and blew the other into the wind as he turned up the Callahan drive. He fished a plaid handkerchief from his overalls and wiped his nose before coming to a stop in the yard. It was Friday morning, and he was making his regular stop at Red's place.

Hank was sixty-three years old and had been making the same milk run for nearly forty years. Even before he inherited the route, he could remember as a boy riding with his father on top of an old buckboard wagon pulled by a couple of Andalusian draft horses. Each stop added full cans of fresh milk. By the time they reached the cheese factory over in Blaine, the horses were often ringed with sweat.

Hank knew every resident by name and most of their parents and even grandparents. Red Callahan's father bought this farm from Ed and Edna Groshek when the couple became too old to work it. None of the five Groshek children were willing to stay put

210

and become farmers. Sometimes he referred to the farm as the "old Groshek place" when chatting with neighbors and friends down at the tavern in Danish Corners.

Despite the cool temperature, Hank was sweating beneath his woolen shirt as he opened the door to the truck and stepped onto the soft gravel driveway. Two men from the Army were hiding in his cab. They refused to tell him what the nature of their business was, but insisted it was important and official. All he could figure was that it had to do with the POWs. Hank was not a man to give in to subterfuge, but there was a war on and the world had shifted a bit, so he agreed to their demands with little argument.

When Red heard the truck pull into the yard, he scooped up a glass of warm milk just pulled from one of his Holsteins and strolled out of the barn. Hank loved to sit for a spell and eat one of Emily's morning buns washed down with fresh, warm milk before driving on.

"Morning, Hank!" Red's voice frightened a flock of starlings from the yard, and they burst over the roof of the machine shed. "A bit cool this morning, eh? Keeps the bugs at bay."

"Nippy," said Hank. "Don't have to hurry the milk to the dairy when it's cool like this." He shook Red's hand.

"Come on in. We'll rummage around the kitchen and see what goodies Emily's baked up."

"I'd love to, but can't this morning, Red."

Red pulled up short and wrinkled his nose. "No? Humm. Well, here's a cup of warm milk. Certainly you have time for that."

"Yeah, of course." Hank slurped it down in two gulps. "Nothing better to keep the muscles strong and the mind right."

"Been a pretty good week," Red offered. "Had a couple new calves, and the sweet summer grasses are makin' the milk flow and the cream thick as pudding. Got about ten cans in the milk house for you."

A small shed had been constructed under the windmill, used to pump groundwater into a holding tank. The water came out of the ground at forty degrees and fed into the tank, which was about twenty inches deep. Metal milk cans, once filled and capped, were placed in the cool circulating water to keep the milk temperature constant. The milk could be stored for several days without going sour. There was a small Ashley woodstove at one end of the shed and a small woodpile for those bitter winter days when heat was needed to keep the water and the milk from freezing.

Hank looked over to the milk house but didn't say anything. He kicked at the gravel and pulled his handkerchief from his pocket, wiping his brow. He was uncommonly quiet.

"Got a joke for me this morning, Hank?" Red rarely had to pry a joke out of him. In fact, Red couldn't remember a time when he didn't offer one, though sometimes they were a repeat. Hank seemed to be caught a bit off guard. "Not like you to let the cat get your tongue. Feeling okay?"

"Fine. Just a bit tired, I suppose." He leaned up against the front fender of the Ford sixteen-foot flatbed. There were already a half-dozen gleaming milk cans strapped in the back right up against the cab. "Those two farmhands gonna give us a hand? You know my back ain't what it used to be."

Red turned and glanced over at the barn. "They'll be along in a bit. They were just turning the cows out to pasture and shoveling a little fresh manure." When Red turned back, Hank was mopping his brow again. "So . . . let's hear the joke of the day."

"Alright, here goes." Hank shoved his handkerchief into his back pocket and pulled on the brim of his cap. "Paddy just returned home from his honeymoon with Molly, his new wife, when she asked him . . . 'Who do you think I would rather be stranded with on a deserted island? You, your dad, or your grandpa?'"

"Don't know," said Red.

"Well, Paddy didn't have to think but answered right away, 'Me, of course, seein' as I'm your new husband.' 'Nope,' answered Molly, 'I'd rather be with your grandpa.' 'My grandpa!' said Paddy. 'What does he have that I don't?' Molly smiled and said, 'A boat!'"

Red laughed till he coughed into his elbow.

Hank shifted from one foot to the other. "I heard that one from Bill Feeney over at the dairy. His parents came from Ireland." He chuckled for a moment, but then his smile disappeared and he asked, "Where are your two workers? I'm kinda in a hurry. Gotta take my wife to her sister's later this afternoon. Gladys' sister is not feeling all that well."

Red raised his eyebrows. "Oh, sorry to hear that. I'll see what's keeping the boys while you back the truck around." His voice trailed as he strode away.

Hank climbed into the cab on the driver side as Sergeant Stanley and Private Hazen slipped out the other door, scurried over to the milk house, and hid behind the open door. Hank started the engine and pulled forward, then back, as he slowly positioned the truck. He hated the idea of being dishonest even if it was his patriotic duty.

A moment later, Red, Oskar, and Marco appeared at the rear of the truck ready to load the milk cans. Marco and Oskar lifted the cans onto the truck as the two older men watched. When they finished, Oskar helped Hank up so he could strap the cans to the sides.

"Need these two boys for anything else, Hank?" Red asked.

"Nope. I think that's all."

"Okay, boys, you can head back to your chores." Oskar and Marco said goodbye, turned, and started back to the barn. When they were about halfway across the yard, Rose flew out of the house and jogged over to the truck with a piece of paper in her hand.

"Hank! I have a message for you. Just came over the telephone."

Startled, Hank lifted his hat and sat on the edge of the flatbed. "Me? Who would want to talk to me?"

"It's a bit puzzling to me too," said Rose, "but here goes. It says there are two POWs that have disappeared from the Larsen farm, and you are to get over there right away." She let her hand with the paper drop to her side. "Came from a Mrs. Welch at the fairgrounds, sounded rather official. She was nearly screaming."

Hank scratched his brow and tilted his head forward. "I don't even stop at the Larsens' anymore. They sold their milk cows a year ago. He just has pigs and sheep, I think."

Suddenly, Stanley and Private Hazen rushed out of their hiding place in the milk house. "That message is for me!" Stanley shouted. "Give me the paper, Rose."

Both Red and Rose jumped when Stanley appeared. "What the heck are you doing here?" asked Red in a high-pitched voice. "And why were you hiding in my milk house? Who's this other guy?"

Stanley pulled the paper from Rose's hand without answering and scanned it quickly. Hazen introduced himself and explained why they had ridden with Hank, who was commanded to keep quiet. "It seems the two POWs you have working for you, Mr. Callahan, are not involved in this escape plan," said Hazen. "In fact, it appears we have been led to the wrong farm on purpose while the real escapees are on the run."

"Shut up, Hazen," growled Stanley.

"Sorry, Sergeant." Hazen's cheeks glowed like campfire embers.

Stanley, on the other hand, was fuming. "Goddammit, Hazen! We were tricked by a couple of fucking Huns!" He turned to Red. "Mr. Callahan, I need to borrow your pickup truck and head over to the Larsens'. Actually, that's an order, not a request. Give me the keys!"

"Now just a minute . . ." Red spit out.

Rose put her hand on his arm. "Let him go, Uncle."

Red stared into Rose's eyes, which were large as quarters. Her face held a fierce expression. He turned to Stanley. "Okay, but my truck better come back in one piece." He plucked the keys from his back pocket and flipped them over to Stanley, who dropped them, which added to his anger.

"Goddammit! Let's go, Hazen." Stanley let Hazen drive. When they backed out of the shed, the truck suddenly stopped. The passenger window came down, and Stanley hollered, "Callahan! Where the fuck is the Larsen farm?" After Red gave directions, the truck roared down the driveway, sending the maple seeds back into the air once again to pinwheel softly to the earth.

"I'm real sorry, Red," said Hank as he stepped down from the truck. "I hated to be dishonest with you, but I didn't have much choice. Those two Army characters showed up at my place at five o'clock this morning and insisted I let them ride along. They were hell-bent on catching your two farmhands red-handed." He scowled. "I told that sergeant your two boys were the nicest guys around and I didn't think they would be doing anything to cause trouble, but he wouldn't listen."

"You made up that story about your wife and her sister?" Red asked.

"Sorry 'bout that."

Red patted Hank on the shoulder. "Not your fault, Hank. Stanley's got a bug up his rear about the POWs working here and tries to do whatever he can to make their lives miserable."

"How about a morning bun, Hank?" Rose offered. "Aunt Emily made a fresh batch this morning, and I'll bet they're still warm." Her face flashed a welcoming smile.

"Thank you, missy. I believe I earned it."

"Marco and Oskar, you come too," Rose said.

A half hour later, Rose cleared the dishes and hugged Hank as he stood in the kitchen doorway. Red said goodbye, touched his index finger to the brim of his cap, and watched Hank's truck lumber down the driveway, turning north on Butternut Road.

After their morning buns and coffee, Marco and Oskar headed to the machine shed where they picked up a post hole digger and crossbuck saw. Red directed them to the south pasture to cut up a box elder tree that had fallen over a section of barbed fence. "Probably went down in the thunderstorm the other day. I'll drive the AC out later with some extra wire and fencing tools."

Red took a moment to settle into the rocker on the side porch and put his feet up on the railing. The sun had broken through; the lavender irises stuck out their white tongues and the blood-red peonies in Emily's side yard showed off their summer finery. The trumpet vine was finally filled out with thick, green leaves and hanging heavily from the trellis at the end of the porch. The bridal wreath along the clothesline posts was awash with thousands of tiny bright-white flowers. In less than a week, the longest day of the year would be upon them and the days would grow shorter. Summer was just under way, and yet cruel Mother Nature allowed the end to invade Red's thoughts, and he hated to think of it, each winter seeming to get longer. He loved the month of June, the time of bright renewal and colorful rebirth. He looked forward to the planting of corn and oats and clover just to see all the tiny plants poke up out of the black dirt. He took pride in growing healthy things to eat, watching the animals grow, knowing he played a small part year after year in making his world a better place.

Crossing the yard, he neared the door of the garage when a barn swallow swooped down and almost clipped the brim of his hat. "Easy, boy, I'm not gonna hurt you. Just want to close this door." The swallows had constructed their half-moon nest just under the eaves and caused a small riot each time someone approached. Why they couldn't move down the way a bit, Red couldn't figure. But he loved to see their aerial acrobatics, purple backs and brown throats soaring like sea glass in the sky. The parents were busy feeding the fledglings. He could see four or five tiny golden beaks resting on the rim of their muddy nest. Red chuckled and said out loud, "Okay, okay. You can stay as long as you like. The insects you eat are a fitting way to pay the rent."

Watching the swallows with such interest, Red didn't notice his pickup truck rolling into the yard. Stanley was at the wheel, Hazen in the passenger seat, and two POWs sitting with their hands tied behind their backs in the open box. The truck's brakes squealed as it rolled to a stop. Stanley clambered out of the cab and stretched his arms above his head, then reached back through the window, found his hat, and fixed it smartly on his head. "Truck's back in one piece, Mr. Callahan," he announced proudly, "as promised."

"I see." Red slowly walked around and rested a foot on the back bumper. "Who'd you pick up?"

Private Hazen came around from the passenger side, the lip of his hat cutting a straight line across his forehead. "These are the two culprits who tried to make a break back to Germany."

Red rubbed the stubble on his chin. "Wonder how they were planning to do that. Seems to me they'd have trouble getting out of the county, let alone the country."

Rose heard the commotion and walked out of the kitchen onto the porch. When she saw Stanley and the men in the back of the truck, her face grew anxious. She pulled her apron off and lowered it over the porch railing, then stepped quickly down the steps and hurried across the yard.

"What's going on, Uncle?" Rose asked, ignoring Stanley as she stared at the two POWs, their heads hanging low, their wrists in handcuffs. One had blood stains on the corners of his mouth and along the buttons of his shirt.

"These two thought they were headed home early," exclaimed Stanley. "But, of course, they were sadly mistaken. No way was I going to let any of my charges escape." His grin was as wide as a jack-o'-lantern's.

Private Hazen said, "The one on the left, the tall one with the blond hair and freckles, he was found in a chicken coop in the backyard of the Larsen farm."

"Can you imagine?" Stanley added. "Thought he would outsmart us by waiting with the hens till dark and then make a run for it. Mrs. Larsen's little house poodle knew something was up and kept barking at the henhouse door."

"That's right," said Hazen. "Then Mr. Larsen figured something was wrong and peeked in to see what the ruckus was all about, spotted that freckled one, and called the camp."

Stanley continued gleefully, "I ask you, Rose, who tries to escape by hiding in a henhouse with the chickens? Not too smart, eh? Downright stupid, I'd say. But then I've been telling you all along these Krauts who thought Hitler was the next great messiah aren't real bright. Some master race, huh? About as clever as the Rhode Island Reds he bunked in with."

Rose looked at the two prisoners, her face seeming to sag with sadness. "What about the one with the blood? What did you do to him?"

Stanley grinned and hopped onto the back of the truck. "This guy?" He gave him a kick in the shin. "His name is Weishaple. This whole charade started because he didn't like working at the Big Falls canning factory. He came to see me a couple days ago, acting as a snitch. He wanted to trade information about an escape attempt for a better job assignment. What a fool! Look where it got him."

"Why the bloody face?" she asked.

"He tripped." Stanley reached down and pulled Weishaple to his feet. "Hazen! Give me a hand." Private Hazen pulled out his revolver and jumped onto the back of the truck, lifting the other POW to his feet. "Take these two down the driveway and wait there for the bus," Stanley commanded. "It should be coming anytime now."

Hazen leaped to the ground and helped the first POW climb

down. Weishaple tiptoed to the edge of the box, expecting Hazen to give him a hand. Instead, Stanley gave him a kick and sent Weishaple headfirst into the driveway. Rose shouted, and Red put out both arms to try and break his fall but was too slow. Weishaple rolled onto his back and groaned. Small stones were imbedded in his nose, and he spit blood and gravel from his mouth.

"Stop!" shouted Rose and took a step toward Weishaple.

"Don't touch him, Rose! That's an order!"

"Why do you have to be so cruel?" Rose lamented.

Stanley stood over Weishaple, who continued to spit blood. "I found him hiding in a culvert under the road in front of the Larsens' place just like the rat he is." He reached down and pulled Weishaple roughly to his feet. "When I flushed him out, he took off running across the oat field, but he hit a muddy spot and tripped, and that's when I caught up to him and cuffed him. Big plans to escape ending in a muddy oat field." Stanley stared into Weishaple's bloodshot eyes, his jaw not more than six inches from Weishaple's jaw. "You won't be running anytime soon, asshole. You'll be in isolation till the Army ships you outta here."

Rose pleaded, "Let me patch him up. I have lots of bandages..."

"No, Rose," Stanley commanded. "He'll be alright till we get back to the camp."

"It'll only take a few minutes."

Stanley ignored Rose and shoved Weishaple toward the private. "Hazen, take these two now before I lose my patience and do some real damage."

"Yes, sir."

"I'll bring Callahan's two POWs and meet you at the end of the driveway in a few minutes. Get going!"

"Yes, sir." Hazen herded the prisoners down the driveway like a border collie bringing in the sheep. If one stumbled, he pulled him back and headed him in the right direction.

Stanley turned to Red and asked, "Mr. Callahan, where are your two farmhands?"

Red cleared his throat, then replied, "Still out in the south pasture repairing the fence."

"Go get 'em. I'm taking both with me."

"But it's not nearly time. I got my second milking coming up."

"You'll have to take care of that on your own. I'm bringing all the POWs into camp immediately. I need to interrogate every last one to find out if there are any other harebrained schemes being planned." Red protested, but Stanley was adamant, so he hustled off to find Oskar and Marco.

Rose's face was as tight as a wood carving when she turned on Stanley. "You didn't have to hurt that man. He was helpless already with those handcuffs still on."

"That POW tricked me and embarrassed me in front of my men. I can't let him or any of the other prisoners forget who's in charge." Stanley bent over and wiped dust off the crease in his slacks. "Besides, I wanted you to see what happens to anyone who tries to escape."

"You pushed him off the truck on my account?"

"When a prisoner breaks the rules, he suffers the consequences." Straightening up and fixing his cap, he added, "Lest you forget, these men are enemies to America. Whatever happens to Weishaple . . . well . . . he brought it on himself."

Rose turned toward the house and took a step to leave, but spun around quickly and flashed dark, cobalt eyes. "There's no reason to be cruel." She spit the words as though they were bugs caught in her mouth.

"Discipline, not cruelty, that's how I see it. But no matter, they'll all be going home now the war's over. If they think they've been ill-treated while in Wisconsin, they can lodge a formal complaint with the International Red Cross, your parent organization, right? Maybe you can write a letter to the peace lovers who issued that fancy uniform you wear so often. See if the folks in Washington care. These POWs' concerns don't measure up anywhere close to the civilians coming out of the camps in Poland or Germany."

"I know the conditions here are more accommodating compared to European camps..."

"Or Russian camps."

"...or Russian camps. But they are still prisoners, separated from their homeland, their families and loved ones. It wouldn't hurt for you to show a little more compassion."

"True. It wouldn't hurt, but it's not necessary either. I'm tired of local folks thinking these are just nice young men who got caught up in a tornado and dropped here outta the sky. If you put a gun in their hands, they would shoot you and me as quick as you can blink. They had their choice to resist or go along with the Nazi party line years ago. As long as they wear U.S. government-issued PW shirts, they are scum to me." He turned his head and whispered, "They're worse than a common murderer or child molester."

"That's an *awful* thing to say. You've been around these men for over a year, and if you are honest with yourself, you'd admit they're not dangerous." Rose's cheeks flushed crimson, and her eyebrows pinched close together.

"So you say."

"So anyone with an ounce of decency says," she barked.

Stanley turned his back to her. "Go on back to the kitchen, Rose. This is government work, and despite your fancy uniform, I don't think you have the stomach for it."

Rose stood her ground and glared at Stanley. She couldn't think of anything more to say but would not back up an inch.

Red walked between Oskar and Marco as the three approached the pickup truck. Rose turned on her heel when she heard her uncle and fell in step with him.

Stanley pulled two pairs of handcuffs out of his back pocket. "Turn the prisoners around, Mr. Callahan."

"Is that really necessary?" asked Red. "These boys aren't gonna try any funny business. They've been here all day working."

Stanley ignored Callahan's remarks and shouted, "Turn around, you two!" Marco and Oskar did as they were told. After Stanley had them secured, he pushed them in the back and started off down the driveway. Suddenly, he commanded the two POWs to stop. He turned around and shouted at Red as though Rose wasn't even there. "Tell your niece she should be thankful men like me are keeping this area safe from dangerous enemies. She can look under her bed without fear; the mighty German soldiers we've all seen goose-stepping on those newsreels are nothing more than weaklings willing to keep company with chickens." He laughed the laugh of the triumphant bully. Then he pushed Marco and Oskar in the back, and the three trotted out of sight.

Rose clutched her uncle's hand tightly, anger seething from her fingers to her toes.

31

DANIEL

2019

"YOUR FATHER CALLED while you were visiting over at the BRC." Denise set the glass saucepan on the stove and turned the burner up from simmer to boil.

Daniel stood over the silverware drawer and pulled out two forks, two knives, and two spoons. "What did you tell him?"

"Tell him?"

"About my time over at the BRC."

"Not much. He asked why you were going over there, but I thought it better for you to explain. If you want to, that is."

"Maybe." He used a clean dish towel and wiped each piece of silver, holding it up for inspection. Then he placed them on the kitchen table in perfect setting, with the knife blade turned inward and the fork on the left.

"Finish the salads, please," Denise said. "There are two bowls of greens on the counter and a couple hardboiled eggs on the cutting board. I bought the eggs today from Mrs. Nevers, the librarian I work with."

"They're cage-free?"

"Of course they are. She and her husband Steve are very proud of their ten Plymouth Rock hens. They raised them from chicks, you know. She told me today that her husband treats them like pets, so I'm sure the eggs are as organic as it gets."

Daniel sliced the first yolk in half and lowered his head to inspect. "This yolk is nice and dark. That means the protein content is high."

"Good to know. I feel healthier already."

Daniel continued cutting each section into thin half-moon slices and placing them in a perfect geometric pattern on the edges of the bowls. "Tomato?" he asked.

"In the fridge, and a part of a red onion too. Look in the drawer."

"How old is the onion?"

"Not as old as you. It'll be fine." She listened to the rhythmic chopping as she stirred the whole wheat pasta noodles. After adding a dash of Pacific sea salt, Denise wiped her hand on her red-and-white kitchen towel. "Don't you want to know what else your father had to say?"

The onion had been reduced to tiny squares, and the tomato, like the eggs, thinly sliced. "Did he want to know where to send my graduation gift?"

Denise waved a hand in front of her face. "He says he's planning to come to the ceremony. He hopes to drive and get here on Saturday, June 6th, the day before graduation."

"D-Day. Operation Overlord. That's appropriate. An invasion of the Allies, you and your ex-husband against the weakened enemy."

"Hey! That's not fair!"

"Tell me why he's really coming?"

"I told you, to see you graduate."

"He can livestream the event."

"He wants to be here in person. Parents escort their graduate across the stage, right? He wants to take part. He certainly doesn't want to see me." She drained the pasta in the sink and splashed cold water over the noodles, then poured them into a bright-orange bowl, placed a pat of butter on the top, and set it on the table. "Ready with the salads? I'm famished." She sat down and pulled the chair up close.

Daniel placed the salad bowls perfectly between the knife and fork, then pulled out his chair and settled in. He stabbed a forkful of greens, added tomato and egg, and hoisted the works to eye level for a final perusal. "Am I supposed to be pleased?" He started to chew; 25 times per mouthful was his rule.

"Why wouldn't you? He is your father, after all. Most parents want to be present when their children attend an important ceremony."

Another forkful and another 25 chews later, he said, "I've seen him in person for 2 hours and 32 minutes in the last 18 months. I don't think his interest is born out of sincerity."

"No? Why else would he come all the way from Ohio?"

"Guilt. I've read up on divorced parents; most accept their parental responsibilities until their children reach age eighteen and then excuse themselves from the lives of their offspring. My father got an early start on the *moving on* phase."

Denise set her fork down and wiped her mouth with one corner of the dish towel. "My, aren't we the sourpuss. I thought I was the one who's supposed to be cynical and angry with the outcome of our marriage."

"You can."

"I've moved on from anger. Granted, I'm saddened, but I want to wake up and face each day with a bit of optimism. I don't feel like joining your pity party."

"He doesn't even know me." Daniel set his fork down and stopped chewing. "He'll talk about his health, his job, how the weather is in Ohio, and then he'll be gone." He placed his salad bowl to the side, spooned a heap of pasta onto the stainless steel plate, and buttered and salted the steaming noodles. "Where will he stay? That is, if he actually comes."

"At the Best Western. He's only planning to stay for a night or two. We can be civil. I know I can. After all, I want the weekend to focus on my graduating son, Oakwood High's valedictorian." She let a smile spread quickly.

"What did you tell him about Mark?"

"Mark? Not much. Just that you're learning German and joined a writing group."

"He probably laughed when you told him the club was made up of ancient men and women."

"I didn't say anything of the kind. As far as he knows, the group could be school-oriented and made up of your peers."

"He would think that. Nothing but *normal* for his son. If he lived here, he'd know my peers are not nearly as interesting as the ART group. I should introduce him to Mark. Maybe he could learn something about believing in a person, about accepting human differences, about being a real parent."

"Hey . . . hey, be nice."

Before meeting Mark, Daniel had wondered if he'd ever feel a real connection to another human being, outside of his mom. As a child, he'd yearned to feel the warmth of his father's love. When he looked into his father's eyes, he was desperate to see himself reflected back, but all he saw was his father's unease and self-denial. When he went to his father, he pulled away. Over time, he had come to feel insubstantial—not invisible, exactly, but not quite seen either. Over time, he grew deeply angry with his father.

"I should take him over to meet the whole ART group, for that matter. I'd love to hear what John Mancuso would have to say about a father abandoning his son. My *concerned* father would need a good set of earplugs."

Denise set her silverware down and rubbed the towel across her lips. "Are you saying you want your father to meet Mark and the others?"

"No!"

"Just checking."

When the meal was over, Denise collected the dishes and placed them in the sink, put the extra pasta in a plastic container, and slid it into the fridge. "Do you want any ice cream? I bought your favorite!"

"Pistachio?"

She put her hands on her hips and gave him a silly look. "Funny. I know you're allergic to nuts. No, I bought Neapolitan from the Co-op. It's hand-churned and made with local strawberries." Her voice was imploring. "I even have some waffle cones."

He stood and stepped toward the door. "I know how much you want to please me, Mom, but right now I have a story to write and a dad to forget and a valedictorian speech to start. Maybe later." And he retreated to his bedroom.

32

JOHN AND MARK

2019

JOHN SLIPPED INTO ROOM 409 AND PLUNKED DOWN ON THE BED. "You know, I've never heard you talk about your POW experience. I mean, I know you were captured and all, but I don't know any of the details, and it's killin' me. It's none of my business, and you can tell me to shut up, but besides being a loudmouth, I can, at times, be a *curious* loudmouth.

He leaned back on the bed and pulled his feet out of the silly moccasins before stretching supine, then twined his fingers behind his head and continued, "Most guys I know would be hangin' their war experiences around their neck like a St. Christopher medal. I once worked with a guy who still wore his dog tags."

Mark set aside his book of poetry by Mary Oliver on the table next to his chair. "Comfy?"

"Fine, thanks."

"Sure I can't get you another pillow or a cold drink?"

"No, I'm good. Just curious, that's all."

Mark pushed his glasses to the top of his head and pulled the handle of his La-Z-Boy so his legs shot up like a couple of smooth barkless sticks. "Funny, I was just reading a poem about curiosity."

"Really?"

"The author says it's a wonderful characteristic to have and most people of greatness in the past were curious about the world around them."

228

"I'm not a person of the past just yet."

"She writes about the way we are inside, our inner thoughts and emotions, the things not seen but felt. You know, honesty, dedication, sibling affection . . ."

"Ya lost me there."

"We're still trying to figure out what makes us human, I guess."

"When you or the poet finally figure it out, let me know. I don't understand any of that deep thought stuff. I just want to know about your war years, at least the POW part. After all, everybody knows you're a hero."

"That hero stuff is overblown, and you know it."

"Maybe. But I'm still curious."

"I didn't do anything to deserve being called a hero in the war. I kept my head down and didn't get killed, end of story. I was captured by the enemy like a zillion other guys and survived my time as a POW. Sure, sometimes it was rough, but who hasn't experienced tough times in their lives? You were in Korea. That qualifies you to be a hero by some."

"Hah! That puny war. It was FUBAR of the first order. If you didn't freeze to death, you were lucky."

Mark paused, then shook his head. "If you want to know a real hero, look to your paramour, Eva. She comes here nearly every morning to be with her mother, takes her to Saturday temple, reads to her every night, brings her and the rest of us baked treats, buys her mom new clothes, cleans her dentures, and always has a smile and a good word for everyone. Not to mention she's been doing it for years. I don't think I could be so dedicated and give so much time to someone else. She's the epitome of a heroic person."

"Eva is a great woman, no argument there. But she wasn't a soldier on the front line."

"Is that the qualification? Because if it is, I knew quite a few guys on the front line who were horses' asses."

"But they weren't captured and held as a POW for years."

"Not *years*, nineteen months."

"If you say."

Mark pulled the glasses from his head, folded them, and dropped them into his flannel shirt pocket. "Speaking of the Army . . ."

"Were we?"

"I want you to promise me something, something I want you to do after I'm gone."

"What if I die first?"

"Well, then you're off the hook."

"Okay, I promise." After a thoughtful pause, he added, "Within reason." John's eyes turned dark and his pupils tiny as ink spots. "What is it?"

"Have you seen those military cemeteries with rows of white crosses?"

"Sure. There's a big veteran cemetery in Milwaukee, right outside the VA hospital. It's got rows and rows of those crosses."

"Don't let me be buried under a white cross."

"Is that a decision I can make? Don't you have some family that may have a say in where you should go? Me and you are buddies and all, but . . ."

"No family, no close friends. They're all dead."

"No one, huh?" John scratched his chin. "Why don't you wanna be buried in a military cemetery with military honors?"

"I hated being a soldier. I hated the war."

John shook his head and sat up, letting his legs dangle over the side of the bed. "That's natural, Mark. Most people hate war. My time in Korea was the worst time of my life. People who glorify war are slobs who never experienced the wrong end of a loaded gun. I take it you didn't enlist?"

"I was drafted."

"Okay, but so were thousands of others. You were just doing your duty. You got a raw deal, what with being a prisoner and all. I'd think you'd want people to remember you as a military hero."

"Stop with the *hero* stuff!"

"Sorry."

Mark took a deep breath and let the air come out slowly. "Forget it. You don't have to apologize, John, not to me." He realized this was an argument he could never win. Most people want to accept their own version of reality, and most want to believe heroes exist as sure as there are Elysian Fields after death.

"Then I won't . . . apologize, I mean." For a long moment, both men sat in silence. In a soft voice, John asked, "Okay, if you're not a hero, and I question that, do you know any heroes?"

"They're dead."

"All of them?"

"As of this minute, yes, all of them . . . except Eva, as I said."

"Who, besides Eva, qualifies in your book?"

It took Mark a good minute before he answered. "A person whose life's work is significant to others in a positive way. A scientist, a musician, an astronaut, a missionary . . . someone who dedicates his or her work and their lives for the betterment of humanity. Not a person who's trained to shoot and kill and drop bombs from forty thousand feet, even if captured by the enemy and treated as a POW . . . that doesn't make a hero out of a person."

John shook his head and conceded. "So, where do you want to be buried?"

"Anywhere fitting, you decide, though I would like to be under a tree or at least in some shade. I've had enough of the hot sun in my life, and being in shade would be refreshing. I know that sounds corny, but the glaring sun and heat bring bad memories. After I go, I want only cool breezes." Mark smiled wistfully and let his head fall back as far as the chair would allow.

"Shade it is. I can make sure that's done. If you do go first, what about your possessions?"

"Goodwill."

John's mouth opened as wide as an egg. "Really? Don't you want anyone to have your personal stuff?"

"I don't have any personal stuff of real value. I have enough money to buy a cemetery plot, maybe enough to cater a meal for the ART group—you can do that as well. Invite Daniel if he's still around. You can ask Helen to help with the personal stuff if it's a problem for you."

"Okay. I'll have to write all this down. I'm beginning to think it'd be a lot easier if I'd just go first." He looked over at Mark, and they both giggled.

33

ROSE AND MARCO

Summer 1945

DURING THE NIGHT, MARCO WAS SICK. He had to make at least a half-dozen trips to the latrine, and by the time the sun popped up, he was sweating and enervated. Oskar came to his cot and immediately recognized that his friend was miserable. "Marco, you look awful."

"I can't go to work today, Oskar. Every muscle in my body hurts, even my eyelids. I think I have the flu." He pulled his blanket up to his chin and closed his eyes. "Just let me stay here. I'll be better by tomorrow, I promise," he whispered.

Oskar stepped back a foot or two and scratched at the scar on his left ear. "I'm going to go and get some breakfast and bring back something for you, and then we are both going to the Callahans."

Marco turned on his side away from Oskar. "I don't want anything to eat, and I don't want to go to work."

"We'll see about that when I get back." Oskar strode out and over to the chow line. He filled his plate with an extra helping of scrambled eggs and took two pieces of toast and two apples, putting the extras in his pocket. After he downed the eggs and a glass of milk, he hurried back and sat on the edge of Marco's cot and pulled Marco up by the shoulders. "Come on, get dressed. You can't stay here."

The camp's sick bay was a tiny Quonset hut erected behind the office building, a classic case of out of sight, out of mind. Those

POWs who were ailing could check in, but few did unless it was a last resort. The medical staff was a party of one, a middle-aged nurse named Bernice Poklasny. She had little time for malingerers and a deep dislike for followers of Hitler in general. Bernice and her parents emigrated from the Netherlands at the end of the nineteenth century and scratched out a living on a rocky forty acres near Stevens Point. She received her nurse's training in Marshfield and worked in a hospital for several years before doing in-home care.

When the Army offered her a job, she took it, telling everyone it was her way of helping the war effort, but in truth the government pay was what convinced her. She had many relatives who still lived in Amsterdam and the area around, but none had been heard from for months. She worried about their safety and could be accused of taking out her frustration and anger on those POWs who were sick enough to come under her care.

"You know if you go to the sick bay, for even a few hours, Stanley will find out," Oskar said.

"I know," replied Marco. "But I feel so weak."

Nurse Poklasny had made it quite well known that any POW who sought the sick bay as a resting zone was immediately reported to Sergeant Stanley, who was sure to make a quick appearance. With his clipboard in hand, he would reassign the malingerer to one of the least desirable contract jobs—hefting milk cans at the dairy, stacking logs with a lumber crew, or spreading manure by hand at a Green Bay stockyard.

"When we were in Africa, you made sure I recovered so we could stay together," Oskar said. "Now it's my turn. Up you go!" He slipped his muscular forearms under Marco's armpits and in one fluid motion had him standing at the edge of the cot. He located Marco's boots and slid them under his feet. "Step into your shoes." It was an order. "I'll help you to the bus, and when we get to the

Callahans, Red won't mind if you rest. Maybe Emily will make you chicken soup. I hear that it can cure anything."

Oskar put his arm around Marco's shoulders and helped him clamber down the steps and across the camp yard. It was 7:15 and overcast. The smell of rain was strong, and the breeze out of the east had picked up within the hour. Several starlings were lined up on the telephone wires like musical notes. When the bus pulled up to the gate, Oskar and Marco were first in line to board. After Oskar's name was checked off, he stepped up into the bus and pulled Marco with him, lowering him onto a bench seat with a window that opened, just in case. Oskar took an apple from his pocket. "Eat this. My mother always said apples are the best medicine."

Marco turned his ashen face toward the window and raised his arms in protest. "No food, Oskar. Not yet. I might throw it up, and the bus driver would be forced to turn around."

Oskar leaned in and whispered into Marco's ear. "Remember when we were on the ship? I was seasick for the first few days, and to help settle my stomach, you made me think of things that were flat and solid. Remember? And it worked. I thought of our hayfields, the horizon, the road to town, all sorts of flat things." Marco nodded, his eyes tiny slits, while Oskar droned on, "A line of oak trees with deep roots, telephone poles standing at attention as far as the eye can see, rows of corn in straight green rows, think the same kind of thoughts, Marco, and we'll be at the Callahans before you know it." Marco belched and then let out a long sigh. He rested his forehead against the slippery window and shut his eyes.

Twenty minutes later, Oskar and Marco stumbled up the driveway leading to the white clapboard house with its wraparound porch and side-yard garden. Iris spears and early-season mums and delphiniums stood tall while peonies and bleeding hearts bent low from recent rains. The two men walked slowly around to the kitchen entrance and stepped gingerly up the wooden stairs that squeaked with each footfall. Emily opened the screen door when she spied Oskar, welcoming him with an animated smile. "Good morning, Oskar!"

Before he could say anything, Oskar broke into a winsome smile as his nostrils flared, drawing in the sweet smell of fresh bread.

"Morning," Oskar finally said, his arm still in support of Marco.

When Emily caught sight of Marco, her face dropped into a serious state. "Uh oh, somebody isn't feeling well, I can see that." She placed her palm on Marco's brow and looked into his rheumy eyes. "This way," she said imperiously. She led them through the kitchen and down the hall to the parlor. "Lay him on the couch, Oskar, and then take off his boots. I'll be right back with pillows and a blanket." Her shoes clattered like drum beats as she hustled up the wooden stairs to the bedrooms.

"I told you," Oskar said. "She'll take good care of you, and Rose too. Red and me will take care of milking. You know I can do the chores of two men. I have to carry your weight most of the time anyway." He winked and dropped the boots onto the navy-blue rag rug.

Emily spread a log cabin summer quilt over Marco and positioned his pillow. "I'll bring some tea and honey. You just rest." She tapped Marco's shoulder to reassure him. "Probably just a twenty-four-hour bug. Lot of it going around." She headed for the kitchen, then stopped. "If you need to use the bathroom, you know where it is. Don't be afraid to holler if you need help with anything."

"Thank you," Marco said weakly.

Emily curled her finger at Oskar. "This way." She pranced into the kitchen, Oskar following like a well-trained hound. She placed a loaf of fresh bread and a bowl of raspberry jam on the table. "He'll be alright, Oskar. He just needs rest and a few of my homemade recipes."

"You are . . . very kind."

"Go ahead, cut off the *shatzl*. That's what you call the end crust, right? The *shatzl*?"

"*Shatzl*, yes. My favorite."

"Red's too. But he can cut the other end. I don't care much for the crust anyway. Go on. It's all yours."

Rose showed up sometime after lunch. Marco had been dozing but opened his eyes when he heard footsteps. "Someone's not a hundred percent, I hear." Rose pulled a small oak rocking chair with a cane seat up close to the couch. She wore a pair of faded bib jeans and a white cotton shirt. Her hair smelled of fresh soap and was pulled back in a tight braid with a pink scarf tied on the end.

Marco smiled and sat up as best he could. He was delighted to see her despite still being a bit queasy. "Only about fifty percent," he replied, "but better than I was when I woke this morning."

"My aunt's cooking has that effect on most people."

"I didn't think I could eat anything when I got here this morning, but the soup she made me and the fresh bread, well, I couldn't resist, and I've kept everything in my stomach."

"A good place for it."

"I hope Red isn't upset. I mean, because I couldn't work today."

"I talked to him, and he said everything is going fine. Seems Oskar is willing to do anything extra. You have a good friend in Oskar, and my uncle sure has taken a shine to that man." Rose rocked forward, her cheeks the color of two Jonathan apples.

"Everybody loves Oskar . . . except . . ." They both uttered "*Stanley!*" at the same time and laughed.

When they caught their breath, they sat quietly, relaxed and comfortable in the presence of each other. Their privacy was intimate and almost overwhelming. Marco summoned up the courage to talk about the future. "Rose, you know we, that is, Oskar and me, we have no future back in Germany."

Rose straightened and tilted her head slightly. "You said that before, and I feel terrible about it." There was another long pause. "What are you thinking about the future?"

"We want to stay here."

"In Wisconsin?"

Marco focused on Rose's eyes, which glittered like polished silver. "Yes, Wisconsin, but more specifically, here in Kocher Valley. We love it here." The floodgates opened, and Marco couldn't stop. "We have no home. We, or at least I, want to see more of . . . you, Rose . . . and of course Red and Emily and the farm and Oakwood. But . . . mostly I want to stay because of you."

Rose tilted back as far as the rocker would allow. Her lips were closed, and her eyes darted around the room. She breathed deeply, and her cheeks turned a deeper red. "You want to escape?"

"Not exactly." Marco was sitting up now, his shoeless feet flat on the rag rug. "Usually when a person escapes, he, or she, runs away from the place they are being held captive. But we want to stay." His voice got louder and more animated. "We don't want to run away. We don't want to return to a place that has no future. It's simple, really. I see my life here, with you . . . and your family."

Rose was shaking her head, not from disagreement with his words, but perplexity. "How? How can you stay? The Army wants to ship you out, and it won't be long now."

Marco looked up to the ceiling and took a deep breath. "I don't know for sure, but I've been thinking, the war in Europe is over, so I don't see why we're not like the soldiers being held captive over there. We'll be turned loose at some point. We'll be like them, displaced persons, only in America."

"I don't know." She stood and began to circle the parlor, and when she spoke, she stumbled over her own words. "I . . . I want you to stay . . . I mean . . . I don't want you to go home. I don't want you to simply leave and never be heard from again." She pulled out a red-and-white hanky and blew her nose. "Ahhh! I don't know what to think!"

Marco flopped back against the pillow. "It won't be easy no

matter what happens, but we can figure out a way ... to ... to ... be together. I know we can."

She stared into his eyes, and a calmness came over her face. "I would like that, Marco, I truly would."

"Thank you, Rose. I was hoping you would say that." He put on an ear-to-ear smile.

Rose returned to the rocker, perched on the edge, and took Marco's hand. "What can I do?"

"We'll need a place to hide, at least for a while, and identification papers, and clothes."

"I can help with some of those things, but I don't think my Red Cross uniform carries enough weight to secure papers."

He chuckled and said, "I have an idea for how to get papers, but it might require the help of your uncle. Do you think he'll help?"

"You know Red has taken you two under his wing as though you're family. He'll do what he can."

Emily called from the kitchen, "Rose, time to gather the eggs! Leave that boy to rest."

Rose stood and moved the rocker back to its proper place, then turned to Marco and winked. "We'll talk more before the bus comes."

He heard her footsteps echo through the kitchen and the screen door slam. His heart was still pounding. He pulled his legs back up onto the couch and closed his eyes, but instead of sleep, he heard the voice of his father the day he left for basic training. *"In times of war, people find out the truth about themselves. Be brave, son, and let yourself be guided by courage."*

Marco smiled inwardly, knowing it would take courage to stay in America, to stay with Rose, but with her help, he believed it would happen. And Oskar and Red, they would help too.

34

MARCO

June 1936

"FERRY TO HARWICH LEAVING IN TEN MINUTES." The announcement came from a short, thin man in a dark-blue uniform carrying a red-and-white megaphone. He circulated the crowd and repeated the announcement in German, then French, and finally English. Passengers of all stripes, carrying bundles and leather bags and even small pieces of furniture, lined up behind a chained-off entrance to the gangplank. There were young mothers holding tiny children, old women with heads wrapped in thick scarves, over-dressed in long woolen coats much too warm for early June. These women, mostly Jews, pulled heavy suitcases tied up with rope, the clasps not strong enough to keep the stuffed contents from falling out.

Many in line were fleeing the wrath of the encroaching fascist policies in several countries. Their fear was palpable. They believed they may never return and wore as many layers of clothing as possible to smuggle out of Europe, much like wearing a suit of armor against the rising hatred. Most kept their eyes downcast and hands firmly glued to valises and canvas bags that often rattled from gold or silver heirlooms.

Several businessmen from Berlin wore three-piece suits and dapper fedoras, smoked American cigarettes, and carried thin briefcases with their initials engraved in gold plating. Small black-

and-red swastika pins were plainly visible on their lapels. They stood apart from the others out of a sense of superiority, and when the call for tickets came, they expected to be taken on board first.

Middle-aged parents speaking either French or German, perhaps Polish as well, formed a wall around their teenaged boys like musk ox, shielding them from the jaws of conscription. England, not yet a German enemy, was a beacon of light and a path of hope for those with the credentials to board. From the UK, many travelers would seek asylum in America or Canada or Australia.

As he neared the entrance to the pier, Johannes Mehlman scowled, then shouted at his son, "Your bag, you forgot your bag!" Eleven-year-old Marco dashed back to the café where they had stopped for a sandwich and pulled his canvas duffel from under the round table. He turned and sprinted, dodging dozens of passengers and colliding with a boy about his own age before returning to his father's side. "Stay close," his father reprimanded, "and don't tell anyone where you are from or where you are going. Understand? No one."

"Yes, father."

"Those men in business suits are not the only Germans in line. I heard others speaking the language as well." Johannes stared down at his son. "If there is to be a war, and I believe it will come soon, we will only be able to cross the Channel if people believe we are English. You must speak only English from now on. Better yet, to be safe, don't speak at all."

Marco nodded and turned away from his father just as the line began to inch forward. His mother bent down and straightened his collar. She wore a tight smile that didn't do a good job of hiding her nervousness. Crossing the Channel, crossing any border for that matter, was becoming more and more difficult. "Just let your father and I do the talking, and everything will be fine," she said softly in an attempt to reassure him. "Smile at strangers but don't say anything."

The ferry from Zeebrugge, Belgium, to Harwich, England, was built to transport railcars and for the first decade and a half of the twentieth century moved freight exclusively. But during the First World War, it became lucrative to ferry up to four hundred English soldiers and supplies to the fronts in France and Belgium.

After the war, the ships made accommodations for passengers, realizing that more profits could be made by allowing civilian walk-ons and freight cars. In 1936, a ferry could carry three hundred passengers and their luggage, though it was still a cramped and often wet and windswept crossing.

The Mehlmans moved slowly toward the quay and approaching gangplank. Two men, wearing dark-blue uniforms with black hats embroidered with red piping, checked papers. Until recently, the process of moving from one port to another had been a formality. The deckhands glanced at the tickets, and people scurried on board. But since the new Chancellor of Germany initiated new identification standards, the authorities everywhere were being more selective. German citizens now had new identification cards and passports indicating their racial characteristics, religious affiliation, and residency.

Johannes Mehlman's grandfather inherited a small family grist mill near Cologne in the middle of the nineteenth century. It became a source of income and stability for decades. Johannes's older brother Fredrick inherited the mill, but Johannes, who was expected to work for his brother, had different plans. He and his younger brother, Alphonse, moved into Cologne and worked for a small printing company, and when the owner retired, they bought the business. The brothers immediately expanded their line of products and markets, and the company grew quickly. Sales in England climbed steadily after the First World War, and Alphonse moved to England to take over the English division.

The Alphonse Mehlman branch of the family moved to

London's East End, historically a German enclave in the burgeoning metropolis, and although anti-German sentiment was high,
Alphonse learned English quickly and insisted his family follow
suit to assimilate as best they could. Marco and his parents visited
every summer for at least a month, and the Mehlman adults urged
that everyone speak English in public as well as at home. Marco's
cousins helped him by playing word games, reciting poetry in
German followed by the English translation, explaining idioms,
and telling jokes in English.

The weather was clear and the winds calm on this warm June
morning. Marco liked crossing the Channel; he watched for seabirds
and porpoise and tried to identify other ships' countries of origin by
the flags they flew.

An older couple, both wearing heavy winter coats and pulling
heavy suitcases, were directly in front of Marco and his parents.
When the couple came up to the checkpoint and handed over their
papers, a moment of silent staring by the uniformed guards halted
the line. Soon, a loud exchange of words, mostly in German and broken English, took place. The elderly couple seemed to speak to each
other in Polish. The inspectors, both in their early twenties, hesitated
and conferred with each other before demanding the couple stand
aside, not allowing them to walk up the gangplank. The older man
held out two tickets and tried to explain. One of the guards pushed
his hand away and pointed to the side, shouting at them to move.

It was at this moment, to Marco's astonishment, that his father stepped forward and asked the older couple if he could help.
Johannes knew enough Polish to be understood and listened as the
man explained. "Our name is Golberg, and we come from Krakow,
so the guards think we must be Jewish. They say they had to turn
away other Jews by the same name on a previous trip because they
were on some sort of list and couldn't enter England. But we are not
Jews. My wife and I have been Catholics all our lives."

Johannes nodded and turned to the inspectors. He spoke in English and explained to the guards the fact that their names may be the same as some Jews, but their religion is quite different. "My name is Mehlman, and my relatives have lived in England for decades, but I don't doubt there are others with the same name. It's a common mistake, and I believe these two are telling the truth."

The inspectors huddled for a moment, and then without a word gestured to the Poles to hand over their tickets and move onto the ferry. The Golbergs didn't hesitate but stepped quickly, pulling their suitcases loudly up the wooden gangplank.

Later, on board and safely out at sea, the Golbergs came up to Johannes and thanked him profusely. They wanted to give him a reward, a gift for helping them, but Johannes refused. They bowed and shuffled off.

When the boat pulled into Harwich and the disembarking was well underway, Johannes saw the couple again as they were greeted by several family members wearing yarmulkes, and he smiled to himself as he ushered his son and wife into a waiting car driven by his brother Alphonse.

35

MARCO

1939-1943

THE TRIPS TO ENGLAND STOPPED IN 1939 when Germany invaded Poland, and on September 3rd, England declared war on Germany. It was time for Marco to stop speaking English whenever he left his house and time to hide his love of English breakfast tea and bury his Manchester United soccer shirt at the back of his drawer. He didn't tell his World History teacher he had visited Stonehenge and walked along Hadrian's Wall and viewed reconstructed Viking villages sprinkled along the Scottish coast. Both his mother and father lectured him on the need to keep silent on the family's oversea business. When he wrote to his cousins, he had to wait until his father traveled far from Cologne to have them postmarked. Secrecy and caution became the watchwords.

Marco had close gymnasium friends who knew he had been to England, but he made them swear on an eagle's feather that they would not tell anyone. It didn't take much coaxing since two of his friends, David Moskowitz and Adam Lerner, were Jews and Johan Baxter had an English grandmother. Everyone he knew seemed to have something to hide, and all were willing to play along for safety reasons. To ensure none of his neighbors would talk, Marco joined the Hitler Youth on the insistence of his parents.

"Just nod and wink," said his mother. "You can put up with most anything if you just nod and wink. Don't make waves that may get you and your family into trouble." She pulled her doughy hands from the big tin bowl she used to make bread. Her dark hair had several streaks of gray that she tried to keep harnessed behind her ears, but when she kneaded the dough with her fingers and punched it with her fist, her hair came undone and hung down into her eyes. "You need to have a good education if you are going to make anything of yourself in this world. It's important you do well in school and rise above suspicion." She slammed the dough with a hard left jab.

"If we don't die in a war first," replied Marco.

"Your father survived the last war, and we both made it through the flu epidemic. I think our chances are good."

"Hitler wasn't the boss in those days."

"He wasn't. But we Mehlmans are a hearty stock, and we can make it. Just don't let anyone outside this house hear you say anything negative about the Führer."

"I won't."

"Good boy. I know this is a trying time, but it'll get better."

Marne Mehlman was an optimist. She couldn't help it; her parents encouraged her to enjoy life from an early age. Her father owned a small grocery in a town called Treudorf, population 850, sitting in the cleavage of a verdant valley just a couple miles from the Danish border. The community was made up of Germans and Danes who had settled in the area for centuries before the borders were established. The local cemetery revealed its long history of mixed ethnicity. One half was dotted with headstones reading family names like Krug, Drexler, Graff, Schmitt, and Shultz, while the other half of the plots sported monuments dedicated to the Larsens, Agards, Andersens, Hansens, and Olsens.

Main Street of Treudorf went unpaved until 1920, and most of the shops still sported striped awnings and flower boxes of geraniums protruding from the windows on the second floor. Marne and her sister worked behind the counter at the family dry goods store until they were eighteen. Her father, a devout Lutheran, believed in the goodness of people, and everyone in town knew he would never let anyone go hungry, even if they couldn't pay. He carried credit for poor families for many years without demanding a settlement.

When Marne pointed out that they were losing money on certain accounts, her father remarked, "People will pay me if they can. If not, they will make me much richer in heaven," and smiled softly.

"I hope we don't go hungry," Marne muttered.

"You may not understand now, but the world is a wonderful place, and someday you will understand that respect from others is much more valuable than gold." He stared down at her with piercing emerald-green eyes.

Marne adored her parents and family but had an insatiable urge to explore a wider world. Her parents were strong believers in education and were often engaged in the evening reading a book, newspaper, or magazine. After high school, Marne enrolled in the Cologne Business School for Women and learned bookkeeping, filing, and dictation. After a year's training, she took a job in a local printing shop that was on course to expand by two ambitious and handsome brothers. Johannes Mehlman was a kind and dashing boss, and soon after her employment, they fell in love, their lives forever sealed.

After the dough was cut and rounded and set into the pans, Marne opened the oven and placed all five pans inside, three on the top shelf and two on the bottom. Then she wiped her hands on her black-and-silver apron and pushed her hair behind her ears. "I laid your Hitler Youth uniform out on your bed, Marco, because tomorrow is Wednesday and it would not be taken kindly if you were to forget."

At first, Marco protested wearing the uniform to school. The camping and swimming and hikes were okay, but the propaganda meetings were not. When the school year started, most of the boys wore their uniforms to school on the first Wednesday. He refused. A firm lecture by his parents persuaded him to participate. "It's only for appearances," his father stated. "It won't kill you to blend in with the rest. But it may kill you if you don't."

A week later, he consented and realized the girls who were members of the German Girls League wore uniforms on Wednesday too. In the second semester of the 1941 school year, patriotic songs were added to the curriculum, sung twice a week at the start of first period. Students were directed to stand and at least mouth the words if not sing loudly.

Several teachers demanded all students stand when they entered the room and hold out their right arms in salute. When the teacher barked, "For Germany and Hitler!" the students responded in unison with "Heil!" And class could begin.

Several of Marco's close friends disappeared from the gymnasium rolls before graduation. At first, he believed they had taken graduation tests early or had been admitted to a university. But by second semester of his eleventh year, he realized the missing students were Jews and later learned the Cologne School Board had expelled all Jews from the public schools. Some teachers were also let go. Those who were not Jews but were still turned away may have been seen associating with known Communists. If the Social Democrats wrote an editorial or letter in the newspaper criticizing the government in any way, it was tantamount to treason.

Bernard Hauptman was Marco's favorite instructor. He taught Modern German Literature and Poetry Writing. The approved literary works he could use in class were seriously trimmed by the school board, who were toadies to the Nazi party. Hauptman allowed his students to read additional texts as "supplementary works" and encouraged his students to think creatively, which often led to digressions into ideas both fascinating and progressive, but dangerous. Hauptman was neither Jewish nor a Communist. He didn't openly criticize or use disparaging language against any of the Nazi educational policies. At first glance, he seemed to be a perfect example of the *new* German teacher.

One day, Hauptman was discussing the works of Fredrich Nietzsche when two men strolled into class unannounced. They wore the black dress uniforms of the SS. They didn't say anything but merely nodded at Herr Hauptman, and the three walked out. Marco and the other students rushed to the windows and looked down as Hauptman was placed in the back seat of a dark Mercedes and whisked away. Hauptman, a wonderful teacher and idol in Marco's eyes, was never seen again in Cologne.

The next day in German Lit class, Marco and his fellow students were introduced to a replacement teacher in a brown SA uniform. He was at least sixty years old and hard of hearing. When he read a poem aloud to the class, he stumbled and mispronounced several words. Growing frustrated at his own lack of understanding, he shoved the book off the podium and with his rough hands tore the page from the book. From his briefcase, he produced a copy of *Mein Kampf* and started to read aloud from page one.

Early graduation came in the spring of 1943. Though only completing the eleventh level, boys were turned out to join the army. Seventeen-year-old Marco Mehlman achieved an award for high academic honors. Johannes and Marne were proud and pleased with Marco's efforts to learn and stay out of trouble at the same time.

The Mehlmans celebrated Marco's achievement by dining at The Boar's Head, one of the finer restaurants in Cologne that managed to stay open during the war. Marco ordered sweet and sour pork, cabbage flecked with anise seeds, and brown bread with butter and apple strudel. The war had made many foods impossible to find, so Marco savored every mouthful. After a dessert of chocolate cherry cake, real coffee was served.

"Son, now that your schooling is behind you, and we all hope this war will be over soon, have you given any more thought to what you want to do?"

Marco let his lips linger on the edge of the porcelain coffee cup, then said, "I think I might like to teach."

Marne raised her perfectly manicured eyebrows. "With all the restrictions placed on teachers today? This is hardly the environment for academics."

"I would follow the techniques of Herr Hauptman. He was an awesome teacher."

Johannes leaned over and said quietly, "But, son, look what happened to him. There are a thousand other possibilities . . ."

Just then, two SA officers appeared at their table. The taller man with thick biceps and a barrel chest asked, "Marco Mehlman?"

"That's me," Marco replied, his hand raised slightly.

"The Fatherland needs you," declared the shorter man, sporting a thin, black moustache that appeared to be drawn on his acne-scarred face with a grease pencil. "Make the Führer proud." He laid a sealed envelope on Marco's coffee saucer, saluted, and the two retreated without another word.

Marco knew what the letter was all about.

"They could have waited until tomorrow," said Marne. "The war is not going to be lost or won in the next twelve hours."

"Open it," encouraged Johannes. "Let's find out how long you have."

Marco slid a knife through the top of the envelope and pulled out a single sheet of paper. He perused it quickly and looked to his parents. "I leave in three days."

36

DANIEL

2019

HIS ARMS ACHED FROM TOO MUCH JUGGLING. 43 minutes and 30 seconds, and finally he let the balls drop. Only 10 days until his story needed to be submitted, and he was experiencing writer's block. Like a column of military vehicles out of fuel and stopped in the middle of the road, Daniel's head was choked with questions. He needed answers to move forward.

The first few pages flowed like honey, sentence after sentence, descriptive words, facts mixed with fiction, producing vivid mental images of Mark's physical characteristics. He even wrote about life at the BRC and the community of Oakwood as a whole during the war years 1940-1945. It came together easily early on.

However, his protagonist, Mark, was still an enigma. Daniel had sketched out a dozen questions to ask Mark, but he needed the perspective of others, those who knew him as a young man and later when he was teaching. He wanted to find out about his wife, maybe interview a social friend or colleague. The history of Mark Flour was more difficult to uncover than the genesis of Stonehenge.

One day during his lunch break, he shared his frustration with Mr. Jensen. "You know I'm writing a story for the statewide contest."

"How's it coming?"

"Not as smoothly as I hoped. I know Mark Flour as a ninety-year-old resident of the nursing home . . ."

"He's your main character?" Mr. Jensen asked.

"He is, but I don't know his background, at least not as much as I want. I need more information, firsthand research, eyewitness accounts."

Mr. Jensen was sympathetic but explained that Mr. Flour had retired so many years earlier that neither he nor any of the present teaching staff had worked with him. "I met him a couple of times in social settings, mostly retirement parties, but we didn't exchange much more than pleasantries. After he retired, from what I can gather, he was a bit of a recluse. I never met his wife. I think she's been dead for several decades, and as far as I know, he had no children or siblings, at least no family living locally."

Daniel shrugged his shoulders and set his salad on the desktop. He picked a hardboiled egg out of a plastic container, sprinkled some Pacific sea salt on it, and bit slowly. "There must be someone," he said.

Mr. Jensen took in a deep breath and sighed heavily. "Perhaps Bob Manion. This is just a wild guess, mind you. He was a janitor in this building for nearly fifty years. He might be able to tell you something. He's still invited to all the end-of-the-year faculty parties and is very popular with the teaching staff. I got to know Bob a bit before he retired, oh, about ten years ago, I guess. I still see him once in a while at a high school band concert or football game. He's living right behind the school on Custer Street. He has a little gray-and-white schnauzer and walks it in the morning when most of us are pulling into the parking lot."

Daniel wrote his name in a spiral notebook.

"You could stop in and ask him if he remembers Mr. Flour. He's an affable man."

"I don't like going to strange houses," Daniel said.

"Consider him one of the high school staff. He won't bite."

"But his dog might. And I'm allergic to certain animal fur."

Mr. Jensen scratched the back of his neck. "Would you like me to invite him for lunch, here, with us?"

"Yes."

"Okay. I'll stop by after school and see what he says."

"It has to be soon."

"I know, you're on a deadline. Hopefully he can come tomorrow or Friday."

Daniel wiped the desktop with a Wet One and put his containers in his lunch bag, then zipped his backpack. "I'll write up some questions to ask Mr. Manion." He nodded and walked out just as the bell rang.

The next day at 11:09, Daniel walked into room 1109, notebook in hand, backpack slung over his left shoulder, and juggling balls at the ready in his dungarees. Mr. Jensen was seated behind his wooden desk, wearing a burgundy cardigan sweater with leather patches on the elbows. His penny loafers were resting prominently on a pile of essays covering the early Macedonian Empire. He flashed a welcoming smile and dropped his feet to the floor. "Come in, Daniel."

"I'm already in."

"This is Bob Manion." He swung his arm toward a petite man with silver hair and a full beard.

Mr. Manion was sitting on a yellow plastic chair. He stood when Daniel approached and held out his right hand. He was dressed in jeans and a brown-and-orange checkered flannel shirt, eyes cobalt-blue and teeth straight and too white, probably dentures. His hand sported deep fissures and knuckles that were oversized.

A second chair, green plastic, was a meter from Mr. Manion's, and Daniel sat without shaking hands. "I have some questions for Mr. Manion. Mr. Bob Manion." Daniel focused on the spiral notebook which he had opened, and he held his ballpoint upright in his left hand. "Can we start?"

Bob Manion sat back down and rested both hands in his lap. Mr. Jensen had prepped him about Daniel's habits and idiosyncrasies. He didn't appear nervous at all. "Alright, young man, shoot."

Daniel's eyes darted up, and for a moment, he thought he was asking for a physical display. He looked at Mr. Jensen, who had a soft, lazy smile, almost a smirk. Daniel returned to his notebook and asked his first question. "Mr. Manion . . ."

"Please, call me Bob."

Daniel didn't look up but started again. "Okay. Bob . . ."

"Good."

"Did you know Mark Flour?"

"I did. I cleaned his room almost every afternoon for over twenty years. Lots of the days, he was in his room when I came in, say, about four o'clock or so. We often chatted about this or that. Sometimes he was correcting papers or planning lessons for the next day, so I cleaned the room without talking. He was a good teacher. At least, that's what all the kids and other teachers told me."

"Did you know his wife or any family members?"

"When I first met Mark, his wife had already passed away. But she was a real beauty, I know, because he had a picture of her on his desk. Well, it was not placed on his desk for everyone to see . . . it was hidden."

Daniel stopped writing and looked up. "What do you mean, hidden?"

"It was kinda by mistake I saw it. One day, I was wiping some crumbs from his desk. He often brought cookies or graham crackers with butter; he had a bit of a sweet tooth, I think. Anyway, one day I accidentally knocked over a picture Mr. Flour kept in a small glass frame on his desk. It was a photograph of him receiving some sort of teaching award, and when it hit the floor, the glass shattered. I felt really bad about that. When I picked up the frame, the picture of him getting the award popped out, and then I saw it . . . another photo was hidden behind. That was the picture of a pretty young woman. There were some words written on the back . . ."

"What did the words say?" Daniel asked.

Bob pushed his eyes to the top of his sockets and recited, "My dearest Rose, my dearest love, you are so beautiful and I miss you so much." He settled back in his chair and crossed his arms over his chest. "After all these years, I'll never forget those words."

Daniel raised his head and stared into Bob's deep-set eyes, now glimmering like two sunlit ponds. "Bob, did you ever ask Mark about his wife?"

"I didn't. I figured if he wanted people to know about Rose, he would have put her photo front an' center. I swept up the broken glass and told him about how it fell off when I was cleaning, but I put his wife's picture behind the other like I never saw it."

Daniel breathed in deeply and tilted his head, eyes back on the notebook. "In your words, what kind of a man was Mr. Flour?"

"Humph." Bob's cheeks above the gray beard were flushed a fire-engine red. "He was quiet, kind, never demanding . . . and friendly. He never said an unkind word to me in all the years I worked there. As I said, his students liked him; many came to his room after the last class just to visit or hang out. I had to sweep around them. Made my job a bit more challenging, but for Mark, I would have done anything."

"Did he ever show anger? Did he ever get upset?"

"Nope. Not that I recall. I mean, he could discipline his students when they needed it. His classes always seemed under control."

"Did . . ."

"Wait!" Bob leaned forward and shook his right index finger. "One time, that's right, one time I seen him get testy. It was back in the seventies. There was a war that was just over . . ."

"The Vietnam Conflict," Mr. Jensen interjected.

Bob's eyes shot up. "Right. Anyway, there was an Army recruiter guy that came to Mark's room during the morning, while classes were going on. He wanted to speak to a couple of boys, and Mark would have none of it. I was mopping up a water spill down the hall. I heard Mark telling the Army guy in no uncertain words to leave and report to the office."

"They still talk about that incident around here," Mr. Jensen chipped in. "But I didn't know it was Mark who put his foot down. We have strict policies regulating recruiting these days."

"Well, back then, the Army seemed to think it could do whatever it wanted," Bob went on. "And the recruiter guy didn't want to leave until he talked to the boys. So . . ."

"I heard Mark smacked him," Mr. Jensen said with a sense of astonishment and glanced at Daniel, who still wore a stone face.

"No. Mark wouldn't ever do that." Bob shook his head. "But he did call the principal, who came lickety-split and escorted the Army recruiter out of the area. I asked him after school what that was all about, and he told me he hated the idea of the draft, ya know, conscription he called it. Wished there was no such thing as forcing young guys to go fight. Seemed strange to me, him being a World War II vet and all. And a POW to boot. Though he never talked about his war experiences. I thought it kinda weird, his opinion about the Army, that is, but hey, Mark was such a nice guy I didn't hold it against him or anything."

Daniel studied his notebook, then asked, "Anything else you want to tell me about Mr. Flour?"

"Nothing comes to mind . . . maybe when I get home . . ."

Daniel picked up his backpack and walked swiftly out the door before Bob could finish his thought.

37

THE ALZHEIMER'S ROUND TABLE

2019

HELEN PEERED OVER THE TOP of her turtle shell glasses, holding John's manuscript close to her nose. She squinted as her head bobbed slightly. "I like chapter two, John. You are an excellent carpenter, that's evident. I don't know anyone who can build a house singlehandedly; that's quite an accomplishment."

John cleared his throat and muttered, "I had no business being the general contractor on that job."

"Why do you say that? You provided a house for a whole family, didn't you?" Emma asked.

"I did, but I hardly knew what end of a hammer to hold at that time. I was in my twenties and had been working with a crew of really good guys, men who could build anything. They knew plumbing, electricity, and a well-constructed square corner when they saw it." He held his hands out as though he was preaching. "But me, I was just a gopher." His palms turned skyward. "They'd tell me to pound this nail or cut that piece of wood, and I did it." He shook his head and let his eyes sink to the table. "I had no business, no business at all."

Eva pushed her plate of marshmallow Rice Krispies treats toward John. "So how come you took the job?"

"A friend of my cousin came up to me when I was in the grocery store and asked if I built houses." John raised his head and let a grimace form.

"And you couldn't say no?" asked Marie.

"I wanted to say no, I really did. But Maureen and me just got married and had one kid and another on the way, and I just saw dollar signs."

"Ambition is not always a bad thing." said Eva.

"You're right, I guess. I was too young and stupid to know what I was getting into. God knows we needed the extra money. We hardly had a pot to pee in."

"Well," Eva added, "as I understand it, the house is still standing and some family lives there now. So, don't beat yourself up too much."

"Yeah, it's still there. At least the last time I rode past it was." John bit into a Rice Krispies bar and nodded. "Lopsided corners and all."

"The friend of your cousin threw quite a housewarming party, at least that's what you wrote on page . . ." Emma shuffled papers noisily. ". . . four, and you were invited. They must have been happy enough with your work to ask you to their party."

"I didn't put everything in the story."

"The party didn't go well?" Helen asked.

"Nah, the party was great." John's face brightened. "Lots of beer and brats and hamburgers and potato salads. Quite the shindig, actually. Most of the people there I knew, since they were friends of my cousin. I brought the wife with me, and she got loaded, and we had to leave early, but that's another story."

"So what went wrong?" Eva asked.

"See, I was in the kitchen getting a beer out of the fridge, and when I turned, I knocked a glass of beer over, spilling it all over the Formica counter."

Marie looked up at her daughter. "I spill something at every meal, it seems."

"It wouldn't have been a big deal except the beer ran off the countertop like Niagara Falls. It was so uneven, a carpenter's nightmare."

"I can see how that could be embarrassing," added Helen.

"I don't make a habit of admitting to being wrong, but I spent most of the week after the party fixing mistakes I should have done better the first time around. If it weren't for that beer spill, the family would've spread the word that they had a horrible home builder and my reputation would've been in the toilet."

"Good for you!" Marie said. "You did the right thing. And I'm sure you didn't lose any customers."

"I guess. Main thing is I learned and didn't make as many mistakes in the future." John fell silent for a long moment, brooding. "Leastwise, not carpenter mistakes. Wish all my mistakes were as easy to fix as an uneven countertop."

Marie's eyes lowered in sadness. "What else went wrong, John?"

"I made a bigger mistake, and it was my own fault." He faltered and let his hands fall to his lap. "I was all about work and the guys, and stopping at the tavern afterwards . . . and eventually . . . I lost, lost my wife and . . . lost my kids."

The room grew still. One of the overhead fluorescent tube lights flickered, followed by a ticking sound. The analog clock showed three minutes to five.

"But that's a story I might . . . and I'm only saying I might . . . share some day."

Eva picked her mother's glasses off the end of her nose and polished them with the sleeve of her light-maroon sweater. She placed them carefully back where she found them. Meanwhile, Marie bit off a tiny piece of the Rice Krispies bar as though she needed to make the rest of the bar last all night long.

Emma's chair squealed when she turned to look at the clock. "Daniel will be here in exactly . . ." She scrunched up her nose. ". . . two minutes."

"Does he know about Mark?" Marie asked. But before anyone could answer, she dropped the Rice Krispies bar on the table, and it broke into several pieces. "Oh my. I'm sorry."

Eva gathered the pieces and placed them on her mother's napkin. "No harm, Mother."

"Helen?" John asked. "You say anything to the kid?"

"I was hoping his mother received a call from Mrs. Andrews, our social worker. That's what social workers are supposed to do. She knows Daniel is a friend of Mark's." Her fingers curled on the tabletop like a nest of worms.

"Well, if he doesn't already know about Mark, the kid's gonna go apeshit when he hears."

"Thanks, John," Helen scowled.

"Just calling it like it is."

"Is Mark up to seeing anyone?" asked Eva.

"I stopped in his room for a few minutes before coming over here," Helen replied. "He was awake and lucid. All things considered, I think he would enjoy a visit."

"Even Daniel?" asked Emma.

"Him most of all," bellowed John. "Mark and the kid have a special relationship. Don't ask me why; they're like popular opposites, but they get along."

"That's *polar* opposites," Helen interjected.

John wrinkled his nose. "What does the North Pole have to do with it?"

Eva suddenly lifted her head and raised both hands palms out, announcing loudly, "Hello, Daniel."

Daniel walked into the room and stood at the place usually occupied by Mark's wheelchair. He was wearing faded dungarees and an orange-and-maroon polo shirt. His backpack was slung over his left shoulder, and his cheeks were flushed and eyes fluttering. He seemed to sense that something was awry. "Mark's not here," he said flatly.

Those sitting around the table seemed as mannequins, or mimes, unable to move or speak, conveying their anxiety in their stillness. Finally, Helen broke the silence. "No, he's not here. He blacked out Saturday night at dinner and was taken to the hospital. He's back now and resting comfortably."

Helen's words seemed to open the floodgates, and John blurted, "He's in the *Mortuary* because he's got cancer, least that's what the hospital docs say. He's in tough shape. Ain't no other way to say it, the guy's hurting."

"It was a mess, alright," Marie added. "He fell over right at the dinner table."

John slapped the table, and everybody winced. "Splat! Right into the Manhattan clam chowder."

Marie continued, "I picked his head out before he drowned. It was awful."

"I think he can beat the cancer," John said with confidence. "It's the clams. He's gotta be allergic to the clams."

"Don't be ridiculous, John. The diagnosis is pancreatic cancer. Clams had nothing to do with it," Emma insisted.

"Ahhhh!" John swiped at the air and turned away. "What do doctors know? Could've been rotten clams."

Daniel was staring at his low-cut Converse tennis shoes. When he lifted his head, he scrutinized the faces of the others and asked, "John said a mortuary. A mortuary is a resting place for the dead. Is he dead?"

"He's not dead, far from it," Helen reassured him.

John butted in, "The staff calls it the Mortuary 'cause when residents go there, they come out with a sheet over their face, if you get my drift. It's a room full of gadgets and tubes and crazy equipment."

"It's like a hospital room where a person can receive critical care," Emma confided.

John chimed in, "Until you don't need care no more."

"The prognosis?" Daniel asked no one in particular.

Helen spoke up, "He's weak and full of tubes . . ."

"Like a human Chia Pet!" John hollered.

Helen continued, "But I visited him a couple hours ago, and he was awake and talking. I think you can see him."

"Don't be afraid. Go to him," Marie encouraged. "He wants to help you win the writing contest."

Without another word, Daniel turned and left the room. The fluorescent ceiling light was blinking faster, and the clicking sounded louder.

"There he goes, the boy wonder writer who needs to end his story, to the man whose life is coming to an end." John picked up his manuscript, took two Rice Krispies treats from the plate, and shuffled out before anyone could respond.

38

DANIEL AND MARK

2019

THE ROOM THE STAFF CALLED THE MORTUARY was located at the end of the hall on the first floor. It was equipped with an oversized hospital bed, oxygen, two sinks, and shelves of gauze, bandages, linens, rubber gloves, and extra blankets. It had no windows and extra fluorescent lighting that bounced off the scrubbed floor. If it was intended to be bright, it was, for the glare was almost overwhelming.

The outside door had a large sign which announced PRIVATE, and Daniel halted before opening. He was anxious to talk to Mark, but afraid in what shape he might find him. Daniel knew the effects that harsh drugs could place on the body. Would a sharp mind become addled? Would Mark be drooling at the corners of his mouth? Would he even remember Daniel and the story he was writing? He pulled the juggling balls out and pushed them up the sleeve of his sweatshirt, just in case. Then he opened the door a sliver and stepped in.

The door closed quietly behind him. A large hospital bed was in the center of the room, flanked by several monitoring devices. The room temperature was high and felt even warmer as a humidifier was running in the corner, making the air moist. Mark appeared to be sleeping, his head turned away slightly and his blanket pulled tight to his neck.

Daniel couldn't shake an odd feeling coursing through his veins. Two months ago, he had been on familiar turf, planning his daily routines at home and at school, viewing familiar television programs, reading and writing science fiction, and, of course, bolstered by the daily support and interaction from his mother. But now he was consumed with the lives of a group of residents in their eighties and nineties dealing with end-of-life issues. In this nursing home of all places, he was struck by the realization that people can't run from themselves regardless of their physical or mental makeup, no matter their age.

There were times Daniel really thought he'd be able to forget himself and wake to a life filled with *normality*, i.e. close friends, a functional family, job opportunities, and little or no loneliness. Didn't most people think that? If you didn't like the life you were dealt, there was always the option of running away from yesterday's cruel opinions and bullies and crushing social constraints. He had a recurring dream about his sister, what she would be like as a teenager, how she would look and what her interests would be. He saw the two of them laughing and keeping secrets from parents and peers. She was a confidant. She accepted him wholeheartedly. He wished to return to the dream each night if for no other reason than to have someone to talk to.

But in the morning light, with eyes still crusted from sleep, his dreams evaporated like the steam from the teapot, and the same problems raised their ugly heads. His school days were spent in avoidance, socially at least. A few precious moments with Mr. Jensen and his books and writing were the only avenue of contentment. For three and three-quarters years of high school, this had been his world.

But it changed the moment he walked into the BRC. Mark and the ART group allowed Daniel to believe he could change. If not now, then one day. It could happen. Hopes of *fitting in* had lain dormant for years but were not unfounded or entirely forgotten.

The ART group accepted him as a seventeen-year-old teenager with autism born with an awesome brain and the ability to rearrange his shadow.

His time spent with Mark made him temporarily forget his own troubles and realize that Mark's fate as a seventeen-year-old conscript sent to a foreign desert in a lousy war carrying a gun to shoot other young men was a far scarier experience. This old man in the Mortuary bed survived, and so could he. At this very moment, the strange feeling of confidence gave him goose bumps by making him believe in himself and his ability to stand tall in the faces of those who would heap pity on him.

Mark opened his eyes and turned his head. "*Guten tag*, Daniel." He pulled himself up and raised the head of the bed. An IV tube was dangling from a metal stand, and the pouch of clear liquid allowed a slow drip to flow through the needle taped to his wrist. "Come in. Come in. Don't be a stranger. It's still me, at least for the present." Mark's voice was weak, but his smile was strong. His eyes were shiny, the color of chipped coal.

Daniel walked slowly toward him.

"I was hoping you'd visit. I thought maybe you'd be afraid to . . . well . . . just be afraid. Anyway, pull up a chair so we can talk."

Daniel stared at the bed and IV and turned slowly to survey the rest of the room. Then he pulled a blue plastic chair to Mark's bedside. After he set his backpack down, he pulled the juggling balls from his sleeve.

"I don't think you'll need those," Mark said. "I'm not crossing the River Styx just yet."

Daniel stared into Mark's watery eyes. "Do you have any gold coins?"

"Sorry, no," he cackled.

"The ferryman on the River Styx won't take you without payment," Daniel said.

"Good! I have no money." Mark flashed a smile. "I'm a pauper, a ward of the state, and hope to remain that way for some time."

Daniel managed a thin smile too. He pushed the juggling balls back into his sleeve and pulled out his spiral notebook. The creases on Mark's forehead and the bluish half-moons under his eyes were distinct. "You don't look too good."

"I had an episode on Saturday night," Mark said.

"I know. The ART group told me."

"Of course." With his right hand, Mark pulled the pillow behind his head up a little. "Did the ART folks give you any details?"

"John thinks you're allergic to clams."

Mark laughed deeply until a cough flared up and made him stop. Both eyes let a little teardrop escape from the corners. When he caught his breath, he said, "It's John's way of coping. He's afraid I might die before him. He's lonely and doesn't want to admit it."

"I like John."

"I know you do, and he cares for you too. He's brusque, obnoxious, and can get in trouble with his comments sometimes, but underneath he's kind." Another small tear pushed out at the edge of Mark's eye.

Daniel pulled a pen from the binding of the spiral notebook and opened the cover. With his eyes focused on the lined paper, he said quietly, "Helen believes the diagnosis is pancreatic cancer."

"That's what the doctors say. Tests seem to confirm it." Mark's voice was filled with resignation. "I'll bet you can tell me more about my condition. It's alright if you do."

Daniel recited as though reading a medical journal. "Acute cases of pancreatic cancer can be fatal within a week. The average is two to four weeks. Remission is rare. Drug therapy is recommended but has little effect on longevity . . ." He stopped suddenly and looked toward the ceiling. "I'd like to juggle now."

"Go ahead, I don't mind."

For the next few minutes, Daniel juggled, first sitting in the chair, then standing and walking about the room. When he returned to his chair, he sat and plucked the balls out of the air like a frog flicking its sticky tongue to pull in moths. When the balls were safely stowed in the pockets of his backpack, he picked up his pen again, placed the notebook on his lap, and stared straight ahead.

After a long pause, Mark realized he was waiting for him to continue his story. "We need to move forward, don't we? Tell me where you are in your writing."

A slight nod and tiny upturn from his lips signaled Daniel was ready to get down to business. "I'm embellishing your life with some fictional parts. Mostly historical fiction. Since I didn't live when you were young, I have to imagine what it was like and what people might say, and how people dressed, and what was important in their lives."

Mark pulled himself up even straighter, shaking the IV stand. He coughed for a moment, then cleared his throat and spit into a folded gauze pad. When he finished, he said, "Let me recap what I've told you so far and what I believe you've written, and if I get it wrong, you can tell me. Okay?"

"I'm ready."

"Is the main character in your story a young man who was drafted into the army during the Second World War?"

"Yes, he is."

"And was this unfortunate soldier captured by the enemy and sent off to a POW camp in another country?"

"He was captured in North Africa."

"A dismal place. And after the war, doesn't he become a high school language teacher?"

"Teaches German for nearly forty years."

"And doesn't this soldier, later a teacher, retire to a retirement community to live out his remaining days surrounded by a bunch of memoir-writing author wannabes?"

Daniel turned a page in his notebook and let his finger trace the lines on the page. "Okay."

"Just okay?" Mark held a tight frown. "You don't seem too excited about your protagonist's life adventures. How come?"

Daniel sighed loudly and stood. He watched the tiny drops of clear liquid slide down the plastic tube into Mark's vein. He turned to Mark with a face full of consternation. "Seven million American men were in uniform during World War II, and over 120,000 became POWs. My main character could have been any one of those. I need more details and more tension to make my story become something other than the plight of POWs in general, which can be found in Wikipedia."

Mark pursed his lips and let his chin sag to his chest. "I warned you my story was dull."

"But it's not the whole story!" Mark had not heard Daniel raise his voice before. His frustration was palpable. Daniel continued in a demanding tone, "What haven't you told me?"

"What makes you think there's more?"

Daniel circled the chair, then slapped the notebook on the seat and walked over to the cabinet with the medical supplies. He opened a drawer and looked down on scissors, a stethoscope, a blood pressure cup, thermometers, and other rudimentary instruments. A moment later, he closed the drawer and walked back to his chair, pulled the notebook to his chest, and sat down heavily. He put his hands and the notebook in his lap and looked at the ceiling and breathed in deeply. "Photos."

"Photos? What photos?"

"The photos that aren't in room 409. The photos of your wife, family, army buddies, and most important . . . Mark Flour in uniform."

"What are you saying? I have no photos."

"I haven't been in a lot of homes in my life, I admit, but everyone I ever visited has personal photos hanging on walls or resting on coffee tables or framed above the fireplace. You have none." He brought his gaze from the ceiling and bore in on Mark. "You were a POW. There should be pictures of you, framed newspaper accounts with local politicians, black-and-white photos with war buddies, color photos of you receiving citations, you and . . ."

Mark stopped him. "Enough! I junked that military stuff decades ago."

Daniel's voice rose even higher as his eyebrows flew up. "Why?"

"I told you, I hated the army."

"But you were a . . ."

"Don't say it!" Now it was Mark's turn to raise his voice. "I was not a hero!" He said each word slowly and emphatically. "I was a survivor, that's all. People want heroes, I get that, but I'm not their man."

"John thinks . . ."

Again, Mark interrupted. "John represents a whole tribe of people who need to emulate the characteristics of others. They want to live vicariously through the lives and deeds of men and women who find themselves in a point and place in history that forces them to do things they otherwise would never think to do. And most of the deeds are foolhardy, but some, precious few, are heroic. He thinks of me as someone I'm not. I don't want to hurt his feelings, but if I were honest, wholly truthful . . . I . . . I can't explain it to him . . . I think . . . well, I think the truth would hurt him," Mark said and closed his eyes. "I don't want to hurt anyone."

Daniel closed his notebook. "I know you had a picture of your wife hidden on your school desk. I interviewed a former custodian, Bob Manion."

Mark was taken aback for a moment. "Bob Manion. I haven't seen him in years. You saw him, and talked to him?"

"Yes."

"How is he?"

"Okay. It's safe to say he's . . . older."

"That he is. What did he say about my Rose?"

"Not much. He discovered, quite by accident, the hidden picture of your wife you kept on your school desk. At least, he thought it was your wife."

"It was my wife, Rose, alright. I have that photo, still hidden. I may show it to you someday. What else have you learned about me on your own?"

After a moment, Daniel continued, "I hacked into your medical records and found you have private health insurance as well as Medicare, but no history of VA visits or any medical opportunities offered by the military. You also have no Army combat life insurance policy in force today, and you didn't take one out in the '40s . . . nothing. Ninety-eight percent of soldiers who went overseas took out a combat life insurance policy. Am I looking in the wrong places?"

"You won't find anything," Mark whispered. "And you're confused, I can imagine. You're a smart young man who has collected the facts, arranged the numbers in an algorithm, and they don't add up. You aren't used to working a math problem when the answer keeps coming up wrong. The Mark Flour you've come to know is not the Mark Flour the data supports. His history is all wrong, at least the history you were able to find. I'm sorry, Daniel. Your brain must be like the hamster on the wheel."

"I don't have any pets. I'm allergic to most fur."

Mark laughed despite himself and flashed a smile. "Must have been difficult for a nature lover like you. I notice how often you stare at the birds on the feeder and the trees and flowers outside."

"I watch the nature programs on public television every week wishing I could be closer to the animals."

There was a long moment of silence before Mark said with emotion, "You have made my life in the past few months so interesting, so challenging. I hate the fact it can't go on much longer."

The two fell into their own thoughts. Daniel opened his notebook and doodled with the pen. Mark looked up and studied his IV pouch. He put his finger to his lips, then turned quickly to Daniel. "Let's go for a walk!"

"Are you sure?"

"I'm sure. I'm sick, not dead."

Daniel helped Mark into a wheelchair. Then he pushed the chair and the IV cart to the door. Daniel struggled to open the heavy door and get the wheelchair and the IV cart out, but when he did, Mark laughed and shouted, "I am Lazarus! Look at me! I've rolled away the tombstone!"

Daniel couldn't help but snicker. "I wish John could see you now. He doesn't think anyone leaves the Mortuary unless they're covered in a white sheet."

Mark raised his arms as high as the IV would allow. "I am Steve McQueen in *The Great Escape*!"

"I watched that movie six times."

"Mush, Sancho Panza! Onward we go to defeat windmills."

"I've read *Don Quixote* in Spanish."

"I am one of the escapees of Alcatraz, on my way to the sunroom!"

"I think they drowned at sea," Daniel countered.

"Supposedly."

"Right. *Supposedly*."

"They might still be living among us. Maybe John . . . he's led a checkered life. He could have found a way to break out of prison . . . or . . ."

"Or . . ."

". . . or maybe he talked his way out."

Daniel laughed a full-throated laugh. "Who else?"

"I am the ghost of Hamlet's father come back to reveal the truth!"

"Nice! His brother was a nasty man."

Together they walked the hallway, reeling off as many references of dead souls come back to life or famous escapes from dire circumstances as they could. Their smiles were plastered on their faces, and the staff and residents they passed were speechless.

When they wheeled into the sunroom, Daniel pulled close to the picture window. Mark exclaimed, "Here! Here! Stop here. Open that window."

Daniel unlocked the window and flung it open as far as it could go. "How's that?"

"Oh, it feels so good to breathe fresh air." After several deep breaths, Mark went on, "Thank you, Daniel. Thank you for helping me escape that dreadful room and dreary thoughts of my past, if only for a few minutes."

Daniel pulled up a wooden rocking chair with bright yellow cushions. "Has your past been that bad?"

Mark shrugged and turned to catch a glimpse of a pair of barn swallows as they soared across the azure sky. His head bobbed back and forth, watching as they did aerial tricks. "I knew a farmer, many years ago, who was fascinated with swallows. I caught him talking to them once, as though they were close friends. He was a kind man, a good man, who . . ." Mark's words drifted off like the last notes of a piano sonata.

"Who?"

"I'm sorry. I was just lost in a memory. What was it you asked?"

"Your past, was it so difficult?"

"No, not entirely. Parts. But then that's what life is in the end, isn't it? A sum of many parts?"

"I don't know. I'm only seventeen. The average male lives to age 79 and 4 months."

Mark showed a hint of a smile. "Of course, how could you know, you have a lifetime to figure it all out."

Daniel looked perplexed. His eyes moved from side to side,

scanning the trees in the courtyard. "I want to understand. I'm trying to decipher some of your early experiences. But I can't seem to make it work."

Mark drew his breath in and let it out with a loud wheeze. He tilted his head slightly. "To write the end of your competitive story, we need to go back to the beginning, the beginning of my life. Ready?"

"Yes."

"Do you know when and where I was born?"

Opening his notebook, Daniel offered, "Google search says Saint Joseph's Hospital, Kenosha, Wisconsin, on January 8th, 1924."

"That's what my birth certificate says as well. But it's a forgery. I was born in a city called Cologne, Germany. Not far from the Dutch border."

Daniel furrowed his brow and let his voice drop. "You were born in Germany?"

"That's right."

"To German parents?"

"Full-blooded."

Daniel scrutinized his notes, turning the pages furiously. He didn't know what to ask next. Suddenly, he blurted, "But you speak English."

"My father and his brother ran a printing business. My father ran the Cologne office. My uncle moved to London and opened a branch office there. We visited England every summer, and that's where I learned English."

"But later you must have emigrated to the United States."

Mark's face seemed to go flat and his thoughts distant. His voice was heavy with sadness. "In a manner of speaking."

"By ship?"

"In the bowels of a converted freighter. I was loaded on board without luggage, along with a few hundred of my closest comrades, all dressed in the same government-issued fatigues. We sailed for nearly two weeks, with only one hour a day on deck to inhale the salty air. My ticket was free, and there were no Russians in sight. I counted myself fortunate when we passed the Statue of Liberty in one piece."

Daniel held the pen tightly and touched the end to his ear. "What year was that?"

"1943."

"I'm still confused."

"I thought you were good at puzzles?"

"I'm not as smart as people think."

"Just like I'm not as heroic as people think."

"Touché," Daniel said.

"And you are not as weird as others might think. You want what most young people your age want—acceptance, happiness, a chance to show your gifts." Mark added, "Your brain power is your shield. We all put up a shield at times to keep the pain and bad memories from penetrating our hearts."

"Do you have a shield?"

"I do, sadly. Made from lies, mostly."

It was time for the juggling to begin. Walking from window to window, Daniel held a tight face as though it were carved in wood. He followed the balls in flight, but his brain was deciphering all the clues Mark had given. Finally, Daniel stopped juggling and sat down in the rocker opposite Mark and whooped, "You were a German soldier!"

39

ROSE

June 1945

RED WAS SITTING IN THE OAK ROCKER on the side porch with a tall glass of lemonade. He took his red-and-white kerchief from his neck and wiped his brow. The humidity was thick, and the corn was loving it. He turned to set his glass down but wiped away the ring of water first. Then he stuffed the kerchief in the top pocket of his bib overalls.

Rose was sitting on the top step with her back to one white post and her feet halfway up the other. She wore a sleeveless turquoise blouse and beige work pants rolled up at the cuff. Her hair was pulled back in a ponytail tied off with a piece of linen. A row of tiny sweat beads lined up above her top lip, and her eyes were dark and her cheeks pinched. "I'm hoping you understand, Uncle Red, ever since Mom and Dad passed away, I've trusted Aunt Emily's and your judgment and your wisdom. You both have been so kind to me. But I need to move on, no, I *want* to move on with my life."

Red brought himself to the edge of the rocker, both work boots squarely on the pine boards painted metallic gray. "You have brought Emily and me nothing but joy since moving here, Rose. If we were ever to have a daughter, we'd want her to be just like you. But I gotta admit, this plan of yours . . . well, it scares the bejesus outta me."

Rose put her thumb against her chest. "It scares me too. But I believe it will work, and in the long run will bring us happiness." The freckles on her forehead and nose turned darker.

"I don't know," said Red. He picked up his glass and drank it to within a swallow of the bottom. "Your aunt and I have tried to keep you safe and help you to make good life decisions. This idea, this plan of yours, is risky. It could bring the whole Army down on you, and on us too."

"It could." She stood and looked out over the straight rows of corn now showing their first large, dark emerald leaves. "My dad always told me nothing of value is worth striving for without taking a risk." She turned to Red. "If you don't want to help, I understand, but I want to go forward."

Red rubbed the gray whiskers on his chin and blurted, "Are you in love with this man? Just tell me if you are. It would help to ease my mind."

"I can't say for certain. I think so, or at least with time I think so. What I do know is I don't want to lose him." She shook her head vehemently. "I don't want him shipped to a country in ruins and never heard from again. That much I do know."

"Well, I agree with you there. I like him, and Oskar too, and wish they could stay on for years. Best workers I've ever had. But I'm afraid the Army doesn't agree." He finished his lemonade and sat deep in the rocker. "They want every one of these blokes to be shipped back, you know that. Maybe they could return in a short time through the proper channels?"

"And if they can't?" Red shrugged, and before he could say another word, Rose went on, "Marco is a good man. He wants to stay. Why can't he be allowed? He looks like any of the men around here, talks like them, has two arms and two legs and two eyes."

"He's a German," Red reminded her.

"So was my grandfather!" She was up and pacing. "Grandpa was born in Germany, and we loved him. He was the kindest, most gentle man I've ever known, and patriotic. He flew the American flag till it turned to rags. He loved baseball with a passion, was a devout Catholic, and ran a general store. He raised eleven children and encouraged each one to receive an education to enhance their lot in the American dream."

"I knew your grandfather, Rosie. He was a nice fellow."

"So is Marco. What's the difference?"

Red's face took on a serious look. "The war. The politics. The fact that he was born on the wrong side of the Atlantic in the last few decades. The fact he was drafted into the army of Hitler. And, of course, was captured and is a prisoner. That's quite a difference."

"Of course you're right. I understand, but it won't stop me from wanting him to stay and wanting him to become a permanent fixture in both our lives," she said.

"Being a POW is no small thing."

Rose sat back down on the steps, her back to Red. "Caring for someone deeply is no small thing either."

After a moment, Red asked, "And what of Oskar? What will happen to him?"

"He'll go back with the other POWs, probably to France. He doesn't know enough English and could be discovered easily."

"So when the time comes, it'll be goodbye to Oskar?"

"For a while. When Marco and I find out where's he placed in Europe, we'll petition for his release and be his sponsors in the States. We think we can make a good case to let him out. After all, there are millions of displaced persons looking for a home."

"Most DPs are civilians."

She turned to look at Red. "Now that the war is officially over, he's a civilian."

"A civilian who served in the German army."

"His dream is to come back and work on the Callahan farm. To work with you."

Red chuckled. "As I said, he's a great worker, but I think he's motivated to stay more by your aunt Emily's liver and onions and fresh bread. I can understand that motivation." He chuckled louder.

"So?" Rose implored. "Will you help?"

"I have never been able to say no to you, Rosie."

She rushed to hug him.

40

MARK AND DANIEL

2019

DANIEL HELPED MARK INTO HIS HOSPITAL BED. Then he positioned the IV cart back where he found it. Mark sighed and put the headrest down until he was almost supine. "I'm a little tired," he croaked. "Breaking out of the Mortuary took more effort than I thought." He closed his eyes and breathed deeply. When he opened them again, he said, "Maybe all those zombies in the movies look so haggard because the journey back to the living is not easy." Daniel came around to the foot of the bed and pulled a blanket over Mark's feet. "Thank you, my good man. To me, if only for a short while, it was The *Greatest* Escape."

The afternoon had turned into early evening. A nurse came in to check on Mark's vitals, then changed his IV pouch and reset the pump while Daniel kept vigil. When the nurse asked Mark if he wanted to order something for supper, he said he wasn't hungry, but maybe would later. She asked Daniel if he wanted anything from the kitchen, but he shook his head. She left the room quietly, promising to return within an hour.

"Your mom," Mark said softly. "Does she know you're still here?"

"I called her while the nurse took your temp. She understands."

"From what I can gather, your mom seems to be a wonderful woman. She's produced an amazing son." Mark was staring at the ceiling as he rambled on, as curious about the boy as the boy was about him. "Tell me about your father. Do you see much of him?"

"He's coming to the graduation. But I haven't seen him for 212 days."

"He's still living in Ohio?"

"Yes. With his *normal* wife and *normal* children."

"When he comes to your house, will you have to get the juggling balls out?"

Daniel replied coldly, "No. I think of him about the same way I think of a passerby on the street. I gave up on his parental concern a long time ago. He's acting on guilt alone. I may as well be living on the moon as far as he's concerned."

"I'm sorry for you. When I was a teenager, my parents meant everything to me. They were supportive and loving, and, if anything, they spoiled me whenever they could. After I was taken prisoner, I lost track of them for a long time." He paused to gather thoughts, then said, "They've been gone for nearly forty years, but I still miss them."

Not sure what to say, Daniel picked up his notebook and sat in the bedside chair. "Can we continue with your story? I'll take notes as you talk."

"Of course. I've lost the strand. Go ahead, ask me anything you want. Now that you know I was a German soldier, I feel the truth seeping out of every pore in my body. Maybe that bag of fluid dripping into my veins is truth serum."

Daniel gave the IV bag a curious look, then opened the spiral notebook and took up the pen. "You were a German POW and came to America in 1943?"

"That's right. We, that is, my friend Oskar and I, and hundreds of other prisoners were shipped here to America, and then by train to Wisconsin. Oskar and I were captured before we even saw much fighting. When we joined the army in North Africa, the major battles were mostly over and the Afrika Korps was in retreat. The war for us was a series of endless marches and daily skirmishes until we were finally captured and sent to Italy and then shipped here."

"Were you mistreated as a POW?"

"Mistreated? No, to the contrary, we were fortunate. We could have been sent off to Russia or some other country where the POWs died like flies. For the most part, we enjoyed our stay in Wisconsin. Oskar and I worked on a dairy farm not far from where we are sitting today. We fell in love with our captors. Oskar was treated like a son by the farm's owner and his wife. I fell for the owner's niece." Mark paused and turned to look into Daniel's eyes, which were wide and filled with excitement. His pen was scratching furiously. "Oh, there were some difficult times as a POW, and a few people who made us miserable every chance they could. But we survived the time unscathed. Unfortunately, Oskar had to go back to Europe after the war while I stayed here to grow old without him."

"That makes you unique among the 120,000 American POWs," Daniel said with a sly grin.

"You have a kind way of saying I was a wolf in sheep's clothing. An enemy on American soil."

"I didn't mean . . ."

"It's okay."

"John thinks you are a real *American* hero."

"John and I have talked about heroism. He wants to believe so badly. He grew up on a steady diet of Marvel comics. His heroes conquered the Nazis and Japanese in every issue."

Daniel snickered. "You're a living example of irony."

Mark giggled back. "Make sure to have some electric paddles close by when John reads your story. His heart might give out."

"I promise." They laughed together. "Can I get you water or anything to drink?"

"No thanks, I'm fine." Mark took a couple deep breaths and hit the button to put his headrest up a bit. "The pack of lies that have collected like a stone on my back for nearly seventy years is dissipating with every truthful word. On we go, Sancho, there are more windmills to conquer!"

"*Yawohl, meine Deutsche soldat!*" And they laughed again. This time, it was Daniel who needed a drink. He skipped over to the sink, found a paper cup, screwed up his courage, and drank the tap water quickly. Then he hurried back and started in again. "So, you didn't return to Europe?"

"After the war, I managed to stay right here in Wisconsin, though it took a series of deceits and forged papers, drugs, and co-conspirators to pull it off. Knowing English helped. In fact, it was crucial."

"Over the years, didn't anyone suspect you were an ex-German POW and not an American POW?"

"When a person living in a small town for years is revealed to be a POW, no one digs too deeply into the details. The truth is, I was a World War II POW. I let people think what they wanted and kept the facts to myself. It was a bit unsettling at times when patriotic groups wanted to honor me at some parade or Veterans Day gathering. I refused most of the time but was always polite."

"There must have been some people who knew you were a German soldier. Your wife? Other POWs? Army guards? Somebody."

"The people who knew and helped me stay in America all died years ago. After I moved from one community to the next, people didn't care or didn't think to suspect. There were thousands of young men returning from wartime duties from all over the world in the late 1940s. It was easy to just blend in."

"Did you kill anyone in the war?"

Mark pointed a trembling index finger at Daniel. "You asked me that once before."

Daniel slid his pen behind his ear and leaned back in his plastic chair. "I thought you were an American soldier then, not a *Deutsche soldat.*"

"I know young people are fascinated with war, my brainy friend, but how would it make a difference? Everyone bleeds the same."

"On Lightstar 8, it's easy to know who is evil and who is not."

Mark grinned and said, "I'll bet it's easy to find a prom date on Lightstar 8 as well."

The pink in Daniel's cheeks rose. "I wouldn't know, I haven't . . ."

"And I didn't kill anyone on either side of the lines," Mark interrupted. "I never even shot my rifle, and it's a good thing too because I was a horrible shot and a horrible soldier in general."

"You were a horrible German soldier but a hero in America."

"America is the land of opportunity!" Mark replied, tongue in cheek.

"How does that make you feel, I mean, the irony and all?"

"Conflicted. I tried to lead an honorable life wherever I was." Mark went on to explain his conscription into the German army, the Wehrmacht. He talked on and on about basic training and gave details about being shipped to Rommel's Afrika Korps as a replacement even though the Germans were in full retreat. He described his capture in the desert of North Africa and crossing the Atlantic on the *Ambrose Bierce*. He told Daniel about his close friend Oskar and the troubles they had with Sergeant Stanley and Weishaple and their work on the Callahan farm. He told him about the meals Aunt Emily fixed and the closeness they developed with all the Callahans, but especially Rose. He told him about the day they heard Hitler was dead, the end of the war, and about their fears of going back to a war-ravaged Europe.

Mark paused, took another drink of water, and closed his eyes. Sleep was heavy on his lids.

"Umm, Mark?"

He turned and gave Daniel a perplexed look. "Did I miss something? More details?"

"No." Daniel pointed to the clock. "I have to go. My mom will be here in 3 minutes."

"Right. I guess I lost track of the time. It feels so good to talk about my early life out loud. I'm like that dormant volcano people see every day and don't expect to change, then one day it explodes and everyone wonders why at that moment. You've helped me erupt. Sometimes I can see the past so vividly, the faces, the farm, the desert sand. My heart races when I think how frightened I was at times . . . the fighting in Africa . . . the loss of Rose and family . . . Oskar . . ." He saw the blank look on Daniel's face. "Now I am rambling like a stereotypical old guy reliving the past . . . I apologize."

"No need. I have more questions for the next time." He stood and hefted his backpack over his left shoulder.

"Go! Go! Come back and roll away the stone to my cave anytime. We'll finish. We'll get to the end. I promise. But don't wait too long. You have a deadline . . . no pun intended."

41

SETH

2019

IT WAS WEDNESDAY BEFORE PROM, and Seth slipped into an equipment room off the varsity boys' locker room where several of the Neanderthals had already gathered. He plopped his gym bag on a long wooden bench and pulled out a tall metal canister. The cluster of young men formed a semicircle around their leader. Seth removed the top of the can and gazed inside, then leaned over and put his nose inside the rim. "Ahhh, the smell of money," he said and pulled out a large wad of bills. "Lots of Hamiltons, and even a couple of Benjamins. We are in good shape, boys." The room filled with boisterous cheers when he fanned out the bills and held them high.

A tall boy with black hair as dark as paint and parted down the middle asked, "Is it gonna be enough? We got a lotta expenses."

Counting the bills for all to see, Seth piled them on the bench. "Eight hundred and twenty-two bucks."

"Here's twenty-five more." A boy with gray eyes and a pudgy face came forward and pushed the bills toward Seth. "Got the cash from some freshman asshole who disrespected the football team. Said we were a bunch of *hoodlums*. I'm not sure anybody uses that word anymore, but I didn't like his attitude. He gave it up pretty easy."

Seth placed the twenty-five on the pile of bills. "Any more cash out there?"

A boy wearing faded jeans with holes slivered into the knees and an Oakland Raiders football jersey said, "I ain't got the money now, but a girl in my algebra class is supposed to bring me two Hamiltons tomorrow and the Ritalin I know her brother takes. Seen his stash in the locker next to mine. She'll deliver or I'll tell the teacher she cheats on her weekly tests. She's a grade grubber, so it won't take much for her to cave."

Seth flashed a toothy smile. "That'll put us near nine hundred. Should be enough. Gus?"

"Yeah," answered a sandy-haired boy with oversized ears and a small tattoo of a lizard on his neck.

"You got the beer lined up?"

"Two barrels of Spotted Cow. Plus the stuff you need to make it come outta the barrel," he added. "You know, the pump thing and the spigot thing." The others laughed along with him, one boy punching him on the shoulder.

"Good man," said Seth. "When you picking it up?"

"Saturday 'bout noon. My bro's got a pickup, and he'll help. We'll have it on ice by about two. Should be nice and cold by four or so. Good for a few slams before the dinner dates start."

The room echoed with approval. Seth put the cash back in the tin. "Everyone know where the cottage is?"

"On Legend Lake, right up the road from The Lakeside Bar!" shouted Gus. "Can't miss it. My girlfriend is gonna put balloons and shit on the mailbox. I'm gonna give her an extra special, you know what, for helping out." He stood on the wooden bench and pumped his hips. The Neanderthals roared.

"Hey, what about that Mannheim kid?" one of the Neanderthals hollered. "He's your locker mate, ain't he, Seth?"

"Yeah, he know where the money comes from?" another boy questioned.

Seth snickered and waved his hand dismissively. "You don't

have to worry about that little turd. He and I have come to an understanding."

"Guy's got ESP or something," Gus chipped in. "He's in my social studies class and knows every fuckin' date and fact about every fuckin' war, every fuckin' president, and has all the amendments to the fuckin' Constitution memorized. You name it, and that guy's got the answer. He's an alien if I ever saw one. Maybe me and a few guys ought to pay him a noon-hour visit," he said emphatically, "just to make sure he won't say anything."

"Don't waste your time," Seth replied. "Besides, my prom date is his one and only girl…" His fingers formed quotes in the air. "…*friend*, the one and only, Paige Bartlett. Trust me, he won't say anything."

"She's hot," someone added.

"I suspect Double D will be in his little hidey-hole all weekend," said Seth. "Or better yet, he'll be at the old farts' home staring into space with the toothless crowd." The group laughed again. "He won't show his face. He's weird as a six-toed monkey, but harmless."

"Come Monday, you can give him all the juicy details about his one and only *friend*," Gus said, mimicking the quotes.

"Planning on it. Now, if everyone knows where the party of the century is gonna happen, I guess we're outta here." Seth put the money in his gym bag and zipped it up. "See you all this weekend. Keep cool and bring plenty of condoms!"

They filed out, slapping each other on the back.

42

DANIEL AND MARK

2019

IT WAS WEDNESDAY BEFORE PROM, and Daniel was relieved to be picked up at 3:09. He couldn't wait to flee the endless chatter of what restaurant was the best place to have a fancy prom dinner, or who was going to attend post-prom, or what girls hadn't been asked. The whole event couldn't be over soon enough for him. Despite his mother's provocations, he believed he was saving her money by not attending and paying hundreds of dollars on the outrageous cost of flowers, tuxes, photos, and limos.

He was still adding up all the money he didn't have to spend as he settled into the back seat directly behind his mom. The nineteen-year-old Ford Taurus rattled as they pulled out of the school parking lot. Denise had wanted to purchase a new car for some time, but Daniel insisted the *Taurus*, the *Bull*, was a symbol of strength and safety. Any other car would be vulnerable if caught in an accident.

When Denise sped up, the car made a roaring sound. "Mom, you can get a ticket for noise pollution. You need to have the muffler changed."

"Uh huh. A new car would be much quieter. Maybe a Prius; they don't make noise at all."

"New vehicles are lightweight and made with lots of plastic composites. They crinkle like tin foil."

"If I want to fix the muffler of this old clunker, I'll have to break your piggy bank to do it. How's that?"

Daniel ignored his mom's comment since his mind was racing toward the weekend, his story needing to be postmarked by midnight on Friday. He had 54 hours and 53 minutes to put it all together. He needed closure from Mark. He was zeroing in on the details; just another hour or two of conversation and he would be finished. "Did you say something, Mom?"

"About three blocks back, not important."

"Can you take me directly to the BRC?"

"Are your legs broken?" she asked sarcastically.

"If they were, I would've needed help to get in the car."

"Okay, okay." She looked at him quizzically in the rearview mirror. "Why do you need to get to the BRC so quickly?"

"I need to visit Mark. It's important."

"How's he doing?"

Daniel slumped back and turned to see a line of school buses parading toward the school entrance. He didn't want to think about Mark's condition and didn't want to answer his mom. He closed his eyes and tried to focus on the barn swallows Mark had talked about. He, too, loved to watch their sleek aerial gymnastics, their effortless gliding ability.

"Daniel! Did you hear me?"

"He's okay. That's all I want to say."

For the rest of the ride, Denise and her passenger were silent. She knew the bond was strong between her son and his German teacher, and she feared what might happen when the end came.

Daniel hurried through the lobby of the BRC, hardly giving the birds a glance. He dodged several wheelchairs along the first-floor hallway parked randomly like dune buggies that had run out of fuel trying to cross the Mojave Desert. When he approached the closed door of the Mortuary, he hoped Mark was not sleeping. He was about to pull on the door when it flew open.

"Hey, D-squared. What the hell?"

Daniel's heart jumped into his throat. He forgot Seth had signed up as a co-op student, allowing him to leave school early a couple days a week for the work experience.

Seth had a water pitcher in each hand. "You're kinda becoming a fixture around here."

Daniel said nothing but stepped back and leaned against the wall, his right hand clutching the walking bar. Seth let the Mortuary door close and moved closer to Daniel.

"Got no response for me? Okay, try this out . . . what the fuck are you doing here? Your writing group doesn't set up for an hour or so."

Daniel turned and looked at a Japanese beetle crawling along the top of the handrail ten feet from where he stood. Its metallic-green folded wings shimmered as it crossed a sliver of sun piercing from a west-facing window.

"Hey, Double D, I'm asking you a question," Seth growled. "I expect an answer."

Daniel watched the beetle flex its wings. It was about to fly. He wished he could do the same. The image of a dozen swallows on the wing was forming in his head.

Seth moved into Daniel's space and hissed, "You hear me, turd?"

"I came to see Mark."

"You mean *Mr. Flour*, don't ya?"

"Yes, Mr. Flour."

"You're not working here, Double D, remember that. You got no special privileges," he snarled.

"No."

"You're just here 'cause of that writing thing going with Mark, right?"

"Yes."

Seth relaxed his posture and stepped back. "That's cool. Can't see what's so interesting with these ol' farts, but hey, they're harmless and easy to care for as long as they don't do something nasty in the bed. It sucks when that happens."

Daniel watched the beetle fly onto the sunny window and fold its wings back under its back like a gull-wing sports car. "Is . . . is . . . Mr. Flour sleeping?"

"Naw, Flour's awake. I'm on my way to get him and the old coot in 121 some ice." Seth put the water pitchers on the windowsill below the Japanese beetle. He turned to Daniel and grinned. "Mark just asked me about the prom. Wanted to know if I was going, so, of course, I had to tell him I was takin' the best-lookin' chick in the school. Know who I mean, DD?"

"Yes."

"That's right, you and Paige Bartlett had a thing going once, didn't you?"

Daniel's eyes found his Converse and stared at the white laces as each poked their way through the silver grommets. "We worked on a science project once."

"Yeah, that bridge thing, made outta toothpicks. I remember." He laughed like a hyena. "Stupid project. Teacher should've had his head examined."

"We were . . . freshmen."

"Well, Paige doesn't look like a freshman anymore. Whoo-hee! Does she have a bod! But then, you probably haven't noticed." After a moment, Seth turned and looked at the water pitchers, then back at Daniel. "Say, as long as you're going into the Mortuary, how 'bout filling this pitcher with ice." It wasn't a request. "Helps both of us. I can get a few more minutes on my break, and you can score a few points with Mark before he checks out."

Seth picked up one of the pitchers and pushed it into Daniel's chest. "Here, ice machine is at the end of the hall, that way," he said, pointing with his middle finger.

Daniel put both hands around the metallic pitcher. "Okay."

"I'll take care of 121."

Daniel's mind was calculating. 121 was not a prime number; it was divisible by 11, it was semi-prime, it was 1 plus 1 equals the middle number 2, like 363 or 484. Daniel was a 1, and Mark was a 1, and together they formed a 2 . . .

"Ask me on Monday how the prom weekend turned out. I'll give you all the dirty details."

Daniel wasn't paying attention.

"Hear me?"

Daniel nodded but didn't speak.

Seth turned to leave, then whirled around, saying, "Oh, and you might wanna take notes!" As he strutted away, his laughter echoed down the hall.

Daniel stood holding the pitcher for several minutes. His mind slowed, the numbers fading and the Japanese beetle coming back into focus. He stepped over to the window and let the beetle climb onto his finger, its tiny antennae wiggling as it walked. He cupped the insect in his palm and walked to a door leading to the courtyard, opened it, and let the beetle fly off.

A moment later, he walked quietly into the Mortuary and stood next to Mark's bed, the pitcher in his right hand. "I didn't fill the pitcher with ice."

Mark shoved his reading glasses to the top of his head and let his copy of poems by Billy Collins slide onto his chest. The wrinkles on his face seemed deeper, and his skin had a slight yellow tinge. "Hello, Daniel." His voice was raspy and breathing shallow. He peered at the metal pitcher. "What happened to Seth?"

"He was in a hurry," Daniel answered with a touch of anger.

"Hurry to do what?"

"Extend his break."

"I see." Mark took off his glasses, folded them, and laid them on top of the book of poetry. "Set the pitcher over by the sink and pull up a chair. I can drink tepid water."

Daniel returned with the chair, then sat and pulled his notebook from his backpack and checked his pen. "Seth told me you asked him about his plans for the prom."

"I didn't ask. He droned on and on about how every girl is in love with him. I don't much care about Seth's bravado, but I do care about Daniel's plans for the prom." Mark raised his eyebrows and glanced at Daniel with a look of anticipation.

"No change." His pen was doodling small circles, then large ones.

"He told me the girl he's taking used to be *your* girlfriend?"

"He's lying. It's his way of showing his alpha standing. He wants to make himself seem stronger in your eyes at the expense of a weakling like me. I've never had a girlfriend." Daniel's eyes were still following the pen.

"You don't know this Paige . . . what's her name?"

"Bartlett. Her name is Paige Bartlett," he answered, his voice low and melancholic. "Her mom and my mom are friends. We've known each other since elementary school. Paige and I worked on a science project as freshmen, that's all."

"And she's very pretty, according to the alpha Neanderthal."

"Yes. He tells me how hot she is whenever he can."

Mark picked up his glasses and the book from his chest and dropped them onto the bedside table. When he turned back, he asked, "Can you fill my water glass with the coldest you can get from the tap, please?" When Daniel returned, Mark continued, "The prom is coming up soon, right?"

"4 days and 5½ hours."

"Maybe his dream night with Paige won't go exactly as planned."

'Neanderthals always get their way.'

Mark thought Daniel was speaking from years of experience. "It seems that way, but . . . not always." He let his lips form a slight smile and pushed his head deep into the pillow. Then his smile vanished and he pushed the bed controls, his head and shoulders slowly moving upward as far as the bed would allow. "Enough of the Neanderthals and Seth. How's the story shaping up?"

Daniel reached behind him and pulled his backpack over his shoulder and onto his lap. He unzipped the main pouch and pulled out a sheaf of typed papers. "I brought a copy of what I have so far. Do you want me to read it to you?"

Mark shook his head. "Paraphrase."

"Okay." Daniel gave Mark the bones of his story. He read a few lines here and there to emphasize his points. His writing was crisp, his word choices exact. When he came to the last page, he declared, "You obviously stayed in America, but I don't know how you were able to pull that off. My research says all POWs in America had to return to Europe. No exceptions. But here you are."

Mark's eyes glazed over as he said, "Right. I had help from Oskar and Rose and her uncle."

43

ROSE AND MARCO

Summer 1945

"IT'S NOT TOO LATE TO CHANGE YOUR MIND, ROSE," her uncle said. They were sitting side by side on the front porch steps. It was before noon on a Sunday and the temperature was already over eighty. The sun was filtering through a thick haze of humidity, the air still and the sky the color of false indigo. Bees were hopping from the snowball hydrangea blossoms to the maroon chrysanthemums. The irises along the split rail fence were about gone; only a couple spears showed deep-purple flowers.

Rose leaned her head on Red's shoulder and smiled. "Thank you for everything, Uncle Red, but my mind is made up. I already miss you and Aunt Emily."

"But you need to move on. I get it. We were young once too and in love. When Emily and I moved from Neillsville to inherit the farm, Emily's dad thought I was crazy. He had a small blacksmithing business, you know, and he thought for sure I would move right in and work alongside him."

"You wanted to strike out on your own?"

"Not as much as Emily. She thought this farm was paradise. When we first walked up the driveway, I thought, 'What am I getting myself into?' The house, the fields, the barn had all been let go while my dad was sick. But Emily, bless her soul, she saw the future: a house with fresh paint, a barn full of animals, crops in the fields, and wash on the line. She loved it from the first day and has been happy here ever since."

A purple finch flew under the eaves of the porch. Rose noticed the nest poking out of the corner and three tiny heads straining with open beaks. "I hope my life will follow a similar course, Uncle, I really do. First, though..." She straightened up. "...we have to carry out the plan. Did you have trouble getting the laudanum?"

He waved his hand as though batting at a fly. "No problem at all. Doc Morris has been a friend of mine for years. When I told him my back was killing me, he was only too happy to give me some extra pain medicine."

"And Aunt Emily?"

"I took her into town early and put her on the bus." He pulled his kerchief from his bib pocket and wiped his brow. "She must be close to Stevens Point by now. Gonna stay with her sister for a few days. Sister's gout is really bad this time, so Em will give her a break from doing chores. She knows today is the day the boys are being shipped out." Red thought for a moment, then added, "She was grateful to be away and not have to say goodbye. She's grown awful close to both of them." His face lit up like a Fourth of July sparkler. "Especially Oskar. She loves cooking for that man."

"Everybody loves Oskar," Rose said with a girlish smile. She stood and bounced down the steps and peered out over the cornfield. When she turned back, she looked straight into Red's eyes. "And me?" Rose asked timidly. "Did you tell Emily about my leaving too?"

Red let out a deep sigh. He shifted his weight and wiped his lips on the sleeve of his flannel shirt. "She's gonna be real unhappy when she comes home to find her niece has left."

"You didn't tell her about our plan?"

Tears showed at the corners of Red's eyes. "Didn't have the heart, Rosie."

"I'm not going to be gone forever, Uncle Red. We'll stay at the

Rogers' cottage near Nine Mile Lake for a few months, maybe a year, and then when the war is farther behind us, we'll come visit."

"I understand, I do, but there'll be a lot of tears from your aunt before it sinks in. She's a forgiving woman, and given a little time, she'll open the door to the two of you anytime you come visiting."

"I appreciate that. The last thing in the world I want is to make either of you unhappy, after all you've done for me, and for Marco ... and Oskar too, for that matter. But I don't see any other way ..." Her voice trailed off.

They sat quietly for a few minutes while the adult finches flitted in and out of the nest.

Red stood and pulled Rose close, putting his arms around her reassuringly. "Your aunt and I have lived through two world wars and a Great Depression. We can handle a little separation from loved ones. You need to make your own life together and find all the happiness you can." He hugged her even tighter. "With a little luck, it'll all work out. I don't know how, but I believe in you, and I've come to the conclusion you'll make it somehow." Then he kissed her on the forehead, looked into her eyes, and nodded slightly. He turned and walked up onto the porch and settled in the rocker.

A moment later, Marco and Oskar rounded the corner of the house. Both were wearing their government-issued clothes, the block PW stenciled on the hip of their slacks and the back of their t-shirts; it was the same outfit as when they had climbed off the train in Milwaukee nineteen months ago.

"All the animals are fed and watered," Marco announced. He dusted off the cuffs of his pants and looked up at Red. "We cleaned the shovels and put them in the pump house, and Oskar loaded up the grain cart so you're all set for the evening milking."

"Ah, thank you, boys," said Red.

Oskar smiled and hollered, "I say goodbye ... to cows. Mooo! Mooo!"

Red laughed until a coughing spell stopped him. Rose put her hand on Oskar's arm. "I'm sure they'll miss you too, Oskar."

Red took the kerchief from his lips and said, "The milk production will be down next week, I guarantee it. The cows know when you boys aren't here."

Marco gazed down the driveway and then back at Rose. His eyes were rippling with excitement, but his mouth was tight. "It's almost time."

"I'll be right back with the lemonade." Rose clambered up the steps, opened the screen door, and caught it behind her as though the noise might upset the finches.

Marco turned to Oskar. "Time for you to walk down the driveway and let us know when you see Stanley." Oskar nodded and strode off. Before he disappeared, Marco shouted, "Try not to let him see you!"

After Oskar was out of earshot, Red turned to Marco. "I have faith in your plan, Marco, but whatever happens, take care to protect Rose." He pulled himself out of the rocker and walked down the steps. "I told Rose that we are always available, so if you need a port in the storm, well . . . you can always come here." Red held out his hand.

Marco took it in both of his. "Someday we will return. I'm certain of it. And Oskar, he talks of nothing else."

Both men were smiling as Rose backed out of the door carrying a round wooden tray balancing a large pitcher of lemonade and five glasses. She set the tray on the table and arranged the glasses in a row, then walked to the edge of the porch and gave the directions. "Now, when Stanley shows up, I will pour lemonade in each glass, but the one for Stanley will be this one." She turned and picked up the glass farthest to the left. "Okay?" Both men nodded. "Marco, you tell Oskar when he returns," she commanded.

"I will."

Rose held out her hand and opened her fingers. "Uncle, I'll take the laudanum now."

Red pulled out a dark-brown bottle from his inside pocket. "Doc Morris told me to be careful with this medicine. He said if I took two ounces of the stuff at one time, it'd be enough to knock out a horse. He gave me this shot glass to measure." He handed the glass to Rose. "I would think one ounce should do the trick, maybe a little more for good measure. That bottle holds about twelve ounces."

Rose took the bottle, measured a shot, and a bit more, and poured it into one of the glasses. "Here's to a nice long, long sleep." She turned to Red and Marco. "Now we just need the guest of honor." Her smile faded from anxiety to determination, her eyes now brimming with excitement like Marco's.

Marco asked Red, "What time did Stanley say he would be here?"

"I told him to be here around noon. Told him I had something important to discuss before you boys leave."

"And he agreed?"

"He was only too anxious. I think it'll give him a last chance to embarrass Rose and make you two look like fools in the process. Who knows with that man." He scowled and spit to the side. "I don't think he was kept out of the Army due to a heart *defect* . . . I don't think he has a *heart*, period!"

The sun slipped under a cumulus cloud, and the breeze came up, supplying a moment of relief from the heat. Red and Marco retired to the steps, and Rose settled into the rocker. She peeked at her wristwatch and rocked, then glanced at her watch again and rocked faster.

Marco looked up to Rose and asked, "The stretcher?"

"It's just inside the front door."

"Did you have trouble finding one?"

Rose let her feet come to a rest on the pine boards. "The Red Cross keeps several in the basement of the Lutheran church. They aren't used unless there's a disaster of some kind or other. I don't think anyone will miss one for a long time."

"And your uniform?"

"Pressed and ready. I'll be the smartest-dressed Red Cross volunteer in the county."

Marco smiled broadly. "And the best-looking."

"Here, here," chirped Red.

Even before they heard his voice, they caught Oskar running up the driveway. "He's coming! He's coming!"

Red turned to Rose and reiterated, "There's no shame in backing out now, Rosie."

"Not a chance." Rose got up and stood over the table of lemonade. "But thanks for the sincere offer." Her face glowed with optimism.

Marco put his arm around Oskar's shoulders as the big man panted and worked to catch his breath. Marco pointed to the glass with laudanum and went over the plan one last time.

The brown and battered Ford sedan skidded into the driveway and braked ten feet from the porch. Stanley climbed out amid a cloud of dust. He was wearing his tan dress uniform, polished black shoes, and a felt hat. He brushed the dust from his shoulder boards and sauntered forward. "Afternoon, Callahan."

"I believe a bit of morning's left, Stanley." Red moved down the steps gingerly and held out his hand.

"I guess you're right. Good morning, then," said Stanley, checking his watch. He shook Red's hand as though he was royalty and Red was his serf. Then he tipped his hat and nodded to Rose. "And hello to you too, Rose."

"Morning, Stanley." Her voice was as sharp as the crease in his trousers.

For a moment, there was silence. Oskar and Marco had moved to the side and kept their eyes from staring at Rose or the lemonade. Stanley was beaming with smugness as he looked out over the cornfield. "Good weather for the corn. Should be tasseling out before August. You've been fortunate to have cheap labor, Callahan, I mean, fortunate to make everything look so good. Too bad they won't be here to help with the harvest." He pivoted and caught Red's eyes, which were clear but worried. Stanley's cheeks were red, and beads of sweat could be seen above his brows. "I hope you've said your goodbyes because the bus to Milwaukee is only twenty minutes behind me."

Red kicked at the dirt with his boot, then looked up. "See here, Stanley. I asked you to come by a few minutes before the bus to see if I could get you to change your mind about sending these workers back before the end of summer. That corn you're looking at needs good workers to get it in before the cold weather. My neighbors' too."

"Not going to happen, Callahan."

"A few more weeks till the clover is cut and stored in the barn shouldn't make much difference to the Army. You could put in a request for that much at least. I know you could."

"Wouldn't do any good," he snickered. "The Army's made up its mind. I hope you didn't ask me out here just for that?"

'Well . . . didn't think it would hurt to try." Red mopped his brow again with his kerchief.

"I was charged with thirty-two of these Kraut POWs, and by God, I'm gonna return the same thirty-two. I woke this morning and thought, 'Today is a red-letter day for the whole valley. It's time all the rats are put back on the ship and sent off to the hole in the ground from where they came.'"

Red turned and walked back up the steps. "Gonna make it hard for some of us farmers this fall."

Stanley shook his head. "Shouldn't be, Callahan. Thousands of hard-working American men will be comin' home in the next few months, and lots of 'em will be lookin' for work. And if I may say so, with a good-lookin' gal like Rose around, you'll have guys lined up at your door."

Rose poured the lemonade into the glasses. "Don't be so sure."

"Why not? Swarms of men will be wanting to start a family and settle down. You'll be a fine catch, Rose. Just the right age and looks. Cast her out, Callahan, and you'll reel in a host of hungry workers."

The ears on Marco turned red as fresh radishes. Oskar put his hand on Marco's elbow and gave a squeeze. His face told Marco to ignore the remarks.

Rose kept her anger in check by shrugging her shoulders and offering a drink. "Glass of lemonade, Sergeant?"

Stanley ignored her. "I'm not sure I have the time. There'll be water on the bus."

"I doubt you'll have anything as good as fresh-squeezed lemonade. It's ice-cold, a perfect drink before a long, hot ride." Her smile showed off gleaming white teeth.

Stanley scanned her from head to toe. He stared at her pretty floral dress, then stepped closer, looking directly into her burning green-and-blue eyes. "I guess it would be alright."

She handed him a glass and then asked, "Would it be alright if I gave Uncle and the POWs a glass as well?"

He extended his arms nonchalantly. "What the hell. Might be the last good-tasting drink they'll have in a long time."

Rose circulated, passing out the glasses. Then she stepped back to her place beside the table. "You want to give a farewell toast, Uncle?"

"Huh?" Red cleared his throat. "Oh, yeah, of course." He turned and faced Oskar and Marco, his glass held even with the tip of his nose. "I'm not happy you're leaving, boys, but seeing as I can't do anything about it, here's to a safe journey!" He raised his glass even higher. "And may your future take you to a place of good luck." He clinked glasses with Oskar and Marco and took a sip.

Stanley peered at his POWs as a falcon to pigeons. "And a good riddance to all." With that, he drained his glass and put it back on the table. "Very good lemonade, Rose. Quite tasty." Then he looked back at his charges. "Better than these heathens deserve."

"All God's creatures need a little comfort," Rose said.

"After all the destruction and death their army caused? I'm surprised at you, Rose. I would have thought the newsreels would have convinced even you that these guys represent pure evil."

"They were here most of the war, Stanley. All I saw was the good they did for the farm and my aunt and uncle."

"Yeah, yeah. The same song and dance you've been spouting for months." He rubbed his eyes and turned to Red. "Mind if I sit on the steps, Callahan? Long ride ahead." He staggered a bit, then slumped down, his back against the porch post and his mouth showing a bit of spittle at the corners. "Gonna put 'em on the train . . . then ship 'em back to Europe . . . all of 'em," he mumbled. "You'll feel better when they're gone, Rose . . . I promise . . . I promise."

He raised his arms as if to say something more, then let them dangle at his sides. His eyes closed slowly, and he nearly rolled down the steps before Marco caught his shoulders and held him up.

44

DANIEL AND MARK

2019

"AND THEN WE SWITCHED PLACES. Oskar and I carried Stanley into the house, and I put on his uniform and we put the POW-issued clothes on Stanley. It was easy; we were about the same size. Besides, none of the government-issued clothing was a perfect fit anyway."

"So, in an instant, Sergeant Stanley became a POW and Marco became a cruel, pompous, arrogant, pain-in-the-ass American serviceman," Daniel said with a wide grin.

"Couldn't have described it better myself. Just like Houdini, we did a little switcheroo. When the bus came a few minutes later, Oskar and I strapped Stanley to the stretcher and carried him to the back door of the bus and slid him down the center aisle."

"And the bus driver and other guards didn't notice?"

"The guards and the driver were all new men. We had learned that many returning American soldiers were being hired to transport POWs. They didn't have a clue as to what any of us looked like. When the bus pulled in, I told the driver that the man on the stretcher had come down with a severe case of pneumonia and needed complete rest. Rose, in her Red Cross uniform, backed me up, and the driver was satisfied."

"The other POWs must have known. Didn't they say anything?"

"That was my crowning moment. I stepped onto the bus and spoke to them in German, knowing the guards wouldn't understand. I said that this busload of POWs was going to Milwaukee to board a train for Boston and then to a relocation camp in France. I ordered them to stay silent about the man on the stretcher and obey the driver and the guards. Then I spied an old enemy of mine and Oskar's, a fellow by the name of Weishaple. I walked down the aisle, stopping right in front of him, and looked squarely in his vermin eyes and said loud enough for all to hear, 'If this man or anyone else tries to change the plans I just announced, I will personally have you all rerouted in Milwaukee to a train for New York to board a ship bound for relocation camps in *Russia*.' I let those words hang in the air for a long moment and watched as Weishaple turned away, a sour look on his face, but said nothing."

Mark was smiling now, his eyes dancing with happy memories. "And then the bus was off."

Daniel pushed his pen behind his left ear and steepled his fingers "Quite a scheme. Oskar was on the bus?"

"He was. He gave Stanley a teaspoon of laudanum every few hours. He was Stanley's faithful escort all the way to Boston. When the POWs were taken from the train, Oskar melted in with the other prisoners. When Stanley finally woke up, he was in the Atlantic somewhere trying to figure out how he came to be wearing POW garb with no identification. I'm sure he had a difficult time proving he was the real deal. Over the years, I could hear him shouting... *I'm an American, for chrissakes! I'm not a cabbagehead!*" Mark chuckled through a cough and then went on. "*Someone stole my uniform and papers. Get me away from these lousy Krauts!* I would have given my good right arm to have witnessed that scene."

Mark's smile turned into a deep cough. He covered his mouth with a handkerchief, and when he finished, Daniel noticed a few specks of blood.

Daniel squinted. "Didn't Stanley come after you when he returned?"

"Nope. Rose and I moved away thinking he might come looking, but he never did. After I dropped off *his* thirty-two POWs in
Milwaukee, people assumed Sergeant Stanley moved out of the area.
I believe if he ever surfaced again in Kocher Valley, he would've been
so embarrassed being hoodwinked by a couple of *lousy Krauts*, he'd
never admit the truth."

For a long time, Mark was quiet. His breathing was quick and
shallow. Every so often, a whistling sound would come through his
nose. Then he turned and caught Daniel's eye. "Let's go on with your
story. What else?" His breathing was labored, but steady.

Daniel looked at the questions he had written and asked, "How
did you get a teaching job?"

Mark took a deep breath and let it out slowly. "After the war,
Rose and I moved to Oshkosh. I had decided to be a teacher, and
the university in Oshkosh, well, it was actually a normal school in
those days, seemed to be a good place to start. There were thousands
of men enrolling in colleges on the GI Bill, but unfortunately, my
background was too risky to ask for government help. I simply wore
my Sergeant Stanley uniform into the admission office, and there
were few questions asked. As long as I could pay the tuition, I was
taken in."

"They didn't ask where you went to high school?"

"They may have. But I told them I was drafted before graduation."

"So you don't have a high school diploma?"

"Technically, no." With a silly smile, he added, "I'm probably
the only high school teacher you will meet who doesn't have a high
school diploma."

Daniel sat back, raising his eyebrows, and said with affection,
"You are *my* hero!"

Mark chuckled, then continued, "Oakwood High School was
looking for a German language teacher, and I applied and took the

job in 1955. I worked in the district for forty years, teaching mostly juniors and seniors."

"Did you and Rose have any children?"

"No."

"Did Rose work?"

"She did. First, she became a nursing assistant—nurse's aide, they called them then. Later, she went to night school and became an LPN. She loved helping others. She was, and always will be, the most compassionate and kindest person to ever come into my life. I loved her, Daniel. I loved her with all my heart. I wanted to spend many more years with her, but . . . in 1995, she developed breast cancer and passed away." Mark was silent for a long moment, then asked, "Could I have some water?"

Daniel set his notebook on the chair and poured water into a glass. He turned the straw to meet Mark's chapped lips. A tiny tear had dribbled from the corner of Mark's left eye. "Thanks."

Daniel replaced the glass and settled back into his chair. "I only have a couple more questions."

"Okay."

"Did Oskar ever come back to America?"

Mark's eyes focused on the ceiling while he talked. "My friend Oskar." He took a deep breath and sighed loudly. "My friend hated the war. He despised the idea of hurting any living thing. He loved working on the Callahan farm—the cows, the fieldwork, the cats in the barn, all of it, especially Aunt Emily's cooking. But it's painful to tell his story . . ." There was another long pause before Mark continued.

"When Oskar arrived in France, he was assigned to a large POW camp near the Belgian border. After the war, many of the POWs were reclassified as DEF men. That stands for Disarmed Enemy Forces. When the war was being fought, POWs had to be treated in a certain humane way under the Geneva Convention protocols. The

International Red Cross would inspect camps and try to make sure the rules were applied. But when the war ended, so did the rules, and German DEFs had no rights to proper food, water, or shelter, and the French supplied as little as possible, so many died quickly.

"Oskar's camp was nothing more than a fenced-in open field. Men dug holes in the ground to try and get out of the weather, food was scarce, and medical treatment was almost nonexistent. During the day, DEFs were put to work rebuilding roads, constructing bridges, whatever the French needed or wanted. They became slave laborers not unlike the slave laborers the Nazis used after conquering certain surrounding countries. The end result was that thousands of German POWs died in France.

"As soon as we learned of Oskar's whereabouts, Rose and I petitioned the U.S. Army for his release. He was still classified as a POW under America's jurisdiction. We were sure we could get him out. Remember, I was Sergeant Stanley in those days and wore the uniform to prove it. We pleaded with the Army. We wrote letters, called officials, we even planned to travel to France . . . but . . ."

Mark's eyes closed, and his shallow breathing could be heard in the stillness.

Daniel counted 50 breaths before he asked, "But . . . what?"

After opening his eyes and turning to Daniel, Mark whispered, "Oskar developed typhus and died in the spring of 1946. Years later, I tried to contact his mother and sisters but never found them. I don't know if they ever visited him before he passed away." Mark began to sob. "It's easy to cry when you're old," he said and reached out his hand. "I'll take a Kleenex, please."

Daniel handed him the box, then waited for Mark to compose himself. "Last question. When did you change your name?"

Mark blew his nose and dried his eyes. Then he forced himself to sit up as high as he could. "I shed the uniform of Sergeant Stanley after we found out Oskar had died. Like a snake, I wanted to wear a shiny new coat. I went to the local courthouse and convinced the clerk that my identification papers were destroyed while I was a POW. It wasn't as difficult as it sounds. In fact, it was quite simple by today's standards."

"And the name you chose?"

"Do you know the German word for *flour*, the baking kind of *flour*?"

"It's *mehl*."

"Spelled?"

"M . . . e . . . h . . . l."

"Correct, my fine student. My birth name was Marco Aloysius *Mehl*man. Long before I was born, my ancestors owned and ran a small, rural grist mill. So, to honor my ancestors, I Americanized my name to Mark Flour. F . . . l . . . o . . . u . . . r."

"No American middle name?"

"Ahh, yes, it's Kevin. Kevin was Red Callahan's given name, but because of his hair, everyone called him Red." He smiled wistfully. "Mark Kevin Flour. I liked the sound of my new name, and I believed it suited my history. What do you think?"

"Most people can't create their own name."

"I guess you have to be a POW in a foreign country to make that happen." Mark smiled again and looked into Daniel's face, but there was a sense of anxiety and fear clearly showing. "What is it, Daniel?"

"I have no more questions."

"Enough information for you to write the end?"

"Yes."

"So, what's troubling you?"

"I have to get to the library before it closes. I need to look up a couple things." He pulled up his backpack and roughly shoved the notebook and pen inside and zipped it.

Mark repeated, "What's troubling you?"

Daniel paused, then reached for his juggling balls.

"Tell me what's troubling you. I'm still your teacher, and you're still my student."

"I don't want to say."

"It will be better for both of us if you do."

Daniel looked up at the white ceiling, but there was no Nile to be found. No map of any kind. He was adrift, and he knew it. He could feel his throat constrict, and he had trouble breathing. He sputtered, "This will be our last visit."

Mark turned his head slightly. "You're sure?"

He shifted his gaze to his Converse and said, "My nose rarely lies."

"How does your nose know this is our last visit?"

"I've studied the science of taphonomy."

"Which is the study of what, exactly?"

Daniel lifted his head. "The degradation of the human body as it returns to the earth." A small tear spilled out of the corner of his left eye. He quickly used his hand to rub it away.

Mark pushed his head deep into his pillow. "How much time does your nose tell you is left for me?"

"I'd rather not answer that question." Tears were appearing quickly, small rivulets sliding down his reddened cheeks.

"That's an unfair question," Mark said kindly. "Let me rephrase. Will I be around to read your award-winning story?"

Daniel wiped his eyes and stared at the sink. There was an empty water glass and a coffee cup and a washcloth that needed to be wrung out and hung up to dry. His voice trembled. "I don't think so." He kept his focus on the sink.

Mark blinked several times, then said, "I see. Well, then it's time for me to ask a favor of you. Will you do me a favor?"

Daniel forced himself to look at Mark. "As a rule, I don't like to answer open-ended questions."

"Alright," Mark said. "How much money do you owe me for the German lessons?"

Daniel sniffed and gave a perplexed look. "Was there money involved? I thought we were just conversing."

"Then you owe me for writing lessons and baring my soul so you can win the writing award. I'll take my due in one favor."

Daniel shook his head but consented. "I guess."

"No, no guessing. You need to follow through."

"I will," he said reluctantly.

"It's a simple request. I want you to accept an invitation if it should fall into your lap unexpectedly. Deal?"

"What kind of invitation?"

"You'll know it when it comes."

Daniel stuttered just a bit. "I ... I ... don't know."

"Be bold, take the plunge, and shed your old reptilian skin. You might even enjoy the shiny skin underneath."

Daniel's hands were quivering as he slung his backpack over his left shoulder. He pulled the balls from his pockets and began to juggle. "My mother will be here in 9 minutes."

"I know," Mark said sadly.

"I want to dedicate my story. Would it be alright if I dedicate it to Marco Aloysius Mehlman?"

Mark took a deep breath and let it wheeze through his nose. "That would be the fitting thing for an author to do, dedicate the story to someone, I mean. But I would be eternally grateful if you dedicated it to Rose and Oskar."

Daniel stopped juggling and stood at the foot of Mark's bed. He looked all about the room and then squarely at Mark. "I will." Then he turned and hurried out before Mark could say another word.

When the door closed and the room was silent, Mark whispered, "*Auf Wiedersehen*, Daniel. You have brought me a joy I didn't think I'd ever experience again. *Auf Wiedersehen*."

45

JOHN AND MARK

2019

JOHN POKED HIS HEAD INTO THE MORTUARY and asked, "How you doing, old man?"

"Come in, come in," Mark said weakly. "I'm still breathing, if that's what you mean." He hit the button for the headrest to go up and gestured with his index finger for John to pull up a chair.

"Helen told me you wanted to see me," John said.

Mark's voice was raspy and seemed to come from deep in his throat. "We need to talk, while there's still time."

John was wearing his frayed moccasins and red-and-white striped flannel pajamas under a maroon robe he cinched at the waist. It was late, and the room was dimly lit with a couple night-lights. He sat as near to Mark as he could, then turned his head so his left ear was closer to Mark. "Gotta turn so I can hear better. You know my right ear is shot."

"I know, frozen in Korea, right?"

"That's what I tell everybody, but actually, I got too close to a big artillery gun. Blew the eardrum. I was a kid when I joined the Army. Thought I was invincible." He waved both hands at Mark. "Enough of that. What's up with you? Gonna get over this cancer thing?"

"Not this time, John."

John turned his head to look straight on. "What? You can't go before me. We gotta deal, remember?"

312

"Sorry. My doctor already called hospice."

"Well, find some new doctor. A second opinion, at least. They don't know everything."

"I already received a second opinion, from Daniel. I trust him more than most physicians."

"The kid? How does he know?"

"Never mind, he just knows. He's the reason why I want to talk to you."

John scowled. "It's not right. I told you I don't do *lonely* very well. You can't leave me like this."

"You have Eva. I've noticed how she looks at you. You and Eva will make a great couple. If I were you, I would put your names on the waiting list for one of the independent cottages."

"You think I should?"

"I do. Besides, she will keep you a lot warmer at night than I could."

Suddenly, John smiled a watermelon-rind smile. "I can't argue with you there." But before he could fantasize any more, he said, "Forget me, what can I do for you and the kid?"

Mark closed his eyes and breathed in and out slowly. "Do you remember how Daniel's been the punching bag for Seth and his buddies?"

John leaned back and snickered. "That Seth is a piece of work. Can't believe the thief is still employed here. What are we gonna do about the drug thing?"

"I hope we can solve it, but you have to help me. I've been thinking . . ."

But before Mark could lay out his plan, John said excitedly, "I still have some contacts in the construction business, Mark. I know I could send a few tough guys to pay Seth a visit, rough the turd up a bit. They could send a message that punk won't ever forget." He punched his fist into the side of Mark's mattress.

"Good idea, John, but that approach might take too long to organize." Mark's voice was a mere croak. "Graduation is not far off."

"A few phone calls, that's all."

"Too risky, too many people involved. But I do want you to make a phone call for me."

"You got it. Let's hear your plan."

46

ALZHEIMER'S ROUND TABLE

2019

THE ART GROUP WAS INFORMED OF A SPECIAL MEETING to be held right after breakfast. It was Saturday morning, and a couple morning newspapers were scattered on the table along with several empty coffee mugs.

Helen had spread the word about the meeting, and when the others entered, she was sitting at the table with a large shopping bag resting in front of her. The mood was somber. Even John seemed sullen as he shuffled to take his chair at the head of the table. Eva helped Marie to her chair and pushed it in when she was settled. Emma came in a bathrobe with a bright-orange scarf covering her gray hair.

Helen, dressed impeccably as usual, was in a long gray skirt, white blouse, and light-blue cardigan sweater buttoned to the neckline. She could have been heading out to a trendy restaurant for a power lunch or interviewing for a corner office in a large corporation. But her outfit couldn't hide the dour face and puffy eyes. "I asked you to come here this morning because I had a chance to talk with Mark last night before he passed away."

Marie let out a loud sob, and Eva pulled out a handkerchief from her long-sleeved sweater and handed it to her mother. "Sorry. Please go on," Eva said apologetically.

"Don't apologize, Eva," John said softly. "We all feel the same way."

315

"Mark wanted you all to know how proud he was of the writing project, and he wanted to encourage us to continue without him. He told me in no uncertain words that he enjoyed every minute. He also said he was sorry for not sharing his own writings but hoped Daniel's story would help make up for his lack of participation."

Emma lifted her head. "He helped me become a better writer and a better person. We are all going to miss him terribly."

Marie sniffled several times, then added, "It's like losing a family member."

"Nice comments, ladies. I couldn't have said it better." John turned to Helen. "What else did he have to say?"

She stood up and folded her arms across her chest. "The main reason he wanted to call us together is because he needs help with an upcoming event. He's not here, but we are, and he was hoping we could carry out one last wish of his."

"I'd do just about anything for that man," John said, and the rest muttered their approvals.

Helen continued, "As you know, he spent these last few months working with Daniel, not only teaching him German, but helping him to write a story based on his life. It seems the story is complete, and Mark hopes it will be an award-winner."

John slapped the table. "It'll win! I'd bet on that kid any day of the week and twice on Sunday!" Nodding, he sat back in his chair, his jaw clenched and his eyes dark orbs.

"That young man's got a brilliant mind," said Eva.

"But . . ." Helen leaned forward and put her hands on the table. "We all know Daniel is still lacking a little in the social graces."

"A little? He makes me look like Emily Post," said John.

"So what did Mark suggest?" asked Emma.

"Today is the high school prom. Daniel's mother has been begging him for months to ask a girl to go with him. She believes it's important for him to get out among his peers, but, of course, he's too shy or too afraid or whatever . . . he just couldn't get himself to ask a girl."

"Doesn't he have a girl *friend,* not romantically, but just a *friend*? It doesn't have to be anything more than a date," Emma offered.

"How about a relative?" John asked. "I went with my cousin to my prom. She lived far enough away that nobody knew."

"I get the impression friends are limited, and no cousins live nearby, John. But there is a possibility for a date . . . the only girl he remotely knows is named Paige Bartlett."

Emma looked up with angry eyes. "I know that name. She's going to the prom with that orderly who works around her, that Seth character."

John turned to her. "How would you know that?"

"That's all I've heard him talk about for the past few weeks. He's got big plans for prom . . . he's going with Paige Bartlett, the best-looking girl . . . she's so lucky to be his date . . . and on and on. He's a regular Lothario!"

John's nose was pinched as he asked, "What's that?"

"He thinks he's Rock Hudson or whoever is the male idol for his generation," Emma said. "He thinks he's God's gift to women. What he is is a chauvinist!" The words came out as though she were spitting a piece of foul meat from her mouth.

John looked around the table. "Is being a chauvinist good or bad?"

In unison, the women shouted, "Baaad!"

"Okay." John put both hands in front of his chest. "Okay. I'm learning as we go here. I don't like the guy for other reasons that Mark and I talked about, and I have a lot of words I could use to describe him, but *chauvinist* is not one."

Helen tapped a pencil on the table. "Let me explain what Mark had in mind. His plan includes all of us at the table. Mark wants to find a prom date for Daniel and save Paige Bartlett from a night of regret. First, we have to free up Paige . . ."

"A kidnapping!" shouted John. "I've got a few old ski masks in my closet. No one would know!"

Eva looked at John and smiled. "Your enthusiasm is wonderful, John, but it may be a bit over the top." She turned and nodded at Helen. "Go on, what did Mark propose?"

"Mark laid out a plan, and I must admit, I think it'll work. Let me show you what I have here." She stood and removed two bottles of A&W root beer and one small glass bottle of a dark, oily-colored liquid. She held up the smaller bottle first. "It starts with this: syrup of ipecac."

Emma screwed up her face. "What in the world is that?"

Marie looked up at her daughter. "Did you ever make me take any of that stuff?"

"No, Mother. You never drank that, as far as I know," Eva said softly.

"I know what syrup of ipecac is and what it does." Everyone looked with curiosity at John. He put his big, rough hands on the table and folded his fingers together as though in prayer. "It makes your stomach turn upside down. It makes you vomit until there's nothing left to throw up. It makes you sicker than a mongrel dog for at least a day, maybe two." John stared down at his thumbs. The others were waiting for an explanation, but when none came, Helen took over.

"We're going to make Seth drink this so . . ."

Emma queried, "How are we going to *make* him?"

"Sit on him and pour it down his gullet," offered John. "That's what he deserves."

Helen wrinkled her brows and then explained, "We won't *make* him. We hope he will drink it willingly. That's where the root beer comes in. See, Mark learned that Seth loves root beer and he also likes to show off by slamming drinks. You know, guzzling as much as possible in one take. Anyway, I thought we might invite Seth to have a send-off toast in Mark's honor, and we'll all drink a glass, except . . ." She held up one of the empty glasses. "His will have a little of this as a booster." She picked up the syrup of ipecac and smiled broadly. "If we get the results John told us about, he'll be too sick to go to the prom, and Paige will need a last-minute replacement date."

Marie let out a loud, "Ahhhh . . . of course. Daniel."

"Of course," added Helen.

"I like this plan. It's nasty!" John said with enthusiasm.

"Wait a minute. Even if we get Seth out of the picture," said Emma, "how do we know Daniel will even want to go to the prom? Seems to me he's pretty committed to not going. I mean, Paige is probably a nice girl and all, but . . ."

Helen interrupted. "Because Mark assured me that if Daniel receives an invitation, he's convinced he will honor it, something about shedding his old skin. I'm not sure what that means exactly, but a week ago, Mark bought a prom ticket, and to make the night special, he purchased a gift card to Che Lasalle restaurant."

"Very swanky place." Eva nodded. "I've been there, once."

"After we give Seth his potion, and assuming it works quickly, I'll call Daniel's mother and tell her Seth is *indisposed* and let her know I have a prom ticket and gift card addressed to Daniel. My guess is she'll be dancing on the rooftop thinking her son will go to the prom! The rest will take care of itself," Helen concluded.

John said emphatically, "I can guarantee Seth will never want another root beer as long as he lives."

Emma was still unsure. "Today is Saturday, the day of the prom. Do we even know if Seth is in the building?"

"He is," said Helen. "He's working a few hours this morning, and I already asked him to join us here. In fact..." She glanced at the clock. "He should be here any minute." She turned and ordered John, "Go to the door and keep watch while I pour the drinks."

"I can help," said Emma, and she ambled over to the cupboard above the sink and came back with a stack of paper cups and a spoon. She lined up six cups and watched as Helen filled all but one with soda. Then Helen opened the smaller bottle and ladled three spoonfuls of the dark syrup into the A&W and stirred it up.

"Put in another just for good measure," Emma said.

"Here comes the famous guzzler," John sang out and hurried back to his chair.

Seth strolled in just as Emma finished handing out the cups filled with root beer. Two cups stood in front of Helen, and she poured the root beer into the last. Seth stopped behind the chair usually occupied by Mark. "Whoa, looks like somebody's having a party! What's the occasion? Social Security announce a big raise?" Seth snickered at his own humorous attempt.

Helen spread her arms and indicated the open chair. "Seth, thank you for coming. Please have a seat. You probably know, Mr. Flour passed away last night."

"Yeah, sure, one of the RNs filled me in. Too bad, I liked the guy, ya know." He glanced at Helen with a quizzical look. "Did you want me to start movin' his stuff out of his room or somethin'? I can get one of the four-wheel dollies and put his crap, I mean personals, in storage. Just take me a jiffy."

"No thanks, there's plenty of time for that later. I asked you to join us because Mark left a little something for you before he passed. Something we could all enjoy."

"Cool. He left me something, huh?" He rubbed his hands together. "Probably not a bundle of Benjamins."

"Right, not that," replied Helen.

Marie looked at Eva. "What are Benjamins?"

Eva put her arm around her mother's shoulders. "One-hundred-dollar bills, Mama. Benjamin Franklin's picture is on them."

"Oh, my. That's a lot."

Helen spoke up, "Mark let all of us know how much you love

root beer, Seth, especially A&W root beer, so we thought you might join us in sharing a final toast in his honor."

Seth jerked his head back slightly. "Sure, let's do it."

Helen continued, "I opened one of the bottles and poured everyone a cupful. There's still one bottle unopened that I'll put in the refrigerator. You can take it home with you when you leave."

"Sounds good. I'm outta here by noon, got a big day and night ahead."

"Prom night, kid?" John asked with false sincerity.

"Should be a blast."

Helen walked over to Seth. "Here's your glass." She set his drink in front of him and returned, sat down, looked over at John, and nodded.

John held up his glass, and the others followed. "I'm not one for makin' speeches, but I think we can all agree that Mark was a heroic man in many respects and will be missed by all." He hesitated for a few seconds, then peered into Seth's eyes and challenged him. "Mark mentioned you were the slammin' king of your high school, Seth. So, as we say farewell to Mark, you can go ahead and chug it, if you can?"

"Oh, yeah, nothing to it."

"To Mark!" John said, his paper cup held high. The others all joined in and hailed their friend.

Seth lifted the cup dramatically to his lips and in one long gulp took it all in, then wiped his lips on the sleeve of his shirt as though he were in an old Western movie. "That's good stuff. Not as good as real beer, but that's coming later."

After the others sipped on their cups and then replaced them on the table, John spoke up. "We hear you're takin' a real nice gal to the prom."

"She's hot. Could've had the pick of the litter . . . and she certainly made the right choice."

"You beat out all the competition?" asked Eva.

"Oh, no, I was talking about me. Of all the girls who wanted a date with me, I chose Paige Bartlett. She's the lucky one!" His mouth curled up as wide as a happy-face sticker.

Eva let her smile fade quickly, then said through tight lips, "Oh, I see. *You* were the *big catch*."

Seth stood and pushed his chair in with a noisy scratch of the floor. "If that's all you wanted, I got a lotta chores before I hit the road." He threw his thumb over his shoulder and backed up a few steps.

Helen bowed slightly. "Thank you for joining us, Seth. It's heartening to know how much you valued Mark while he was with us."

"Yeah, okay."

"Enjoy the prom tonight," Emma said with a phony smile.

Seth took a couple of steps toward the door and then stopped. "Ohhh . . . ahhh . . . the A&W doesn't seem to go with eggs and sausage." Suddenly, his face turned white and seemed to be made of silly putty, flexing in several directions and causing deep creases. He grabbed at his belly.

Eva looked over at Seth but didn't move. "You're probably just a little nervous. It can happen before a big date."

John stood and held his arm straight out, pointing with his index finger at Seth. "Gas! That's what I think. Kid's got gas! Won't kill ya, Seth, but sure feels bad. Why not rest in the break room? They got a couch there."

Seth took a couple of uneven steps with his palm wavering over his mouth. "Good idea, not feelin' so solid here."

"Can I help?" John shouted.

"No thanks, Mr. Mancuser, I can make it." He scuttled off like a wounded crab looking for a place to hide.

John walked over to the door and hollered after him, "Pepto-Bismol might help! And by the way . . . it's Mancuso, Mancuso!" He turned back to the ART group. "Stupid kid's been working here for nearly a year and still doesn't know my name. Deserves everything he gets. And trust me," John said gleefully, "he'll be feeling like death warmed over about right now."

Helen stood and gathered the cups, then walked over and put the unopened A&W in the fridge and poured the rest of the opened bottle down the drain. "Alright, everybody, I think it's safe to call Daniel's mother. Operation *Prom* is well underway."

"I like this plan," announced Marie. "I think it will work. And I am so happy that Mark took the time to help his young friend. He would be proud of us."

Eva smiled and helped her mother into a wheelchair. Emma stood and turned to leave. John too. But they stopped suddenly when Helen asked, "Before you go, John, could you tell us, if you don't mind, how is it you know so much about syrup of ipecac? It's not a household drug."

John turned and sat back in his chair with a loud groan. He breathed in deeply and let it out with a sorrowful sigh. His voice trembled a bit as he spoke. "It's the drug that saved me. You all know since reading my stories that my personal life is, or was, a train wreck, and that's putting it mildly. When I first came here, I was confused. Sure, I had a mild stroke and my brain was jumbled for a few days before I ended up here, but that wasn't what really hurt. Maureen had divorced me years ago, and my kids, they're scattered all over creation . . . they rarely call or stop in. I was a poor parent, I admit, and an awful husband. 'Bout the only thing I've ever been good at was using my hands to build things." He paused as the analog clock ticked loudly.

"When I couldn't build houses anymore, and my kids didn't talk to me . . . well . . . I just got confused. And after being here about a month, I got so confused that one night I took a whole bunch of pills. Lucky for me, Mark came into my room to check on me . . . he was good at doing that. He hardly knew me then, but he could sense I was hurting. He was a true hero to me.

323

He found me on the floor and called the nurses, and they gave me the same stuff Seth is dealing with—syrup of ipecac. Mark saved my life. Not just that one night, but ever since. We talked, a lot, and he made me realize there's still a lotta good stuff to live for."

With that, John looked squarely at Eva, who smiled back and nodded. A single tear rolled down her left cheek as she leaned onto the arm of her mother's wheelchair. John used a paper napkin to clear his eyes. "I'll miss Mark more than you all will ever know. Lucky for me, he, and syrup of ipecac, not only saved my life but opened up my eyes to a whole new world."

John picked up a used paper cup and held it high. "Fear not, Mark, I will honor your wishes as you asked. Happy Trails, buddy." Then he dropped his head and sobbed into his shirtsleeves.

47

PROM

2019

TINY, WHITE CHRISTMAS LIGHTS were woven into a portable arch in front of the heavy wooden doors of the Riverview Country Club. Cutouts of mermaids riding on seahorses and Poseidon on his dolphin were attached randomly to the arch. Over the door itself was a long banner with the high school crest and the theme of the prom: *Dreams Under the Sea*.

A small, white wicker table and matching chair were placed alongside the arch for Lenore Ryan, who greeted the guests and collected the tickets. Lenore had volunteered to chaperone and be the greeter each prom for over a decade. It was a chance for her to get dolled up in an outfit that could only be referred to as a prom dress for a middle-aged woman.

She wore a canary-yellow dress with puffy chiffon sleeves, a satin bodice cinched at the waist, and a hemline that reached down to her ankles. It was cut as low in the front as Lenore dared, showing just a touch of cleavage. She wore a string of faux pearls with a brushed-granite stone pendant and matching pearl drop earrings. She had a pair of long, white gloves, but they were folded on the table. If the night turned too chilly, they might come in handy.

As the pairs of students strolled up the red-brick walk, she greeted them loudly with compliments on their dresses, hair, tuxes, corsages, whatever jumped out at her. She spent so many hours and so many days listening to the miseries of students' dysfunctional families, addiction problems, economic woes, bully reports, unwanted pregnancies, and on and on that for one night, she put the troubles aside, treated herself to a fancy dinner, and greeted the students in an idyllic setting. Her smile was incessant.

Some of the students hired limos to cart them from home to restaurant to the dance. Many of the students who owned their own cars, mostly secondhand or cheaper models, borrowed a parent's car, so higher-end autos, washed and shiny, gleamed in the decorative lighting of the parking lot. The air was clear and summery, warm for the middle of May. A horned moon played hide-and-seek through high, wispy clouds. Occasionally, a southerly breeze tickled the cutouts on the arch, and for a moment, the dolphins swam and the seahorses gently rocked their long-haired ladies.

Lenore greeted a sharply dressed couple, she in a purple-and-green cocktail-length clingy dress and he in a tan tux with a bow tie that matched her dress colors. She stepped ahead and held open one of the red wood doors, encouraging them to enjoy the music and dancing. When she turned back, she saw Denise Mannheim dressed in a white blouse, a fetching multi-colored scarf, and a maroon skirt. With a quizzical face, Lenore scurried back to her table and said, "Hello, Denise."

"I bet you didn't expect to see me tonight."

Lenore sucked in a breath as she stammered, "I ... I didn't. But I'm happy you came." She looked past Denise and asked, "Are you alone?"

"No, I certainly am not," Denise said proudly. "Daniel and his date will be here in a moment. He's inspecting some flowers in the center circle of the drive. Caladiums, I think he called them."

Lenore's hand flew up to her chest. "Daniel? You're kidding! With a date?"

"That's right," said Denise, her smile as wide and pointed as the crescent moon.

"How did this happen? Do tell."

Denise stepped off the brick walk onto the dewy grass. Lenore followed her, and the two sat on a white wrought-iron bench. "It all happened so quickly, I hardly believe it myself. I received a phone call a little before noon ..."

"Today?"

"Yes, today, from one of the residents at the Bethlehem Retirement Community." She stopped suddenly and put her hand on Lenore's arm. "You heard Mark Flour died yesterday?"

Lenore frowned and lowered her head to one side. "I did. Such a shame. He was such a good man and so kind to Daniel."

Denise nodded. "Daniel was terribly upset. I know he was hurting. He stayed locked in his room, finishing the story he and Mark had been working on, and he didn't even stop for supper. We had to get his story postmarked by midnight, and he barely made it."

Lenore put on a sympathetic face. "Daniel will be fine, I'm sure of it." There was a short pause. "But the phone call ... ?"

"Right, right. The caller, I think she said her name was Helen, told me Seth Wenton got very sick at work and was throwing up to beat the band and wouldn't be able to attend the prom."

"His date was ... Paige Bartlett!" Lenore almost screamed.

"Now she's Daniel's date."

"My god! How did that come about?"

"Well, first I called Paige's mom to make sure Paige still wanted to go to the prom—of course she did, having purchased a dress and flowers and all. Barbara Bartlett was thrilled with a replacement. Seems she wasn't too keen on Paige going with Seth Wenton in the first place."

"Good for her. But how did you talk Daniel into asking her?"

"That's the weird part. Helen from the BRC was sending over an invitation to the prom and a gift card to Che Lasalle, paid for by Mark Flour. At first when I told Daniel about Seth being sick, he had no interest in calling Paige, but when I mentioned it wouldn't cost much because there was an invitation waiting for him care of Mark Flour. Well . . . he hesitated for about thirty seconds and then picked up the phone and called Paige. I'm a skeptic when it comes to miracles, but I believe I witnessed one today."

"Amazing, Denise. I am so happy for you." She gave her a big hug, almost lifting her off the ground. "What about Seth? Is he very sick?"

"I phoned his mother too. She called the clinic and said it's probably a flu bug of some kind and he should be fine in a day or so. Turns out she was very supportive; she realized Paige had put out lots of money and didn't want the *poor girl* to waste it by sitting home. Her words, *poor girl.*"

"Congratulations."

"And, despite Daniel's unwillingness to be photographed, I told him I wouldn't chauffeur him around unless I could take as many photos as I wanted." Denise triumphantly held up a camera as though it were an Olympic gold medal.

Lenore suddenly turned her attention to the walkway. She spun Denise around as she announced, "Speaking of the lovely couple, here they are." They stepped back onto the brick walk. "Hello, you two. Paige, you look stunning, and Daniel, handsome as ever." Lenore couldn't have been more complimentary if she tried.

Paige smiled demurely. "Thank you, Mrs. Ryan."

"Ditto," said Daniel.

Denise moved around, taking as many candids as she could get before they entered the building.

Paige was beautiful. She had shoulder-length blond hair hanging in tiny curls, hiding her delicate ears and falling quietly on her lightly tanned, bare shoulders. She wore a form-fitting dress the color of wood violets and sported a beautiful corsage of tiny yellow roses and white carnations. Her blue eyes sparkled, and her smile was blinking on and off like a lighthouse beacon.

Daniel looked taller than his six-foot frame in a black-and-white tuxedo, compliments of his mother's last-minute scouring of every rental store in town. His hair was shiny and combed, and his breast pocket sported a deep-red handkerchief. He did, however, win the fight over shoes and wore his black-and-white low-cut Converse sneakers. Oddly, they looked casual and sporty at the same time. Even his mom smiled when he was fully dressed.

Lenore stepped closer. "My job this evening, along with greeting each couple, is to collect tickets."

Daniel pulled the tickets from his coat pocket.

"Thank you, Daniel." She turned and swept one hand in front of her, speaking in a deep voice, "And my other job is to tell you to have a wonderful time." She showed all her teeth when she smiled.

"We will, Mrs. Ryan. Thanks."

"Ditto." And they walked toward the door.

"Oh," said Lenore, "I almost forgot. Your tickets entitle the two of you to the post-prom, held at the VFW Hall starting right after the dance and running till 4:00 a.m."

Daniel looked over at Paige, who smiled and nodded excitedly. Daniel smiled back and looked to his mom. "You don't have to pick us up at midnight, Mom. We'll find our own ride home."

Before Daniel saw the stunned look on his mother's face, he turned toward the door and shouted over his shoulder, "Take the night off, Hoke!"

Denise almost collapsed into Lenore, who was holding her hand over her mouth and giggling.

48

DANIEL

2019

DANIEL'S FATHER WAS TALL, DARK-HAIRED, BONY-FACED, and had an uncanny likeness to the photo of Abraham Lincoln hanging in Mr. Jensen's classroom. His skin was rough and pock-marked, and his five-day-old beard was blotchy with white circles like the rear end of an Appaloosa horse. He appeared the Thursday before graduation at the front door with an old leather satchel and wore a Cleveland Indians baseball cap. Denise led him to the kitchen, where Daniel was already seated for supper. It was 6:07.

"I thought you were going to drive?" Denise said. "I would have picked you up at the airport if you had called."

"Last-minute change," he answered. "My car's not in the best of health, and I didn't want to take the chance. Plus, we only have one car, so Monica would be without transportation if I drove."

"Uh-huh," said Denise, scowling. "Well, you're just in time for supper. Daniel, please set another place for your father."

"Hello, Daniel. Congratulations on your upcoming graduation."

Daniel stared at Anton Mannheim for a moment. Then he gave him the slightest nods, set his fork full of pasta on his plate, and headed to the cupboard for another place setting. "How was your flight?" he asked flatly as he turned back to the table.

"Bumpy," his father said. "Seems every thunderstorm from here to Ohio was in our flight path." Anton sat down and pulled his chair up to the table. The chair let out a loud screech on the tile floor. He stared at the bowls of salad and platter of linguini noodles on the table. "Everything looks wonderful."

Denise passed Anton a bowl of pasta tossed with a garlic and sesame seed oil dressing. Daniel set down a small plate of fresh carrot sticks, celery sticks topped with natural peanut butter, and white radishes cut in slices.

"Would you like a glass of water?" Denise asked.

"No, thank you. I had a beer on the plane."

Daniel returned to his seat and picked at the whole grain pasta. His fork scraped loudly against his plate like a nail on a chalkboard. Denise gave him a piercing glance. "Sorry," he said quietly.

Denise turned to Anton. "We appreciate you making the effort to come for Daniel's graduation. The ceremony should be exciting, seeing as Daniel is valedictorian, as you know . . ."

"Wonderful honor," Anton threw in.

Denise continued, ". . . and therefore he has to give a speech. But the principal has made it clear that all speeches will be short."

"No more than 300 words. He wants to look over the content beforehand," Daniel said coldly.

Anton flicked his eyebrows. "How long is 300 words?"

Daniel stopped chewing and said through clenched lips, "3 to 5 minutes."

"Anyway," Denise went on, "the whole affair should take no more than an hour, according to Mr. Tobias, the principal, and he runs a tight ship. Right, Daniel?"

"There are 130 graduates, Mom. Assuming they all attend and walk up to the podium with parents, each will take 30 seconds on average to navigate stairs, handshakes, and photos. That alone will take 63.5 minutes. No way will the ceremony be over in an hour."

Denise let her head nod to the side in resignation and sighed heavily. "Okay, ninety minutes then. That's not bad. It starts at two, so we should be home by four. I have a special dinner all planned with Daniel's favorites—free-range chicken in a lemon and mustard sauce, homemade potato dumplings, and fresh peas from Tyner's farm market. I ordered the peas this morning." Her smile showed her gleaming teeth.

Daniel pulled his fork from his mouth and tried to smile, but it faded into a frown. He stabbed a round slice of a Cherry Belle radish and made a loud crunching sound as it disappeared in his mouth.

Anton sat back in his chair and brought his hands to the side of his plate. "I need to talk to you about the timing of Saturday's festivities." Both Denise and Daniel looked at him with a sense of foreboding. "I received a text from Monica while the plane was in the air. It seems our youngest daughter has come down with a bad cough, and Monica needs my help. She hasn't been sleeping too well as it is, what with getting up to feed the baby in the middle of the night and all." The refrigerator motor kicked in, and the humming seemed more like a car with a faulty muffler. "So, I changed my return flight time to tomorrow afternoon at four. I'm sorry, Daniel."

For a moment, Anton didn't think he had been heard. Denise looked over at the stove as though she had left a burner on. Daniel sat with a blank expression.

Finally, Daniel said, "The graduation is Saturday. If you leave at four tomorrow, you will be 22 hours short."

"I know, and I truly planned to stay through Saturday. But . . ." His hands were raised in defense. ". . . the best-laid plans . . ." His voice trailed like a caboose in fog.

The pink in Denise's cheeks turned a deep crimson. "Why am I not surprised."

"I'm sorry, Denise, it just didn't turn out."

"Kind of like our marriage and family life, huh?" she spat. "It's your son I'm concerned about, not me."

Anton turned to his son, but Daniel was already on his feet, plate in hand, heading to the sink. "I prefer these noodles, Mom. Better than the last batch. Did you get them at the Co-op?"

"I did, they're made with kale and spinach. Did you hear your father?" He rinsed his plate and headed for his room. "Daniel, where are you going?"

He didn't turn back but stared at the wall. "I have to work on my speech."

"Don't you want to visit with your father? You just heard him say he's leaving tomorrow," she said, her voice imploring him to stay.

"I know, Mom. 17 hours and 33 minutes from now. That's 2 hours and 25 minutes more than the last time." He walked down the hall and disappeared behind his bedroom door.

49

DANIEL

2019

THE FRIDAY BEFORE GRADUATION, all senior classes ended by noon. After a picnic lunch held outside on the soccer field, seniors were to meet in the library with the principal for final instructions and practice marching into the gym.

At 12:45, Principal Tobias stood on a wooden library chair and called for quiet. "Make sure your robes are pressed and don't forget your caps and tassels. We don't have any extras, so if you leave anything at home, you're outta luck! Wear appropriate clothing underneath your gowns; we don't want any streakers!" His levity did not go unnoticed.

"Damn," one girl shouted and snapped her fingers. "I was so looking forward to a naked afternoon jog!" There was a general sound of snickering and light applause.

"Alright, alright," Mr. Tobias said. "Calm down. When we leave the library, I want you all to line up alphabetically. Your parents will accompany you to the front of the gym, and then they will split off and sit in the bleachers. Mrs. Rice . . ." He peered out over the crowd. "There she is." He pointed to a short, plump woman with a clipboard in hand and reading glasses hanging around her flabby neck. "Mrs. Rice has a list of all the parents who are planning to escort their son or daughter to the podium. If you have any changes to that list, let Mrs. Rice know before you leave this room. I don't want any surprises." With that, Principal Tobias turned the rehearsal over to the senior teachers.

Daniel was leaning against a window on the far wall next to the nonfiction books. He sidled his way toward Mrs. Rice and said over her shoulder, "I have to make a change."

She turned sharply. "Daniel, I didn't see you. What's the change?"

"My father will not be at the graduation ceremony."

She scanned her list and put her finger on Daniel Mannheim's name. "How about your mom, Denise? Is she still coming?"

"Yes."

"Okay." She erased Anton Mannheim. Then she looked up to Daniel. "Is he ill?"

"No." Daniel hesitated. "He's traveling." And with that, he slithered through the throng, avoiding contact wherever possible, and headed for the gym.

50

GRADUATION

2019

THEY WERE LINED UP ON THE STAGE like bowling pins: school board members, principals, student leaders, salutatorians, and valedictorian. The other graduates paraded down the center aisle two by two alphabetically, like a legion of returning soldiers. The crowd hooted and whistled. Fortunately for Daniel, the student speakers were allowed to come in a side door and climbed onto the stage without much notice. The dais was decorated for the occasion in royal-blue and white bunting. Helium balloons of similar colors were tied to every available railing. Three or four balloons had already broken loose and were hovering against the ceiling tiles.

If Daniel hadn't been valedictorian, he would have been paired with a football jock named Nicholas Manchester. Nick was tall, with a thick muscular neck and brown spiky hair, and talked with a slight lisp. He was a card-carrying Neanderthal.

Daniel smiled inwardly when Nick filed close to the stage with his alphabetical partner, Shelley Minten, a preppy girl who dressed to the nines for every occasion. She was frowning because she was forced to wear a simple royal-blue gown and tacky cap. She would not give Nick a passing glance because she believed he was bound for a greasy job and a clapboard ranch house with a detached garage. Her sights were set on a newly built house with brick accents not under

3000 square feet, overlooking Lake Michigan in Door County or in a tony Milwaukee suburb.

There were over 1500 people crammed into a gymnasium that the fire code said could only handle 1250. Daniel made a mental note to tell Mr. Tobias as soon as the ceremony was over. The temperature was rising with each extra body. Dark sweat rings already appeared on short-sleeved shirts and sleeveless dresses. A few overweight men had moisture lines forming on the backs of their shirts.

Daniel wore his gown and cap but tucked the tassel under the cap so it wouldn't tickle his ear. It was a ridiculous outfit, and he wished he could skip the whole affair and have the school district snail mail his diploma. That would bring his high school career to a fitting conclusion. He knew he would enjoy a letter or package in the mail more than being propped up in front of a senior class that for the most part ignored, bullied, or misunderstood him. But here he was, watching the ark fill up two by two.

He had to give a speech. It wasn't as though someone put a gun to his head, but it was tradition and an honor, he guessed, to be on the podium. Mostly, he was fulfilling his mom's dream, and that was more important than his anxiety. Besides, he had his juggling balls in his pockets. Just in case.

He looked out in the crowd and found his mom. She was wearing a light-yellow blouse and gray skirt. She had purchased shoes for the occasion and had visited the beauty parlor earlier in the day. He smiled at her, and she smiled back. He wished he could do more to make her happy. Not that she wasn't happy now, but she had spent so many years watching over him, foregoing chances to make friends or travel or join social clubs.

His relationship with his mom was uncompromising, and they were always supportive of each other, yet he worried about her. He knew all about autism—the research and symptoms, the long-term studies, the breakdown in racial and ethnic groups, the difference in geographic pairings. He knew it all . . . but it didn't help with his anxiety toward his mom. She had sacrificed so much, and he didn't want to embarrass her. He would give his speech to please her, but he would do it his way.

"Thank you all for coming today." Mr. Tobias's voice squeaked, then settled over the loudspeaker as the crowd became quiet. It broke Daniel's reverie. He was going to have to speak in about 12 minutes. He had his speech rolled up in his hand and started to unroll it. Mr. Tobias had perused it yesterday to make sure there was nothing objectionable. Daniel had no intention of using it.

After the Pledge of Allegiance and the pep band's version of "The Star-Spangled Banner," the president of the school board stepped to the podium. Mr. Koopman was a short man whose girth almost exceeded his height. He had white hair that needed trimming on his otherwise round, cantaloupe head. His voice was soft, and when he tried to be emphatic, it came out as a shriek and difficult to understand. He gave the same speech every year, utilizing stereotypical phrases like "We will miss you, but you will be replaced," and "Best of luck with your future choices," and "It's been an honor to preside over such a wonderful occasion as this graduation."

When he finished, it was time for the student speeches. Two salutatorians did a tag-team speech, recalling both the highs and lows of their four years in high school. One girl took the negative, which was intended to be humorous, and the other girl the accomplishments. Daniel couldn't help but see the two angels perched on the shoulders of Dr. Faustus, bickering back and forth, *You enjoyed it! You hated it! You enjoyed it! You hated it!*

Then it was time for the student council president, Millie Shapman. Daniel sat behind her in Calculus. She was pretty and quiet and very serious. She never talked to Daniel unless passing back papers. But he had overheard conversations she had with others about problems in the student parking lot, or random locker searches, or what the school could do to help cut down carbon emissions. Her speech was short, clever, articulate, and well structured. *Someday she may run for a political office,* Daniel thought.

Mr. Tobias stepped back to the microphone and pulled it upward by at least 12 inches. "Thank you, Millie. That was a wonderful and thought-provoking speech." The crowd had folded the programs into fans, and hundreds were fluttering as bat wings in the stuffy, humid air. Many of the graduates and parents were checking their phones. Millie may have given a thought-provoking speech, but there were plenty who thought Facebook, ESPN, Twitter, or Instagram were more important.

"Now, it gives me great pleasure to introduce the 2019 valedictorian. This young man received all As for four years and had exceptional attendance, missing only three days of instruction. Please welcome ... Daniel Mannheim."

The audience gave its tepid approval. They seemed to be clapping more in anticipation that the end was coming so they could get on with the main attraction: house parties, bonfires, and gift giving.

Daniel walked slowly to the podium and stared at the microphone for a full 30 seconds. He pulled on his royal-blue gown trimmed with gold cords and drew out the three juggling balls. He could juggle for his three minutes and sit down. There would be nothing objectionable about it. He looked at each ball carefully and then set them on the podium one at a time.

The crowd quieted, put down their electronic devices, and seemed to take a collected breath to focus on the podium, wondering, waiting for something astonishing to happen. Daniel kept his eyes on the three balls. The entire room became as silent as a cave. Mr. Tobias crossed his legs and folded his hands in his lap. The stains under his arms turned dark.

Daniel cleared his throat, looked toward the rafters, and finally spoke. "I am here to give a speech." His voice was flat, but loud enough for all to hear. The gym was built with exposed steel beams that had been painted the same royal blue as the graduation gowns. One balloon bobbed and spun in a circle, its string caught in a ceiling fan.

"When my three minutes are up, 2300 new babies will have entered the world . . . the polar ice shield will have shrunk by two-hundredths of an inch . . . the Earth will have rotated 3800 feet . . . all while I'm standing here in front of 147 graduates in our tiny city in one of 50 states on 1 of 7 continents." He lowered his gaze and looked again at the three balls.

"Life is not infinite. We are on this planet for a fraction of a second in the Earth's life span. If you want me to give advice on how to achieve financial success, social happiness, and relief in stressful situations, I suggest these." He picked up the balls, stepped to the side, and started to juggle. At first, the audience tittered, then laughed, and finally clapped.

After a moment, Daniel plucked the balls from the air, stepped back to the podium, and set the balls carefully on the podium tray.

"I am a person with autism. I have a brain that's different from yours." He was staring at the Oakwood High crest on the wall above the last row of graduates. "I have an ability to see things and memorize things and understand things you can't. I am not an outlier, nor a freak of nature, any more than a person born with perfect pitch, or incredible running speed, or a musician who can play any instrument without reading music, or a person who can love others without hesitation.

"The world is a biosphere made up of complex forces. It takes 20,000 bees to make 10 pounds of honey and 100 gallons of sap to make 1 gallon of maple syrup. It takes students with all types of abilities to make up a graduating class. I am only one.

"Recently, I wrote a story about a man who fought in World War II and was captured and became a POW for 19 months. He was only seventeen when he was conscripted, forced to serve. He had no choice. The world can be dangerous. The world can be hurtful. How many of us could survive for 19 months as a prisoner in a foreign country, no cell phones, no family, no electronics of any kind . . . yet this man didn't become angry and hateful. When he escaped from the prison, he used his entire life to teach and help others. This man died recently. He was my friend. He understood me and my autism. I hope the Oakwood High School graduates of 2019 don't have to be ninety years old before a person with autism or any other difference can be their friend."

The overhead fans hummed loudly, and a few chairs squeaked as the gym remained silent. Daniel stood looking down at the three juggling balls. He picked each one up and examined it like a farmer candling the eggs. He then turned and looked at Principal Tobias, whose face was drawn and his lips tight. As principal, he didn't want his ceremony to become a disturbance of any kind. The school board president was mopping his sweaty, bald head with a brown-and-white handkerchief.

Daniel turned back to the audience and said, softly, "There are three things I will leave behind as I pass through the doors of Oakwood High School." He held up the first ball. "*Fear*. I will no longer fear any of my peers." He raised the second. "*Insecurity*. I have found people who accept me and will help me reach my future goals." He raised the third ball. "*Guilt*. I am proud of who I am and will never again apologize for my gifts." And with that, he strode over and dropped the three juggling balls one at a time into the lap of a startled Principal Tobias. He then returned to his seat and leaned back, watching the balloon go round and round like one of the fourteen moons of Neptune.

No one clapped. Unsure if the speech had concluded, the crowd waited for the next move. After stuffing the balls into his sport coat pockets, Mr. Tobias returned to the podium. "Let's give Daniel a big hand."

When the clapping subsided, the principal called up the senior class faculty advisors to help in the handing out of diplomas. When each graduate's name was announced, he or she was accompanied by parents, guardians, or grandparents. Hands were shaken, photos snapped, and the next grad came forward.

Daniel concentrated on his black-and-white Converse for most of the first half of the alphabet. When the line of Ms stood up from their folding chairs and moved forward, he walked off the dais to meet with his mom. She was beaming with pride. Standing next to her was a man, his head down, dressed in an old brown suit and polished black shoes. At first, Daniel thought his father had returned, and a shock of fear ran down his spine. When the man looked up, Daniel smiled and walked to greet him.

John Mancuso was nervous, walking slowly but firmly. "I hope you will accept my being here," he said. "I'm not your father, and I'm not Mark, but I would be honored to walk up to the stage with you." His voice trembled a bit, and his hands were at his side.

Daniel stepped between his mother and John. "Thank you for coming, Mr. Mancuso." He held out both elbows, and his mother and John locked arms with the valedictorian.

After the conferring of diplomas, the crowd filtered into the commons where cookies and soft drinks were available, courtesy of the junior class. Families and friends milled around for more pictures and well-wishes. Some of the grads circulated, handing out invitations to their graduation parties. None approached Daniel, except for Paige. She was still wearing her cap and gown as she sidled up to him. "I loved your speech," she said with an honest face.

"Thank you."

"I wish I had the courage to say the things you said." She smiled and looked into Daniel's eyes to find that he was staring back.

"You have the courage to talk to a person of autism. That's more than most."

Paige invited him to her graduation party at her house. She told him her dad had cleaned the garage and set up tables and chairs, and her mom had been cooking all week. "Would you please come?"

"I will," he said without hesitation.

Then she turned her attention to Denise. "Mrs. Mannheim, my mom asked me to ask you if you would like to come to my party too. She would love to talk with you." There was a plea in her voice.

"Of course, Paige, I wouldn't miss it. And congratulations to you as well."

The blush in Paige's cheeks turned from pink to scarlet. "Thank you, Mrs. Mannheim."

Denise snared John's arm and pulled him closer. "May I bring a friend of mine and Daniel's, Mr. Mancuso, to your party?"

"Of course," replied Paige.

John stepped forward and introduced himself, then asked, "Were you Daniel's date for the prom?"

"I was." Paige looked to Daniel. "We had a great time, didn't we, Daniel?"

"Ditto," Daniel answered.

"I see now that Daniel had the prettiest date in the senior class," John said, "and the nicest." He loosened his tie a bit. "Thank you for letting me come to your party." He took one step back before asking, "By chance, I know this is a bit out of the ordinary, but . . . are you serving any bratwursts?"

Paige answered excitedly, "My dad is cooking the brats right now. Oh, and there's plenty of beer."

"Hot damn! I need to get out more." Everyone laughed, even Daniel, his face warm and rosy in the fluorescent lighting.

Paige said her goodbyes and drifted into the crowd. John looked over to Daniel and gave him a silly but sincere grin. "Well done, young man." Then he added to the ceiling, "Well done, Mark. Bully for you!"

Before they left the mob in the commons, Lenore Ryan waved

from across the room and wiggled her way to join them. "Daniel, congratulations! I am so proud of you. Your speech was ... well ... so you. Just wonderful and poignant and what needed to be said." She turned and gave Denise a big hug. "You should be so proud."

"I am. Thanks, Lenore, for everything." She turned and introduced John.

"John Mancuso, from BRC?" Lenore said excitedly. "How nice of you to come and support Daniel."

"He's a great kid. It's my pleasure." John was enjoying the moment. "And we're going right from here to a graduation party."

"Wow." Lenore pulled in her lips and chortled. "Aren't you the lucky ones!"

Suddenly, Officer Rivera, the police liaison officer, came up behind Lenore. He was dressed in his navy-blue uniform with black belt and silver piping along the slacks. "Sorry to interrupt, folks, but Lenore, could I have a word?"

"Sure." She turned to Denise. "I'll be right back."

A moment later, she returned, carrying a diploma in her left hand. "Sorry about that. Always something."

Denise gave her a quizzical look. "Nothing to do with Daniel, I hope?"

"No, no, this diploma is for a student who wasn't able to be here today."

"Seth Wenton, he's waiting his arraignment," announced Daniel. Denise gave him an incredulous look. "How did you ..."

"Police records are accessible online, Mom."

In a hushed voice, Lenore confided, "Seth was picked up by the police a couple days ago. Seems they finished their investigation about drug stealing and selling activity that led back to Seth and a few others. Evidently, it happened right before the prom."

John Mancuso punched his fist into his palm. "Got what he deserved!"

"What do you know about this?" Lenore asked.

John motioned with his fingers for the others to huddle toward him. When they stepped closer, he said, "Mark Flour knew the father of the young policeman you just talked to, Officer Rivera." He pointed at the PLO officer now near the doorway. "His father was a student of Mark's years ago, a good student too, according to Mark. Anyway, before Mark passed away, residents at BRC found out Seth was stealing pills from them, so I called the officer's father, Mark's ex-student, and explained the whole thing. A few days later, a couple detectives showed up at the BRC, and boy, did we give 'em an earful on that Wenton kid."

Lenore shook her head in amazement. "Officer Rivera wants me to keep this ..." She held up the diploma. "... until the courts decide on Seth's fate. I'll put it in my office before I forget. See you at Paige's party." Lenore made her goodbyes and scurried off.

John, Denise, and Daniel gathered their things and walked through the front doors of Oakwood High. The June 6th sun was bright, and the humid air hung like a gray film. John walked with renewed energy; he liked the hot weather. He turned to Daniel and said, "When I was building houses in weather like this, I could sweat off five pounds in a day. Unfortunately, by the time I stopped for a few beers after work ... well ... I put it right back on."

"8 to 10 glasses of water is required for men on a hot day," Daniel added.

"Beer's mostly water, isn't it?"

"Ninety-two percent on average."

"Well, I can't do that anymore anyway," he said dismissively. "I have two beers now and I'm under the table."

When they arrived at their car, John asked Daniel, "You got any plans for a summer job?" Daniel looked at his mom and shook his head sheepishly. "I've never had a paying job."

"Well, apparently there's an opening at the BRC for a health aid.

Seems one Seth Wenton won't be back anytime soon." John grinned, and his eyebrows shot up as he opened the door of the front passenger side. "Just sayin.'" And he slid in and slammed the door.

Daniel looked at his mom, who was smiling as wide as Neptune's universe. "Mom, I think it's time I learned to drive a car."

EPILOGUE

2019

JOHN WALKED WITH EVA OUT OF THE BETHLEHEM RETIREMENT COMMUNITY after the ART meeting broke up. The day started dreary, low-hanging clouds and a wispy fog forming a circle around the sun. By noon, the sun had poked through the cirrus clouds, and by early evening, the temperature was still in the mid-seventies. The white blossoms of the crab apple trees lining the parking lot were alive with bees of all kinds. The daylilies were open wide, their orange-and-yellow petals stretching skyward, and the smell of freshly mown grass was strong.

John opened the door to Eva's car and waited for the heat to escape. He breathed deeply and smiled across the roof, watching Eva as she folded herself behind the steering wheel. On the way to Riverside Cemetery, he talked nonstop about the Oakwood High graduation, the party at Paige's, the brats and beer, the card and money collected from the ART group that he presented to Daniel, and the pleasure he had walking on the stage with the valedictorian. "I'm not a smart guy, Eva, but I felt like Einstein at that moment." Eva listened and nodded and smiled.

John had not felt so alive in a long time. His energy and positive outlook were infectious, and Eva was thinking of future outings, maybe even dancing at the Long Lake Casino on a Saturday night. She was thrilled with John's suggestion that they put their names on the waiting list for one of the independent cottages on the BRC campus.

"I was so proud that you escorted Daniel. That was a wonderful thing you did for him."

"It was for me too, Eva," John said. "It was a great day for me too."

The car stopped in a shady area not far from Mark's grave. Three or four magnificent oaks with branches crisscrossing the area were nearly leafed out. Eva and John walked together to the foot of the grass-covered grave sporting the lone American flag and simple headstone.

Eva handed John a cardboard tube and watched as he walked to the headstone and unfurled the contents, bent over, and pushed the wooden pole sporting a new German flag into the ground equal distance from the American flag. He stepped back to Eva's side and took her hand. "Now it's complete," John said.

"We'll miss you, Mark," whispered Eva. "You brought two countries together . . ." Her eyes fell affectionately on John ". . . and two people."

AUTHOR'S NOTE

The characters in this story are fictitious, but the events are based on historical facts. Between four hundred thousand and half a million World War II POWs came to America from 1942-45, with all but two states in the lower forty-eight housing some. Wisconsin held nearly 20,000 POWs, mostly Germans and some Italians, the majority arriving in 1943 and 1944. Camps for the POWs were sprinkled throughout the state and by design were in rural areas.

The U.S. Army had little fear that the POWs would escape or cause trouble of any kind, but rather the Army feared reprisals by local residents. Therefore, newspapers were ordered not to carry stories or report on the locations of POW encampments. The punishment for breaking the censorship could result in the closure of the newspaper.

Many local farms paid a marginal daily fee for POW workers, as did canneries, orchards (especially in Door County, Wisconsin), and municipal road crews. Strong bonds often formed between Wisconsinites and the POWs, and long after the war, letters, phone calls, and other communication between parties continued. Some people even planned vacations to visit their friends in their home countries.

There are no records of any POWs remaining in Wisconsin immediately after the war. Records show that all POWs were sent back to Europe. Conditions as described in the book about camps in Europe, especially France, are based on facts, as many German POWs from the Wisconsin contingent, upon their return to Europe, died from disease, malnutrition, or extreme living conditions.

ACKNOWLEDGEMENTS

I am lucky to have an editor, Rick Simmons, who is willing to read and help with changes over several drafts. He pored over each chapter, sentence by sentence, offering positive encouragement every step of the way. As I agonized with the writing, he was my personal coach, motivating me to dig deeper and find better ways to express my thoughts. I can't overstate how grateful I am for Rick's unfailing patience and the confidence he showed in me and the novel.

I also wish to thank Mark Polebitski, who answered all my technical questions and suggestions on layout and format. And, of course, my partner Mary, for allowing me the expense of time and resources to make this novel happen.

And finally, I want to thank director Monica Reeves of the Waupaca High School Drama Department and Amy Holterman, director with the Waupaca Community Theatre, for taking a chance on this story and bringing a version of it to life on the stage. The play, *Two Flags for Marco*, was a rousing success and by many accounts was the finest regional performance to be done in a long time. The cast, the set, and the technical innovations thrilled the audience for each performance. The talk-back sessions stimulated many audience members to share family or even personal experiences with the themes of the story. Most local residents, even those old enough to have lived through the war years, were unaware of the role Wisconsin played in the housing of captured enemy combatants.

For more information on the history of the thousands of German prisoners of war brought to Wisconsin during the Second World War, I suggest Betty Cowley's book *Stalag Wisconsin*. Many other fine resources can be found in most community libraries on autism and the WWII years in Wisconsin.

PATRICK PHAIR is a retired English teacher who has published poems, plays, and this his debut novel. His writings explore what happens to normal people when they collide with those whose experiences are driven by conflict or ostracism. He lives with his wife Mary in central Wisconsin.